SIMON RAVEN was born in London in 1927. He was educated at Charterhouse School and King's College, Cambridge, from which he graduated in the Classics. After university, he joined the Army as a regular officer in the King's Shropshire Light Infantry and saw service in Germany and Kenya where he commanded a Rifle Company. In 1957, he resigned his commission and took up book reviewing. His first novel, *The Feathers of Death*, was published in 1959. Since then he has written many reviews, general essays, plays (which have been performed both on radio and television), plus a host of successful novels including the highly acclaimed 'Alms for Oblivion' series.

The Survivors is the tenth and final volume in the 'Alms for Oblivion' series.

Also by Simon Raven

Novels

The Feathers of Death
Brother Cain
Doctors Wear Scarlet
Close of Play

'Alms for Oblivion' Sequence

The Rich Pay Late
Friends in Low Places
The Sabre Squadron
Fielding Gray
The Judas Boy
Places Where They Sing
Sound the Retreat
Come Like Shadows
Bring Forth the Body

Essays

The English Gentleman
Boys Will Be Boys

Plays

Royal Foundation and other Plays

Simon Raven

The Survivors

PANTHER
GRANADA PUBLISHING
London Toronto Sydney New York

Published by Granada Publishing Limited
in Panther Books 1977
ISBN 0 586 037136

Granada Publishing Limited,
Frogmore, St Albans, Herts AL2 2NF
and
3 Upper James Street, London W1R 4BP
1221 Avenue of the Americas, New York, NY 10020 USA
117 York Street, Sydney, NSW 2000, Australia
100 Skyway Avenue, Toronto, Ontario, Canada M9W 3A6
Trio City, Coventry Street, Johannesburg 2001, South Africa
CML Centre, Queen & Wyndham, Auckland 1, New Zealand

First published in Great Britain by
Blond & Briggs Ltd 1976
Copyright © Simon Raven 1976

Made and printed in Great Britain by
Hazell Watson & Viney Ltd
Aylesbury, Bucks
Set in Linotype Pilgrim

Contents

Ulysses : Time hath, my lord, a wallet at his back,
Wherein he puts alms for oblivion . . .

SHAKESPEARE : *Troilus and Cressida*
Act III, Scene iii

PART ONE

THE INHERITANCE

'SHIT,' said Captain Detterling.

He spoke loud enough to be heard by the Bulgarian delegation at their table ten feet away, and in a tone that made his meaning very plain even to those of them who did not understand his vernacular. None of them, however, even so much as twitched. They simply sat on, attentive yet relaxed, their eyes fixed with bland and total respect on their Bulgarian comrade who was speaking up on the platform.

'It is the function and duty of all writers,' came the anxious voice of the English translator through Detterling's earphones, 'to participate in the political instruction of the people, in the ideological exemplification, that is, of the way in which the people must go. As for what way this is, doubt is no longer permissible or pardonable, unless it be caused by ignorance. It is therefore the duty of the writer to remove this ignorance, to assist in the struggle' – here the translator hesitated for some seconds – 'to promote the amplification, the universal comprehensivization, of Socialist Doctrine and Principle.'

God, thought Detterling, what does this drivel sound like in other languages? He switched the arrow on the dial in front of him to Italian. A voluptuous voice fervently caressed the long abstract words as though about to bring them to orgasm. A degenerate tongue, the Italian, Detterling thought: its constant juxtaposition of the diminutive with the grandiose transposes everything, whether the most noble utterance or this jargon which we're hearing now, to the same level of trivial hysteria. No wonder the Italians are at once so conceited and so futile; their language compels them to live a libretto.

He turned the arrow to French. Absolute silence; how appropriate – French, a precise and civilized language, had no equivalent for this rubbish, so the translator, one assumed, had simply given up. German : great throatfuls of congested inflections, ejaculated in a tone at once whining and aggressive. He removed his earphones to hear what the speech sounded like in Bulgarian itself, and hurriedly put them on again. Finally, for want of an alternative, he turned the arrow back to English.

'Now is the time,' twittered the English translator (a female with an upper-class accent) 'for all writers in the so-called "free" countries of Western Europe and America to impeach the false and bourgeois, so-called "liberal", concepts of freedom, in the name of which the capitalist masters of these countries contrive to hoodwink and prey upon the masses, and to proclaim the true freedom, which is conceived and actualized by the aspirations of the toiling proletariat.'

'Shit,' said Detterling once more.

The Bulgarians again ignored him, and all other ears in the chamber were blocked by earphones. Detterling sighed and turned to Fielding Gray, who was sitting next to him at the British delegates' table. Gray raised his one small eye in interrogation and eased back his headpiece to listen.

'Time for fresh air,' said Detterling into the pink and crumpled ear.

'Ought we to go out in the middle of a speech? Discourteous to the speaker?'

'He's already been going on for twenty-five minutes. That's discourtesy if you like.'

So Fielding Gray, amid glances of angry disapproval, followed Captain Detterling out of the Sala dello Scrutinio, in which the deliberations of the Annual Conference (1973) of the International PEN Club were being conducted, and into the courtyard of the Doges' Palace. Without a word they crossed the Piazzetta and settled themselves in the late afternoon sunlight that still loitered in front of Florian's.

'Seventy writers all in the same room,' Detterrling groaned at last, 'and most of 'em foreigners.'

'You didn't have to come.'

'I thought I ought to see you all at it, just the once. As you know, I'm only really interested in the social goings-on.'

'They're even worse. You have to talk to people.'

'That's what I intend. I might pick up something useful.'

'Like what?'

'I might induce one of those ageing lady novelists to promise Stern & Detterling their memoirs.'

'Most of 'em are too drunk to write any.'

'They'll have kept diaries over the years. Or even better, I might get a manuscript from one of those Communists.'

'Not if you can't be bothered to listen to their speeches.'

'*That* was an official Communist. I'm interested in the kind that are planning to escape to the West and would be glad to find a little money and reputation waiting for them.'

'That kind aren't allowed out to affairs like this.'

'It's coming to affairs like this that turns them into that kind. They get a whiff of lovely bourgeois decadence, and then there's no holding them.' Detterling broke off to order two John Collinses. 'Stern & Detterling,' he said, turning back to Fielding, 'is prepared to sink quite a bit in a book by a renegade Communist. That's the main reason we're here in Venice.'

'Gregory Stern said you were both here to attend that exhibition of European Book Production on San Giorgio.'

'*And* to find a renegade Communist at the PEN Conference.'

'You'll be lucky,' said Fielding. 'Every Communist writer here, however well regarded by the Party, has a kind of personal commissar in attendance. To see he doesn't hobnob with characters like you. You're a Tory M.P., remember. They've done their homework about all that, and no writer from behind the curtain, not even a potential renegade, will dare come within a mile of you. Any budding Pasternaks will have to be found by Gregory ... who, incidentally, seems to be spending his entire time riding round the place in gondolas.'

'That's Isobel's fault. She says that Venice is dying and they must look at it all for the last time.'

'Isobel may have a point, I fancy. But I can't think the end will come *quite* as soon as she implies. At least I hope not,' said Fielding, 'as I've more or less decided to stay on for a year or two after the Conference is over.'

'For a *year* or two?'

'I like decaying cities, and even dying ones, so long as they don't positively collapse on top of me. And *pace* Isobel, I don't think Venice will do that just yet. Another thing,' said Fielding, caressing the cool shaft of his John Collins: 'tax.'

'Trouble with the Inland Revenue, old man?'

'Not yet, and I don't mean there should be. If you stay out of the way long enough, you don't have to file tax returns for the period of your absence. It's now September 1973. If I stay abroad until June or July 1975, say, I could save myself a lot of money.'

'Funny. I never thought of you as being in the tax-evasion bracket.'

'If it's legal, it's called *tax-avoidance*, Detterling. And I promise you I'm going to be strictly legal from now on. Too much worry the other way, believe me.'

'So you have done some fiddles in your time?'

'Just one. Back in 1970, when I was working on Corfu with those film people, I got them to pay me in Zürich. Ten thousand pounds odd I've got there – and not a penny can I bring to England. One more reason for staying abroad a bit.'

'But if *I* understand you, old man, it's income tax you really want to save. How's your income got so large all of a sudden? Time was when your novels barely kept you in booze.'

'If you'd looked at your firm's accounts lately, Detterling, you'd know what's happened. My novels, as you observe, merely make gin-money. But the book on Conrad which you and Gregory commissioned for your Modern English Novelists series has turned into a gusher. The American rights alone,' said Fielding bitterly, 'are worth nearly twenty thousand quid. I shan't need to work again for years.'

'You don't sound very happy about it all. Funny,' said Detterling, 'I always thought that Modern English Novelists series would be a loser. Good for prestige, but a financial loser.'

'You must have heard what happened?'

'No. I've been away six months, remember, fact-finding for Canteloupe and that Ministry of his.'

'But Gregory must have written – or told you since you got back?'

'There was some letter about tarting the series up. And Gregory did mumble something the other day about a gratifying response. But he was so eager to go off in his gondola with Isobel and Baedeker that he never got round to details.'

'Well, he tarted the series up all right. He turned my book into a plushy great slab of a jet-set job with 128 pages of plates, most of them in colour. Isobel's idea. She'd been on about it a long time.'

'Where did he find the money to go in for that sort of publishing?'

'I thought some of it might be yours.'

'Oh no. I made my deposit in the firm years ago, and that was that.'

'Perhaps he got some from Isobel – she had quite a bit when

her father died. In any case, he found it. And *I* found,' said Fielding Gray, 'that my loving and dedicated literary study of the life and work of Joseph Conrad had been transformed into a kind of Bumper Annual Omnibus, full of tit and botty pics of South Sea Islanders.'

'And now here you are, flying from the tax-man in consequence.'

'I don't say I'm not glad of the money. Early middle age is an expensive time : one is old enough to have taste and still young enough to have appetite – a costly combination.'

'Then why are you being so sour with Gregory for putting all this cash in your pocket?'

'Because he turned a serious book into something trivial.'

'He didn't change your text, did he?'

'No. He just made sure that no reputable critic would give it serious attention. In the circles which I'd hoped to impress, my book on Conrad will just be written off as another piece of smarty-pants publishing.'

'You can't have it both ways, Fielding. You can't get rich *and* be a Doctor of Letters.'

'Oh, I know that. It's just that this way of getting rich seems so particularly shabby. Instead of being read by a few critical and appreciative people, and receiving in return a modest sum of money honestly earned, I am being paid a huge sum of money in return for being read by nobody. For nobody *reads* a book with that sort of get-up, Detterling; it just lies around to be glanced at. But even though I know this – and here's the really horrible thing about it all – I have nevertheless been developing a curious and most unwholesome conceit of myself; because a book with my name on it is selling by tens and hundreds of thousands, I have started to invest myself with great importance – although I know, in my heart, that it is spurious.'

Fielding Gray drank at his John Collins; Detterling attempted no comment beyond a sceptical smile, as if to say, 'Stop posing.'

'No, no,' said Fielding, who read the smile aright; 'I mean what I'm saying, Listen, Detterling. As part of the sales campaign a certain amount of "lionizing" was organized for me – luncheons at the Connaught and so on. And do you know, I began to take the treatment quite seriously. Every now and then I had to shake myself all over, in order to remind myself that I wasn't the lion they were pretending I was, that I had simply, by pure chance, got caught up in a commercial process.

And as the process intensified, so did I deteriorate. I forgot to remind myself of the truth; for hours, days at a time, I really thought I was the great writer they said I was. This sort of thing destroys a man, Detterling. I told you just now that I won't have to work for some time; but the truth is that I should find it almost impossible to work if I had to. My whole life lately has been a round of fêtes and speeches; I've been doing nothing whatever except sit in Buttock's Hotel and listen for the telephone to summon me to press interviews and television studios, and indeed I'd got to such a pitch that I felt bored and insulted if it didn't ring every ten minutes. That's why I came to Venice. September is not much of a time for literary lions in London, so I thought, "I'll go to the PEN conference in Venice, they'll be all over me there".'

'And have they been?'

'No,' said Fielding abruptly. 'They're silly enough in their own way, but they've too much sense for that. They don't go in for straw lions. So I'm beginning to be sane again – sane, but very sour, as you say, not because I'm denied the false praise that was ruining me, but because I'm denied the small degree of genuine recognition which I should have for my text on Conrad. The PEN people haven't been taken in by the ballyhoo, but because of the ballyhoo they haven't troubled to read my text either – and they're just the kind of people who should be appreciating it.'

'I can't think,' said Detterling, 'why you want their appreciation. All those dreary, unctuous Reds, pissing out great pools of stale propaganda.'

'There *are* more desirable elements in the PEN Club.'

'Like those lady novelists you just accused of being tiddly all day long? But I take your point,' said Detterling. 'You're a poor little rich boy whom nobody loves – or not the right people and not for the right reasons. Boo-hoo, Fielding, boo-hoo-bloody-hoo. Pull yourself together and start another book.'

'That's one reason why I'll probably stay on in Venice. There'll be fewer telephone calls to distract me, and I'm hoping this city will show me something to write about.'

'It might,' said Detterling. 'If you stop whining and start looking, it just might. Good afternoon, Isobel ... Gregory ...'

Fielding and Detterling rose and rearranged chairs. Isobel Stern wrapped her long, gangling legs over one; her husband

Gregory sat primly on the edge of another. Detterling beckoned a waiter and ordered more drinks.

'Phew,' said Gregory; 'we have walked all the way from the New Ghetto.'

'What happened to your gondola?'

'Isobel dismissed it. She said we must see that part of Venice on foot. We must look close with our eyes, she said, to see how it is crumbling. I tell you, Fielding, Detterling, it is not crumbling, it is suppurating.'

'Doomed,' said Isobel.

'The Venice in Peril Fund—' Fielding began.

'—What fund?' said Isobel. 'Only peanuts, unless the Italian Government does its bit. And can you imagine those greedy wops spending money just to save something beautiful? They'd sooner put a motorway through the place.'

'And ruin their tourist trade?'

'They hate tourists. They think of them as people who have come to see a corpse.'

'Who *pay* to see a corpse.'

'Only they don't pay enough any more, and the corpse is taking up the best bed. The Italians would sooner have a nice, juicy, living slut in it,' said Isobel, 'something they can fuck.'

'Isobel, my wife, what *do* you mean?'

'I mean, Gregory my husband, that the eyeties are sick of Venice and want something modern instead. Something which appeals to *them* for a change: speedways and football stadiums and enormous swimming pools. Or failing those, a lot of factories in which they can make money. Anything, in fact, but what they've got.'

'Poor Fielding,' said Detterling. 'He's just decided to live here for a bit, and I don't think speedways and factories are quite what he's looking forward to.'

'You are going to live in Venice?' said Gregory to Fielding.

'For a year or two, perhaps.'

'You've made him so rich by the way you've promoted his book on Conrad,' said Detterling, 'that he can't afford to live in England.'

'No good ever came of living abroad,' said Isobel. 'A man should stay where he has roots.'

'Ah,' said Detterling, 'Fielding thinks his roots are being poisoned. Gregory has corrupted him, he says, by turning him from a poor novelist, who worked quietly in the country, into a gilded metropolitan celebrity. He must stay abroad to escape further contamination.'

'Contamination?' said Gregory. 'What nonsense, Fielding, is this?'

Fielding, whose head was turned towards the glittering façade of St Mark's, brought it slowly round and directed his eye straight at Gregory.

'It's true,' he said. 'I can't sit still, I can't be quiet, I can't work. And all because of this sham success with Conrad. I've started to think and behave like a matinée idol ... preening myself on doorsteps and waiting for the cameras to click.'

'Balls,' said Isobel. 'All you need is a good kick in the arse.'

'Please, Isobel. Is it the money,' said Gregory, 'that has done this?'

'No. I've earned big money before for a time – working on films. But there what I did was genuine, in its kind, and I was not corrupted. This is different; because what we've done – what you've done – with this book on Conrad is pure faking. You've faked me into fame, Gregory, and made me into something which I both adore and totally despise.'

'The tragedy of the year,' said Isobel: 'poor little Fielding sobbing his heart out because he's suddenly famous and rich. See what you've done, Gregory? You and your vulgar wife. Listen, you,' she said to Fielding: 'it was my idea to jazz that book up because I smelt money in it and it's high time Gregory made some. If I'd left it to him he'd have gone on printing nice, liberal, literate and wholly unsellable books until he wound up in the gutter. And don't think Detterling would have bailed him out. Detterling's as mean as a crab-louse.'

'Steady on, old girl,' Detterling said.

'So Gregory needed to do something different,' said Isobel, 'and I showed him how, and now we're all making a packet. If you don't like the money, Fielding, don't go on squealing about it; just give it back.'

'I've told you, it's not the money I mind—'

'—It's the damage to your poor sensitive soul,' Isobel sneered. 'For Christ's sake don't be so silly, Fielding. Just go home to England and get on with another book.'

'There isn't another book,' said Fielding stubbornly. 'I can't see it anywhere, not yet. But I might find it here, and here, as I told you, I'm staying.'

'In Venice.' Isobel shuddered. 'It's ... it's like being in a graveyard full of broken tombs. Rather pretty to look at on a bright day, but to live in ... Fielding,' she said, suddenly changing her tone to one of persuasion and affection, 'listen to what I'm saying. Can't you smell death in this place?'

Fielding shrugged at the suggestion but smiled in response to her obvious concern for him.

'I'm staying, Isobel,' he said. 'I think it may suit me.'

'Well, don't say I didn't warn you. I tell you this town is rotting to death ... in spirit as well as fabric. I feel it, Fielding.'

'Isobel is sometimes psychic,' said Gregory in an apologetic voice.

'I'm making Gregory take me home,' she said: 'I can't stand any more of it.'

'When?' said Detterling sharply.

'Tomorrow.'

'You never warned me,' said Detterling to Gregory.

'I did not know until Isobel told me.'

'A fat lot of help that is, Gregory. We're here to find new authors, remember? And now you're deserting me before we've even started.'

'You must manage by yourself, my dear. After all, you have deserted me for all of the last six months.'

'I was doing this enquiry for my cousin Canteloupe.'

'None the less deserting me, my dear. But since we're on the subject, I confess I'd be intrigued to know exactly what you were up to.'

'Yes,' said Fielding. 'What were you up to, Detterling? You've always kept clear of Government office: why did you take this on?'

'This was not a Government office.'

'A job for a Ministry ...'

'Strictly unofficial. I wasn't paid – though Canteloupe subbed up for my expenses. Out of his own pocket. I wasn't really working for the Ministry of Commerce but for Canteloupe personally.'

'Cut the small print,' said Isobel, 'and tell us what you did.'

A deep bell began to toll from the Campanile.

'Curfew,' said Fielding.

'Only a show for the tourists,' said Isobel, 'but one day soon it'll be the real thing.' And to Detterling: 'Come on, Detterling. What was the dirty work you did for your noble cousin?'

'I never said it was dirty, and I only took it on to oblige Canteloupe. It was, in fact, an enquiry into something that had already happened.'

I see,' said Isobel. 'Cleaning up an old pile of dirt instead of starting a new one.'

'On the contrary. Just making sure that there wasn't any dirt . . . or at least none visible.'

'How dull.'

'Far from it. In the summer of '72,' said Detterling, 'Canteloupe's Under-Secretary, Peter Morrison, pulled off a very neat coup at the Trade Convention in Strasbourg. No need to go into details. but the end of it was that Britain sold a huge amount of a new light metal alloy which we were keen to push – and one of the reasons we sold so much was that Peter had managed to discredit the products of our competitors. I can't tell you how he did it, but it was by means of a clever trick which Peter and Canteloupe think they might use again, with certain variations. Before they can do that, however, they have to be sure that no one has rumbled the trick . . . indeed that no one even suspects there *was* any trick. That was where I came in : they needed a substantial sort of chap with all the entrées – an M.P. like me – but one who doesn't count in that world and therefore wouldn't be noticed, to go all round the world listening in to what was being said about the '72 Convention and to find out if anyone was harbouring nasty thoughts about the sale of our light metal alloy. I was to be a fly on the wall – and I wasn't at all keen to take it on, because in my experience even the most discreet fly is apt to wind up under a swatter. But Canteloupe made a family obligation out of it, and I've always been interested in Peter Morrison's stratagems, so on condition that Canteloupe paid for me to do my travels *en prince* I agreed to have a try at it. And here I am, as you see, still unswatted, and happy to be able to report that no one appears to have spotted what Canteloupe and Morrison have been up to. So,' he said to Isobel, 'no dirt to be cleaned up; not so far, anyhow.'

'Such hazards you went through,' said Gregory. 'I trust the Most Honourable the Marquis Canteloupe was happy with the news you brought home to him.'

'Insofar as he can be happy about anything. Canteloupe, just now, is batting on a very dodgy wicket. He can't last much longer at the Ministry.'

'Despite the success of our light metal alloy at Strasbourg?'

'That was over a year ago,' said Detterling ,'and Britain cannot live by light metal alloys alone. The cry is going up for a younger man who is – what's the jargon? – more in tune with the technological era in which we live.'

'Not that anyone will do any better,' said Gregory Stern. 'Even the most brilliant technology, with the most abrasive young Minister behind it, will be little good unless the people are prepared to work and the Unions to co-operate. Just now I see no work, no co-operation anywhere.'

'The people are bored,' said Isobel. 'They want some excitement. The only way of getting it is to precipitate disaster, and that's what everyone is busy doing. Demanding everything and giving nothing, and sitting back to see what will happen.'

'Ai-yai,' said Gregory : 'death in Venice, doom in Britain.'

'And trouble on its way to this table,' said Isobel, as two Carabinieri, wearing cocked hats and short swords, halted by them and saluted. 'What have you boys been up to?'

'Signor Capitano Detterling?' one of the Caribinieri said carefully. 'Membair of the Ingleesh Parli-a-ment?'

'I am he,' said Detterling.

Both men saluted again; one of them opened the pouch on his belt and produced an envelope.

'Thank you,' said Detterling, and took it.

The Carabinieri exchanged glances, then saluted once more and slithered away through the surrounding tables.

'Oh dear,' said Detterling softly, 'listen to this. "CANTELOUPE DIED AT DESK FOUR OF CLOCK THIS AFTERNOON CARDIAC THROMBOSIS STOP PETER MORRISON." He must have had it sent over some special network. Rather flattering that those police chappies knew who I was and where to find me.'

'They always know that kind of thing in Venice,' said Fielding; 'rather frightening if you ask me. I think,' he said, 'that there's another sheet in that envelope.'

'Yes . . .'

Detterling unfolded a second message. He blinked, grinned rather wolfishly, then shook his head in puzzled acknowledgement.

'It's from the lawyers,' he said. 'They lost no time, I must say.' He shook his head again, as if speculating on the logistic problems which the lawyers must have overcome in order to effect so swift a transmission. 'Peter rang them at once, I sup-

pose, and they must have asked him to relay this message to me
the same way he sent his own.'

'It must be very urgent.'

'Not exactly. But certainly exigent.'

'Well, what is it, Detterling?'

'Not Detterling,' said Captain Detterling, in a still, small
voice: 'not any more. You should call me ... Canteloupe.'

The Marquis Canteloupe was dead : long live the Marquis Canteloupe. In point of fact, as Fielding remarked to Detterling the
next morning, both custom and courtesy forbade him to assume
the title until his predecessor was buried. Detterling countered
this by producing a telegram which had arrived from the lawyers
a little while before and informed Detterling that under the
terms of the deceased's will there was to be no burial service and
that circumstances (mercifully unspecified) made it advisable to
inter the body that very morning. Thus Detterling was spared the
inconvenience of an immediate journey to England to attend
the obsequies, and might call himself Canteloupe from that
minute.

'But of course,' he said, 'I'll have to go home in a week or so
in order to see into it all.'

Meanwhile they began to piece together, from the copious
letters and telegrams which arrived in the next few days, what
had happened to bring about Detterling's unlooked-for inheritance. Canteloupe's son and only child, the Earl of Muscateer, had died many years since while an Officer Cadet in
India; and until a very few days previously the heir presumptive
had been Canteloupe's brother, Lord Alfred Sarum. But Lord
Alfred, they had now learnt, had expired suddenly while at-
tending his 113th drink cure, and since all Canteloupe's other
siblings were also dead, this had opened up the field a bit, as
Detterling put it. Yet the field, on inspection, proved to be
exceedingly thin. Cousins or uncles Canteloupe had none –
except for that branch of the family which descended from his
great-great-great-great-great aunt, Lady Julia Sarum, who had
married a certain Adolphus Detterling, of Richborough in the
County of Kent, Esquire, in 1810. Of this line the only survivor
was now Captain Detterling, and of course he could inherit only
such titles as might descend through the Lady Julia, his great-
great-great-great grandmother.

The lawyers, nosing into the matter after Lord Alfred's death, had at first opined that there was only one of the family peerages to which Detterling might succeed – the Barony of Sarum of Old Sarum. The two Viscountcies (Sarum of Sherwood, and Rollesden-in-Silvis) could certainly not be transmitted through the female line; nor could the Earldom of Muscateer. There remained only the Marquisate, a rather late creation (1799), of which it was assumed that it could descend only through issue male. However, a junior partner of antiquarian tastes, idly reading through the original letters patent which conferred the Marquisate, came across a clause which assigned a special remainder, in default of heirs male, to the eldest daughter of the 1st Marquis and to heirs male in direct line of succession from her. This eldest daughter was in fact the Lady Julia Sarum (later Detterling) aforementioned, and an examination of the family records made it clear why the special remainder in her favour had been arranged : for the 1st Marquis, at the time when he was so promoted for his highly confidential services to the Crown, had no son (his only male child having died while abroad, two years previously) and a lunatic wife. In the event, however, the special remainder was not invoked, as the mad marchioness had killed herself by jumping from a window, and the Marquis had married again and contrived, albeit very late in life, to father a boy. Only now, some 170 years later, was the remainder suddenly applicable, vested as it undoubtedly was in Captain Detterling, who accordingly became, by virtue of it, 6th Marquis Canteloupe of the Estuary of the Severn.

'And also,' as Detterling explained to Fielding Gray, '19th Baron Sarum of Old Sarum, by reason of a different and more usual kind of remainder which Henry V assigned to all female descendants of the 1st Baron.'

'But the Earldom and the Viscountcies,' said Fielding, 'are definitely extinct?'

'A pity, that,' said Detterling : 'but it doesn't do to be greedy. There are plenty of goodies without those.'

The goodies not only included the Marquisate, the Barony, Canteloupe's house and park in Wiltshire, the theoretical right to every carp ever caught in the Severn, and a superb collection of rude books; they also comprehended Cant-Fun & Co. Ltd, one of the slickest and most successful 'Stately Home' carnivals in England, so organized as to screw the maximum of cash out of a credulous public and to inflict the minimum of inconvenience on the Marquis himself when in residence. In recent years Cant-

Fun had paid for the entire upkeep of the Wiltshire house and estate, had shown an average profit of £300,000 annually, and had been so cunningly engrafted into the main body of the Canteloupe finances that death duties, as Detterling now learned from the accountants, would be extremely modest.

'It seems,' said Detterling to Fielding, 'that I've not really inherited Canteloupe's estate but the Chairmanship of the Company that runs it.'

'Cant-Fun,' Fielding said. 'Only your cousin could have thought up a name as vile as that. The old philistine. Do you remember how he tore up that rose garden right in front of the house to put in an Amusement Arcade?'

'That was in his unregenerate days,' said Detterling. 'He got quite civilized towards the end. There was a man he met called Balbo Blakeney – a Fello of Lancaster – who knew about houses and gardens. Balbo came to stay once or twice and showed him how to camouflage Cant-Fun. You'd hardly know it was there now, if it wasn't for the prole infants screeching. And I suppose that's a small price to pay for getting away with the death duties.'

'I still don't quite see how that works.'

'I don't actually inherit the *property*, or not so that I own it personally. Everything's tied up in the Company, which in some aspects is like a kind of Trust. There's a Board responsible for it, and I become Chairman of the Board, and as such I draw a vast sum in salary and expenses, enough to cover anything I could want within reason and indeed well beyond it. But the point is that every penny of the capital belongs, not to me, but to the Company. Everything I get, including the right to live in the house, I get because I'm the Chairman, not because I'm the Marquis Canteloupe.'

'No,' said Fielding : 'the Marquis of Cant-Fun.'

'If you're going to make jokes like that, I shall think you are jealous.'

'Of course I'm jealous. I've always coveted a coronet myself.'

'Stick to your writing, and you may get a crown of laurel.'

'But not a Chairmanship to subsidize it. . .'

There was a knock on the door of Fielding's sitting-room, and a flunkey in liveries bowed himself in with a letter. This turned out to be for Detterling.

'I must say, they do us well here at the Gritti,' said Detterling when the flunkey had gone. 'The minute a letter comes they bring it to you – wherever you are in the hotel.' His face clouded a little. 'But how do you suppose,' he said, 'that they knew I was in your room?'

'I told you the other day, when the Caribinieri delivered those messages in the Piazza. In Venice they always know where important people are. It's been their speciality for centuries.'

'You won't mind that ... when you're living here?'

'I'm not the 6th Marquis Canteloupe. They won't bother me.'

'Such modesty. You were right. Venice *is* doing you good. But don't overdo the self-abasement. It can be quite as unwholesome as its opposite.'

Detterling opened his letter. 'From Carton Weir,' he announced.

'What's he on about?'

'Canteloupe's death – the manner of his dying.'

For a minute or two Detterling read in silence. Then, 'Listen to this,' he said. ' "... The odd thing was that for some weeks the old boy had been in the best possible form. Back in July he'd been pretty depressed about the way things were running ('It's enough to put one off one's drink,' he said once, and indeed it even seemed to be doing that), but about three weeks ago he perked up again and was full of ideas for the future. I think he was encouraged by the final report you sent in after your tour, telling him that no one seemed to have spotted the way he finessed the opposition at Strasbourg. 'We're not done for yet,' he said, and held a series of long conferences with Peter Morrison, at the end of which they'd both go away grinning like two cats who'd been at the baby's bottle. No doubt about it : he was in the pink. And then a few days ago his brother Alfred died – but he took that in his stride. 'I've hardly seen him in twenty years,' he told me; 'silly, boring drunk – a good job he can never inherit.' And after Alfred's funeral : 'That's the last of my brothers and sisters gone,' he said; 'I've beaten the lot. A pretty poor lot they were, but I'm a long way the oldest, and it's something to have seen them all underground.'

' "And then he settled down again to do his plotting with Peter, and went on as merry as a martlet. The day he died he came into the Ministry at ten, looking fitter than ever. 'What have I got on today?' he said. 'Lunch with Sir Geoffrey Bruce-Cohen, Minister,' I told him : 'at the Ritz.' 'Right,' he said : 'after I've had lunch with the old Shylock I'll just pop over the Park to see Maisie. So don't expect me back till tea-time.' But as it happened he was back by half-past three ... and looking rather dismal. 'Lunch go off all right, Minister?' I said. 'Lunch went off all right,' he said; 'the trouble is that *I* didn't go off all right when I went to see Maisie afterwards. Soft as a fish-cake.' 'Cheer up, Minister,' I said : 'we all have our off days.' 'I was looking forward to it like anything,' he said, 'all through lunch. But when I got there, I might as well have been made of plasticine.' Then the phone went, and it was Peter Morrison wanting him. 'Not just now, Carton,' he said; 'tell him to drop in at four. Now be a good fellow and leave me in peace.' So then I left the poor old dear at his desk. Nothing else for it, I thought; he'll get over his depression by and by.

' "But when I showed Peter in at four",' Detterling read to Fielding, ' "he was sitting there dead. Peter took over then – called a doctor, rang the solicitor, sent those messages to you in Venice. Congratulations, by the way; I'd no idea you were in line for the title.

' "You're not the only one to benefit : as you may or may not have heard, they've given the Ministry to Peter. Rather to my surprise he's taken me over along with the rest of it. I never thought he really liked me or trusted me, and I was all ready to pack up and go, but almost the first thing he did after they appointed him was to send for me and ask me to stay on. 'I'm going to need you, Carton,' he said; 'you understand the way we work.' Flattering. Or was it? Anyway, I'm still in my old billet, so all's well that ends well, you might say. Except that I miss Canteloupe so dreadfully. He was often absolutely foul to me, and not a day passed without his telling me I was a fat old fairy, but we were together a very long time and he was such fun to be with. . ." '

'So Peter's fallen on his feet,' Fielding said.

'He was always bound to. But he hasn't had everything his own way lately ... what with his elder boy gone potty and his land in Norfolk threatened. They're going to develop in that area, I'm told.'

'I stayed with him there once, years ago. It was a very ... seemly place. I wouldn't like it to be spoiled.'

'It won't be, now he's Minister of Commerce. Somewhere else will just happen to turn out more suitable. Time to go, Fielding.'

'Go? Where?'

'This PEN Club party you said there was this evening. I'm

still looking for Communists with manuscripts ... or at least lady novelists with memoirs.'

'You're going to go on with all that?'

'Certainly I am. I'm fond of Gregory and I'm fond of publishing,' said Detterling, 'and I shall have time on my hands. My seat in the Commons is gone and I don't suppose being Chairman of Cant-Fun is very hard work.'

'You'll be sitting in the House of Lords ...'

'Not much going on there. Off to the party,' said Detterling. 'Now Gregory's been dragged home by Isobel, I've got to do the work for us both.'

The PEN Club party was being held in the Sala dell' Albergo of the Scuola San Rocco. No sooner had Detterling and Fielding got inside than they were boarded by two lady novelists, one middle-class and the other proletarian. Since they were too young to have written any memoirs worth mentioning, and since their books were already published by Stern & Detterling in any case, Detterling, who was anxious to break new ground, made some effort to circumvent them. But both of them were very excited, in their different ways, by his new title (intelligence of which had speedily run through the conference) and were also covertly fascinated by the celebrity, however meretricious, that had been recently attained by Fielding. So they made a strong frontal movement, trapped Detterling and Fielding firmly underneath Tintoretto's *Ecce Homo*, and settled down (as it seemed to Fielding) to make a night of it.

'Bloody lucky to be having this party here,' said the proletarian, who was missing two important front teeth: 'half the museums in Venice have been boarded up.'

'No staff,' said the bourgeois: 'museum curators in Italy are wickedly underpaid.'

'No cash to pay them, dearie. All drained off into the pockets of the politicians... Tell me, Lord Canteloupe: what does it feel like to be a Marquis?'

'After walking all the way here,' said Detterling, 'it feels thirsty. If you'd let me get through to the bar—'

'—No need for that,' said the bourgeois severely. 'The waiters are coming round as quick as they can. In a crush like this it will help everyone if you stand still.'

She then began a long lecture to Detterling on the iniquity of hereditary titles, while her colleague told Fielding all about her next novel, which was to contain several blow-by-blow descriptions of intercourse between an agricultural labourer and his nine-year-old daughter.

At long last, a waiter proffered a tray of tiny glasses of highly coloured liquids.

'John Collins?' suggested Detterling. The waiter shook his head malevolently. 'Gin and tonic? Vodka and lime? Whisky-soda?'

'You'd better settle for Martini Rosso,' said the prole, taking a glass and passing it to Detterling; 'the rest are poison.'

She passed another to Fielding, who accepted it glumly.

'Attaboy,' she said: 'there's Sydney Offal. You know Syd?'

'No.'

'Syd's a Yank. Longest prick on the conference.' She began to enlarge on the theme, breathily, while the bourgeois ordered Detterling to renounce his peerage, on the subject of which she was clearly manic. Detterling let his eyes wander, in search of discontented Communists or stylish Edwardian ladies, but saw only a scrawny Irish poetess with mauve hair who was straddling a chair and crying while a plump Italian critic gesticulated and pirouetted in front of her.

'. . . And a pair of ghoulies like basket balls,' the prole was saying, as Fielding fiddled with his empty, sticky glass and prayed for rescue . . . which suddenly came darting from the region of *Christ before Pilate* in the form a very young girl, who slid between Fielding and the prole like an eel and coiled herself around Detterling.

'*Lovely* Captain Detterling,' she said; 'I'm Baby Llewyllyn. I met you last year at Grantchester.'

Baby Llewyllyn, Fielding observed, must now be about thirteen; she had gay little breasts, a page boy hair-cut, and long, loose stripling's thighs, about a furlong of which were visible beneath a tartan mini-mini-skirt and above matching tartan knee-socks. Like her mother, Patricia, she was strongly made as an entity yet curiously flabby in parts; the flesh of her thighs, though it looked spare and firm at one moment, could be seen to spread and wobble at the next, as she pressed her length against Detterling's; and the joints of her arms and legs had a quaint, gangling action which recalled her mother's sister, Isobel Stern.

'Poppa's here,' she said. 'He's just coming over.' And then, with hostility, 'Who are these people?'

'These ladies are Acarnania Mayling,' said Detterling, indicating the bourgeois, 'and Jessica Fubs.'

'I know about them. Poppa says your books are soft, sticky crap' – to Mayling – 'and yours are hot, runny crap' – to Fubs.

'And this gentleman,' said Detterling, as Mayling and Fubs withdrew snarling, 'is Major Fielding Gray.'

'Poppa's spoken of you too,' she said.

'So what kind of crap are my books?'

Baby laughed happily.

'He doesn't tell me that, because he says you're an old friend.' She prised some of herself off Detterling and clamped it on to Fielding. 'He says he *loves* you,' she said.

Before Fielding could comment on this remark, which gave him great pleasure, Tom Llewyllyn came up.

'Evening, Canteloupe,' he said quite seriously, 'evening, Fielding. I hope Baby's behaving herself.'

'Magnificently,' said Fielding. 'She's just routed Fubs and Mayling.' Dear God, he thought, you do look old; you're forty-five, as I am, and you look over sixty ... stooping like a hump-back, wrinkled and scraggy at the neck. 'What brings you here, Tom?' he said. 'We didn't know you were in Venice.'

'We've only just come and not for this PEN thing, though as I'm a member I thought I'd just drop in this evening. We're having a little holiday, Baby and I.'

'I've got poppa all to myself,' Baby said.

'Yes,' said Tom, begging his two friends with his eyes not to ask where his wife, Patricia, was. 'But not for long, poppet.' Baby pouted fiercely, but Tom went on firmly, almost sternly, as if determined to make his point clear beyond possible doubt. 'Baby must go back to England for school in a few days,' he said. 'I'm staying on here. I've got a Sabbatical Year from Lancaster, and I've decided to spend it researching into the decline and fall of the Serene Republic.'

'Good, oh good,' said Fielding, pursing his tiny warped mouth in his gladness. 'I'm staying on too.'

'Right,' said Tom after a pause, as if he had summed and discounted possible objections and was now giving his (slightly reluctant) permission. And then, as if realizing that this was niggardly, 'Good, Fielding,' he said.

He's worried, thought Fielding, lest I might disrupt his life here in some way; he may 'love' me, as Baby says, but he's never really trusted me since I let him down over that Greek affair in

1962... Further speculation along these lines was interrupted by the reappearance of the waiter with the tray.

'Perfectly revolting drinks,' said Tom. 'Do you think we might go somewhere else and have dinner?'

'There's a buffet,' said Baby, who liked to show she was well up with what was going on.

'A cold buffet,' said Fielding, 'they shuttle the same stuff round from function to function until at last it gets eaten.'

'That's settled then,' said Detterling, who had decided that the auspices of the evening were against his finding any literary prospect worth waiting for. 'I know rather a nice place near the Rialto Bridge. You must all three be the guests of Cant-Fun.'

'Cant-Fun?' said Baby.

As they walked to the Rialto Bridge, Detterling explained Cant-Fun to Tom and Baby. Baby took a very intelligent interest.

'So what it comes to,' she said, 'is that you pretend to the Government that you only live there because you run the Company.'

'That's about it.'

'But you won't really run it, will you? I mean, I know you're called the Chairman, but there'll be lots of other people doing the real work.'

'There's a Board. Trustees – or that's what they amount to. Solicitors and so on.'

'But if they ever turned nasty,' said Baby, 'they could stop you from being Chairman?'

'Shrewd point,' said Fielding.

'We shall be very careful,' said Detterling, 'that no one nasty gets on to the Board.'

'I should hope so. Because when you have a son,' said Baby, 'you'll want to arrange for him to be Chairman after you die.'

'I suppose so. I can't say I've thought of that much.'

'But of course you'll want to have a son,' said Baby, and squeezed Detterling's hand, 'so of course you'll have to have a wife. I think that I should *love* to be Lady Canteloupe.'

'I'll bear you in mind.'

'I think you're so sexy.'

'That'll do, Tullia,' said Tom, 'you've made your point.'

'Tullia?' said Detterling.

'Baby's real name. I use it if she's being silly or childish.'

'I wasn't being silly or childish,' Baby giggled, 'I was being grown up.'

Whereupon they arrived at the restaurant. By the time they had surveyed the place and engaged a table (*al fresco*, by the side of the Grand Canal), Baby had dropped the topic of her matrimonial ambitions and redirected her talents and energies to the task of planning her menu.

'Parma ham and melon, tomato soup, ravioli, grilled scampi, and roast veal,' said Baby when invited to order.

'Are you sure that will be enough?'

'With pudding and cheese, of course.'

While Baby went through her first three courses, the others, who were waiting to begin at the scampi, drank long iced drinks such as had not been provided by the PEN Club and talked of the historical research which Tom was to do in Venice.

'The decline and fall of the Serenissima,' said Fielding, 'rather a long order?'

'I don't propose myself as the Gibbon of Venice,' said Tom. 'I merely intend to pick out and analyse certain moral and political mistakes which have from time to time damaged the Republic. For example: Ruskin maintains that in one sense the Republic started to decline very early – as soon, in fact, as it lost the first fine fervour of its primitive Christian faith. Most scholars see this as an absurd exaggeration, and point out that this was just the stage at which Venice started to flourish as a mercantile and imperial power. But I think that Ruskin deserves a certain, admittedly much qualified, support. One result of the falling off in faith which Ruskin so much deplored was that Doge Dandolo was condoned and applauded by his people when he perverted the Fourth Crusade into an expedition for the conquest of Constantinople. Splendid, said all the Venetians: lots of lovely Byzantine loot, large territories won from the Roman Empire of the East – to say nothing of fat fees for shipping the Crusaders where they hadn't intended to go. But in the end what Doge Dandolo really achieved was the laying open of Byzantine territory, not so much to the Venetians, who hadn't enough citizens to administer it, but to the Turks, who were thus enabled to expand in wealth and power until they became the Republic's most ferocious enemy. And so an early failure in morals and religion led, over the centuries, to commercial and strategic disaster.'

'It's like poor Mummy always used to say,' said Baby, looking up from her soup: 'we are "tied and bound with the chain of our sins".'

Not the least astonishing thing about this observation, Fielding thought, was the way in which Baby referred to her mother as being totally finished and done with, if not indeed actually dead. But once again he saw that Tom's eyes were pleading that nobody should enquire about Patricia, so he coaxed the conversation away from this dangerous area and back to Tom's academic affairs.

'What do they say about this at Lancaster?' he asked. 'Are they happy you should spend your time on this subject?'

'I've got a Sabbatical Year,' said Tom, 'and I'm free to use it as I wish.'

'That wouldn't stop Provost Constable giving his opinion.'

'He takes the view that since my book on power has been well received, I can safely be left to choose my own subjects for the future.'

'A gross *non sequitur*,' said Detterling, 'but then I never took Constable very seriously. The man has a massive complacency which he deludes himself into thinking of as moral integrity.'

'You could be right,' said Tom, 'but a lot of important people share his delusion. He's to have a Life Peerage very soon.'

'From a Conservative Government?'

'Why not? It makes the Tories feel good to create a socialist peer from time to time, and Constable's socialism is safely back in the Attlee vintage. The great point is,' said Tom, 'that Constable will oppose all modish and egalitarian schemes of education, and will do so the more impressively for speaking from the Labour benches.'

'Do you value his approval,' said Fielding to Tom, 'of your research here, I mean?'

'Not particularly ... though of course it's convenient. The truth is,' said Tom, 'that I'm not very concerned about my research ... not just now at any rate. What I'm really after is an excuse to spend a year in Venice.'

'Why?'

'Mond,' said Tom, 'Daniel Mond. You remember him, Fielding?'

'Vividly. What has he got to do with it?'

'He'll be joining me before long, I think.'

'I still don't see—'

... But further enquiry into this matter was now prevented by a cry of ecstasy from Baby.

'Ooooh, look,' she piped, 'on the Canal.'

A magnificent gondola was coming from the direction of the

Rialto Bridge; it was now nearly opposite where they sat and about twenty yards out in the Canal. The immediate comparison which occurred to Fielding was with Cleopatra's barge. From the poop to the cabin the hull of the vessel was ornamented, not indeed with beaten gold, but with an intricate lattice of silver that flashed and sparkled in the evening light and, aided by its broken reflection in the choppy Canal, made the rear half of the gondola seem in some sort to burn, on and into the water. The cabin or *felzo* itself was not of the usual near-rectangular structure, but resembled a tiny tented pavilion, such as a pigmy knight might retire into during a tournament, with a mock battlement from which flew a banner displaying a yellow heraldic beast on a red background. There was one gondolier at bow and one at stern; both of them were dressed in red pantaloons and short, tight tunics quartered in red and yellow. Forward of the pavilion two men were sitting on chairs with high, straight backs; and on a couch in front of them sprawled a pretty, dimpled boy, a Cupid of some seventeen summers, drinking from a goblet. As this tableau was ferried past, one of the seated men raised a hand briefly in the direction of the dinner party, but without turning his head.

'Jesus,' said Baby, 'that *boy*.'

She started to skip along the quay on which they were sitting, keeping pace with the gondola and waving across at it. 'You saw who they were?' said Detterling to Fielding.

'One of them. Max de Freville. The one who waved – if you can call it that. The other was in the shadow of the tent. '

'Lykiadopoulos. . .'

'His partner. . .'

'And the third, one presumes, is Lykiadopoulos's current boy. Rather a high standard – I agree with Baby. I wonder,' said Detterling, 'what Max and Lyki are up to in Venice.'

'Will Baby be all right?' said Tom, following her with his eyes. 'What happens along this quay?'

'Nothing. In about forty yards there's a side canal blocking the way. She'll have to come back here.'

'While she's gone,' said Tom rather nervously to Detterling, 'I want to ask you something. You'll have to go home in a few days, you said just now, to see into Cant-Fun and the rest of it?'

'That's right.'

'Can you take Baby back for me and dump her with Isobel

in London? She likes you, and I don't want her to travel alone
– for obvious reasons, I think. I can't go with her myself, because Daniel Mond may be here at any time, and it's important
I should be here to meet him when he arrives.'

Why, thought Fielding, who had already been intrigued by
Tom's earlier reference to Daniel; why can't Daniel take care of
himself for a few hours? But Tom clearly did not intend to say
any more of Daniel Mond just now; it was Baby he wished to
talk of.

'So if you'd see her to Isobel's,' Tom said, 'I'd be most grateful. You see, it's not just that she's so precocious, but she's
innocent with it. She doesn't realize the sort of ... unpleasant-
ness ... which she might get into if she carries on as she does.'

'Don't worry,' said Detterling, 'I'll take her back for you.'

'Thank you,' said Tom.

He looked along the quayside. Under a lamp at the end of it,
Baby was to be seen hitched up over a parapet, showing a pert
little bum and exiguous knickers, and craning down what must
be the side canal of which Detterling had spoken.

'I don't know,' said Tom, 'why she's like she is. Isobel was a
bit the same when she was young, all flirty and knowing, but
not ... not so *radical* about it as Baby seems to be. Mind you,
Canteloupe, she's much better than she was a year ago when
you last met her, but she's still ... rather a worry.'

'So I imagine. What happens when she gets back to England?'

'Isobel will pack her off to school. It's a special sort of school
which I found out about after Patricia – that is, after we decided Baby ought to go away. We were lucky to find a suitable
place for her, for Baby, I mean.' Tom, thought Fielding, has
rather lost his grip over all this. 'They have ways,' Tom said uncertainly, 'of calming them down.'

What ways, Fielding longed to ask; and whom, exactly,
were they calming down? But Baby was now cantering back
along the quay, eager to be at her scampi.

'They went along a little canal up there,' she said, helping
herself to half a pint of sauce tartare, 'and stopped a short way
down it, and got out of the gondola on to some steps. That boy
has got something the matter with his leg. It makes him limp
horribly.'

'Sounds like the Palazzo Albani,' Detterling said. 'I thought it
was empty.'

'Perhaps they've hired it.'

'If so they'll be here for some time. I thought they had their hands full on Corfu. All those hotels they're building there ... to say nothing of their interest in the Casino.'

'The season's almost over on Corfu,' Fielding said.

'But if you're building anything in Greece, you stay close and watch as sharp as Argus. Otherwise not one brick goes on to another. Lyki knows that even if Max doesn't.'

'I think,' said Baby brightly, 'that that boy belongs to one of the gentlemen.'

'That's my guess too,' said Detterling. 'Mr Lykiadopoulos has a tooth for boys like that.'

'Which of them is Mr Lykiadopoulos? The straight one or the small round one?'

'The small round one.'

'Yes,' said Baby. 'He was helping the boy out of the boat. He wouldn't let the gondoliers get near him.'

'What happened then?'

'A sort of Major-Domo man came out of a big door. With a lantern. Which wasn't necessary because there was a light over the steps.'

'Fantasy,' said Tom. 'The gondola, the Renaissance liveries, the Major-Domo, the lantern ... sheer fantasy.'

'They've both got a streak of it. You should see the tomb Max put up for Angela in the British Cemetery on Corfu. But that's a different kind of fantasy from the pantomime we saw just now; this lot smells of Lyki more than of Max de Freville. Lyki always liked Venice ... or what he thought was Venice. I wonder,' said Detterling, 'I wonder what those two are up to.'

Detterling's question was to be answered soon enough. The very next morning, at ten o'clock, the telephone rang in his drawing-room and the concierge asked his permission to send up the Signor Max de Freville.

'Morning, Canteloupe,' said de Freville as he was shown in, pronouncing the name in the same tone of polite acceptance as Tom had adopted the previous evening. 'I knew you'd be staying in the Gritti.'

'Good of you to call. When did you and Lyki arrive in Venice?'

'A day or two ago. We only realized you were here when we spotted you and your party last night.'

'I gather you've hired the Albani,' Detterling said. 'Does that flash gondola of yours go with it?'

'That gondola is Lyki's. He had it built to his own specification years ago . . . in 1959, I think, when he was running the Baccarat Bank at the Casino here.'

'Tell him it defies the sumptuary laws of the Venetian Republic. The cabin is not of regulation design, and that metal-work all over the hull is an exhibition disallowed even to noble-men.'

'Do the sumptuary laws still apply? I thought they went with the last Doge.'

'Perhaps they did and perhaps they didn't. But the Venetians are in a very odd mood, Max, and this is no time for conspicuous display by foreigners.'

'I'll tell Lyki you said so. But I don't think he'll take any notice. You know what Greeks are, Canteloupe: no tact and no taste.'

'Since we're talking of taste and tact, how are you and Lyki getting on with your plans to wreck Corfu?'

A hurt expression appeared on Max de Freville's face. The deep furrow, which dipped from his nostrils to the corners of his mouth, opened like wounds.

'You know I'm trying to play that down,' he said morosely. 'Angela's always hated what we're doing to the island, and I'm trying to placate her by limiting our operations.'

'From what I hear, you're building as many hotels as ever. You've even put one on the beach at Ermones. Nausicaa's beach,' said Detterling. 'You wouldn't even leave that alone.'

'Lyki insisted and I couldn't stop him. But I'll tell you what,' said Max de Freville, becoming visibly more cheerful, 'that hotel at Ermones may well be the last. Things are falling apart on Corfu. Greek inflation is making nonsense of available capital, and there aren't enough tourists even to fill the hotels that are up already.'

'Why so pleased about it, Max? You surely don't want to go broke?'

'I shan't go broke. We've got other investments – including a large share of that film of the Odyssey which was made on Corfu three years back. I'm told it's doing rather well.'

'It'll need to – if it's to make up for all your hotels going smash.'

'I don't mind being poorer, much poorer,' said Max, 'if only

I can do what Angela wishes – stop Lyki from turning the whole island into a lump of concrete.'

'Then stop him,' said Detterling, uneasily reflecting that Angela had now been dead for nearly three years.

'It's difficult. In name, he's head of the whole concern – I had to concede that to make the thing workable under Greek law. So if he wants to go on building – which he still does – he can only be stopped, in the end, by lack of cash. Which is just what I'm hoping will happen.'

'I see... And so what brings you to Venice?'

'Lyki brings me to Venice. He didn't want to leave me behind on my own, because he's long since rumbled my change of heart and thinks I might deliberately screw things up on Corfu even worse than they are already.'

'Then why did he leave the place at all? What brings *Lyki* to Venice?'

'Ah,' said Max de Freville, wrinkling his nose part in amusement and part in annoyance, 'you may well ask.'

'And shall I be answered, Max?'

'I don't see why not, though it isn't for everyone's ears. Keep it under your coronet, Canteloupe, if you please. The long and the short of it all is that we have, or soon will have, a very trying liquidity problem. New projects, as I say, are likely to be postponed or cancelled – and even then, with the present recession what it is, we shall barely have enough to keep afloat. So Lykiadopoulos has been doing some arithmetic, and taking into account the probable rate of inflation from now on, he has concluded that in order to be safe we shall need another million quid in the kitty by next April.'

'What's all this to do with Venice?'

'He hopes to find the money here,' said Max de Freville. 'I mentioned a few minutes back that he ran a Baccarat Bank in Venice in 1959. He made a lot of money then, and he hopes to make even more now. Tomorrow he's going to see the Directors of the Municipal Casino, hoping to persuade them to let him run a full-scale Baccarat Bank from October through to March, with our assets on Corfu as his security.'

'Dwindling assets.'

'And very rapidly dwindling at that. But although Lyki's worried sick about tomorrow's interview with the Directors, I think he'll have his way with them. Any dish Lyki cooks up has the right smell, and he's a specialist in presentation.'

'But surely,' said Detterling, 'you two own a substantial interest in the Casino on Corfu. Wouldn't it be much easier to set this bank up there?'

'The Casino on Corfu is peanuts. In Venice they still gamble with big money.'

'Big enough to bring him in a million?'

'That's what he's hoping.'

'And what are your hopes, Max?'

'I shall just watch and wait. If Lyki wins his million, then we shall have enough to safeguard our existing installations. So far, so good : there's no getting rid of the bloody things now they're built, so better they're kept going than rot to pieces. What worries me is the chance that he might win much more than we need to tick over and have cash to spare for his beastly new projects.'

'So what you'd like is for him to win enough to keep everything cosy—'

'—Anything up to eleven or twelve hundred thousand—'

'—But no more.'

'That's about it.'

'Unlikely that he'll win more,' said Detterling. 'Eleven or twelve hundred thousand is a very long order.'

'He'll have six months. The minimum stake for the punters will be very stiff. Big Baccarat Banks are few and far between these days, so this one will attract attention; and there's still a lot of people about with money to lose.'

'I get the impression they're no longer interested in losing it. This kind of thing's going out, Max.'

'Going, perhaps, but not gone.'

'All right. Along come the few remaining big spenders and start betting in maximums. How high is that?'

'Five million lire, if the Directors will allow it. Ten million on special days.'

'Three and a half thousand quid, that makes, and seven thousand for festivals. Suppose they get lucky and clean Lykiadopoulos out?'

'They won't do that.'

'How can you be sure?'

'I've known Lyki for a very long time. However lucky other people get, he always gets luckier.'

'That's sheer bravado, Max. Lyki can be broken like anyone else. What happens if he is?'

'We'll see when the time comes.'

'You seem very fatalistic about it all.'

'Why not? I don't see much future left, Canteloupe, for our kind of people. It's all coming to an end for us. Closing time in the Playgrounds of the West, as somebody once said. But there is just a little while left, and now I'm going to spend the next six months of it in a beautiful palace in the most beautiful city in the world. I'll settle for that – and leave the problems till they come. The chances are there'll be nothing I can do about them anyway.'

He smiled at Detterling, who shook his head in deprecation. But Max went on smiling, and gradually a dreamy look – almost, Detterling would have said, a soppy look – spread all over his face.

'But there is one problem,' Max went on, 'which I shall attend to immediately. The state of this city. I'm going to see what I can do to help the Venice in Peril fund. Angela will like that; the place has always been one of her favourites. I'm going to look around and see what, in my opinion, are the things which most urgently need doing, and then decide which of them, from a practical point of view, *can actually be done*. There's a lot of such things which can't possibly be done because it's too late and the cost's too high; but there's also a lot of quite important jobs which could still be managed, even on the relatively small sums which I can contribute. I shall raise what I can and send it in to the fund, with a special report, recommending where and to what my money would be best applied.'

'Why bother?' Detterling drawled. 'If the Playgrounds of the West are closing, as you say, and if, in any case, people like you and me are going to be turned out of them, why spend money and effort on their preservation?'

'I want Angela to see that I have tried,' said Max in a shrill voice. 'I know I shall be beaten in the end, but to please *her*, Canteloupe, I must try. Anyway, I shall need some occupation,' he went on, in a somewhat saner tone. 'I have no real part to play in Lykiadopoulos's arrangements for this bank.'

The telephone rang. Detterling picked up the receiver and listened.

'Very well,' he said, and rang off. 'Fielding Gray,' he said to Max de Freville. 'Are you prepared to be civil to him?'

'More or less. Whatever he did to Angela, he's had his punishment. I know she's forgiven him.'

'Good,' said Detterling evenly. 'He's staying in Venice for some time, and now I come to think of it, you might get him to help you conduct this survey of yours. He'd be useful, and it would do him good.'

'Has he the right kind of approach? Literary tastes rather than visual, I should have thought.'

'At any rate, try him.'

'All right, I'll try him. When he gets here, I'll take you both off for a look at the Albani. If he is appreciative ... in the right way ... then he could be my man. After all, he's very sensitive – or so Angela's always said.'

At the same time that morning as Detterling and Max de Freville were talking in the Gritti, Daniel Mond finished his packing in Lancaster College, Cambridge, and telephoned to engage a taxi to meet him presently at the Porters' Lodge. Everything was in order : he had been granted leave of absence by the Provost; he had informed his bedmaker and said all his goodbyes; he had arranged that someone else should take his tutorials in mathematics when Full Term began; and he had sent a telegram to Tom Llewyllyn in Venice, warning him that he would arrive by the late afternoon train on the next day. Now all that remained was to make sure that he left behind nothing which he would be needing. He carried his suitcase from his bedroom into his sitting-room, and looked carefully round.

It was astonishing, Daniel thought, how little he had acquired, apart from books, since he first came to live in this set in 1953. Twenty years, and all he had achieved by way of decoration was a mediocre print of the college chapel, an eight-day clock (a present from a pupil) which no longer worked, a framed photograph of Tom Llewyllyn and himself standing on the college bridge, and the regimental badge, mounted on a small wooden shield, of the 49th Earl Hamilton's Light Dragoons.

One by one he looked at these. No; nothing he would need. Time to go.

But as he walked towards the door, he halted, put down his case, and returned to look once more at the mounted badge. 'The old skull and coronet,' he muttered to himself, and thought of Corporal-Major Chead and Trooper Lamb and Mugger in the stores; of Giles Glastonbury and Geddes the Squadron barber, of Mick Motley and Captain Fielding Gray. What was it Corpy Chead had said when he gave him that badge years ago? 'You can polish all you want, friend ... but that skull will keep on grinning.' Yes, that was it. I wonder, he thought, what Corpy Chead is doing now.

Time to go. He put out his hand almost guiltily, took up the wooden shield, and slipped it into the pocket of his jacket. He carried his suitcase outside on to the stairs, closed the inner door, hesitated briefly, and then sported the oak. But did one *sport* it, he thought, when one was going away? Or did one sport it, properly speaking, only when oneself was inside and behind it? In which case, he supposed, when one was going away one merely closed it. In any case at all, his oak was now shut.

He stepped out over the dewy autumn grass by the river, walked slowly up the path which went by the Provost's Lodge and the College Hall, then on to the lawn of the Great Court, and paused by the central statue of the Founder. 'Beate Henrice,' he whispered, 'ora pro nobis', although he did not believe in God. As he walked on, Jacquiz Helmutt came in through the Porters' Lodge. Since Daniel had said good-bye to Jacquiz the previous night, it was rather embarrassing to meet him like this, so he smiled vaguely and made to walk straight on; but Jacquiz confronted him full-face and barred his way.

'Good-bye again, Danny,' Jacquiz said. 'I hope you'll soon be feeling better.'

'Thank you, Jacquiz,' said Daniel, the tiny voice grating from his ruined throat.

'Give Tom my best wishes and have a nice rest in Venice. We'll miss you when Full Term starts. Any idea when you'll be back?'

'At God's good pleasure,' rasped Daniel thinly, although he did not believe in God.

'Er – well – au revoir,' said Jacquiz, and moved away quickly, as if he had suddenly thought of something important which he must do at once.

Time to go.

The Porter on duty was Wilfred, who smiled and waved at Daniel in his usual friendly way but did not, being a man of rare courtesy, bother Daniel with questions either about his going or his coming back.

'Taxi's ready waiting, sir,' said Wilfred. 'Want a hand with your case?'

'No, thank you. It's very light.'

'Well, sir : cheerio.'

'Cheerio, Wilfred,' Daniel said.

The taxi was waiting on the college stones outside the Lodge. Had he remembered to pack his thick fawn jersey with the roll collar, the one that Mrs Constable, the Provost's wife, had given him? 'For protection against the fen air,' Elvira Constable had said : 'it's very treacherous.' And so, Daniel thought, was the air in Venice. But there was nothing he could do about the jersey. It would look odd if he opened his case on the stones to find out whether it was inside, and in any event he could not go back for it now.

The Palazzo Albani, as Max de Freville explained to Fielding and Detterling on the way there, was up for hire because Benito Albani and his wife, sole surviving members of the Venetian branch of the Albani dei Conti Monteverdi, had left Venice some years back and gone to live in Siena, where the family had its origins. Not only was the Palazzo for hire, it was also for sale if anyone would buy it; but this was not in the least likely, since the building, while undeniably both curious and attractive, was also sprawling, intricate, unsound, incommodious and exceedingly expensive to maintain. It was, said Max, only through the perverse whim of Lykiadopoulos that they had taken the place; however pleased with it he (Max) might be for antiquarian and aesthetic reasons, it was, from a domestic point of view, at once an extravagance and a nightmare.

Max's judgements, both adverse and favourable, began to receive illustration from the moment they disembarked from their motor-boat on to the steps of the entrance in the Rio Dolfin. As Baby Llewyllyn had observed the previous evening, there was a lantern over the entrance; but what Baby had not been able to see from a distance was that this was at the centre of a circle formed by seven small projecting stones, which were carved into grotesque but very humorous miniatures of the seven deadly sins.

'How Ruskin would have hated them,' said Fielding. 'He always deplored the way the Venetians saw vice – as funny instead of wicked.'

Max gave Fielding a thoughtful look. The Major-Domo on whom Baby had reported, splendid in wig, yellow coat piped in red, and silk breeches and stockings, opened the door from within and walked backwards, with arms spread daintily, bowing. They were now in a large, crude hall which, Max explained, took up the whole of the ground floor, having been used for many centuries, in accordance with the Venetian custom, as a warehouse. It was now absolutely empty except for one wooden bench.

'Quite uninhabitable,' said Max: 'cold, damp and hardly any windows. God knows what kind of state the Albini's merchandise got into when it was stored here ... but of course the water kept much lower then.'

'The Albani weren't above trade?' asked Fielding.

'No Venetian has ever been above trade... There's another door at the far end for pedestrians, leading into the Calle Alba, but it's not at all the thing to arrive or leave on foot.'

They went up a flight of plain stone stairs, which lacked rail or balusters, along a stone corridor, through a padded door, and into a circular anteroom. The few chairs looked as though they would collapse if an infant sat on them, and the hangings (Fielding noticed) were frankly tatty. There were no windows, only doors, since the anteroom, Max told them, was dead in the centre of the piano nobile and was surrounded on all sides by other rooms, a ceremonial dining-room to the left, kitchens to the rear, and for the rest Max's own sitting-room (which looked out over the Rio Dolfin), his bedroom, bathroom and dressing-room, and a small den in which his manservant performed the offices of valeting. The guided tour was clearly to be of 'public' rooms only, for Max did not offer to show them his own set but led them straight into the dining-room on the left.

This was spectacular. It ran the whole length (from the Rio Dolfin to the Calle Alba) of the Palazzo, making a long rectangle which was broken only by a convex curve, formed by a segment of the anteroom, in the central portion of the inner wall. All along this wall were bracketed candelabra, those on the circumference of the curve being of nine branches (in tiers of five, three and one) and of sumptuous design. The doorway (in the centre of the convexity) was surmounted by a pediment which displayed a frieze of the deserted Ariadne; Ariadne herself, weeping and rending her piquant breasts, stood upright from base to apex, while Theseus' ship was slipping away into the left-hand angle and Bacchus and his crew were distantly emerging from the angle on the right. The tale was continued in the pediment which topped the high mantel over the fireplace at the far end of the room: in this frieze Ariadne and

Bacchus and his entire gang, including the obese Silenus, were involved in a complicated orgy, a great feature of which was the rapt expression on the face of a leopard who was being orally pleasured by a pre-pubescent but priapic faun.

'*That*,' said Max, 'the Albani had to keep covered. By Dogal decree.'

All of this was beguiling enough; but the chief excellence of the room lay not in the room itself, not in the candelabra nor in the friezes, nor even in the magnificent black table that ran on legs carved as gods and heroes for thirty yards down the middle; it lay in the view which was to be had from any of the seven windows which were set along the outer side wall. Framed between thin stone shafts which supported ogival canopies, they were absolutely plain both in surface and in substance; and what one saw through them was this :

On the right a wall, which rose sheer beside the waters of the Rio Dolfin to a height of twenty feet and was an immediate continuation of the façade of the Palazzo. To the left of this wall, an enclosed garden. In the centre of the garden a gravel path, forming a perfect square and flanked by rose bushes and statuary; within the square an unkempt lawn; and at its centre a fountain – a nymph pouring from an urn, looking sadly at the ground as well she might, for her urn was dry and no waters ran. Outside and all round the square, a pretty wilderness of shrubs and tall grasses and trees, ilex and lady-birch, apple and cherry; and through the wilderness little tracks (much overgrown) running to little clearings (now hard to define) in which were garden seats of elegant design and tainted metal. To the left of the garden a wall (on the other side of which, thought Detterling, must run the Calle Alba) matching, in height and texture, the wall which separated the garden from the Rio Dolfin. At the far end of the garden the tall side, masked by trees up to forty feet but above that absolutely blank, of the next building along the Rio.

And there was one thing more of note. On the far side of the formal square path, set well back in the wilderness and surrounded by a cluster of tiny plane trees, stood a round tower. This was perhaps forty feet high, pierced by small but frequent windows, and crowned, like the turret of a French castle, by a cone which bore a weather-vane, this being in the shape of a mounted and fully armoured knight, the point of whose lance indicated whence the wind blew to Venice.

'What's that?' Detterling asked of Max de Freville. 'A summerhouse?'

'A pleasure pavilion. Supper-room on the ground floor, well-appointed bedroom above it. Built by the same Albani as commissioned the Ariadne friezes. Young Piero – Lyki's boy – wanted to have it for himself when we got here, but Lyki likes his boys under his eye and under the same roof, so he told Piero that the tower wasn't hygienic – no plumbing. Piero said he could use a commode, as they did in the days when it was built, and Lyki said that Piero wasn't living in the slums of Syracuse any more and must forget the filthy habits he learned there, and there was nearly a nasty row. Luckily Piero's a sensible little boy, so in the end he shut up and moved in where Lyki told him – on the third floor of the Palazzo. Lyki's on the second. We'll go on up there now.'

'So the tower in the garden is empty,' said Fielding, as they walked up the plain stone stairway to a stone corridor on the second floor. 'Just as well perhaps. Let the ghosts take their pleasures undisturbed.'

Once again, Max gave him a thoughtful look; then he led the way through a padded door into an anteroom very much the same as the one on the floor beneath.

'Same arrangement all the way up,' said Max. 'On the right are Lyki's private rooms, and on the left a drawing-room.'

Lykiadopoulos, rotund and glossy, came out of a door on their right and bounced up to them as if made of rubber. Although his acquaintance with Detterling and Fielding was very slight, he greeted them with enthusiasm.

'My dear Lord Canteloupe, my dear Major Gray. Welcome to our beautiful house. But there is nothing worth looking at on this floor, we shall go up to see the portraits ... and you shall meet our Piero.'

They mounted a third flight of plain stone steps, went along yet another stone corridor, through yet another padded door, and into a third circular anteroom.

'Piero,' called Lykiadopoulos in a high voice, 'you may come out, my birdie. Come out and meet our guests.'

After a few moments a door in front of them opened and the boy Piero, wearing wide blue trousers and a short yellow jacket of velvet, limped across the ante-room towards them.

'You are welcome,' he said to Fielding and Detterling in a low, modest voice.

His thin childish face and long dark hair, which swept back over his ears and tapered to a little tail down the back of his neck, reminded Fleming of an acolyte he had once seen in a Beardsley drawing of Venus at her toilette. But unlike the acolyte Piero did not simper or leer or giggle; when introduced to Detterling and Fielding he shook hands very correctly and looked them both gravely and full in the face.

'Your friends will want to see the portraits,' he said to Lykiadopoulos, and led the way out of the anteroom and into a chamber identical in shape and dimensions with the dining-room on the first floor. It was absolutely empty, except for a long row of portraits down the inner wall.

'The Albani portraits,' said Max de Freville.

'All by mediocre hands,' said Lykiadopoulos, 'and not valuable, but a complete record of the family, from the man who built the Palazzo down to the man who is hiring it to us today.'

'*Simpatici*,' Piero said. 'They have pleasant looks, have they not?'

Slowly they moved from the fifteenth-century Albani who had founded the Palazzo, past a number of calm and knowing faces, until they came to a picture much larger than the rest, a family group which must have been painted (Fielding reckoned) towards the end of the eighteenth century. Father and mother seated; two small children on the floor in front of them; a boy of about Piero's age, and of somewhat the same grave yet childish cast of countenance, standing behind the mother; a girl perhaps a year older, very fresh in the cheeks, standing behind the father; and, standing behind and between the boy and girl, an alien figure – a young man in his middle twenties, comely enough to look at but conveying with his green eyes and strongly set mouth a definite impression of pride and even arrogance that was wholly lacking in the other persons in the picture or in any of the Albani portraits which Fielding and Detterling had yet seen. For while the Albani faces down the centuries suggested that their owners were given to the quiet and steady pursuit of tasteful and available pleasures, the features of the young man at the rear of the family group indicated an inclination to whim and a readiness to dictate.

'Who's that?' Fielding said. 'A stranger in the nest.'

'We do not know,' said Piero. 'The husband and wife are Fernando and Maria Albani. The two little ones are twins, Francesco and Francesca. The girl, the eldest child, was called Euphemia, and the boy, like me, Piero. But the man between them, *bello ma non simpatico*, him we do not know.'

'Funny,' said Detterling : 'he has a look of Canteloupe's dead boy, Muscateer. Mind you, Muscateer had a much kinder face and he was only nineteen when he died; but still, if he'd grown, he might have been rather like that.'

'Your memory goes back a long way,' said Max. 'Canteloupe's boy Muscateer died in 1946.'

'I watched him dying,' Detterling said.

'Who was this . . . Muscateer?' Piero asked.

Fielding started to explain. Captain Detterling, now Lord Canteloupe, had been a distant cousin of the late Lord Canteloupe, who had had a son called Lord Muscateer, who had died of jaundice while serving his King in India.

'Jaundice,' said Piero, as they lagged behind the rest of the party, 'what is that? A plague, a fever, such as kills men in hot countries?'

'No. Hepatitis. An illness of the liver . . . hepatico,' Fielding hazarded.

This Piero understood.

'One does not die of that,' he said.

'Muscateer did.'

'In India. . . Poor Muscateer, so far from his home. Why was he named Muscateer,' said Piero, evidently anxious to know, 'when his father was named Canteloupe?'

'In England,' said Fielding, 'the eldest son of an important lord is called by the second of his father's titles.'

'I see. And this Captain Detterling, now Lord Canteloupe – has he a son?'

'No. He is not married.'

'But when he marries and has a son, that son will be called Muscateer? Because Captain Detterling is Lord Canteloupe, is also Lord Muscateer.'

Piero was so pleased at having mastered the principle that Fielding had not the heart to explain why it did not, in the case of Detterling, apply.

'I wish *I* was called Lord Muscateer,' Piero went on. He touched Fielding's arm and led the way across the room to the windows which looked down on the garden. 'Look,' he said : 'that tower. That would be my castle. To be called Lord Muscateer and live in a little castle. . .'

'You live in a very fine Palazzo.'

'Yes, but for how long?'

Piero glanced down the room towards Lykiadopoulos, then turned his face to look levelly at Fielding. Fielding, who took the point, gently shrugged his shoulders.

'Mr Lykiadopoulos,' said Piero, 'is kind but very strict. He would not let me live in the tower. He will not like you and me talking too long now. Come.'

Piero and Fielding walked down the room to join Lykiadopoulos, Detterling and Max in front of the final portrait, that of Benito Albani, absentee owner of the Palazzo. Fielding looked at the typical Albani face: agreeable, sceptical, placid, indicative of a self-indulgent disposition kindly and carefully schooled by its possessor.

'Why did he leave for Siena?' Fielding asked.

'They say,' said Max, 'that he found Venice no longer to be real. The Albani have always dealt in terms of realities, and Benito was put out when none was left. I'm told he said that living in Venice was like living in a dream, which did not suit him, as dreams cannot be controlled by intelligence.'

'A pretty cool lot, these Albani.'

'*Ma simpatici,*' insisted Piero.

'One can be both.'

They all walked down the stone corridor towards the stairs. There was yet another flight going up, and Detterling, who was in the lead, made to ascend this.

'No,' said Lykiadopoulos with (Fielding thought) unnecessary earnestness. 'There is only the servants' rooms up there. The attics.'

Piero looked at Fielding and gave him, for whatever reason, a wide grin. This was the first time Piero had smiled, and on the whole, Fielding felt, he did better not to; he smiled like a whore, venal, insinuating, obscene. But it seemed that Piero knew this himself; for after only a split second the grin disappeared totally and Piero became his grave and modest self again. I wonder, thought Fielding, what he found so funny as to make him forget himself; what can there be up that stairway?

Clearly he was not to find out. For,

'Now you have seen all,' said Lykiadopoulos, leading the way quickly down the stone steps. 'I have work. Max will telephone for a motor-boat for you.' He stopped suddenly and turned, then called up to Piero, who stood uncertainly on the top stair of the flight.

'Do not come down, little one,' Lykiadopoulos called. 'You will only tire your poor leg. Our guests will forgive you, that you do not see them off. Go to your room.'

'When will you take me to the Piazza?'

'This afternoon, this evening. Now go to your room.'

Piero lifted a hand, to salute Detterling and Fielding, and limped away down the corridor.

'Nicely mannered boy, that,' said Detterling as they all continued their descent.

'Yes. Good morning, Lord Canteloupe, Major Gray.' Lykiadopoulos turned down the corridor which led to his own apartments. 'You will forgive me that I too do not see you off. There is a lot of work.'

'Funny,' said Detterling, as Max led him and Fielding on downwards : 'he seemed delighted to see us, but now he can't get rid of us too quickly.'

'He didn't like it,' said Fielding, 'when you tried to go up to the attics.'

Max twitched slightly at this observation, as if he both resented it and appreciated the acumen behind it.

'It's only,' Max said in a cajoling voice, 'that's he's nervous. He's got a lot on his mind – this interview with the Directors tomorrow, and all the preparations he'll have to make to get his bank set up. When that's all settled, we'll both want to see a lot of you here. We'll give a dinner soon. I'm hoping,' he said to Fielding, 'to go about Venice these next weeks seeing what a bit of money might do to stop the rot. Canteloupe here thinks you might be interested in helping me.'

'Why not? If you can let bygones be bygones, so can I.'

'Then you'll hear from me later. But one thing, Fielding. When you come here, do not interest yourself in Piero.'

'I suppose I can be civil?'

'Civil but distant, if you please. Anything else would anger Lyki; he knows your sort. As I say, Lyki's got a lot on his mind just now,' said Max de Freville, 'and it would be ... unfortunate ... if he were to get upset.'

When Daniel Mond arrived in Venice the next evening, Tom and Baby met him at the station. Baby kissed Daniel shyly and chastely (for he always had a quietening effect on her) and Tom picked up his suitcase.

'Not much luggage,' Baby said.

'Not much need,' said Daniel.

But lightly burdened though they were, Tom hired a motor-boat (largely because Baby's conduct on public transport was not always discreet) and from this they disembarked at a quay near the Campo di San Giovanni e San Paolo.

'We're in the Pensione San Paolo,' said Tom, 'just behind the church.'

'I always liked this part of Venice,' said Daniel, 'even that brute Colleoni.'

'I think Colleoni's lovely,' said Baby. ' "A brow like Mars to threaten and command".'

'The trouble is,' said Tom to Daniel, ignoring Baby's cultural show-off, 'that the San Paolo is closing for the winter in a few days. We'll have to look out for something else.'

'Anything quiet will do.'

They booked Daniel in at the Pensione San Paolo, then returned to the Campo and sat down at a table, in the shadow of Colleoni, for a drink. A few minutes later they were joined by Fielding and Detterling, in accordance with an arrangement made with Fielding by Tom that morning.

'He'll be tired,' Tom had said on the telephone, 'but he'll be glad to see you. Please be very easy with him. And please bring Canteloupe with you.'

'He hardly knows Canteloupe.'

'That's just the point. It'll make it all look more natural and casual than if you come alone.'

'I don't see it.'

'If you come alone,' Tom had said, 'it'll look as if you've come especially as an old friend for a privileged inspection.'

'Tom . . . you're not making much sense.'

'Never mind, Fielding. Just do as I ask.'

And so Fielding had done. But as he arrived with Detterling now, and looked at Daniel, who gave a serene smile of greeting, he wondered, rather crossly and not for the first time, what all this fuss and fiddle-faddle were about. If Daniel wished to join Tom in Venice, why could he not have fixed a definite date and just come, like anybody else? Why had Tom been kept waiting on Daniel's pleasure, uncertain when Daniel would arrive and yet insistent that he must be there to meet him? And why so much solicitude about how and with whom Fielding should present himself to Daniel that evening?

'Canteloupe will take Baby home when he goes,' Tom was

now explaining to Daniel, 'so I can stay put in Venice from now on. We can start looking for digs in a day or two and move into them when Baby leaves.'

Daniel nodded. He seemed to take it for granted (Fielding thought) that some such arrangement should have been made about Baby and that from now on Tom should be entirely at his disposal.

'What a pity,' said Baby to Detterling, 'that we can't go home on a boat. That might take *weeks*.'

'Alas,' said Detterling courteously, 'the world is too much with us.' Then to Tom, 'What's all this about looking for digs? I thought you were settled.'

Tom told him about the closure of the San Paolo.

'This habit of closing places out of season is getting to be an absolute curse,' Detterling said. 'It means re-engaging the servants every spring – or worse, engaging new servants – so that they don't begin to understand what they're doing until the season's nearly over again.'

'I think,' said Tom, 'that the San Paolo is closing for modernization.'

'Which means there'll be four rooms the size of boot cupboards for every one room they had before.'

'Very optimistic,' said Fielding, 'to spend money modernizing a hotel in Venice just now.'

'But the fact is,' said Baby, who had an eye to essentials, 'that it *is* being closed and Poppa must find somewhere else. And just as well, if you ask me. The San Paolo's a real dump. There was a spider dropped out of my shower.'

'Speak no ill of the San Paolo' said Tom. 'Once, when I was an undergraduate, the owner lent me enough money to feed myself on the way home to England. Currency was very tight in those days, and he knew he couldn't possibly see me or his money again for at least a year.'

'If he's an old friend,' said Daniel, 'he might suggest somewhere for us to go.'

'He sold out and vanished years ago,' said Tom, 'though I still stay there for old times' sake.'

'You know,' said Detterling, 'I think I might have the answer for you.'

'Somewhere quiet and moderately priced,' said Daniel. 'Which will take us for an indefinite period.'.

'And I must have a table big enough to spread my work on,' said Tom.

'And so, one assumes, must Mr Mond.'

'Mr Mond,' said Daniel, 'can do such work as he has on his lap.'

'Well, I think I know something,' said Detterling. 'Something which meets all your conditions and is rather out of the ordinary too. I can't promise, but I can let you know about it for certain in twenty-four hours.'

'Very kind, Lord Canteloupe,' Daniel murmured.

'The least I can do. The last time you needed my help I rather let you down. In Baden Baden, if you remember?'*

'Very clearly. But I don't know that it was your fault. Anyway, it was a long time ago . . . over twenty years.'

'I shall try to do better by you this time,' said Detterling. 'Please leave it to me.'

'It is,' said Tom, not looking at Detterling but gazing warily past him at the pedestal of Colleoni's statue, 'perhaps more a matter for Daniel and me.'

'You can always go somewhere else,' said Detterling coolly, 'if you don't like the place I hope to arrange.'

'What do you hope to arrange?'

'I'd sooner not say until I'm sure I can arrange it.'

'Rather odd of you,' said Tom in a brittle voice.

A football, kicked by one of a crowd of little boys who were playing in the Campo, bounced into Tom's lap. He stood up and threw it angrily from him, over the rails which guarded Colleoni's plinth. The boys looked at him reproachfully, and one of the eldest began carefully climbing over the rails to retrieve their toy.

'Poor little boy,' said Baby annoyingly.

'You shut up.'

'Tom,' said Daniel, and rested his hand for a second on Tom's shoulder. 'I'm rather tired and I'd like to go in and rest.'

'Sorry,' muttered Tom.

Daniel finished his drink and rose.

'I understand, Lord Canteloupe,' he said to Detterling, 'why you don't want to tell us what you have in mind for us. It's rather special, isn't it, and you don't want us to be disappointed if you can't, after all, arrange for us to go there?'

'That's about it,' said Detterling, looking pleased.

*See *The Sabre Squadron* p. 216 and *passim*.

'Then kindly go ahead and do your best,' said Daniel. 'It's very civil of you to offer. If you say it's special—'

'—Out of the ordinary, I said—'

'—Out of the ordinary, then I'm sure we shall like it if we can have it.' And to Tom, 'It will save us both a lot of trouble.'

'Of course,' said Tom. 'I was being silly. Come on, Tullia. We'll go in now with Daniel.'

'I want to stay with Lord Canteloupe,' Baby said.

'Go with your father when he asks you,' said Detterling levelly.

Baby went. Detterling and Fielding remained sitting tête-à-tête in the Campo. An empty barge passed down the nearby canal in the dusk. The little footballers were suddenly gone. A man and a woman in black crossed the Campo very slowly and went into the entrance of the Scuola San Marco, between the two vast sheets of sacking that hung on scaffolds in front of the façade.

'I'm told that façade has been hidden for nearly a year,' said Fielding. 'God knows when they'll finish whatever they're doing.'

'Pity.'

'Yes. Though of course the sacking is not inappropriate, since the Scuola is now a hospital. One always tends to forget that.'

'I don't suppose the Venetians forget it.'

'No... What did you make of Daniel Mond?'

'A mild man. A peace-maker,' Detterling said.

'We certainly needed one just now. I wonder what's got into Tom. His behaviour was most peculiar – like an affronted nanny.'

'No doubt it will all be made plain in time. Anyway,' said Detterling, 'it's none of my business. But I do like Mond, from the little I've seen of him, and that's why I volunteered to make arrangements about their diggings. I've had rather a nice idea.'

'What is it, Canteloupe?'

'You'll know as soon as they do ... if it comes off.' Detterling picked up his empty glass and clinked it against another. 'Time to get back to the Gritti,' he said.

'Why can't you tell me what you're trying to arrange for them?' said Fielding huffily.

'You're getting as prickly as Tom.' Detterling paid the waiter who had answered their summons. 'I prefer not to discuss my vision – for vision it is – until I have been able to realize it. A very sound rule, Fielding; you, as an artist of sorts, should be able to appreciate that. An unrealized vision is very vulnerable: it is easily spoiled or dirtied, easily reasoned or mocked away. One should keep it secret until one has given it a form solid enough to stand against the malice of time and chance ... and the human race. '

However anxious Detterling might be to guard his vision, he had no choice but to discuss it with those on whose good will he must depend to give it substance. The next morning he went to see Max de Freville and Lykiadopoulos in the Palazzo Albani.

'The word "Casino",' he began deviously, 'has three meanings in this country: an establishment with gaming-rooms; a common brothel; or, in a prior connotation, a "little house" (diminutive of "casa") built for the purposes of more or less disreputable private pleasures.'

'I dare say,' said Max. 'What of it?'

'But the pleasures need not necessarily be disreputable,' Detterling continued. ' "A little house" could be used to enjoy the pleasures of reflection, scholarship or conversation. Or, indeed, of quiet habitation.'

'No doubt. What is the point of this exegesis?'

'The point,' said Detterling, 'is that you and Lyki possess just such a little house or casino – that tower in your garden; and that I know two people who would thoroughly appreciate it. Should they be allowed to live there, the arrangement would be ... aesthetically apt.'

There was a long silence. Max looked at Detterling with suspicion, as though fearing that he was perpetrating some obscure joke. Lykiadopoulos was poker-faced.

'Who are they?' he said.

'Tom Llewyllyn is here in Venice – you saw him dining with me the other night. He has been joined by his friend Daniel Mond, a mathematics don of his college. They are looking for somewhere to live quietly together during the winter.'

'I know neither of them,' said Lykiadopoulos.

'But Max knows Llewyllyn, and I know both. I can vouch for them. You would be doing more than a kindness; by installing them in your tower you would, let me repeat, be creating an aesthetically pleasing scene.'

'Not very pleasing for them,' said Max. 'There is no running water for a start.'

'You have servants who could carry them water. They would rather like that. It will remind them of their undergraduate days just after the war, when the young gentlemen still had bowls and ewers in their bedrooms.'

'And chamber-pots,' said Max. 'They'd be needing them too. Where would they empty them? These days one cannot ask Italian servants to carry full jerries about.'

'Ah,' said Detterling. 'As to *that*, I thought some chemical device might be installed. I'd gladly pay for it, and there is plenty of time to have it done. They wouldn't want to move in till their hotel closes next week.'

'Very obliging of them,' said Max. 'Meals?'

'This part of Venice is full of cafés and restaurants.'

'I do not quite understand,' said Lykiadopoulos. 'What are they doing here, these two friends of yours?'

'They both have cause to spend the winter in Venice. Tom Llewyllyn has research to do. As for Mond's reasons, they have not been told to me and it would be discourteous, I fancy, to enquire very closely into them; but I think they are of a kind that might entitle him to consideration.'

'Are they poor, that you wish us to lodge them in such quarters? That tower is for summer pleasure,' said Lykiado-poulos, 'not for winter dwelling.'

'They are not rich but neither are they poor, and they could certainly afford a decent hotel for as long as they will be here. But the thing is,' said Detterling, 'that they both have – how shall I put it? – a flavour of the medieval scholar, or even of the monk, about them. So they will not mind, in fact they will rather enjoy, a little discomfort, and in any case they will soon make themselves snug. And then the cloistered setting ... a little tower in a walled garden ... will suit their temperaments. Of all people in the world, they will understand what such a place has to offer.'

Lykiadopoulos nodded.

'Very well,' he said, 'and why not? It will take perhaps a week to arrange that beds and furniture may be placed there, and that this sanitary "chemical device", for which you say you will pay, may be satisfactorily installed. Tell your friends they may move into our garden casino after one week. And during that week they shall come here to dinner so that I may make their acquaintance first.'

'You're sure you want them here?' said Max.

'Not particularly. But I want to stop Piero's hankering. Day after day he is at me, "why can he not live in that tower?" If it is full of other people, he will know he cannot live there and will be quiet. So that is settled, Max. And now,' said Lykiadopoulos, beaming on Detterling, 'since we are talking of casinos, I have interesting news. Those responsible for the Municipal Casino here have finally acceded to my request that I run a Baccarat Bank this winter.'

'When do you start?'

'When they change over from the Summer Casino, out on the Lido, to their winter premises on the Grand Canal. In just over three weeks.'

'On the Grand Canal? It's still the Palazzo Vendramin they use?'

'Oh yes indeed.'

'As far as I remember,' said Detterling, 'the gaming-rooms there are very pretty but rather pokey. Where are they going to fit you in?'

'That is a problem. Hitherto there have been Baccarat Banks only out on the Lido. To accommodate a table for eighteen persons and myself and the croupiers – to say nothing of the spectators – is not easy in the present rooms in the Palazzo Vendramin. So they are to open a new chamber one floor up, and I am to bear one half of the expense.'

'I don't see why you should,' said Max. 'They'll be taking five per cent every time your bank wins a coup, which will amount to a huge sum before the winter's done. The least they can do is fit up a suitable room for you.'

'Ah, but I am being very fussy, Max my friend. I am insisting on the most luxurious fittings, and on special arrangements for the service of food and drink so that my clientele do not have to descend to the bar and buffet below.'

'I still think the management should pay. They'll collect the profits from the catering.'

'Maybe not all of them,' said Lykiadopoulos. 'It is one of the many details that have still to be settled. But the important thing is that in principle we are agreed that my bank should commence on October the sixth. Already advertisements are being prepared, and letters will be sent to prominent gamblers on the books of the Casino.'

'What one must ask oneself,' said Detterling, 'is will enough of them come?'

'Why should they not?'

'Venice can be very putting-off in the winter, very damp and bleak – and all the worse now it's positively falling apart. And then there is always the danger of another 1966. But I think your worst enemy,' said Detterling, 'will be indifference. People just don't seem to go in for persistently high play any more – or at any rate not as persistent and as high as you'll be hoping for. The big games have all dried up in London. The high tables in the French Casinos are very poorly attended, by comparison with ten years ago. Somehow the whole thing seems to be losing its appeal. It is no longer considered amusing to drop really big money at the tables, or not by those that have the big money to drop. The rich, as a breed, are changing: they have become ... less visible, tighter and more discreet. They've had to, in order to survive.'

'And you, Lord Canteloupe,' said Lykiadopoulos, 'have you become tight and discreet?'

'I always was,' said Detterling. 'You ask Max. He'll tell you how tightly I used to play in his chemmy games in London back in the fifties. I never risked more than a few hundred the whole evening, and very seldom that. Eh, Max?'

'But you did come and play. Shall you have a go at Lyki's bank when it starts?'

'It would be a pleasure to see you there,' said Lykiadopoulos. 'The presence of an English marquis on the opening night would do much for the tone and would attract extra customers.'

'I might drop in as time goes on,' said Detterling. 'But not until much later in the winter, and certainly not on the opening night. I've got to go home and look into my new estate. Tight and discreet, you see. I'm flying back to London next week.'

'Please tell me exactly when,' said Lykiadopoulos. 'I want to arrange a day for this dinner your two friends are to come to.'

'I'm flying next Wednesday.'

'Shall we say Monday for dinner then? The seventeenth. We will make of it a farewell for you, a welcome for your friends, and also a celebration that I am given permission for my Baccarat Bank.'

'Can we ask Fielding Gray?' said Max. 'I want to talk to him about our inspection of Venice.'

'Certainly we can ask him, Max my friend. But I hope you are not preparing to be *too* liberal in your gifts to the fund for preservation.'

'Liberal or not,' Max answered sharply, 'I shall be giving only my own money.'

Lykiadopoulos shrugged gently, as if to imply (Detterling thought) that Max's money, as an entity separate from their joint interests, no longer existed. Max coloured.

'My money,' he insisted, 'or money that I myself have raised for Venice. There must be ways of doing that.'

'Most of them are being thoroughly explored by others,' said Lykiadopoulos smoothly. He turned to Detterling. 'Then that is settled, Lord Canteloupe. Dinner on Monday the seventeenth. You yourself and Major Gray, and your two friends who are to come into our tower. You will kindly engage them for me. Eight o'clock for eight-thirty.'

'Just one thing,' said Detterling. 'Can Tom Llewyllyn bring his daughter?'

'His daughter?'

'The little girl you saw from your gondola the other night. She's called Tullia – usually known as Baby.'

'Baby,' said Lykiadopoulos in quiet deprecation.

'She ran after us that evening,' said Max, 'and absolutely goggled into the gondola.'

'It was a very intriguing sight,' said Detterling, 'for a child of her age.'

'It was very rude behaviour for a child of any age. Also' – Max glanced at Lykiadopoulos – 'I fancy she's rather ... forward ... for hers.'

He's trying to ingratiate himself with Lykiadopoulos, Detterling thought: he's trying to make up for that spat about the money by warning Lykiadopoulos that Baby might raise naughty ideas in Piero. Max, thought Detterling, must be very much under Lykiadopoulos's thumb – or even his heel. Aloud he said:

'I'm taking her back to London with me on the Wednesday. We can't just leave her alone on the second last night of her holiday.'

'Do you promise that she will be ... *sage* ... if she comes?' asked Lykiadopoulos.

'She'll be good,' said Detterling. 'I'll tell her she's invited as a special treat before she goes home, but that the invitation is conditional on her behaving quietly. She understands that kind of bargain.'

'Does she?' said Lykiadopoulos. 'I'm told that very few of the young understand bargains these days and even fewer trouble to keep them.'

'She'll behave nicely if I ask her to,' said Detterling, 'for my sake.'

In fact he knew very well that Baby, though anxious to please him *ceteris paribus*, could not be relied on to behave nicely for his or anybody's sake. By issuing his guarantee he had put his personal credit with Max and Lykiadopoulos very much at risk. This he had done, not out of affection for Baby, but out of his sense of what was fair and proper: it was neither fair nor proper that any thirteen-year-old girl should be abandoned for a whole evening just at the end of her holidays; therefore Baby must come to this dinner; therefore he, Detterling, was prepared to enter into an undertaking, though he knew it to be imprudent, on her behalf. Whatever happens, he thought grimly, she'll enjoy the party: she's the kind that always does.

Lykiadopoulos, who had been watching Detterling's face, now nodded at him slowly, as if to say that he was privy to Detterling's process of thought, which he respected as a man of feeling but somewhat resented as Baby's future host.

'Very well,' he said with courteous reluctance. 'Ask Mr Llewyllyn to bring Tullia on the seventeenth. In view of her extreme youth we will dine earlier than I said before. All should come at seven o'clock for seven-thirty. Informal dress...'

'... So I suppose this will do,' said Baby Llewyllyn to Detterling, pulling at her tartan skirt.

'You wouldn't by any chance have something a bit longer?'

'No. My only other one is even shorter. Don't you like seeing my legs?'

'I'm thinking of Mr Lykiadopoulos. He might think that that outfit could, let us say, *confuse* Piero.'

'Piero?'

'The boy you saw in the gondola.'

'What a pretty name. Why does he limp, that boy?'

'I haven't asked. Come on, we're there.'

Detterling and Baby jostled their way off the vaporetto and stood looking up at the façade of San Giorgio Maggiore. Detterling had called on Tom and Daniel earlier that morning, to tell them about the dinner at the Palazzo Albani, and had found Baby kicking her heels in the foyer of the Pensione. Apparently Daniel wasn't feeling well and Tom was busy looking after him; and so Detterling, acting on the same principle as had made him insist that Baby should be asked to Lykiadopoulos's dinner, had volunteered to take her on for the day.

'How lovely,' Baby said now. 'Thank you for bringing me. I've seen San Giorgio from over the water, of course, but never close to.'

'Funny. I should have thought your father would have brought you.'

'Oh, Poppa doesn't care for Palladio. He thinks his buildings are smug.'

'But you like them?'

'I find them ... satisfying,' Baby said. She took his hand. 'Come on,' she said, 'let's go inside.'

She continued to hold his hand as they walked into the church, but he did not find this embarrassing. She was not up to her tricks, he realized; she was simply being friendly. Perhaps he was beginning to have a good effect on Baby; he certainly hoped so, as he did not want any trouble on the way back to London.

'We must see the Tintorettos,' Baby was saying, 'in the chancel. At least, most of the work is by Tintoretto, but he was very old when he painted them, so some of his pupils probably had to help.'

'You seem to know a lot about it.'

'I read it up in the guide book. One should always read the guide book,' Baby instructed him, 'before going to a place, to prepare oneself, and then again when one gets back, to remind oneself what one has seen and fix it in one's head.'

'A very good rule. Did you make it up for yourself?'

'No. Uncle Gregory Stern told me. He often takes me to see things. I think he fancies me.'

'Don't talk like that, Tullia,' said Detterling, in a tone so sharp that it surprised both of them.

'Why not?' she said, letting go of his hand. 'If it's true.'

'Because it isn't true, and because in any case it spoils things. You ... you spoil yourself when you talk like that.'

Baby gave Detterling a long and careful look.

'You mean,' she said, 'that you don't like me when I talk like that. But I've done it before, and you haven't complained. Why start now?'

'Because I didn't care before. That is, I hardly knew you before. I've been thinking,' he hurriedly changed the subject, 'about that dinner. You'll want to look grown-up.'

'Do *you* want me to look grown-up?'

'I think the best thing,' said Detterling, evading the question, 'will be a trouser suit. That will be very sensible from every point of view.'

'I haven't got a trouser suit.'

'I'll get you one.'

'Thank you,' she said coolly. 'Now look at these Tintorettos. The guide book says they're best seen from the altar rails.'

There was something here that puzzled him, something small and innocuous, yet which offended his sense of logic.

'Tullia,' he said, 'you haven't got that guide book with you?'

'No, my lord.' She laughed and spread her hands, then took one of his again. 'Uncle Gregory says one should always leave the guide book at home, because otherwise one will probably lose it somewhere and guide books are very expensive. Uncle Gregory,' she said, 'is a generous man but mean in small matters. Still, he's quite right about this, because if you bring the book you keep looking at it and not at what you came for.'

'But if you haven't got the book with you now, how do you know about these pictures?'

'I told you just now, silly. I read about them before we came, like Uncle Gregory said to do. Now please be quiet and look at them.'

'But Baby,' he persisted, 'you didn't know I was going to bring you to San Giorgio until we left your hotel. So how could you have re—'

'—I knew I would be coming here last night,' she said patiently, 'though I didn't know it would be with you. So I read all about it before I went to sleep.'

'*How* did you know?'

Baby shrugged.

'One does sometimes,' she said. 'Auntie Isobel says it's the same with her. Now please be quiet, my lord, and let's look at these lovely pictures.'

'These pictures, my birdie, you are forever looking at these pictures,' said Lykiadopoulos to Piero, who was gazing at the family group round Fernando and Maria Albani. 'They are not well done. This one is one of the worst. By the end of the eighteenth century there were few good artists in Venice, and the man who painted this was not among them.'

'I am puzzled, Lykiaki,' said Piero. 'That young man at the back does not belong. Who is he?'

'You have asked me before, and I have told you: I do not know, and it cannot matter.'

'Lord Canteloupe said he was like his cousin Muscateer, who died in India.'

'A fancy.'

'Lykiaki,' said Piero, turning from the family group, 'why can I not have that tower – just during the day? I could go there when you are busy.'

'What would you do there?'

'I could make it a pleasant place to be in. Arrange it and decorate it . . . if I may have a little money.'

'A little money you may have perhaps, my birdie, but you may not have the tower. Others are coming to live there. Two friends of Lord Canteloupe.'

Piero glowered with disappointment.

'What friends?'

'Two *professori*. An old acquaintance of Max, called Tom Llewyllyn, an historian, as I think. And a mathematician called Mond.'

'Why would two *professori* want to live in that tower?'

'Lord Canteloupe says they will appreciate it.'

'So would I . . . appreciate it.'

'The matter is settled, Piero. The two *professori* are coming to dinner on Monday, and with them Lord Canteloupe and the writer you have met here with him – Major Gray.'

'The man with the wounded face.'

'Also a little girl, Mr Llewyllyn's daughter. She was the one who waved at our gondola the other evening.'

'Is she coming to live in the tower?'

'She is going back to England, to school. Why do you ask?'

'Because she is a very pretty little girl,' said Piero.

'What is that to you?'

'I shall enjoy looking at her.'

'Look all you wish, my birdie, and let it stop there . . . unless you would sooner be back in Syracuse than here in Venice.'

'What harm can looking do if she is going back to England?'

'None. I tell you, you may look all you wish. But do not touch, Piero *mio*. Little girls are not for touching.'

'Why should I want to touch?'

'Because you are hot, you boys from Sicily. But hot boys from

Sicily who touch little English misses' – Lykiadopoulos lingered on the words with some relish – 'end up in prison.'

'I know what you would really like, Lyki *mou*. You would like for me to touch her, and for her to touch me, while you were watching. You would like to see my fingers go into her tight little knickers, and her hand reach to stroke my—'

Lykiadopoulos slapped Piero very hard on one cheek.

'You have sung enough of that song, my birdie. Of course,' said Lykiadopoulos calmly, 'you are quite right. But we may not think of such things.'

'We may think of them, if we may not do them. But I would gladly do that, or anything you wanted, to give you pleasure. I am here to give you pleasure, Lykiaki, and yet you ask nothing of me. All the time I have been with you, many months now, you have asked me to do nothing. What do you wish of me?'

'To be my little lame birdie, that is all. Time was, Piero *mio*, when I would have demanded pleasure from you every day, every night. But now it is enough to know that you are there ... and to know, also, that you are hot, oh, so hot, but cannot touch anyone else because I will not allow you.'

'And yet you say it would give you pleasure to watch me touch someone else. So why do you not do this? You are rich, it is easily arranged, a girl, or another boy if you wish, or a man—'

Once again Lykiadopoulos struck Piero on the cheek.

'I said, enough of that song. These things are not permitted, for they are sin, and though I have sinned myself in the past, I shall sin no more and I shall save you from sinning. Your poor ruined leg shall be a token that you are not for coupling, and that you are bound, by the will of God and by your fear of me, to be for ever clean.'

After a long silence, Piero said :

'I would sooner love you than fear you.'

'Your fear is the expression of your love.'

'A sad way of loving.'

'The most desperately and deeply felt, the most profound way of all. Only through abiding fear can there be abiding love ... the love I wish from you.'

'Can I not love you just because you have been kind to me?'

'You can love me for that, but not only for that. You must also fear and obey. And one of the things in which you will obey me is this : you must not sulk because you cannot have the tower, and when these *professori* come to dinner, *caro*, you must show them that they will be most welcome there.'

'I shall do my best,' said Piero, 'since you have asked me.'

'My birdie, I have commanded you,' Lykiadopoulos replied.

'And so,' said Piero to Daniel Mond, 'now that you have seen the tower, you will be glad to live in it?'

'It looked enchanting in the dusk. And Mr Lykiadopoulos has made very handsome arrangements inside it.'

'You will be all right with paraffin lamps?'

'I like them. They remind me of when I was a soldier.'

'You, a soldier?' said Piero dubiously.

'Well, not exactly. But once I spent some days with soldiers on a big manoeuvre. We had paraffin lamps in our tents. They made a small circle of very clear light, I remember, light you could easily read by, but they left the rest of the tent dark and mysterious. And yet one felt completely safe inside the circle . . . as though there were an invisible wall, put there by a magician, to keep out the creatures of the night. It was a very cosy experience.'

'I think I know what you mean,' Piero said, and started to smile at Daniel. Almost as soon as his smile began, however, he closed his lips sharply to shut it away, as if he had suddenly remembered, Daniel thought, that he had carious teeth or rotten gums which he must on no account reveal. But since he showed his teeth and gums quite unashamedly when he was talking, it could not be these that troubled him. So why, Daniel wondered, is he afraid to smile?

'Why do you smile?' Daniel asked.

'I did not smile.'

'You were just going to.'

'I was thinking . . . in my home in Syracuse we had paraffin lamps because there were no other kind. So I knew what you meant when you said their light made one feel so safe – though of course we longed to be rich and have the electricity.'

'You speak English remarkably well, for a boy from Sicily.'

Again Piero started to smile and again he clamped his lips shut.

'There you go again. You were just going to smile at me, but you stopped. Did you think I was making fun of you? I meant it. Your English is excellent.'

'I have had opportunity since ... since I knew Mr Lykiado-poulos.'

'Good. Then smile.'

'No. Why should I?'

'If you don't, I shall think I have offended you. Please smile.'

'Very well,' said Piero, and smiled. Daniel, despite himself, shrank slightly, and as the others at the table observed the smiling boy, they stopped talking, one by one. A long silence followed, which was at last broken by Baby Llewyllyn.

'Christ,' she said, 'what's up with you? You look like Lazarus saying "Hullo there" from his grave.'

Up to this stage of the evening, everything had gone smoothly. Tom and Daniel had been shown the tower and were as pleased with it as Detterling had hoped. For Lykiadopoulos had taken trouble and shown taste: each of the two main rooms had been furnished and arranged as a bed-sitting-room for one person; they were well warmed by oil heaters, comfortably carpeted, prettily hung about with pictures and curtains, and immacu-lately clean. ('This is what I should have wanted to do,' Piero had said aside to Lykiadopoulos, 'but with my own hands.') The chemical sanitation (which came with Detterling's compli-ments, as promised) had been installed in what had once served as kitchen and pantry to the former dining-room (now to be Daniel's apartment) on the ground floor; Tom would have to walk downstairs from his own room and then through Daniel's in order to come to it, but a certain amount of inconvenience was to be expected of such an establishment, and Tom and Daniel had known each other too long and too well to worry about niceties of privacy. For the rest, hot water would be brought over from the Palazzo every day at 8.30 a.m. and 7 p.m.; baths were to be had on request in Max's bathroom ('Or in mine,' Piero whispered to Daniel); and for meals Tom and Daniel would quite simply go out, proceeding through a door in the garden wall which opened into the Calle Alba. He would give them the key of this door, Lykiadopoulos said, as soon as they moved in – which, it was agreed, they were to do on the Wednesday afternoon, after Detterling had been seen off with Baby. This settled, and certain minor problems, such as the col-lection of laundry, having been raised and resolved, the party had crossed the garden to the Palazzo ('I wish I could live in that tower, it's so *snug*,' Baby said) and mounted to the dining-room on the first floor for dinner.

A round table had been set for the party's accommodation between the head of the long table and the fireplace, in which there was an extravagant log fire. They dined by the light of candles which had been carefully deployed (Detterling noticed) so as to leave the obscene carving on the pediment above the fireplace in complete darkness, out of respect, no doubt, for the tender years if not the innocence of Miss Tullia Llewyllyn. Baby, seated on the right of Lykiadopoulos, got along very well with him. Modest and composed, looking three years older in her new trouser suit than she did in her tartan outfit, she behaved beautifully and conducted a knowledgeable conversation with her host about the Titians in the Accademia, comparing them with those in the National Gallery in London. In other respects also the dinner had gone on swimmingly. As delicious courses and exquisite wines came and went, Fielding Gray and Max de Freville discussed their forthcoming excursions in Venice; Tom and Detterling discussed Tom's research and the future publishing ventures of Stern and Detterling (Detterling had still not found either a Communist who wished to default or a Senior Lady Novelist with available memoirs); and Daniel had been very contented to talk with Piero of the tower and to try to make out something of the boy's provenance. Later on, conversation had become general, had for a while waxed genial, and had then reverted, without any sense of strain or failure, to the former duologues. Everything, in fact, had been as friendly, as civilized, as enjoyable as the most dutiful host could hope or the most exigent guest require ... until, that is, Piero began to smile at Daniel's behest and Baby broke the ensuing silence by comparing the boy from Syracuse with the risen Lazarus.

'Or Lazarus rolled into Mary Magdalene,' Baby now emended herself, 'if you see what I mean.'

They all did; for Piero, as Fielding Gray had noticed on his previous visit to the Palazzo, smiled like a whore, a whore, moreover, who was desperate for custom. But offensive, not to say cruel, as Baby's remark undeniably was, and embarrassing, even excruciating, as the situation had suddenly become for Piero, it should not have been beyond the powers of the six very experienced men who were also at the table to set matters right. One child caried away by wine and by her personal success in conversation with her host, had shown off, gone too far, and in so doing had insulted another child: nothing here surely (thought Detterling) which a little adult tact and firmness could not correct. The trouble was that too many adults now applied themselves, too obviously and too earnestly, to mutually contrarious processes of correction.

Daniel, full of guilt at his own clumsy persistence in demanding a smile of Piero and thus initiating the incident, was the first to try.

'Very odd,' he said, 'the effects produced by candlelight. Chiaroscuro can make a nightmare of the most familiar domestic scene.'

This, though somewhat donnish, was not all a bad improvisation. All might have been well, had not Tom, much ashamed as a father, leaned right across the table to Baby and told her very sharply to apologize; and had not Lykiadopoulos, much affronted as a lover, said that evil lay in the eye of the beholder. Max de Freville then added his quotum to the prevailing distress and anger by observing that it was nice to see Piero smile 'for a change', as he often wondered why he never did so. While everyone began to digest the several injurious implications of this kindly intended remark, Detterling decided on a policy of total silence and Fielding Gray determined on one of total candour.

'Don't let's be silly about this,' he said. 'There's something badly wrong, physical or mental, with every single one of us at this table. I myself have a hideously deformed face, a self-pitying disposition, and a near-absolute addiction to drink. Max is pathologically obsessed with a dead woman, whom he couldn't fuck when she was living; Lykiadopoulos hopes to make money by preying, in the meanest and nastiest way, on the most contemptible failing of his fellow-creatures; Daniel talks, or rather croaks, like a sick frog; Canteloupe is callous, cowardly, corrupt and viciously smug; Tom could only ever copulate with his wife when she put on an act like a kitchen-maid in heat for the butcher's boy (quick, quick, we can do it under the stairs); and Baby is a greedy and conceited little bitch. So why, in this company,' he said to Piero, 'it should worry you or anybody else that you happen to smile like a seventy-year-old street-walker I cannot begin to imagine.'

Having delivered himself of this lot, Fielding rose from the table.

'If you'll all excuse me,' he said, 'I'll go upstairs and look at those portraits.'

'I think I'll come too,' said Baby. Her cheeks were shining and she looked very excited.

'Tullia—' Tom began anxiously.

'—She'll come to no harm with me,' said Fielding as he made for the door. 'These days,' he turned to add, 'I can't get hard after seven in the evening. Liquor.'

'I didn't mean—' Tom began again.

'Yes, you did. That's what the trouble is with the wretched child. You keep thinking she's going to get up to something, and she senses it and starts thinking so herself. It's your thoughts, Tom, which are infecting her. Treat her normal and she'll behave normal.' And to Baby, 'Come on, then, if you're coming.'

'I meant,' said Tom, 'that in your present mood you may say some more unpleasant things to her. More things like all you've said already.'

'In my present mood I shall say only the truth – which is all I've said already. If you don't want her to hear the truth, tell her to sit down.'

'Go with him,' said Tom to Baby.

'I was going anyway.'

She walked down the room to Fielding, who opened the door for her.

'See you all later,' she said.

'Well,' said Lykiadopoulos after the door had closed, 'he's quite a speaker, that Major Gray. He's quite right about my Baccarat Bank, of course : it really is a most despicable proceeding.'

Slowly they began to collect themselves while Lykiadopoulos, the perfect host, kept the conversation going by discoursing of the preparations for his despicable Bank.

'Nice looking lot,' said Baby to Fielding as they walked down the line of Albani portraits : 'fond of a little fun, I'd say.'

'You'd be right,' said Fielding. They paused before the picture of a sixteenth-century grandee who held a rose in one hand and the lead of his pet monkey in the other. 'Expensive fun at that,' Fielding added.

'And knew a thing or two about how to get it. But these paintings aren't up to much,' Baby said. 'That monkey could be made of straw for all the life it's showing.'

'The Albani, though they were wealthy and loved pleasure, had a mean streak in them. They liked getting things at a cut rate. In the sixteenth century they could have found a very good portrait painter, but they used this one – Rocco da Malamocco – because he was a distant connection and was prepared to knock off ten per cent.'

'Rocco da Malamocco,' Baby rhymed. 'What a very silly name. How do you know all this?'

'I've been investigating the Albani. There's a very good public library here – the Biblioteca Marciana – full of annals of the city and its families. "*Insignis et iucundus,*" says one chronicler of this fellow in the picture, "*pecuniae tamen cautor*: distinguished and agreeable but sparing of his money". Another writer calls him "*avarus*", but he was an enemy.'

'*Avarus,*' said Baby : 'grasping?'

'Worse; downright greedy.'

'Ah,' said Baby, 'like me.'

She grinned at him and hooked her hand into his arm, propelling him on to the next portrait.

'That was quite a mouthful,' said Baby. ' "Greedy and conceited", you called me. Do you really think that?'

'You're certainly greedy for food—'

'—That's because I don't get enough love,' she said slyly.

'And you're conceited about your appearance.'

'Do you like my trouser suit?'

'I prefer the little-girl get-up.'

'You like little girls?'

'Yes.'

'Even when they're greedy and conceited?'

'I like looking at them, Baby.'

'Good,' she said. 'I enjoy being looked at. All girls do. There's nothing unnatural about it – though Poppa seems to think so.'

'He's afraid that if you overdo your enjoyment, you may run into a nasty spot of trouble.'

'I should just run out again, from anything nasty. You know, one thing you said was quite right. If only Poppa wouldn't worry about me, there'd be nothing to worry about. He makes me nervous, though I love him very much. But he doesn't love me all that much, I think, although he fusses; he only brought me to Venice out of a sense of duty, because of Mummy and everything that's happened just lately. I expect you know all about that.'

Fielding didn't, having not seen or heard of Patricia Llewyllyn since 1971, and he longed to ask Baby to bring him up to date.

But he felt this would be unwise and unkind. Although he had spoken so frankly before her, in the dining-room, about her parents' past relations, that had been in the heat of the moment and he was now inclined to regret it. Baby, for all her apparent sophistication, was very young, and he was beginning to understand what Tom had meant when he claimed that beneath all the tartish antics the child was still innocent. For while Baby knew that people often behaved in an abandoned way and did very peculiar things, she also believed (or so Fielding sensed) that it was all jolly and kindly and pretty, all in delicate shades of pink and cream like a tasteful pornographic painting, that it was soft and giggly, jokey and tickly, in a word, idyllic. Lust (as opposed to mere randiness), dirt, disease and stink – these had no place in Baby's tender little Eden, nor did violence or betrayal, pain or *tristitia*. 'I should just run out again, from anything nasty,' Baby had said. But would she see it coming? Would she start running in time? All in all, Fielding felt, he must be very careful with Baby: not indeed fussy, like Tom, but sympathetic. There was no unsaying what he had said in the dining-room but he was most reluctant, now, to draw Baby into what was evidently, to judge from Tom's reticence about Patricia since he had appeared in Venice, a very perilous area. Perhaps Baby was equally reluctant to enter it, for she was already sailing off on a new bearing.

'... You know,' she was saying breathlessly, 'I sometimes think Poppa likes Daniel more than he likes anybody. Not that I mind, but I do feel a bit jealous of them being together in that tower. They'll buy a kettle and give little tea-parties, and you'll come and so will Piero, though not Mr Lykiadopoulos or Mr de Freville. And you'll all sit there, waiting hours for the kettle to boil on one of those oil-heaters, talking men's talk as the evening comes down on the garden; and later on you'll wonder where to go out to dinner, and Poppa will wrap up Daniel against the cold when it's time to go, and Piero will be sad because he'll have to have dinner in the Palazzo with Mr Lykiadopoulos instead of coming with all of you, but he'll cheer up when Daniel asks him for tea again the next afternoon.... And all the time I shall be hundreds of miles away in England, trying to do my prep or whatever they call it at my new school, but thinking of Venice, thinking of you and Poppa and Daniel and—'

'—Stop enjoying yourself, sweetheart,' Fielding said, 'and look at this picture.' He pointed to the family group round Fernando and Maria. 'What do you make of it?'

'Sentimental,' said Baby after some thought. 'Those two little kids might be made of marshmallow. And really bad anatomy. The girl at the back has got a triangular tit.'

'An effect of the draperies, perhaps?'

'Ugly. Bad workmanship. But there is one thing about this picture,' Baby said : 'that young man at the very back, between the boy and the girl. *He* comes alive all right – the only one that does. And very bad news he was, if you ask me.'

'I'd hoped you'd notice him.' Fielding stepped in front of Baby to study the group more closely. 'The trouble is, I can't find out anything about him. A contemporary gossip-writer describes the picture, but simply refers to the fellow at the back as "a friend of the family", without naming him. Yet he must have been a very special friend to be included in a family group. Had the Albani adopted him? Or was he some kind of a very superior tutor? Or was he the *cicisbeo*?'

'What's a *cicisbeo*?'

'The recognized lover – often in the fullest sense – of a married woman. Sometimes he lived with the family and went everywhere with it. The husband would be complaisant, because he would prefer to go out for his goodies; and so the wife would be very grateful for the *cicisbeo's* attentions. He had a definite and respected place in society. In the days of arranged marriages, when husband and wife were often totally indifferent to each other, it was a very sensible system.'

'Well, this one looks like a bully to me,' Baby said. 'A bully and possibly a blackmailer as well.'

'Someone who'd made his way into the household and couldn't be got rid of?'

'And had them all afraid of him.'

'Yes... A *cicisbeo* who had gone rogue on them, perhaps? I'm inclined to think not, though. The convention required that the *cicisbeo* should be more or less of an age with the lady, and this chap is much younger than the Signora Albani.'

'That wouldn't have stopped him being her lover.'

'It would have stopped him being her acceptable, her *legitimate* lover. In which case he would have been a family scandal. In which case he would hardly have appeared in this picture.' Fielding sighed. 'I must do more research into it all,' he said. 'What do you make of the boy? He was called Piero, by the way.'

'Dripping wet,' said Baby.

'But rather beautiful.'

'A little like Mr Lykiadopoulos's Piero – but brought up soft.
I'll tell you what : – I want to go to the loo,' Baby said. 'Where
is it?'

'They all have private ones in their own apartments.'

'There must be one for guests.'

Baby crossed her trousered legs and lifted one foot from the
ground, miming urgent need.

'If you went downstairs to the dining-room and asked Max
or Mr Lykiadopoulos. . . .'

Baby pouted miserably. 'Infra dig,' she said, 'like a bub at a
nursery party.'

'I know,' said Fielding : 'on the next floor up – the top floor
– there are the servants' quarters. There's bound to be a loo
there, and the servants will still be busy downstairs, so they
won't bother you.'

'Phew, thanks,' gasped Baby and hurried off.

Fielding went on looking at the family group. What was it
Lykiadopoulos had said about the top floor? 'Just attics and
servants' quarters' – only that. But Piero had found something
funny in this remark. So what was up there to amuse him?
Perhaps sharp-eyed Baby Llewyllyn would find out ... a little
girl looking for the lavatory, not knowing which door it was.
Fielding grinned at the alien in the portrait. 'And as for you,
you bastard,' he said, 'I'm going to find you out as well.' He
stood there, gazing into the narrow green eyes of the unknown
young man who was his quarry, and pleasurably wondering, as
the minutes ticked away, what was keeping Baby Llewyllyn for
so long upstairs.

In the dining-room Lykiadopoulos talked on about his Baccarat
Bank.

'There will be two sessions *per diem*,' he said, as he poured
himself brandy and passed on the bottle. 'From half-past four
to seven, and from half-past ten to one a.m., giving time for us to
go through three shoes in each session, each shoe to be of seven
packs. But on the opening day – Saturday, October the sixth –
there will be only the later session, a longer one from ten-thirty
to two, preceded by a gala dinner for specially invited guests.
You're sure,' he said to Detterling, 'that you wouldn't like to
attend?'

'I can't, I'm afraid. I shall be tied up in England.'

'I think I can promise that your air fair would be paid – first-class, of course – if you cared to come out just for that week-end.'

'Very civil of you,' said Detterling, 'but I prefer to pay for my own tickets, especially when they're first-class. It makes life simpler, you see. In any case, I shan't be leaving England at all for at least a month.'

'Then the opening night will be the poorer without you,' Lykiadopoulos deferred gracefully.

'And I shall be the richer without it, I dare say. But I'll try to pop in during the winter, if only for the pleasure of watching you in action.'

'In action,' said Daniel : 'forgive my ignorance, but what does the action in Baccarat consist of?'

Max now gave an account of this, necessarily rather lengthy and provoking little grunts of annoyance from Piero, who interrupted from time to time to protest that the game was merely childish. Daniel, however, being interested in the mathematics that governed games of chance, listened with attention.

'Unless my calculations are at fault,' he said when Max had finished, 'the odds are slightly but definitely in Mr Lykiadopoulos's favour as the banker.'

'Yes,' said Max. 'The only trouble is that every time Lyki wins a coup, five per cent is deducted from the sum won, there and then, to cover taxes, expenses and the Casino's commission.'

'Thus the only party that is sure to win,' said Piero, 'is the Casino itself. The whole affair is not only despicable, as you said, Lykiaki, it is the merest folly.'

'I must be the judge of that.'

'But do you not *know* that it is so?' Piero persisted.

'I know that once before, here in Venice, I won several hundred thousand pounds from such a bank. The stakes were much smaller then—'

'—So now you think you will win more. Suppose you have ill luck,' said Piero, red in the face with drink and irritation, 'suppose God looks down and says, "Why should that fat Lyki win money, who has so much already, I will make it all go to the other players".'

'That would be very unfair of God, my birdie. The other players will be no more deserving than I am, and some of them will be much richer.'

'But still, it might happen. God enjoys being unfair : he

enjoys taking things away from people, even if he only gives them to somebody richer instead. It is the sort of thing that someone who made this horrible world would think to be funny. To those who need he seldom gives, but he takes from all alike – whatever they love most, he takes it. You love most your money, so he will take that. And if he does, it will serve you right.'

'You must make up your mind with whom you are so angry: with me, or with God?'

'With both of you. With God for making a bad world, and with you for making it worse. You have all you need; why not be content with that?'

'Times are difficult, my dear?'

'Not for you,' said Piero. 'If you would only cease from making Corfu hideous with those hotels, you would still have enough money to be happy. It is those hotels—'

'—I do not wish to discuss them in front of our friends—'

'—It is for those hotels, to keep them going, to build up more, that you have come here like a jackal to scavenge.'

'We will not talk of this.'

'Shall we not say the truth? It is those hot—'

'—You are drunk,' said Lykiadopoulos, at last losing patience, 'you are silly with drink.'

'Do not say that.' Piero was now suddenly threatened (Tom thought) with such loss of face as would be unbearable by a Sicilian. 'I am never drunk.'

'You are a little boy, full of ignorance and drink.'

'*Do not say that*,' Piero shouted.

'Shall we not say the truth? The drink is talking from your belly like a devil possessing you.'

Piero's face gobbled with fear.

'That is wicked,' he yelped, making a sign against the evil eye. 'To talk of devils is to raise them.'

'See how he babbles,' jeered Lykiadopoulos, inviting the rest of the table to join him against Piero, 'this brave boy from Sicily who believes in devils.'

'So do you,' said Piero, recovering his spirit. 'I have seen him on his knees,' he said to all at the table, 'trembling and sweating with terror and begging God to deliver him from the evil one. Upstairs, on the top floor, he has a special—'

'—You be quiet,' said Max de Freville. 'Be quiet, do you hear?'

'Trembling and sweating,' said Piero, pointing to Lykiadopoulos. He thrust his face over the table. 'Lykioula *mou*,' he spat.

Daniel, who knew that 'oula' was the Greek form of femine diminutive, patted Piero on the hand and croaked,

'That's enough for one evening. Tell your friend you are sorry, then take me upstairs to see the Albani portraits.'

There was a long silence.

'I am sorry,' said Piero sullenly to Lykiadopoulos.

'No, not like that,' said Daniel, 'say it as you mean it.'

'I am sorry. Lyki, I am sorry.'

Lykiadopoulos showed no sign of hearing.

'As your guest,' said Daniel, 'your guest for the first time, I ask you to accept Piero's apology.'

'If he will say he was at fault, he shall be forgiven.'

'Go on,' said Daniel to Piero.

Silence.

Daniel rose.

'I wish to see those portraits,' he said to Piero. 'We cannot go until you are forgiven.'

'I was at fault,' blurted Piero. He bit his lip and started to cry.

'Tears,' said Daniel to Lykiadopoulos; 'will that do?'

'Tears of sorrow or tears of temper?' said Lykiadopoulos.

'Shame,' said Piero.

Lykiadopoulos hesitated.

'Then you may go with Mr Mond,' he said.

Daniel bundled Piero across the room and through the door. For the second time that evening Lykiadopoulos started to soothe his guests with suitable discourse, this time (in Detterling's honour) about the state of cricket in Corfu and the success of To Krikit Phestibal in which several notable English clubs had fielded elevens against the islanders earlier that very month.

As soon as Daniel and Piero were on the stone stairs, Piero recovered.

'I have never slept with him,' he declared to Daniel.

'I don't care either way about that.'

'But I never have. See,' he said, as they came to the second floor, 'he has his rooms along this corridor here. Mine are above.'

When they had mounted to the third floor, Piero led Daniel into the circular anteroom, then through a door at the far end of it and into a bedroom.

'I sleep here, always here,' Piero insisted. 'I have my own sitting-room on one side of this and my own bathroom on the

other.' He opened doors into both. 'You must come and have
baths when you wish – but better that he should not know.'

'Then better that I should not come.'

'We will see. He is jealous. He wishes to keep me in a prison.
That is why he calls me his birdie : he has me in a cage. Not a
small one, a big one, with trees and flowers – how do you say ?—'

'—An aviary—'

'—An aviary. This palace. A very beautiful aviary; but always,
beyond the leaves and the branches, there are iron bars, network—'

'—Netting—'

'—To hold me in. I cannot leave this floor to go downstairs
but he will know it. He will not stop me, but he will know it
and perhaps he will follow me. I may go into the garden, but
otherwise I may not leave the palace without him.'

'He has said so ?'

'No. But it is so. When I did once go out by myself, he
punished me. I wished to go to the Accademia, for the pictures.
Often I asked him to take me, but he was always too busy, so
one morning I decided to walk there, though it is not easy for
me to walk. When I got there, he was waiting with the gondola.
"You are tired, birdie," he said : "I have come to take you
home." "I wish to see the pictures." "You are too tired. You
shall see them another day with me." And he made me come
back with him. Since then we have not yet been to the Accademia. So instead I look at the portraits here. He is always telling me how bad they are, but never does he take me to see
others.'

'He has a lot on his mind.'

'That Baccarat Bank. Paah. But I should not have spoken as
I did. It will do no good, and I shall be punished again.'

'He forgave you.'

'Perhaps, but he will also punish me. I should not have called
him "Lykioula". Especially not that.'

'If things became really bad, you could always leave him.'

'Leave him ? Where for ?'

'Your home in Sicily.'

'He sends money to my family there. They would sooner have
the money than have me. It is time we went to see the portraits.'

Piero led the way back through the anteroom and into the
long salon where the portraits hung. As Piero and Daniel entered, Fielding Gray turned towards them.

'Is Miss Llewyllyn not with you?' asked Piero.

'She went to the loo.'

'Loo?'

'Lavatory.'

'Which lavatory? There is only mine on this floor, in my bath-room, and she was not there just now.'

'I told her to go upstairs. To the servants' quarters.'

Piero's eyes opened very wide.

'She should not go up there. I mean, there is no lavatory there.'

'No loo in the servants' quarters?'

'No. That is,' Piero stammered, 'their quarters have been changed. Anyway, there is no ... no loo up there now.'

'Perhaps that explains,' said Fielding, looking carefully at Piero, 'why she has been gone so long. I expect she's still look-ing.'

Piero's eyes opened yet wider.

'She has been gone a long time?'

'Nearly half an hour.'

'*Gesu-Maria*,' said Piero. 'You are sure she went upstairs?'

'That's where I told her to go.'

'Then I must find her at once. You will excuse me, Mr Mond, Major Gray.'

He hobbled off with urgency, leaving the door of the salon open in his haste. His footsteps receded over the parquetry of the anteroom floor, signalling his impediment (clack, pause, clack-clack, pause, clack-clack); the padded door, which led to the passage and the stairway, swung to behind him with a muted thump.

'What do you suppose all that is about?' asked Daniel.

'The top floor here is a sensitive area. They let that out with-out meaning to when Canteloupe and I were being shown round the other day.'

'And so ... you sent that child up to find out what's there?'

'Yes. She doesn't know it, of course. She's simply looking for a loo. Or she *was*,' said Fielding with satisfaction.

'You've not forgotten how to use people, I see.'

'I'm curious, Danny. I'm curious about a lot of other things as well. About you, for a start. Before you appeared in Venice, Tom was going on as if you were bringing the crown jewels with you. "I must be here to meet Daniel. No, I don't know when he's coming, but I must be here when he arrives." You'd have thought he was expecting some kind of Messiah. What's the mystery, Daniel?'

'No mystery, Fielding. I've always wanted to spend some time in Venice, and with things as they are I thought I'd better come now.'

'Before the whole bag of tricks sinks into the lagoon?'

'You could put it like that. I've never taken a Sabbatical in twenty years, so the College Council was prepared to release me.'

'You've got a Sabbatical Year, then, like Tom?'

'Not exactly. Fellows proceeding on a Sabbatical undertake to do some special research, for which they would not normally have the opportunity, while they are away. I am under no such obligation.'

'They've given you a holiday? In return for long service and good conduct?'

'They released me for a while,' said Daniel, with an edge of irritation to what was left of his voice, 'because they knew – or at least Provost Constable knew – that I wished to go to Venice while Tom was living there.'

'Tom puts it the other way round. He said, just the other day, that he was living in Venice because he knew you wished to come here. He chose the Serenissima for his research, he said, as an excuse to sit in Venice and wait for you ... and then to stay with you after you came. Which comes first, Danny: Tom's hen or your egg?'

'Why are you so anxious to know?'

'Because I'm looking for a subject for my next novel. I've been rather ... rather sterile ... these last months, and Detterling is anxious to put me to work again. For my own good, he says, and he's probably right. So I'm latching on to anything which I find at all odd, in the hope that it'll give me a start. Your situation and Tom's might give me a very promising start.'

'Oh no, Fielding,' said Daniel with real pain, 'don't put me in another of your books.'

'Not you, Daniel. Your *situation*, I said. That's what I'm interested in.'

'So was it the last time – with *Operation Apocalypse* – or so you've always pretended. But you were so cruel and false, Fielding : cruel and false to *me*.'

'As I've told you before, it wasn't you. It was a character

in a fiction : a mere combination of words.'

'Sophistry, Fielding. Oh Fielding,' said Daniel in a thin, despairing voice, 'please don't use me again. Please.'

Daniel's fingers twitched along the high silk scarf which protected his throat. He had sounded (Fielding thought) like the last satyr in the forest, piping his scrawny dirge while the Christians felled his shrine to build a church.

'Never mind, Daniel,' he said. 'I'll not hurt you. . . . But I'd like your opinion on another little mystery, which could be the sort of thing I need.'

He took Daniel up to the picture of the Albani family group, and began to explain about the stranger in its midst.

'Miss Llewyllyn,' called Piero. 'Miss Tullia Llewyllyn?'

The top floor of the Palazzo Albani consisted of a single-storey penthouse divided by a corridor. On either side of the corridor were three doors, two of those on Piero's left being, as he well knew, locked. He opened the only unlocked door on the left and switched on the light : an unshaded bulb dangled from the ceiling, showing a room empty save for an old rocking-chair. Then he tried, one after the other, the three rooms on his right. Two of them were stacked with empty crates, trunks and suit-cases which had come to the Palazzo in Lykiadopoulos's elaborate baggage train. The third was full of toys, abandoned Albani toys, Piero presumed : two magnificent rocking-horses, a model railway with scenic background on a wide shelf all round the walls, a four-foot long replica of an ocean-going liner (this done with detailed expertise, the kind of thing he had sometimes seen in the windows of the more expensive shipping offices in Syracuse), and a collection of military uniforms, built for a child of seven or eight, which were carefully draped over wickerwork frames in two ranks of four.

But in all of this there was no sign of Baby Llewyllyn.

'Miss Llewyllyn,' he called along the corridor.

If he assumed that Baby was still on the top floor, there was now only one place where she could be. He limped to the end of the corridor, opened a door which faced him, and stepped out on to the palace leads. There was a flat margin, about twenty yards wide, between the four walls of the penthouse and a battlement (fifteen feet high and perforated with narrow Gothic apertures) which rose from all four sides of the palace roof. Somewhere in that leaded margin, he thought, he must find Baby.

'Miss Llewyllyn . . . Tullia . . . *Baby.*'

'Here,' said Baby's voice.

She was peering through one of the apertures which looked
down on to the Rio Dolfin. The opening was taller than she was
and slightly broader. She's had a lot to drink for a little girl, he
thought : she could have fallen through.

'Come away from there,' he said. 'What are you doing on
this roof?'

Baby's dim figure turned from the battlement and skipped
across the leads to join him in the strip of light which was coming through the open door of the penthouse.

'I came out here to widdle,' Baby said. 'There was nowhere
else I could do it.'

Piero winced. Although he had not led a sheltered life, he was
not used to being addressed by young females in such very direct
terms on this particular topic.

'But Major Gray says you've been up here half an hour,' he
said. 'It couldn't have taken you all that time just . . . just to
do it.'

'Ah,' said Baby, 'I've been looking at something.'

'Looking down at the canal?' asked Piero hopefully.

'Of course not, silly. Or not for long. *You* must know, since
you live here. Perhaps you can explain.'

She took him by the hand and led him round the corner of
the penthouse, down that side of it on which were the two
locked rooms. With her free hand she pointed through a window.

'This,' she said, 'I can understand.'

Against the right-hand wall of the room, as seen through the
window, was an altar surrounded and surmounted by eikons,
which glittered dimly, gold and red and blue, in the light of a
sanctuary lamp.

'A shrine,' said Baby; 'a chapel.'

'You should not have seen this. Mr Lykiadopoulos wishes nobody to know of it. Those eikons are very valuable.'

'Well, I shan't steal them. I'd like to look at them more closely,
though. You haven't got a key to that room?'

'No.'

'Well then : come on and tell me about the next thing.'

She pulled him along the wall to the next window.

'Now this,' she said, 'really does need a bit of explaining.'

'This' was a sculpture, perhaps a third of life-size, of a fat and lightly clad lady in early middle age. She was reclining under a cupola, propping her leering face up with one arm and reaching with the other to take a wine cup from a tray which was being held out to her by a group of four skinny boys who had hair-styles rather like Piero's. The boys were quite naked : each of them had one hand under the tray and was using the fingers of the other, with a kind of lewd delicacy, to amuse his already rampant genitalia. This interesting tableau was set on a square dais of wood and lit by four pairs of altar candles, each pair being at one corner of the dais.

'You should certainly not have seen this,' said Piero. 'It is not right.'

'Don't be silly. I know what boys do with those things of theirs – Mummy told me years ago. I often wish I had one my-self,' said Baby; 'it looks great fun.'

'Mr de Freville would be furious. It is his.'

'What is it?'

'This too is a shrine. That sculpture is a copy of the tomb of a dead lady friend of Mr de Freville. The tomb – it is much bigger than this – is in the British Cemetery in Corfu.'

'You mean ... those boys are going on like that in a ceme-tery?'

'That bit is different. In the cemetery the boys do not have ... those things of theirs ... at all.'

'How horrid. That,' said Baby, 'must look really nasty. But this is rather pretty, in a way.'

'When he is in Corfu, Mr de Freville goes every day to the tomb. Here in Venice he comes up to this room instead. The candles are always lit. He ... he talks to the lady,' said Piero. 'I heard him once, one night when I was up here looking down at the canal. Very late it was, three in the morning. He was talking on and on. I could not hear what he was saying, because the window was closed as it is now, but I could hear his voice because it was all shrill. I came to the window and looked through it. He was kneeling by her side, weeping and babbling in this high funny voice.'

'Poor Mr de Freville.'

'You must not tell anyone you have been here. You promise?'

'I promise,' said Baby, crossing two fingers of her free hand behind her back.

'And now we must go before anybody comes. Mr Lykiado-poulos would not like us to be alone together.'

'You're afraid of him?'

'Yes.'

'Come on then. Poor Piero,' said Baby, as they moved away from the window. 'Everyone in this house seems to have problems. I wouldn't wonder if Mr Lykiadopoulos's are worse than anybody's.'

They walked down the corridor of the penthouse, Baby being careful to suit her pace to his.

'What a pity,' she said. 'This wonderful palace, and nothing but misery and worry inside it.'

'It will be better, for me at least, now that your father and Mr Mond are coming to the tower.'

They started descending the stairs to Piero's floor and the picture gallery. Piero released his hand from Baby's.

'I'm sorry,' he said, 'but we are nearly back with the others.'

In the dining-room the conversation had turned on to Daniel Mond.

'A mathematician, you say,' said Max de Freville to Tom. 'Distinguished?'

'Not very. Something went wrong with his original line of research and he could never find anything else. I have an impression that he never really tried ... that he didn't want to find anything because he was afraid lest it might be too dangerous.'

'Dangerous?' said Lykiadopoulos.

'It was all before I first knew him,' said Tom, 'and it's not easy to get him to talk of it. As far as I can make out, he was tipped, back in the early fifties, to be *the* mathematician of his generation. He was a pupil of Dirange's, his research was brilliant, so they say—'

'But you've just told us it went wrong,' said Max.

'Not in the sense that he failed. He succeeded all too well. It turned out that what he had discovered was not just a new operation in pure mathematics, as he had thought; it was something which, potentially at least, had a disastrous application to practical physics.'

'A bigger and better nuclear bang?'

*'Something of the kind, but far worse. Daniel, it seems, deciphered a mathematical notation which had been invented by a German called Dortmund. Dortmund had died without explaining it to anyone, and for years nobody could crack the

*See *The Sabre Squadron*, pp. 8 to 12 and *passim*.

code, so eventually Daniel, the young white hope, was put on
by Professor Dirange to get to the bottom of it. Now Daniel,
as I say, had assumed that it was all to do with some new
theorem of pure mathematics. But it wasn't. What Dortmund
had discovered, and Daniel now uncovered, was a method of
examining the behaviour of particles at any given moment in
their existence ... of examining this behaviour so minutely that
he was on the way to revealing what power ultimately held all
particles, and therefore all matter, together.'

'And so also on the way to revealing what could pull it
apart?'

'Yes. Enormous forces, far greater than those released in any
nuclear explosion, were involved. For Daniel had come close
to finding what it is that binds the entire universe. At this stage,
certain people guessed, more or less, what he was on to, and
put him under pressure to show them the new method. It was
his patriotic duty, they said. On the contrary, he said, it was
his duty to humanity to keep silent. And keep silent he did,
though he half-killed himself – quite literally – in order to do
so. I don't know the details – none of his friends does. But I
know something horrible happened to his throat, which is why
he speaks as he does.... So that is what went wrong with
Daniel's research, and why he never had the heart to take up
anything else. He came back to Lancaster, after it was all over,
and settled down simply to teach conventional mathematics in
conventional areas. And that is all he has done in the last twenty
years.'

'With nothing to show for it,' said Max, 'when he might have
made history.'

'Or perhaps unmade it altogether,' said Detterling. 'His predicament was hardly enviable. But all that was a long time
ago,' he went on, his tone glibly recommending that old, unhappy things should be forgot by all right-minded people. 'Whatever may or may not have happened then, he looks a contented
man to me now. Any man who succeeds in being contented,' he
said to Max, 'is quite successful enough. No need to make history.'

'He has been a fine teacher,' said Tom, 'and he has published
some useful textbooks for undergraduates. For the rest, he has
lived with his friends, and at peace.'

'At peace?' said Lykiadopoulos. He turned to Detterling.
'Contented, you say? Not entirely, I think. Every now and then

his eyes hold great pain. I have only known him since an hour or two, but I have seen this.'

'His throat often hurts him,' said Tom.

'There is also a different kind of pain. Or perhaps not pain: yearning. For what does he yearn?'

'He wishes,' said Tom, 'to be able to believe in God.'

'Why can he not?' asked Lykiadopoulos.

'Because of his early work. It wasn't only that this work might have been used to tear the world apart. There was another, a different horror lurking at the back of it ... a kind of metaphysical obscenity. You see, his method – or rather Dortmund's – would have enabled him to take a particle of matter, and then, by minutely investigating its behaviour and the causes of this behaviour, to follow it back through all its career to the beginning of time ... to analyse what happened at its birth, *i.e.* what happened at the birth of the universe itself. He never tried to do this, or not consciously, because he was afraid. But he thinks part of his mind followed the trail back through time, followed it despite his fear, because one night he had a dream in which he was taken back, step by step, and shown the beginning, the explosion into being, of the universe. *And then he was also shown what had been before the universe.* Just for an instant, before he awoke, he saw what had been before space and time began.'

'And what was that?' said Max de Freville. 'Some kind of primaeval atom from which the explosion had come?'

'No. Nullity. Nothingness. Not even emptiness, for there was not yet space to be empty. It was like sleep or unconsciousness; total non-existence.'

'Which, nevertheless, he could in some sense observe?'

'He ... conceived it. But how, he asked himself, had existence sprung from nullity? Because if there were total nullity, nothing whatever could have been born in it or emerged from it.'

' "In the beginning was the Word",' quoted Lykiadopoulos.

'There was no Word. He was sure of that. No God, no presence, just nothingness. And yet there had been birth; he himself had just witnessed it. He had seen the explosion, and now he was seeing the nullity which alone had preceded it and out of which, therefore, it must have come.'

'God's work,' insisted Lykiadopoulos. 'What else?'

'No. Not God's work,' said Tom. 'God's death. For there could only be one explanation, Daniel decided. The nullity which preceded the universe only commenced when there *was* a universe to precede. The explosion which was the birth of the universe had created nullity in retrospect. Before the universe began there *must* have been something, which we may call God. But God, in creating the universe, had destroyed himself – he had become the universe, and so left a blank, a nullity, where he himself had once been.'

'But surely,' said Max, 'if Daniel was privileged to go back before the universe began, he must have found the God, or the Something, that was there before it.'

'No. Because although he was allowed back into the past, he was of the universe and therefore went back into the past as it had become since the creation of the universe. Once God had become the universe he could no longer project himself back into the past, for Daniel's benefit, or appear as he had in fact been in that past. God was now the universe; what had been God was now nullity to those allowed back to see it. Or that was how it seemed to Daniel. It was the only way of explaining how total nullity had produced a universe.'

'A stupid nightmare,' said Lykiadopoulos. 'But even if the nightmare was a vision of the truth, Mr Mond can still believe in God, because he says that God became the universe. Therefore the universe is God.'

'No. In becoming the universe God abdicated. He destroyed himself *as God*. He turned what he had been, his true self, into nullity and thereby forfeited the Godlike qualities which pertained to him. The universe which he has become is also his grave. He has no control in it or over it. God, as God, is dead.'

'Yet we are all bits of him.'

'Bits of his corpse. Not of the true God.'

'Why did God do it then?' said Detterling. 'Why did he commit suicide?'

'Daniel says the only person who could answer that question would be the true God who no longer exists to answer it. It is conceivable,' said Tom, 'that he got bored with his own perfection.'

When Piero and Baby returned together to the portrait gallery, Daniel and Fielding were still standing in front of the Albani family group.

'Ah,' said Fielding to Piero, 'you found her.'

'Yes,' said Piero flatly.

'Then should we not,' said Daniel, 'be getting back to the rest of the party?'

'Hang on a mo,' Baby said. 'I haven't yet seen all the pictures.'

After briefly recharging her memory of the family group, Baby began on the nineteenth-century offerings, Fielding hovered after her. Piero joined Daniel.

'I shall let you know,' whispered Piero, 'if it is all right for you to come to my rooms. Mr Lykiadopoulos told me to make you welcome, but I am not sure how much I shall be allowed to see you.'

'I'm very tired,' grated Daniel; 'please let us go downstairs.' Then, seeing that Piero was hurt by his neglect of the whispered confidence, 'If I cannot come here,' Daniel managed, 'you can always come to the tower.'

'If I am allowed . . .'

Daniel took hold, rather heavily, of Piero's arm. As they began to move towards the door, Piero staggered slightly on his bad leg.

'I am sorry,' he said; 'please do not let go.' He looked nervously back at Fielding and Baby. 'You will be coming now?' he called.

'In a minute,' Baby carolled. 'He's scared,' she said to Fielding, 'that I might go upstairs again. Or show you what's there.'

'What is there?'

'I shan't tell you. I promised Piero not. And besides,' she teased, 'it was mean of you to tell me there was a loo up there.'

'Wasn't there?'

'No. I had to go out on the roof.'

'So one can get on to the roof, can one? What else did you find out?'

'That Piero is a very polite, kind boy, and he's afraid of Mr Lykiadopoulos, who is very religious. That Mr de Freville is very sad about a lady who died a while ago, and comes and talks to her statue. 'There,' said Baby: 'I haven't actually broken my promise, have I? Anyway, I had my fingers crossed.'

'I knew that lady,' Fielding said.

'She's the one you mentioned downstairs? The one he couldn't fuck when she was alive, you said. Why couldn't he? Your turn to tell me something.'

'I think he liked her too much,' Fielding speculated. 'He knew that if he fucked her it would be different, and he wanted it to stay the same. He—'

—Clack, pause, clack-clack, pause, clack-clack. Piero coming back along the corridor to move them on.

'Go on,' said Baby.

'He didn't want to try to have too much,' said Fielding. 'He was right. I loved somebody once, and my mistake . . . my lethal mistake . . . was to try to have too much.'

'Quick, Major Gray,' came Piero's voice down the gallery. 'Quick, to the stairs. There is something wrong with Mr Mond.'

Daniel was in the pine forest near the Warlocks' Grotto, where he knew he must meet Captain Fielding Gray and his driver, Trooper Lamb. They were to picnic in the Grotto, near Dortmund's grave. Fielding and Lamb were driving up the track (with the picnic hamper) in Fielding's land-rover, but Daniel had chosen to walk up the hill through the trees.

But now he could not find the way. The trees were in circle upon circle around him, all evenly spaced, and in the gap between any two of them stood another sentinel just behind, so that after a few yards their ranks were impenetrable by the eye and for all Daniel knew they might spread away to the end of the world. His only hope was to pick the right direction in which to make for the Warlocks' Grotto, where he would find food and wine and Michael Lamb and Fielding Gray.

'Fielding,' he called.

But the trees would not let his voice through any more than they would let his eye.

'Oh, Fielding. . .'

And now he could hear the howling of the dogs, still distant but nearer every second. Which way should he run? If he could hear the dogs, surely Fielding could hear him.

'*Fielding.*'

But he knew he was not heard, or not by Fielding.

Daniel ran. At first he thought he was running away from the howling of the dogs, but soon he realized that the howling was all round him, filling his ears, his head, his throat with noise and pain.

'Fielding, oh Fielding,' he sobbed, 'why did you let me come alone?'

He sank down towards the soft floor of pine needles. He would lie here till the dogs came. But even this brief comfort was denied him, because the floor of the forest was as hard and cold as stone.

'Oh, Fielding,' he moaned.

'I'm here, Danny,' said Fielding. 'Help me get him down the stairs' – this to Piero. And to Baby Llewyllyn, 'Tell someone to ring for a doctor.'

'You shouldn't move him,' Baby said.

'I'm all right,' said Daniel. 'Just one of my spells. No doctor, please. I'll just stay here a moment, and then we can go on down.' His face was running with sweat and his colour was grey-green. 'No fuss,' he croaked; 'but ask them to have a boat ready so that I can go home.'

Baby went on down to deliver the message. Piero squatted on the stairs behind Daniel and began to massage his neck, one hand resting lightly on each shoulder, the thumbs working from the shoulder-blades to the top of the spine and then round to the ears.

'Daniel,' Piero said; 'Daniele.'

Slowly the colour came back into Daniel's cheeks.

'Daniele. Oh, Daniel. Daniele.'

Ten minutes later the dinner guests were embarked from the Palazzo Albani and were waved on their way by Lykiado-poulos and Max de Freville, though not by Piero, who retreated to his rooms as soon as the boat was announced. They got Daniel back to the Pensione San Paolo without any further trouble and saw him to bed. Then they went to Tom's room for a night-cap. Baby served the drinks from Tom's dressing-table: whisky for the grown-ups, cola for herself.

'Daniel likes that tower,' said Tom. 'Good.'

'Piero will be good for Daniel,' said Fielding.

'And Daniel will be good for Piero,' said Baby. 'Piero is afraid of Mr Lykiadopoulos. Daniel will protect him.'

'Tell them what you told me,' said Fielding to Baby, 'about when you went to the loo.'

Baby told them. She did not tell them exactly what she had seen, because, as she explained, she did not want to break faith with Piero. But she had had her fingers crossed, and so she might tell them as much as she had already told Fielding.

'Yes,' said Detterling when Baby had finished, 'Lykiadopoulos has always been pious on the side, and Max's thing about poor Angela is obviously getting worse and worse. When I saw him in Corfu last year he was only visiting her grave. But now it seems he tries to cart her about with him. A statue, you say?' he said to Baby.

'A small one,' said Baby. 'I don't think Piero would like me to say more. Nor would Mr de Freville. '

'Thank you, Tullia,' said Tom, 'that was all very interesting. Now say goodnight.'

'Must I?' Baby wheedled.

'Yes,' said Detterling.

Baby kissed her father on the lips and Detterling on his cheek. As she came towards Fielding Gray, he held out his hand for her to shake, thinking that she would not want to kiss a face like his. But she ignored his hand and kissed, not indeed his face, but his hair.

'Nice hair,' Baby murmured, and quietly left the room.

'Baby did well at dinner,' said Detterling. 'Kept her end up with Lyki. A pity about that gaffe with the boy, but he seems to have forgiven her, telling her all that about Lyki and Max. You tore us all off a pretty fierce strip,' he said to Fielding.

'I was sick of all that pussy-footing. No one saying what he meant. I had a whole lot more of it from Daniel later on.'

'Don't you bully Daniel,' said Tom.

'I wasn't. I was just asking him a few questions – about why he's come to Venice and so on. He was as sly and shifty as a sewer rat.'

'Your enquiries were impertinent.'

'Why?'

'Fielding,' said Tom, 'can't you see that Daniel is vulnerable? That attack he had tonight before we came home—'

'—He's always had attacks of one kind and another ever since I've known him – even before that business with his throat. He was always being sick or turning green or starting to cry or—'

'—Fielding. Are you so totally dedicated to yourself that you notice nothing at all about other people?'

'I notice what they tell me. Daniel said it was "just one of his spells", not to fuss. No point in calling a doctor, he said.'

'No, none. You see, Fielding, every now and then his throat hurts him so much that he faints, as he did tonight. Nothing a doctor can do. He has a drug to deaden the pain, but he takes it as seldom as possible because it makes him – well – peculiar, inconsequent, and he prefers to be of the company, to understand what's going on. So he delays taking his drug for as long as he can, and then the pain comes at him.'

'Well, I'm very sorry to hear it.'

'You must hear more. What have you noticed of Daniel's ... demeanour ... since we have been here?'

'Whatever this pain in his throat, he looks pretty contented most of the time. Sometimes he seems quite fatuous with content, positively gorged with it.'

'Yes. That is the effect of the drug. If he gets the dose just right, he is in a comfortable, drowsy state but fully able to follow conversations and so on. Contented. But if he has taken too much, or if he has only just taken it, he is what you call gorged or fatuous and I should call vague or withdrawn. That is what he is anxious to avoid.'

'Will his throat ever get better?' Detterling asked. 'I should have thought Venice was the last place to bring it. All this damp. This bad, marshy air. Polluted too, these days.'

'He wanted to come to Venice for the peace.'

'That I understood. That's what made me think of that tower for him. But in the circumstances, is Venice wise?'

'It's what he wants,' said Tom. 'That is why I arranged to spend the winter here. So that when he came, there should be somebody here to take care of him.'

'If you want to do that,' said Fielding, 'get him out of Venice. Canteloupe's obviously right.'

'Where should I take him? Venice or Cambridge are the only places he wishes to be, and he cannot stay in Cambridge for fear of embarrassing them. While he is taking this drug, he cannot be relied on to teach effectively.'

'Anyway,' said Fielding, 'Cambridge and the fens are just as bad for throats. For heaven's sake, Tom, take him somewhere suitable. Up in the mountains, perhaps ... or somewhere warm. The doctors must know what would be best.'

'They say Venice is best, because it is what he wants. When a man must be dead in a few months,' said Tom, 'you no longer bother about giving him healthy air. If you love him, you give him what he wants.'

PART TWO

WINTER QUARTERS

A sad tale's best for winter.
I have one of sprites and goblins.

Shakespeare, *The Winter's Tale*
Act II, Scene i

'GOODBYE, Poppa ... Daniel ... Fielding.' Baby Llewyllyn
waved at the receding group on the steps of the Gritti. The three
men in the group waved back and turned away. 'Goodbye,'
called Baby, and choked ominously.

'Come and sit down,' said Detterling, and led her into the
cabin of the motor-boat which he had engaged to carry them
across the lagoon to the airport. 'There,' he said : 'don't cry,
or you'll have me starting.'

'I can't imagine you crying,' snuffled Baby, and managed a
smile.

'I do from time to time, I assure you. Heigh-ho,' he sighed
after a pause, 'goodbye to Venice, and nothing achieved.'

'What did you hope to achieve?'

'I was meant to be looking for authors. Renegade reds at the
PEN conference, or old ladies who were tickled in their cots by
Henry James. But I've been too frivolous to find any.'

'You haven't been frivolous at all. It's just that too much else
was going on. Your being made a lord so suddenly, and then
that gang at the Palazzo, and getting that tower for Poppa and
Daniel.'

As they passed the cemetery island of San Michele, they
watched some men in black unload a coffin from a funeral barge
on to the landing stage.

'Tricky work,' said Detterling; 'they wouldn't want to drop it
in the water.'

'That reminds me,' Baby said. 'That lady Mr de Freville used
to be so fond of. Angela ... ?'

'... Angela Tuck.'

'You said, and Piero said, that he goes to her grave on Corfu
to tell her things. What sort of things, do you think?'

'He's unhappy because Lykiadopoulos makes him do things

she wouldn't have liked. Putting up ugly buildings near beaches, cutting down trees for roads and car parks. . .'

'Why doesn't he stop Mr Lykiadopoulos?'

'He can't. Mr Lykiadopoulos is stronger.'

They passed an islet on which was a tumble-down farm-house and a few acres of reed and wild grasses. A boathouse sprawled down a mud embankment and into the lagoon, the waters of which filled it to within a few feet of the roof.

'I should like to live there,' said Baby; 'on that little island, in the farmhouse. In a way, it would be rather like living in that tower in the Palazzo garden.'

'I know what you mean.'

'It was kind of Mr Lykiadopoulos to let Poppa live there with Daniel. But I do not like Mr Lykiadopoulos. He won't do any harm to Poppa or Daniel, I think, but he is bad for Piero and Mr de Freville. And it may be,' said Baby, 'that he is bad for you.'

'What harm can he do me? I shall be in London.'

'But you'll be coming back to Venice,' said Baby. 'You'll be coming back to make sure Daniel is all right in that tower.'

'Perhaps, yes.'

'Then please be careful, my lord, of Mr Lykiadopoulos.'

'You don't have to call me "my lord". In fact you shouldn't.'

'I like to. Sometimes it's a joke; sometimes it's because I like to. You *will* be careful of Mr Lykiadopoulos?'

'You mean . . . I ought to steer clear of his Baccarat Bank?'

'No,' said Baby, 'I don't think it's exactly that. It's another danger. '

'Danger?'

'It isn't clear. It's still some way off, you see.' A gondola nosed out of the tall reeds to their left; a man in a grey cap sat fishing from it. Baby came close to Detterling. 'It isn't clear,' she repeated, 'but it's there.'

'Thank you for letting me know.'

'Don't make fun.'

'I wasn't making fun.'

For a while they sat in silence as the motor-boat swished along a channel through the reed beds. Then Baby said :

'Poppa will be with Daniel. Uncle Gregory and Auntie Isobel will be kind to me, of course. But . . . ?'

'. . . Yes. I shall come.'

'Often?'

'If you wish it.'

'If you please, my lord,' Baby said.

'I do hope Baby's going to be all right at this school,' said Detterling to Gregory and Isobel Stern in their house in Chelsea.

They had all had a delicious dinner cooked by Isobel, after
which Baby, worn out with flying and with eating, had volun-
tarily retired to bed.

'She's got to go somewhere,' said Isobel gloomily, 'what with
Tom off in Venice and Patricia ... well ... permanently out of
the way.'

'What exactly happened about Patricia?' asked Detterling.
'I was in the East when she was taken off, on my mission for
poor old Canteloupe. I never heard the full story.'

'Boys, my dear,' said Gregory: 'young ones. Lots and lots of
young boys.'

'But surely, you don't have a woman put away ... "permanently" ... just because she likes boys?'

Since neither Isobel nor Gregory seemed eager to answer,
Detterling now began to approach the question from another
angle.

'Fielding Gray said something rather curious in Venice the
other day,' he told them. 'He said Tom liked Patricia to behave
like "a kitchen-maid in heat" – that it was only any good for
Tom if she did behave like that.'

'She got to like it too,' said Isobel flatly. 'Then Tom stopped
liking it – or anything else in that line, so I gather – about six
or seven years ago. He left her high and dry. Or rather, high
and wet.'

'Oh Isobel my wife, such a vulgar thing to say of your own
sister.'

'Go on, Isobel,' said Detterling.

But once again reluctance prevailed, and once again Detterling was compelled to abandon the direct approach and come
crawling in from the flank.

'Well, how was it,' he said, 'that Fielding Gray knew all about
the "kitchen-maid" bit? He's a very old friend of Tom's, but I
can hardly think Tom told him.'

'Patty told him,' said Isobel. 'They had an affair together.'

'I never knew that.'

'Even you, Canteloupe, do not know everything,' Gregory
said.

'It was in the summer of 'seventy-one,' said Isobel; 'they had a nice little bunk-up down at Broughton Staithe.'

Clearly, thought Detterling, Isobel had little objection to talking about her sister's peculiarities or infidelities *as such*; it was only about this business of the 'boys' that she was reticient. Well, let her get on at her own pace, he thought; she'll have to come to it in time.

'Tom was at some conference of history dons,' Isobel was saying, 'and Patty took Baby to Broughton for the sea air. Fielding was alone in his house there (it was long after Harriet had pushed off) writing his book on Conrad. And then one day he met Patricia and Baby as they were trailing across the golf links to the beach. Up till then they'd hardly known each other, and Patricia hadn't even registered that Fielding lived at Broughton – or so she told me later, and I believe it. But now . . . well, they took one look at each other over Baby's head, and what they both read in the other's face was, "God, I need some sex and you'll just about do for it." They didn't need to say anything explicit, they couldn't in front of Baby; they simply exchanged a few vapidities, in the course of which he mentioned where his house was. So that evening, after Baby was in bed in their lodgings, Patricia tramped along the lane to Fielding's house, and two whiskies and fifteen minutes later he was riding her past the post for the first time. She couldn't stay long because her landlady locked up at eleven – typical of Patty, to be too mean to stay in a proper hotel – but that suited Fielding down to the ground. He didn't want a lump like her in his bed half the night – she knew that well enough for herself, she told me; which was another thing typical of Patty – she was dead honest when you came down to it. So it was hot, quick, sloshy short-timers every evening for the ten days she was in Broughton, and when, after a week or so, he didn't come up to scratch too easily, she used to excite him by telling him about what she did with Tom – or *had* done with Tom before he gave out on her some years before. And on the last night, when that no longer worked, she told him about some horny undergraduate she'd had it off with a time or two. . .'

Isobel paused, but now that she was well into her narrative she was bound, as Detterling had foreseen, to continue. Just as a driver, who has many excellent reasons for stopping the car, nevertheless finds himself compelled to drive on, despite his hunger for lunch, despite the squeals of the children who are clutching their parts in the back, until he comes to the ideal place to halt; so Isobel must now keep going, whatever her misgivings, until she reached the only destination that was fully appropriate – the end of Patricia's story.

'So when Patricia went back to Grantchester,' Isobel went on, 'they said good-bye and thank you, and that, one might have thought, was that. No harm done, quite the reverse. Both of them much the better for it ... but neither of them likely to go trekking all across Norfolk and Cambridgeshire for another helping. It had been very convenient, and now it was over. The trouble was, it wasn't over with Patricia. Not that she wanted Fielding again, for he was nowhere near being up to her demands; and yet he had not entirely failed her; he had responded, for a time, with just enough skill and enthusiasm and what she called *inspiration* to hint to her how fascinating sex could be, and indeed *would* be, given a man of Fielding's strange and creative sexual aura who was twenty-five years younger. In short, Fielding had roused her imagination more than he had pleased her body. He had made her hunger for someone who must certainly be younger and stronger and far more beautiful than he but must *also* have his – Fielding's – uncanny talent for investing sexual activity with a new and enchanted atmosphere. This she found hard to describe, but it seems to have been a failing she had with him that she was taking part in something insidious and forbidden, not just ordinary mutual pleasuring or copulation, but something deliciously and magically perverse, like a mythical piece of metamorphosis or incest, which was at the same time both unnatural and paradisial. With Fielding, however, this feeling never anything like reached the heights (or depths) she thought it could have reached, because his physical performance was so lax. Where was she to find someone who was both physically proficient *and* endowed with Fielding's brand of sorcery?

'Now, I've already told you that in order to excite Fielding, to get him going when he was bored with her, she'd reminisced about her goings-on with an undergraduate. He'd been gone from Cambridge for some time, this young man, but now she began to wonder if she shouldn't look for another one like him, because a clever and sympathetic undergraduate might be able to provide just this extra sexual dimension for which she was hankering. The trouble was, it was rather unfair on Tom to go drumming up young men on his college doorstep; and anyway she wasn't all that to look at any more, so she might have a lot of difficulty pulling them in. But she had a really murderous itch on, poor Patty did, like Pasiphaë for her bull or Phaedra for Hippolytus, and somebody young and beautiful she must have ... somebody young and beautiful and as enchantingly perverse as Fielding Gray.

'Then she remembered something she'd once heard about adolescent boys. They're so randy, she'd heard, so full of fresh juices, that they don't much care what they do or whom they do it with provided they get a nice feeling at the end of their pricks. Unlike twenty-year-olds, who are beginning to discriminate, they just want to come as often as they can and never mind where. That's not saying, of course, that they'll do it with any old slag who comes up to them – they're too wary for that – but once they know who a person is, and so long as that person behaves pleasantly and is presentable in the broadest sense, they don't at all mind being invited to hang their trousers up to dry when they come in out of the rain and being given a nice long rub down. And then they're pretty to look at, and they can go on and on, and, above all, they're accustomed to take orders at that age and indeed prefer to take them; so that although she could hardly expect them to manifest of themselves that weird and arcane *esprit* of which she'd had such tantalizing whiffs from Fielding, she knew they would happily comply with whatever she suggested in her pursuit of it. She would have to conjure up the demon herself, but at least a fresh eager boy (provided she didn't frighten him) would give unstinting co-operation.'

'And so,' said Detterling, 'she started spotting out adolescent boys up in London. Since she was a well-mannered upper-class woman, when she chose to be, and quite definitely "presentable in the broadest sense", they soon came round to her all right. And then, of course, they came round to her London flat.'

'Who told you?'

'Jonathan Gamp. Over a year ago. But,' said Detterling, 'the story was, then, that her little friends were all over sixteen, which made it legal, and though she sometimes asked two or three of them to come along at the same time, she handled them all too discreetly to give rise to scandal.'

'She handled them strictly one at a time, if that's what you mean. Apparently group sex wasn't her answer. There was no question of illicit orgies.'

'Then why all the bother later on?'

Isobel took a deep breath.

'Have you ever seen that picture by Bronzino in the National Gallery?' she said. 'It's called Venus, Cupid and − What's the rest, Gregory? You'd know.'

'Venus, Cupid, Folly and Time,' Gregory said.

'Apt,' said Isobel crisply. 'Well, there's a little smirking cherub throwing rose petals about and a horrible old man lowering in the background. Venus is kneeling down among the rose petals, and Cupid is bending over to kiss her. But it isn't going to be just a nice kiss for Mummy, it's going to be something very different, because they're both smiling in that certain way, and Venus is already popping her tongue out, and Cupid is fondling one of her tits. He's about fourteen, Cupid is, and a real dish, with his plump curvy rump sticking out behind him, and his whole body all silky and sexy and taut. You can't see his cock because it's hidden between his thighs, but there's a tiny wisp of dark hair running out which is more suggestive than any penis ever painted. So that's what the cherub is smirking about and the old man is lowering about: Venus and her newly pubescent son are just about to have it away among the rose petals. There's a light, bright, thrilling madness about it all − just the sort of thing, Patricia told me, that she got hints of when she was with Fielding. And as time went on, what she began to want was what was happening in that picture: to frolic among the rose petals, not just with any adolescent boy she managed to pick up, but with her own pubescent son ... which, as you well know, she has not got.

'Then in 1972 something new started up, something about which she did *not* tell me herself. Baby reported to Gregory on one of their outings that Mummy had taken to having very funny conversations with her, "telling her things", as Baby put it. After a little probing, it emerged that Patricia, under pretence of telling Baby the facts of life, was describing her own fantasies. She told Baby that if she'd been a little boy, Mummy would have shown him what to do now he was growing up, and she gave a pretty detailed account of the imagined course of instruction. You see what she was at? She was trying to get the incestuous kick she wanted by corrupting her own child − only verbally, but quite effectively for all that. Naturally enough − *un*naturally enough − Baby got a lot of ideas into her head and started to behave a bit oddly. She noticed how excited Patricia became during their sessions, and she also noticed that Patricia was going off to London increasingly often, so she put two and two together and started her own line in fantasies about what her Mummy was up to in the big city. This made her behave odder, and the end of it was she was sent home from school in the middle of one bright morning, carrying a polite but firm letter for Tom which said that she'd better not come back the next day – or ever. At this stage Tom, who already knew that something was wrong but had deliberately tried not to realize what, was compelled to have a show-down with Patricia. How much he got out of her I do not know, because by this time I was out of Patty's confidence – I'd told her rather sharply to pull herself together and she'd bitterly resented my "unkindness", as she called it. Anyway, whatever Patty told Tom, the upshot was that he engaged a governess for Baby and encouraged Patricia to stay out of the way in London ... which she began to do for longer and longer periods, until by the beginning of this year she was hardly in Grantchester at all. Baby was jealous about this at first, but she got fond of the governess, and started to simmer down, and there's been a marked improvement in her ever since.'

'There certainly has,' said Detterling. 'I went to see Tom and Baby in Grantchester back in May last year – just after Baby was sacked from school, it must have been. Baby was a really atrocious child, and poor Tom looked about ninety.'

'Both of them started to recover as soon as Patty removed herself to London. Gregory and I helped a bit – we've always been fond of the child, even at her worst, not having one of our own. We used to take her on holidays and expeditions and so on when the governess had time off. I think it did her good to be away from Tom as well as from her mother. Tom means well by Tullia, but he broods over her.'

'Agreed... But meanwhile,' said Detterling, 'what of Patricia? She was living alone in London, I suppose ... and you and she weren't talking?'

'No. I made one last effort, but she just wouldn't see sense. All she kept saying was, "I'll find him. I know I'll find him." "You be careful where you look," I said, and was told to get out and mind my own business. There was nothing I could do. There was no question, yet, of having her confined unless she went of her own will. You see, she'd done nothing – nothing palpable – which could be put up against her. It's not against any law to talk to your daughter about sex or to entertain sixteen-year-old boys in your flat, if they're willing to come there. And willing they certainly were. A couple of 'em were moving up the stairs as I went down after my last missionary visit, and they were positively pink with pleasure. So after that I just settled down to wait for whatever was going to happen.' Isobel paused and drank some whisky from her glass. Then, 'Lobes,' she said suddenly, as if announcing an important clue : 'ear-lobes.'

'What?'

'When Patty and I get really excited, we nibble and we nip. We particularly like nipping ear-lobes. Right, Gregory?'

'And very nice it is, Isobel.'

'Gregory may enjoy it,' said Isobel to Detterling, 'but there are those that don't, as you'll see in a minute. Well, time went on, and then one afternoon about three months ago, midsummer's day it was, the telephone rang and there was Patty clacking away on the other end of it. We hadn't spoken for weeks, but now here she was, positively honking with excitement. She'd found what she was looking for, she said, and she wanted me to come round to her place and see him. Why? I asked her. So that I could see for myself, she said, that she hadn't been wasting her time. So that I should understand that those that seek will, in the end, find. That dream she'd had, of being Venus in the Bronzino picture – that dream had come true. I could come and see for myself.

'So I went. Rather fast, because I didn't like the sound of it. Light, bright madness, I said to you just now about that picture; well, there was all of that in Patty's voice. When I got there twenty minutes later, the door of her flat was ajar and she was looking out of it, wearing slacks and a shirt (which didn't suit her) and with her finger over her lips.

' "He's asleep," she whispered; "come and see."

'On the bed, lying on his side, was a perfect little beauty, limbs like Cupid in the picture, the same round and rather fat bottom, the same silky flanks, and a little dark bush, hardly more than a fleck of it. And the face in profile on the pillow . . . well, it was a pretty close boyish approximation to Baby's. This boy could have been Baby's brother; and so Patricia had her dream, she had a son, a son whom she could . . . "show what to do now he was growing up". By the look of it, she'd been showing him pretty energetically, because he was absolutely flaked out.

' "How old?" I said.

' "Seventeen."

' "You're sure?"

' "Yes. I know he looks much younger, but I've seen his pro-
visional driving licence. I always make them prove they're old
enough."

'This made me burst out laughing. Poor old Patty, I thought,
a gone woman if ever there was one, but still retaining this one
vestige of caution and respectability, clinging to this one last
rule as a bankrupt clings to a teapot that the sheriff's men have
somehow overlooked.

' "Shush," she said; "you'll wake him."

' "Where did you find him?"

' "At the Baths. He's got a half-holiday from school."

'Yes, I thought, you'd know all about half-holidays by now,
when to go to the Baths.

' "Well," I said, not knowing what else to say, "don't do him
to death. He looks absolutely whacked.'

' "That's the swimming," she said. "I haven't done anything
yet. I'm waiting for him to wake up."

' "He knows what he's here for?"

' "Oh yes. He let me undress him. He liked that, but he asked
if he could go to sleep before – you know."

'By this time I thought our absurd conversation had gone on
long enough. The plain facts, whatever Patty's fantasy might be,
were these : she was about to take her pleasure with a healthy
and willing seventeen-year-old boy, who was having a nice rest
on the bed first. That was all. Nothing to be done. No sense in
making a fuss. I'd just better go away and leave her to it. To
tell the truth I was getting rather excited myself—'

'—Oh Isobel, Isobel,' Gregory said.

'Sorry, my old darling, but that boy was such a peach, such
a soft fleshy peach with down on, and looking at him lying
there just waiting to be eaten was more than I could stand. So
I said good-bye and good luck to Patricia, and I went . . . leaving
her to her big moment.

'And a really big moment it must have been,' said Isobel. 'I
suppose all the ingredients were just right. Youth and strength,
both refreshed by sleep. Beauty. The eerie feeling which she
remembered having with Fielding and had always wanted
again – the feeling of taking part in a forbidden yet divine mystery : in this case, Venus making love to her own son. And then
think of the sheer perverse lustfulness of it all. Patty peeling off

her slacks ... standing over the bed ... coaxing the cries of
pleasure from the little boy whom she imagined as flesh of her
flesh... Oh yes,' said Isobel, 'she must have had a very big moment indeed. You see, Canteloupe, for all our love of nipping
and biting, I've never drawn blood – have I, Gregory? – and
Patty once told me that though she did sometimes bite through
the skin, it was only a little way and only if she was very excited indeed. But this time,' Isobel said, 'this time with the boy
from the Baths who looked like Baby,' Isobel said, '*this time,*'
Isobel said, 'she bit his whole right ear off and bloody near
killed him with it. When she came to and realized what she'd
done, she bandaged him somehow with a towel, and she called
an ambulance, and the ambulance men called the police, and
the police called me and Gregory, and nobody thought of calling
Tom, and in the middle of the hubbub she gave a little moan,
just a tiny moan, and told them to take her away.'

'And so now,' said Detterling after a long silence, 'she'll be
in an asylum for good and all?'

'For as long as anyone can foresee. Apparently she thinks,
now, that that boy really was her son. She thinks she seduced
and nearly killed her own son, and she's torn between terrible
remorse and desire to make it up to him – by seducing him all
over again, but this time without savaging him. I suppose the
shock finally did for her – when the blood began to spurt...'

'How much does Baby know?'

'She's been told there was a horrible accident,' said Gregory;
'that Patricia among others was very badly injured and is unlikely ever to come back from hospital. She seems to accept
that. She's had the great good sense not to ask any questions.'

'One thing is clear,' said Detterling: 'she's much better off
without her mother. And I don't think she'll suffer from being
away from Tom for a bit.'

'Tom's jittery after everything that's happened,' said Isobel,
'and who shall blame him? God knows what ideas Patricia
put into that child's head before she left home.'

'Better forget about all that and let her forget it. She looks
a tough child to me,' Detterling said. 'If she's treated just like
anyone else, and doesn't feel that anxious eyes are following
her the whole time, she'll be all right.'

'Well, we shall see what we shall see,' said Gregory, who
seemed a trifle irritated at the confidence with which Detterling was prescribing.

'What is very important,' said Detterling, 'is this school she's going to. What's it like?'

'That's the trouble,' said Isobel : 'it's one of those expensive places where the rich park their problems. God knows how Tom can afford it.'

'Some of his early books are in the fashion again,' Gregory said; 'he's making very nice money out of them this year.'

'More's the pity,' said Isobel, 'if it means he can go on sending Baby to this school. It's the sort of place,' she explained to Detterling, 'which is battened on by psychiatrists who pay the head a fat commission for recommending that the children should have treatment. All fads and no learning.'

'That's the last thing Baby needs. A psychiatrist would just stir her up again – and then announce she needed ten years' deep analysis.'

'Tom's told them "no psychiatry". We made him. But we couldn't get him to send her to a normal school,' said Isobel, 'though these days, with a bit of push, she could probably be got into one. He thinks she may still be ... peculiar ... and he wants a school which offers special care for peculiar children.'

'Of course she'll be peculiar,' said Detterling, 'if she realizes she's being specially cared for.'

'So we told Tom. He wouldn't agree. He's got dreadful guilt about what happened – he thinks he betrayed Baby and Patricia by his own neglect – and he wants to feel he's doing something out of the way, *i.e.* something very expensive, to make amends. Self-sacrifice, you see.'

'Only it's not himself he's sacrificing, it's Baby.'

'Well, one will see,' said Gregory, still sounding as if he resented Detterling's interference.

'Yes, one will see,' said Detterling, 'and very soon at that. She's asked me to go and see her.'

'We shall all go to see her,' said Gregory stiffly.

'Well then,' said Detterling, deciding that a little soft-soaping was now called for, 'Tom trusts you and Isobel more than anyone on earth. If you tell him that this school is definitely not doing her good—'

'—That we cannot tell him until we know it to be so. I do not understand why you are so ... taken up ... with my niece Tullia. You hardly know her.'

'I saw a bit of her in Venice,' said Detterling carefully, 'and I rather liked what I saw.'

'Oh. And what of your other business in Venice? Finding authors for us. You had, perhaps, a little time left over for that?'

'That was your business too. Only you ratted on it.'

'Boys, boys, boys,' said Isobel. 'Such speech we cannot have,' she said, imitating Gregory: 'there must be civil words.'

'Of course there must,' said Gregory: 'more whisky, Canteloupe?'

'If you please. Quite a lot. As it happened,' said Detterling, 'I became rather preoccupied with one thing and another, and anyway all that PEN crowd went away not so very long after you did. But I've briefed Fielding to keep his eye open for us—'

'—That is no good. Writers do not procure the services of other writers any more than bishops procure the services of saints. There is too much professional jealousy.'

'Well at least,' said Detterling, 'Fielding seems to be working again. Or on the verge of it. He thinks he's on to a new story.'

'What kind of story?'

'Mystery man in a family portrait – late eighteenth-century. No one seems to know who he was or why he's in the picture. Obviously it must have been known once, but none of the surviving records have anything to say about the chap. Why not?'

'Is this fact or fiction?' asked Gregory.

'Fact, so far. If Fielding can't find out anything more, he'll have to make up the rest. But if he can discover who the fellow was there might be an amusing biography in it.'

'If he was someone who is worth a biography,' said Gregory.

'If he wasn't, there can still be a good novel.'

'I think,' said Isobel in a thoughtful voice, 'that for all our sakes Fielding Gray should not start writing a costume piece. If he makes it up, it will probably be ridiculous, and if he finds out what really happened, he may disturb troublesome ghosts.'

'Good heavens, Isobel my wife, is no one ever to do research for fear of raising ghosts?'

'Sad,' she said. 'Such sad ghosts.'

'What are you saying, Isobel?'

Isobel did not answer.

'Isobel ... *Isobel* ... what is this you are saying?'

Isobel shook her head.

'It is not clear to me,' she muttered. 'I am very tired and I must go upstairs.'

'Bloody blue murder,' said Max de Freville to Fielding Gray:
'to do anything for this heap would cost millions.'

This "heap" was the Palazzo Castagna-Samuele, a high and
narrow seventeenth-century edifice languishing over a scurfy
little Rio and long since ready to subside into an easeful death
by drowning. Max and Fielding were surveying it at an angle
from the Ponte del Ghetto Vecchio, their view being somewhat
impeded by assorted articles of underwear which hung drying
on a line slung athwart the waters of the Rio.

'It might be possible to restore the façade,' said Fielding,
'without bothering about what's behind it. The façade is all that
matters here.'

'That way, the whole damn city will turn into a façade.'

'I know. Half the buildings have been rotten inside for decades.
This one certainly has,' said Fielding, 'so there'd be no cause to
feel guilty about abandoning the interior.'

A loose shutter, caught by the evening breeze, flapped feebly
back against the wall, showing a window behind which was
utter blackness. The sun caught the window, which responded,
or rather failed to respond, like the pupil of a sightless eye to
an optician's flashlight. Then, after a few moments, the sun
sank behind the ragged roof-line of the buildings behind them.
Although it at once became very chilly on the bridge, neither
man moved: for the sickness of the Palazzo Castagna-Samuele
compelled respect as well as melancholy; and just as Max and
Fielding would have felt it impolite to walk noisily or eagerly
from the bedside of a declining man, so they would now allow
themselves only the most gradual and decorous, almost im-
perceptible, withdrawal from the house which they were examining.

'What sort of state do you suppose the foundations are in?'
asked Max.

'They could be better than the fabric. They were built to with-
stand water, whereas the fabric was not designed to resist all
this filthy air pollution from Mestre. At any rate it might be
worth having a survey done. If you could raise a respectable
sum for the Fund and also send in a surveyor's report which
said the foundations were in quite good nick, they might put
up the balance needed to restore the façade.'

'How important is this building?'

'As architecture it's no more than merely handsome. But it
has a curious history. A Jewish doctor, Josephus Samuele, built

it for a courtesan called La Castagna. Since Jews were not allowed to build palaces – only tenements – and since they were forbidden to have carnal intercourse with Christian women, including whores, there are some interesting questions to be asked.'

'Like, why was Samuele allowed to get away with it?'

'Yes. One answer is that he was the confidential physician who was treating the Doge's daughter for the clap. According to another story, La Castagna had a reputation as a witch, so no one wanted to offend her or her lover.'

'Wouldn't they have burnt her?'

'One would have thought so. But according to this version, she put it about that she was the reincarnation – or even the zombie – of Medea herself, the Queen of Witches, and as such indestructible.'

'A likely tale.'

'The chronicler Andrea di Cannaregio says it was widely believed. In any event, the Inquisition was told to lay off La Castagna, though there may have been several different reasons for that. Apparently she was pretty generous with her favours even after she moved in with Samuele, who was a complaisant protector if ever there was one. One theory says he encouraged her to have as many affairs as possible, and then hung about behind the curtains taking notes and making sketches, as he was a pioneer sexologist who wanted to record variations in coital behaviour. Unfortunately La Castagna burnt all his papers after he died. Like most harlots, she was subject to fits of prudery.'

'I don't know that any of this justifies expensive restorations to the Palazzo.'

'Oh, his descendants were a pretty odd lot too. They included a distinguished architect who is reputed to have bought the children of poor parents in order to bury them alive under the cornerstones of his building – an ancient form of sacrifice which was intended to propitiate primitive gods of earth and weather. He built several villas in the Veneto, all of which have survived in good order, so the superstition may have had something in it.'

'Where do you pick up all these stories?'

'The Biblioteca Marciana. It's full of gossiping histories and the like. The nuisance is, I can't find out anything at all about the one person I'm really concerned with just now. I mean that stranger in the picture in your gallery – the late eighteenth-century family group of Albani. I know a good deal about the picture, who painted it and so on, and quite a lot about Fernando and Maria Albani, and the ages of all the four children – but not a word can I find, anywhere, about that stranger at the back of the picture. All the records and references are written as if he simply didn't exist, as if there were only the six Albani figures in the painting and no one had ever seen a seventh.'

'It's getting late,' observed Max, dropping his voice to a whisper as if afraid lest the Palazzo Castagna-Samuele might hear him; 'we'd better be going.'

They moved slowly on across the bridge and down a broad Calle. Golden Hebrew letters arched over a door on the corner in front of them; a very small boy scampered past with a little round cap on his head and ringlets hanging over both ears.'

'Orthodox,' said Fielding. 'There can't be many of them left. Who *can* that man be,' he said, turning earnestly to Max, 'that man in the picture?'

'Why are you so keen to find out?'

'Because everything is against my finding out. Because there's a conspiracy of silence on the subject.'

'Benito Albani – the one who let the Palazzo to Lyki – he may know.'

'Do you know his address?'

'Only that he lives in Siena. But Lyki will have the exact address – or the lawyer's. I'll get it from him and send it to the Gritti for you.'

'Not there. I'm moving out. Into the Gabrielli for the winter.'

'Yes,' said Max, part as in malice, part as approving a sensible course of action; 'the Gabrielli will only cost you half.'

'It's not that. It's just that the Gabrielli is more appropriate. Middle-class people like myself,' said Fielding, 'even when they're highly paid writers, have no business in places like the Gritti for very long. To stay there for the winter would be to promote myself above my proper station – an easy and tempting thing to do when one is abroad, but dishonest and destructive.'

'All those years with Hamilton's Horse,' said Max, 'and you still think of yourself as middle-class?'

'In origin. You should have seen my parents... Anyway, please send Benito Albani's address to the Gabrielli. I'll have moved in by tea-time tomorrow.'

'I can't guarantee to send it tomorrow. Lyki's in a tremendous whirl, getting ready for this Baccarat Bank. Sometimes I don't see him for twenty-four hours on end.'

'As soon as you can then.'

'I'll do my best. But there's another thing about Lyki which won't help. He's in a very uncertain temper – and not just because of the Baccarat Bank. I think . . . that Daniel Mond bothers him. Tom and Daniel have been in that tower for over a week now, and everything's going well on the surface, but I think that Lyki is – well – discomposed by Daniel. It's as if he suspected that Daniel saw too far into his concerns.'

'Daniel will have no interest whatever in Lyki's concerns.'

'I know that. So does Lyki. But what he feels – he hasn't put it into words, but I've known him for years and I can usually tell – what he feels is that if Daniel ever should take a look at his affairs he's capable of seeing much farther into them than Lyki would care for.'

'What is there to see? Baccarat, Piero, hotels in Corfu – all rather out of the ordinary run, I grant you, but nothing, by contemporary standards, to cause serious trouble or discredit.'

'In the end there's always something to cause serious trouble or discredit. You know that.'

'Yes. . . On second thoughts, save yourself the trouble of sending that address to the Gabrielli, and leave it with Tom and Daniel in the tower. I'll be popping in on them in a couple of days.'

'Warn Daniel to be careful ... not to annoy Lyki in any way.'

'Daniel always annoys a certain kind of person, which kind includes Lykiadopoulos for one and myself for another. He is good, Daniel is, and he makes the likes of Lykiadopoulos and me feel guilty and inferior. That's all this whole thing of Lyki is about. Tell him to do as I do – to try to treat the uneasiness which Daniel arouses in him as therapeutic. I'll be coming along to the tower for a dose of this purgative therapy on the afternoon of the day after tomorrow,' Fielding said, 'and I'll very much hope that by then you will have found me Benito Albani's address.'

In order to reach the tower in the garden of the Palazzo Albani, it was necessary, unless one had a key to the door which led into the garden from the Calle Alba, to go through the

Palazzo itself. Fielding decided it would look better to arrive there by water. When he informed the Major-Domo, who met him on the landing stage, that he wanted 'i signori Mond e Llewyllyn', the man gave him a look as of one who was being put upon and showed him through to the garden with neither the respect nor the elegance which he had manifested on previous occasions.

Fielding decided to say nothing of this to Tom and Daniel. What he did say was that it would be tiresome having to go through the Palazzo every time he came to see them.

'I know,' said Tom; 'but Lykiadopoulos insists on our keeping the door into the Calle Alba locked up.'

'There's no bell there?'

'No. When you're coming in future, you must let us know roughly what time. Then I can wait by the garden door and let you in when you knock.'

This settled, Fielding enquired after Tom and Daniel's domestic arrangements. These, it appeared, were satisfactory: the tower was warm, the sanitary device was up to its office, and the beds were comfortable. Hot water came in from the Palazzo at the stipulated hours, borne by a cheerful female from the kitchen who had taken a maternal fancy to them. For the rest, they had decided to use Daniel's room, the one downstairs, for 'entertaining', and they had purchased a kettle. This Tom now filled from a white ewer and placed on one of the oil heaters to boil.

And how did they pass the day? Well, they went to a café in the Calle Alba for coffee at nine-ish, read during the morning in their separate rooms, had a light lunch at another café which did snacks, slept a little in the early afternoon, then went on a local sightseeing expedition (to the Frari, perhaps, in which there was enough to be seen to last them a lifetime), and came home at about four-thirty for tea. More reading after tea unless, as today, there was a guest; a bath at seven-thirty for one of them (they took it in turns) in Max's bathroom; then dinner in one of the restaurants near the Rialto, and back home to whisky and bed.

'Very quiet, you see,' said Daniel.

'I suppose you see quite a lot of Max and Lykiadopoulos?'

'No. Max occasionally, when we go to his bathroom. Lykiado-poulos only once, when he came on a rather formal visit to enquire whether we'd settled in all right.'

Odd, thought Fielding (remembering what Max had told him), that Lykiadopoulos should be 'discomposed' by Daniel after meeting him only twice – at the dinner, and on this 'formal' visit to the tower. But never mind Lykiadopoulos for the present. The topic which Fielding really wished to get on to was the far more inviting one of the boy Piero. However, he was wary of naming him immediately lest injurious deductions be drawn by his hosts from his eagerness; and he therefore raised another subject which, he thought, might serve as a way of bringing discussion round to the young Sicilian without indecorous pre-cipitation. 'I hear hooligans have been smashing your college chapel about,' he said.

There had been an item in the English papers about this six days before. The offertory chest in Lancaster College chapel had been busted open and rifled, and a tomb in a chantry off the choir had been, for no ascertainable reason, savaged with a pick.

'We had a letter about that today,' said Daniel; 'from Balbo Blakeney. They think it was done by some of our own under-graduates.'

'But surely,' said Fielding, 'term doesn't start till October.'

'That wouldn't prevent some of 'em from sneaking back to do their dirty work during the vacation,' said Tom. 'There are quite a few students of Lancaster just now who resent the chapel because, they say, it stands for a representative faith and, even worse, causes the college to maintain a private school for the choristers.'

'I thought Lancaster had flushed out all that left-wing non-sense.'

'There's been less of it, but these days you're never quite rid of it.'

'But is there any hard evidence to connect your own students with this affair?'

'Yes. An anonymous note to the Provost said that the money had been sent to Oxfam, and that similar action against the chapel would be repeated unless the choir school was closed by Christmas and he himself gave an undertaking not to accept a Life Peerage. It's pretty widely known that he'll probably be offered one this autumn.'

'I see,' said Fielding. 'The argument is that only a member of the college would care whether he took his Barony or not?'

'What is more, the note bore the motto, "A Red Rose for

Lancaster". There is always a possibility,' said Tom, 'that one of the young and more dissident Fellows had a hand in it. A Fellow might be in a good position to steal a key to the chapel.'

'I don't see Provost Constable scaring very easily,' said Fielding.

'No,' grated Daniel. 'Balbo says that the Provost has hired a private security agency to guard the chapel and track down the offenders; and that he has intimated to the agency that if they find anyone up to any new mischief he doesn't much mind how hard they hit him.'

'He'd better be careful,' said Fielding: 'these days that sort of talk could prevent even a Conservative Prime Minister from giving him a peerage.'

'Constable's too grand a man to care about any Prime Minister.'

'You're on his side in this?' said Fielding. 'I should have thought you would have deprecated violence – and in a sacred place at that.'

'Sacred places, of all places, must be protected. The only way you can be sure of controlling a violent man,' said Daniel, 'is to knock him unconscious. Nothing else is *certain*. And if you hit him too hard and kill him by mistake, he has only himself to blame.'

'Daniel, my Daniel,' mocked Fielding, 'what would the National Council for Civil Liberties say? You're not dealing with criminals, my dear, or hadn't you heard? These fine young men are politically dedicated idealists.'

'Then the harder you need to hit them. Violence is no less to be prevented because it is political in motive, and idealists are far more dangerous than criminals. Criminals stop when they've got what they wanted. Idealists never stop because they can never attain their ideal.'

Daniel put his hand up to stroke the silk scarf over his throat, which had clearly not benefited from the vehemence of his last speech. Tom started fussing around with the kettle, which showed no signs of boiling. Fielding wondered how he could slant the present subject of delinquent youth in general on to the subject of Piero in particular. This had been his aim in raising the Lancaster desecrations, but the turn which the discussion had now taken was unhelpful. Whatever Piero might be, he was clearly neither violent nor idealistic. However, Fielding's prob-

lem now solved itself, in a sense : there was a light tap on the
door, and into the room limped Piero.

'Mr Lykiadopoulos has gone out,' he announced to all
present, 'and so I could come.'

'Good,' said Daniel : 'the kettle's boiling for tea.'

'He has told me not to pester you,' said Piero : 'he says I
must not come to this tower or even go into the garden without
asking his permission first. He would not have let me come this
afternoon ... but now he has gone out to that Casino to make
more arrangements, and he will not know. He thinks the servants will tell him if I disobey him, but like me they are Italian
and they will not betray me to a Greek.'

He did not, however, sound absolutely sure of this.

'As far as we're concerned,' said Tom stolidly, 'you're always
welcome.'

'He says I am a nuisance to you, and that is why I may not
use the garden without asking him first. But really he is punish-
ing me for what I said at that dinner.'

Piero sat down on the arm of Daniel's chair and placed the
finger of one hand lightly over Daniel's wrist.

'Yet he says,' Piero went on, 'that I may go out with you,
should you wish. Although he does not like me to see you here
in the garden or in the house, he says he does not mind how
often we go together to churches or galleries or restaurants ...
should you wish to go.'

'Interesting,' observed Fielding. 'It seems he does not mind
how well you know Tom and Daniel provided you do not know
them on his territory. In other words, he wants them to keep
their distance from him. By more or less forbidding you to see
them here but encouraging you to go out with them, he is sending them a message. He is telling them to look away from the
Palazzo; he is telling them that they will enjoy his confidence,
of which you, Piero, are the symbol, so long – and only so long –
as they turn their attentions away from himself and his immediate precinct.'

'Then why,' said Tom, 'did he allow us to come and live in it?'

'To keep me from having this tower,' said Piero, 'and also,
perhaps, out of kindness. But he did not realize, when he made
the arrangement, what sort of person was coming. He did not
know about Daniel.'

'Did not know what about Daniel?'

'That ... that Daniel sees certain people a long way through their skin,' said Piero awkwardly.

'You flatter me,' said Daniel.

'But now he knows this,' said Piero, 'it is rather, I think, as Major Gray has described. He cannot change the arrangement about the tower, he would not wish to, because he made it with Mr de Freville's friend, Lord Canteloupe; but he does not like ... being looked at ... by Daniel. He does not like to be discussed by Daniel. Now, if I see Daniel and Tom here, on Mr Lykiadopoulos's ground, it is Mr Lykiadopoulos whom we shall discuss, as we are now doing. But if I go with them to churches and museums, there will be other things to talk of.'

'I'd sooner talk of other things now,' said Daniel.

'Very well. Let us talk of the places we shall go to in Venice, now it is permitted. You do,' said Piero, 'you do want to come with me?'

'Of course,' said Daniel.

'The kettle has nearly boiled,' Tom now told them all, 'but there is nothing to eat. I will go and buy some biscuits. Bear me company, Fielding.'

As Fielding and Tom crossed the little wilderness towards the garden wall, Tom said:

'For a little while Daniel will be able to go to places. Later on he will not.'

He took a key from his pocket and unlocked a green door in the wall.

'So then,' said Fielding, 'the less Daniel can leave the tower, the more Piero will want to come to it. Which Lykiadopoulos will not like.'

'He may not mind when he knows what is happening to Daniel.'

'Will he want to have Daniel ... dying in his garden?'

'Daniel says that Lykiadopoulos will not object to that. Nor, he thinks, will Max. Although they are both superstitious men, they are not frightened of death as such, only lest it should deprive them of something. Daniel's death, he says, will deprive them of nothing.'

Tom opened the green door; they stepped through into the Calle Alba; Tom locked the door behind them. Bewildered by the bustle in the Calle after the peace of the garden, Fielding followed Tom in silence until they came to a wide Campo. Just beyond the entrance to this was a little grocery store, the outside of which was much hung about with flasked wine of dubious provenance and thick-skinned salami sausages. While Tom bought the biscuits, Fielding went to examine the well-head at the centre of the Campo.

'What will Piero do,' said Fielding after Tom had rejoined him, 'when *he* knows that Daniel is dying?'

Tom put down his packet of biscuits on the metal cover of the well-head.

'I cannot concern myself too much about Piero,' he said. 'I only hope he won't be a nuisance.'

'You dislike Piero,' said Fielding.

'Yes. But I shall do my best to be pleasant to him because Daniel seems fond of him.

'How deep does that go?'

'You are in a very prying mood today, Fielding. Come on. They'll be expecting us back.'

When Tom and Fielding had regained the garden, Fielding said :

'I should rather like to have Piero. But I shan't even try. You know why not?'

'Because you haven't a chance.'

'On the contrary. My face makes people pity me. You'd be surprised how many people come to bed with me out of pity, or rather, out of a combination of pity and disgust, which they – and I – often find hugely exciting. I might well get Piero that way.'

'All right. Then why won't you try?'

'Because Piero's pity would be of a kind dangerous and degrading to both of us. It would be the pity of the priest for the victim. That's why I asked what Piero will do when he knows Daniel is dying. If he starts to pity him, and if I am right about his particular brand of pity, it could be an ugly spectacle.'

'That's enough for one afternoon, Fielding. I shall be bearing the brunt of all this. I've chosen to do it, so I've asked for everything I get; but you will not make the task easier for me by prematurely airing your clever, beastly theories about what may or may not happen. You will only confuse and depress me. Please leave me to cope with the problems as and when they crop up.'

When Fielding and Tom entered the tower, Daniel said,

'Piero and I have thought of such a good expedition. There's a church called the Madonna dell' Orto—'

'—A long way up beyond the Fondamente Nuove,' said Piero. 'It has a cloister, they say. Daniel would like that.'

'There are Tintorettos,' responded Daniel. 'The kettle is boiling, Tom. It was the church of Tintoretto's own parish.'

'There is a Last Judgement by him,' said Piero, 'all sorts of bodies coming alive again.' He lay down on the carpet and performed a mock-gruesome pantomime of this phenomenon.

'And it is not far from the Ghetto,' Daniel said. 'Perhaps I should see that.'

'I was up there with Max the other day,' said Fielding; 'beautiful but sad. And dirty with it.'

'We could go to the church by boat,' said Daniel, 'and then walk down through the Ghetto to the Grand Canal – it's not too far for us, I think – and catch the vaporetto home... The kettle is boiling, Tom.'

Although Daniel was sitting just by the boiling kettle, he made no attempt, Fielding observed, to do anything about it. Tom, who had been ponderously measuring tea into a teapot, now crossed the room, lent over Daniel with some difficulty to reach the kettle, and carried it back to the teapot.

'It should be a very good expedition,' Tom said. 'Shit. I've forgotten those bloody biscuits. We must have left them on that well,' he said to Fielding.

'We do not much need them,' said Piero, who was now capering about on the carpet and clearly cared for nothing save the projected trip to the Madonna dell' Orto. 'Tell me, Major Gray, when you went with Mr de Freville, did you go to the church or only to the Ghetto?'

'Only to the Ghetto. There's a peculiar palace there which might be restored if the Save Venice Fund ever got the money. I'm not sure whether or not Max thought it would be worth the trouble; he was in a non-committal mood. Which reminds me: did Max leave a note for me?'

'Yes,' said Daniel, taking an envelope from his breast pocket. 'He gave it me when I went for a bath last night. Just as well you mentioned it, or I'd have forgotten. It seems easy to forget things here,' he murmured uneasily; 'messages, biscuits, time itself—'

'—Good,' said Fielding, purposely breaking in on Daniel before he could enlarge his catalogue, 'it's Benito Albani's address in Siena.'

'What do you want with that?' said Tom.

'I thought he might know something about that stranger in the painting.'

Tom began to hand round cups of tea. Piero followed up with the sugar bowl.

'I've not seen the picture yet,' said Tom. 'I didn't get up there that night when we dined, and I haven't cared to ask since.'

'I will show it to you some time,' said Piero.

'Perhaps,' said Tom, offering lemon to Daniel. 'Baby told me about it before she left,' he said carefully. 'She said she thought there might be a good reason why you could not discover any-thing . . . anything about this stranger, I mean. She implied that it was just as well.'

'Come, come,' said Fielding, 'and you a scholar.'

'Someone seems to have taken care,' said Tom, 'that all record of this man should have disappeared. This was almost certainly the work of the Albani family. If so, why should Benito Albani be willing to tell you anything?'

'Because it all goes back over 170 years. At one time the family may have been anxious to suppress information about Mister X, but by now, surely, there can't be anything they'd wish to hide.'

'That depends what it is.'

'Why do you say "Mister X" and not "Signor"?' said Piero.

'Just a manner of speaking. Though come to that he certainly looks more English than Italian.'

'Look,' said Tom; 'it's an intriguing little mystery, from what I've heard, but probably the solution is quite banal. So why not make one up for yourself – if you're going to write a novel about it. You'd do it very well.'

'And that way you would not impinge,' said Daniel, 'on what doesn't concern you.'

'I should like to find out the truth,' Fielding said.

'You've shown very little respect for *that* in the years I've known you,' croaked Daniel.

'I tried to tell the truth about Conrad in my biography. After years of writing novels, you see, I've become rather bored with lies. And so now, Daniel, I should like to follow up an historical truth. You just remarked,' said Fielding, turning to Tom, 'that the truth in this case was probably very banal. But a little earlier,

you told us that Baby reckoned there might be quite a lot to it
—and not very pleasant at that, or so she seems to have hinted.'

'She was showing off to me, I expect. She often does. Anyway
she had nothing to go on.'

'I'm inclined to trust Baby's instinct. She has a good eye,'
Fielding said. 'She may not have had much to go on, but enough,
I dare say, to warrant a polite letter of enquiry to Benito Albani
. . . now that I have his address.'

He flourished Max's note and put it in his pocket.

'But suppose that he is — how do you say? — evading?' said
Piero.

'Not quite: evasive,' corrected Daniel with an encouraging
nod of his head.

'Then I shall at least know,' said Fielding, 'that he has cause
in this matter for evasion . . . and therefore that I have cause for
pursuit.'

'Things are going to be a bit different from now, Corporal,'
said Detterling to his manservant in London.

'So I had surmised, my lord.'

'We shall still keep this place in Albany going for when we're
up here. But quite a lot of the time we shall be at the house in
Wiltshire. Do you fancy being butler there, by the way?'

'Thank you, my lord, but no. Personal servant has always
been my place, and I've no wish to step out of it now.'

'Wise man. Very few people realize that promotion is often
a prime cause of misery, particularly for men in middle age. It
takes them into a sphere which is beyond their competence and
reduces them to nervous wrecks.'

'Exactly so, my lord.'

'So personal servant you'll remain, but I'm going to increase
your money. Valeting a peer of the realm warrants more than
valeting a mere M.P.'

'Your lordship is very generous.'

'No, just much richer. Now then: immediate plans. I'll need
another ten days in London to sort things out with the lawyers
and the College of Arms. If there are no snags, we'll leave for
the country on Wednesday, October three.'

'Are there likely to be snags, my lord?'

'No. If one considers what a devious line of inheritance it is,
it's surprising how smoothly things are going. Most of the stuff
is routine — except for one thing: the patent for the first marquis

was drawn spelling "marquis" with an "i". I want to be marquess with an "e" and a second "s".'

'The two ranks are identical?'

'Yes. But "marquess" looks nicer on paper.'

'There will surely be no difficulty then?'

'You'd think not. But the Heralds incline to the view that I should stick to the spelling in the original letters patent.'

'I see. But I cannot imagine, my lord, that we shall overstay our time in London merely to supervise the substitution of an "e" for an "i" and the addition of a second "s".'

'I suppose not. You know, Corporal, your style has changed. You may not want to be a butler but you're beginning to talk like one.'

'As your lordship observed a few minutes ago, there is a difference between being a valet to a peer of the realm and being valet to a mere M.P.'

'Well, so long as you're happy. . .'

'Never happier, my lord. We are to leave London on Wednesday, October three, you say. At what o'clock?'

'Estimated time of departure, Corporal, is o-nine-forty-five hours.'

'Covers for the furniture, my lord?'

'No. We shall be back and forth pretty often. Which reminds me: I shall probably be going to Venice again in November or December. Some particular friends of mine are there this winter. Do you wish to accompany me or would you prefer to remain in England?'

'I should prefer to be instructed, my lord, rather than consulted. It makes me feel more secure.'

'Very well. I'd better take you. It's the sort of thing they may except of me now. But that's not for weeks yet. Smoked trout and cheese soufflé for lunch tomorrow, please; I shall be dining out in the evening. I think that's all for now.'

'Then have I your lordship's permission to retire?'

'Yes, Corporal. Fall out, please.'

'The personal servant of a marquis, my lord, does not fall out; he retires.'

'Very well; you have my permission to retire.'

'Thank you, my lord. Goodnight, my lord.'

'Goodnight, Corporal.'

For many years now, ever since he had left the Army and come to his present employment, Detterling's man-servant, when bidden goodnight, had turned smartly to the right and marched straight from the room, as was the custom in his (and Detterling's) old regiment. Now and for the first time, however, he put his right hand over his heart, bowed, then backed slowly off (reminding Detterling of Lykiadopoulos's Major-Domo) and did not turn his face from his master until he was out of the door. Oh well, thought Detterling; if that's how he wants to go on, why should I object?

'And so, Max my friend, everything is all set,' said Lykiado-poulos in Venice. 'The guests whom I wished to be invited have all accepted for the dinner on the opening night; all the places at the *Table de Banque* are already taken for the first session; and it is thought that there will be a number of very substantial punters playing from the floor.

'I'm glad you're pleased,' Max de Freville said.

'It is very urgent I should do well, Max. I have had today the figures for our concerns in Corfu. Inflation, over the last two months, has run even higher than we thought. If our concerns are to remain healthy, I must win the equivalent of three million dollars by April.'

'And if you don't?'

'You and I will not starve, my friend; but many of our employees will. I do not want that for my people. We must keep our hotels open on Corfu, and in order to be safe in doing so we must have three million dollars by the spring.'

'Rather more than you were originally aiming at.'

'Because inflation in Greece, as I say, is running even higher than we feared.'

'Three million dollars,' said Max. 'Nearly two thousand million lire. It's a long order, Lyki.'

'There is one new factor in my favour. The management of the Casino have agreed that the maximum stake against the bank for any one individual punter at any one coup should be increased to ten million lire on ordinary days and fifteen million at week-ends and holidays.'

'Fifteen million, eh? Ten thousand quid. Very nice if you're winning, Lyki. But if the cards go sour on you...'

'I shall have bad patches, of course. But with the security that is behind me, I can weather those. In the long run, as you very well know, the odds are with me.'

'But if you had a particularly fierce reverse in the short run?

They're very grasping, the management of this Casino, Lyki: that's why they're letting the stakes march so tall – bigger and better five per cents for them. But on the same reckoning, if they saw you take a real walloping one evening I wouldn't put it past them to ask for a payment in cash. Now, what securities have you given them?'

'The deeds of several of our hotels in Corfu, and of other properties. It would take a very big walloping to come anywhere near reaching what they are worth.'

'Granted. The fact remains that if things go badly for you the management *might* ask for cash at some stage, and once it was known that any of our properties was up for a quick sale, their value would slump like a snowman in Hades.'

'I think, Max, that I can keep the Casino management happy as long as they hold those deeds. There is only one thing which worries me.'

Lykiadopoulos went to the window and looked down on the Rio Dolphin. He gave a very long sigh and broke it off with a quick hiss, like a tyre being tested for pressure.

'Arabs,' he said, turning back towards Max de Freville.

'Arabs?'

'Arabs and their oil money. It is rumoured some may come to play against my bank.'

'Well, that's what you want. Really rich punters.'

'These are too rich. They will *all* of them play in maximums *all* the time. A bad run while I was playing against them could be very painful indeed. And there is another thing. These Arabs – the ones that may come here – were on the French Riviera during the summer playing Roulette and Trente-et-Quarante. When they lost, they would request that the maximum stake should be raised still higher, and that the game should continue beyond the advertised hours. . .'

'. . . Thinking that since their money was more or less limitless, they only needed time to start winning?'

'Precisely. One cannot operate a bank if such privileges be allowed to the punters. The Casino managements in France, I am glad to say, were very firm. They did not raise the maximum stakes and they did not stay open beyond the normal time. But what I am afraid of, Max my friend, is this. If those Arabs come here, and ask *here* that the stakes be raised and the hours of play extended, the Casino management might be inclined to give way. Italians are different from the French in these matters;

they have far less regard for regulation and procedure. And then the management here in Venice would be so keen to please such wealthy clients and tempt them and their kind more and more away from France.'

'If such a thing were to happen, you, as banker, could always insist that the conditions originally agreed should be kept to.'

'Yes, I could – and make enemies of these Arabs. I think they would accept a refusal from the management to change the procedure, but they might not like it if the refusal came from me. Such men make vexatious enemies.'

'In short,' said Max, 'win or lose, those Arabs will be a big pain in your arse.'

'In my neck, if you please, Max. Yes, a very big pain. Because, as you yourself observed, their money is limitless. Every day more of it gushes out of the ground : it is *infinite*. This destroys all the usual assumptions as to the long-term odds and so forth. Once one is dealing with infinity, as every schoolboy knows, the usual laws of mathematics cease to be applicable.'

'What shall you do, Lyki?'

'Wait and see whether they come. They may well not. But if they do come,' said Lykiadopoulos, 'then I must acquaint myself with that branch of mathematics – there is such a branch, I believe – which attempts to regulate the region of the infinite.'

'It's a branch of metaphysics, Lyki, rather than mathematics.'

'Then I shall now go upstairs to my dear chapel and pray for metaphysical guidance,' said Lykiadopoulos. He grinned and waddled towards the door. 'From God at least,' he announced as he departed, 'even infinitude can have no secrets.'

Egregious Sir,
began the letter which Fielding Gray received from the Albani lawyers in Siena :

My esteemed client, Signor Benito Albani dei Conti Monteverdi, has passed to me your recent enquiry and requested of me to answer you.

This we can only do within the competence of our records here in Siena. These demonstrate as follows :

1) In October of 1796 our client, the Conte Monteverdi, then head of the Monteverdi family and a resident of Siena, received a visit from his Venetian cousin, Signor Fernando Albani dei Conti Monteverdi. Signor Fernando carried with him a small

facsimile of the family painting to which you refer. This, he said, he had come particularly to show to His Excellence the Conte; for he wished him to look on the figure of the young man at the back of the picture. This he declared to be an Englishman of the name of Humbert fitzAvon, who was affianced to the Signor Fernando's daughter, the Signorina Euphemia. It was the Signor Fernando's wish that the Conte Monteverdi, as head of the family, should adopt Humbert fitzAvon as his son.

2) When asked why he had brought with him only a picture of the young man instead of conducting him to Siena in person, Signor Fernando Albani averred that it was unwise for an Englishman to travel openly in Italy at that period. It was, he said, the very uncertainty of Mr fitzAvon's situation in Italy which made him anxious that the young man should be legally adopted by the Conte before marriage into the Albani family.

3) When asked for further information about Mr fitzAvon, Signor Fernando stated that he had known Mr fitzAvon in Venice for some two years and was satisfied that he had a respectable fortune at his disposal. He had nothing to say, however, on Mr fitzAvon's standing or relatives in England, and when pressed in this matter could only assert that Mr fitzAvon was a gentleman, an orphan from an early age, and that he had attended Oxford University.

4) Such a meagre indication of Mr fitzAvon's provenance was considered by the Conte Monteverdi to be unsatisfactory. Having first taken the advice of the partners at the head of our house at that time, he declared his refusal to consider any further the adoption of Mr fitzAvon.

In conclusion, my present client, the Signor Benito Albani, has asked me to assert to you that nothing more is known of the matter. It is, however, generally believed in the family that Mr fitzAvon left Venice shortly after Signor Fernando's return from Siena, and that the Signorina Euphemia was subsequently placed in a convent.

> We Beg to Remain,
> Egregious Sir,
> Your most Respectful—

'—Et cetera, et cetera,' said Fielding as he folded up the letter.

There was a thoughtful silence in the Casino dei Due Professori (the name by which Tom and Daniel's tower was now beginning to be called by the inhabitants of the Palazzo Albani and its neighbourhood). Tom lifted the kettle off an oil-heater, warily tested it with his palm, and put it back.

'Nowhere near boiling,' he said.

Piero, who was sitting by Daniel and making sandwiches for tea in the English manner, put down his knife and said, 'In Sicily we say that there are three kinds of truth: the truth one tells to the taxes man, the truth one tells to one's acquaintance, and the truth one tells to God. The first is for deceit and no one would think of believing it, not the taxes man or anyone else. The second is for *bella figura* – what one's acquaintance should think if they are to respect one. Only the third is really true, and not always that, because a certain sort of Sicilian will lie even to God. That letter from the Albani lawyer in Siena is telling you the second kind of truth. They assume you are too intelligent to be satisfied with the first kind, while the third – the real – kind is of course none of your business: so they are telling you the second kind, which is what people tell to their acquaintance and their acquaintance, for the sake of politeness, at least pretend to accept.'

'A plausibly edited version?' said Tom.

'Yes,' said Piero. 'True in what it says but leaving much unsaid. Admitting the existence of shadowy places – to make it seem the more honest – but casting little light among the shadows.' Piero turned to Fielding. 'Yes, Major Gray, they are telling you, there was indeed such a young man as you ask about, rather mysterious, as you say, and for a time he was quite closely connected with our family; but in the end the family's better judgement prevailed to reject him, and after that he disappeared.'

Piero went on making the sandwiches in the way he had been taught by Daniel.

'We have been told nothing positive about him,' said Tom, 'except that he was an English orphan of education and gentle birth with an adequate estate, this latter apparently in money. You see how cleverly the thing has been angled. The young man in the picture, from being a mysterious stranger whose presence might have sinister implications, becomes simply a prosaic and quite well-heeled Englishman of whom the Conte Monteverdi pronounced that he didn't really measure up to Monteverdi standards and must therefore be sent packing. For that's how the matter is now presented: Italian grandees examine and then dismiss an English gentleman who aspired to marry with them. The story not only refutes scandal but actually confers credit on the family for being formidable and fastidious.'

'Exactly,' said Piero. 'It promotes *bella figura*. "Promotes" is right?' He looked at Daniel for approval of his idiom.

'Don't take risks in our language,' Daniel said with a cautionary smile. 'That one came off. Next time you may fall flat on your face – not good for *bella figura*... They make no difficulties, you notice,' he went on to the company at large. 'There is no suggestion that Fielding is sticking his nose where it isn't wanted. A strictly factual letter, purporting to tell him everything on record.'

'But making it very plain,' said Fielding, 'that that's my lot. Where do I go for honey?'

'You could always accept the version you've been given. It *might* be true.'

'No. You've only got to look at that portrait. That young man ... fitzAvon, as they call him ... is not the sort to be seen off just like that by a mere – by a mere—'

'—By a mere bunch of wops?' Piero suggested.

'And another thing,' said Fielding: 'I want to know what happened at the beginning.'

'You mean,' said Piero, 'how Mr fitzAvon ever got mixed up with this particular bunch of wops in the first place.'

'Yes. I don't believe he just picked up somebody's handkerchief while on a Sunday afternoon walk. That picture – he'd thrust his way into it, and all of them, even the two little children, knew it.'

'Perhaps you are reading too much into that picture,' said Daniel. 'Anyway, you seem to be at a dead end now.'

'Try the British consulate,' said Tom. 'As that letter implies, 1796 was not the most propitious time for an Englishman to be in Italy. Napoleon menaced the whole country, and the fall of the Serenissima itself was only months away. Perhaps fitzAvon was on some special mission, or carried special papers ... in which case he would have had to report himself to the British representative in Venice, to say nothing of Venetian officials. There may still be some record in diplomatic or state archives.'

'Yes,' said Fielding. 'According to what Fernando told the Count Monteverdi, in 1796 he had already known fitzAvon for two years. Which means fitzAvon must have arrived here not later than 1794 ... when things were already very tricky in

Italy, so that he might well have had to be specially accredited, but before things finally broke down in Venice, so that records were still being properly kept here. Bureaucrats may help me out where the local historians have failed me.'

'I shouldn't bank on it,' said Daniel. 'Can you really imagine that a file of the kind Tom is thinking of would survive for 180 years? Or that anyone could find it if it had?'

Nevertheless, while Daniel and Piero discussed their forth-coming trip to the Church of Madonna dell' Orto, Fielding listened very carefully to Tom, who now instructed him in the special skills and vanities of bureaucratic archivists and how to exploit these in his search.

Captain Detterling, on arrival at his house in Wiltshire, surveyed it and saw that it was good; he surveyed his furniture, his books, his pictures, his gardens, his home park and his outlying terri-tories, and saw that they were good; he surveyed the Cant-Fun installations and saw that even these, in their fashion, were good : for they had been so cleverly arranged and tricked about on the advice of his late cousin's friend, Balbo Blakeney, that while they might still entice the vulgar, who arrived by the trip-pers' entrance, they were invisible from the drive used by His Lordship or the apartments in which he lodged.

'Lodged', indeed, was the *mot juste*, and here was his only cause for dissatisfaction. As Fielding Gray had suggested in Venice, he was not so much Lord Canteloupe as Lord Cant-Fun. Although the grosser appurtenances of Cant-Fun had been tastefully camouflaged, its influence and organization were everywhere. There could be no doubt of it : the Marquess Can-teloupe (he had had his way with the Heralds about the 'e' and the second 's') was lodger and not lord in his mansion ... which, in any case, was not his mansion; legally it belonged to Cant-Fun & Co. Ltd, and only because he was Chairman of the Board of that company was he graciously (or rather grudgingly, he sometimes thought) allowed a suite, much as in an hotel, for his accommodation. His very servants, except for the Corporal, were on the company pay-roll; and if he could not assert the rights of a proprietor, no more could he assert those of his office as Chairman – because, as he very soon discovered, there were none, except to draw a massive income and operate a vast ex-pense account. He had no reckonable authority; only by cour-tesy of the company was a certain deference conceded to him.

He was asked to render no services, and was indeed competent to render none, He was not even required to sign the company's cheques.

But if Cant-Fun could do without him, it could not get rid of him. The employees might think that they served only the company, but the company, in the last resort, served only the Lord Canteloupe. It existed, in practice if not in theory, only to provide the Lord Canteloupe with money and goods. So cannily had the terms of the trust been drawn that the one right which was his – to be supplied – was inalienable; the lawyers had seen to that. In principle, it was true, the members of the Board might vote him out of his seat at their head; but if they did so, they were deemed also to have voted for a dissolution of the Board itself and with it the dissolution of their handsome salaries. The matter was abundantly clear : Detterling might be without power or function in his domain, but of his revenues he was truly King. These he now surveyed, and saw that they were good.

Thinking his state over, then, Detterling decided, all in all, that it would do. Though resentful, for a while, that no one valued his opinion or sought his decision, he was bound to admit to himself that administration (as opposed to intrigue) was neither to his taste nor to his talent; let those that understood such things get on with them for his benefit. And again, although it saddened him slightly that he was tolerated rather than obeyed in his ancestral (however deviously ancestral) home, he saw the very real advantages of his position; for if he could not command, neither need he care. The company would attend to such tedious chores as maintaining the fabric, restoring the plumbing and seeing to the welfare of the numerous personnel.

And so Captain Detterling surveyed his Marquessate and saw, on the whole, that it was good. He was magnificent yet he was free of responsibility. Free, indeed – but free for what? How was he to fill his days?

Of this he thought as he walked in his rose garden (though it belonged, of course, to the company, trippers were not allowed to obtrude into it, and it might pass, if anything might, for his own) on one blue and elegiac autumn afternoon. He had done with the House of Commons : he was not inclined to attend, more than occasionally, the charade that was now the House of Lords. Although he would continue as an active partner with

Gregory Stern in the publishing house that bore their names, this had always been a hobby with him rather than a profession, and he did not think Gregory would thank him if he made more of it now. Again, while he was a reader of books and a passable amateur scholar of the Greek and Latin classics, his interest in literature was too casual to constitute a *raison d'être*. Charitable works he despised as hypocritical interference; entertaining he disliked, except for small dinner parties; county society bored him, and London society irritated him past bearing. There had been a time when he enjoyed, as he would have put it, 'observing the upper-class scene', but these days most of those in it seemed to him either querulous or trendy, without dignity and without humour, witty indeed on occasion but for the most part lacking the gift of irony, which of all human qualities he valued highest. The only people he still enjoyed observing were certain old acquaintances who had retained a kind of disillusioned elegance over the years; and of these the most rewarding, Somerset Lloyd-James, was dead. With what, with whom should he amuse himself, he wondered, as he watched the sun go down behind the company's trees. Should he travel? But there was little pleasure in the greatest journey unless there was someone to wave one off and wave one home again : someone to miss a little; someone to need a little. He needed, in his middle age, to need someone. Still more, perhaps, he needed someone to need him.

And then, with a sudden stirring of his muscles from knee to navel, he remembered that there was someone who needed him, if only for the time being. He went straight indoors to telephone the Head Master of Baby Llewyllyn's school in Devon, was allowed to speak to Baby herself, and heard her voice rise with happiness as she said, yes, oh yes, of course she could come out with him the next Saturday afternoon.

Daniel and Piero's expedition to the Church of the Madonna dell' Orto started with a disappointment. They had planned to stop at the Accademia on their way and look at the cycle of splendid paintings in which Carpaccio displays the ridiculous history of St Ursula. But although the Accademia was open, the entrance to the room they wanted was blocked.

'*Chiuso*,' they were told bluntly and could get no explanation.

'It is the shortage of staff,' Piero told Daniel, 'though they do not like to say this.'

'That is no excuse,' said Daniel petulantly. 'They should close some less important room.'

'That is just it,' said Piero; 'less important rooms do not need to be guarded so carefully. The Carpaccios must be watched all the time.'

'Then they should find someone to watch them. Good heavens,' grated Daniel as they returned to their boat, 'people come for thousands of miles to see those pictures – only to be told "chiuso".'

'But we have not come thousands of miles,' said Piero soothingly, 'and we may try another day. And this morning, if you like, we may see other Carpaccios at the Scuola San Giorgio near the Riva. It is on our way.'

'I don't want to see other Carpaccios,' grizzled Daniel; 'I want to see the St Ursula ones, and I want to see them now.'

'Stop being a baby,' said Piero, 'and I will show you something special instead.' And some time later, as their boat cruised along the Fondamente Nuove, 'You see that pink house,' he said, 'on the corner of the basin and the Lagoon?'

'Yes,' grumped Daniel.

'It is called the Casino degli Spiriti. It too is among trees and in a garden, like your Casino ... though yours is much smaller. This one is so called because a group of friends would meet here, in the summer afternoons, and walk in the garden talking of philosophy, of the Good and the Beautiful.'

The pink Casino came nearer. It did not look philosophic and intellectual, Daniel decided, but rather jolly in a commonplace way.

'Nevertheless,' said Piero, answering the unspoken thought, 'it was of the deep things that they would talk.'

'I doubt it,' said Daniel, 'if they were Venetians.'

'But it is so, *Daniele caro*. That is why they were called the Spiriti – because it was of such matters that they spoke.'

The boat turned left, out of the Lagoon and into the basin.

'But later,' said Piero, 'there was a story that it is called the Spiriti because ghosts come here, across the Lagoon from San Michele. Fools,' he said; 'there may indeed be ghosts here, but they come from a cemetery much closer than San Michele.'

'There is no other cemetery.'

'I will show you.'

Piero spoke to the boatman, who was about to turn across the basin towards a small canal which opened over to their right. The man straightened the boat and drove on into the neck of the basin and down to a second canal on the right, in the mouth of which he held the boat steady. A small bridge arched almost over their heads, and a cowled Franciscan who was crossing it paused to look down at them.

'That huge building to the left of this little canal,' said Piero, 'that is the old school of the Misericordia. A little way along ... there ... is an angle in the wall which makes an alcove. There is grass as you see, and much thick bramble, and at the edge of the bramble is set a white stone. Do you see it?'

'I see it.'

'Inside the bramble there must be more such stones, although we cannot see them. This little alcove was a cemetery, or so I say, and it is from here the ghosts rise who walk in the gardens of the Spirits.'

'How did you first find this place?'

'I have never been here before. Before you and Tom came, I was not allowed out, you remember.'

'Then how did you know it was here?'

Piero blushed slightly.

'From Miss Llewyllyn,' he said, 'Miss Tullia Llewyllyn. She had been here when she was in Venezia, and she has written from England to tell me of it, as she also told me of the Casino degli Spiriti. She said ... that they are sad ghosts who come from here, and they go to the garden of the Spiriti because there they may feel memories of happiness, not their own happiness because they had none, but that of the friends who walked in the garden long ago. Come, we must go on, or they will close the church before we have had time to see it.'

Again Piero spoke to the boatman. They passed under the bridge, from which the friar had now departed, and after a little while they turned right under another bridge and then left, and stopped by a small quay.

'La Chiesa della Madonna dell' Orto,' Piero said, and raised both arms to greet an opulent façade much encumbered with statuary. 'Miss Mary McCarthy writes in her book of Venice that it is a great favourite with the English.'

'You've been reading Mary McCarthy?'

'Baby Llewyllyn sent me the book with her letter. She says

Miss McCarthy knows much of this quarter and I should read her.'

'Have you got the book with you?'

'No. Baby said I must read it before coming and then again when I get home. While I am here, she said, I must use my eyes. First we will go inside the church, and then we must visit the cloister.'

To Daniel's relief, the interior of the church was less elaborate than its façade. Even so, he found it difficult to understand why the English were supposed to be so fond of the place. Ugly girders traversed the nave above his head; the Tintorettos by the altar were ill-lit and somewhat hectoring in aspect; there was brickwork of an unendearing pink. He told himself that he was in an unco-operative mood, probably because of his earlier annoyance at being cheated of the Carpaccios, and that he must try harder to be appreciative. Piero would be disappointed if he did not enjoy himself. But try as he might, he could not dissipate his hostility to the building and its contents. The marble columns, which much impressed Piero, seemed to him to be dull and (since they needed girders to hold them in place) bogus. The celebrated Cima over one of the side altars he thought artificial and absurd: what were all these saints doing, so superior and self-satisfied, standing under a crumbling colonnade in the middle of nowhere? Why didn't they get moving and do something to prove their sanctity or at least to earn their daily bread? They weren't even talking to one another, merely being pensive – about their own excellence, no doubt.

'I like that little hill town at the back,' said Piero, 'and the landscape is so pretty.'

'But what's the point of that group in the foreground?' snapped Daniel, being pettish and knowing it, unable to stop himself. 'An ecclesiastical corner-gang of useless idlers. What are they *doing* there?'

Piero looked at him in pretended consternation and then laughed.

'What would you expect them to be doing?' he said. 'Masturbating one another?'

The idea of their all beginning to do just that, with the same grave and smug expressions still on their faces, cheered Daniel up. He gave a thin smile.

'That's better,' said Piero; 'now let us go to the cloister.'

The entrance to this was just to the left of the church as they came out of it. The door in the wall was locked.

'Somehow,' said Daniel, 'nothing seems to be turning out quite right this morning.'

'Don't say that,' said Piero, distressed. He pushed miserably at the door, which did not give an inch.

'I never saw a door look more locked. Let's go back to the boat.'

'The boat has gone,' Piero gulped. 'I told the man to go before we went into the church.'

'You let the boat go?'

'I thought we were to walk down through the Ghetto and take a vaporetto home.'

'I'm too tired to walk anywhere.'

'Why did you not say so before?'

'How could I know you were going to be so stupid about the boat?'

'But we had *agreed*, Daniel, that we were to walk down—'

'—Only if we felt up to it. Of all the stupid, selfish, thought-less—'

'—*Prego, Signori*,' said a voice behind them.

The speaker was the cowled friar who had earlier watched them from the bridge near the basin. He was holding up a key and trying to get past them to the door. Daniel and Piero stood aside.

The Franciscan unlocked the door and held it open for them. Daniel and Piero hesitated.

'We may as well go in,' said Piero.

'I suppose so,' griped Daniel.

Nodding their thanks to the friar, they stepped into the cloister. The friar closed the door, showed them how to unlatch it from the inside, and then walked quickly away towards an opening that led off the cloister at the far end. Daniel and Piero stood and looked around them.

'There, *Daniele mio*,' Piero said.

And now Daniel began to understand why the Madonna dell' Orto had always been loved by the English. The cloister was not remarkable; the stonework was ordinary and the plot of grass in the middle was badly kept, consisting mostly of bald patches and sagging weeds: but the place was for some reason deeply satisfying. It was all that such a place should be; its arcades invited one to saunter; its proportions dispensed ease to the mind. Daniel and Piero walked slowly to the end of the gallery which ran along the south wall of the church, then turned right, and came to the opening through which the friar had disappeared. He was standing in a tiny, sawdusty court on the far side of the opening, in conversation with a workman who was hammering tacks into a complicated framework of wood. The workman looked up and saw Daniel and Piero; he said something sharp to the friar but was apparently soothed by the answer.

'He asked why we were let in,' said Piero. 'The friar said we would do no harm.'

'Surely,' said Daniel, 'this cloister belongs to the church. Why should we not come in?'

The friar turned towards Daniel.

'He rents this corner as a workshop from the priest,' the friar said. 'He does not like to be disturbed. If the cloister is open the local boys come in and play football and break things.'

'We shall not play football,' said Daniel.

'So I inferred,' said the friar.

'You speak very good English, Father.'

'Brother. I am English. Brother Hugh.'

'What is he making?'

'He is making an aviary for our island.'

'Your island?'

'San Francesco del Deserto – near Torcello. We have a convent there, which is also a kind of rest-house for our brothers from elsewhere who are tired, and a school of preparation for novices. These days there are few novices. But there are a lot of birds. You may remember that the Founder of our Order was partial to birds. We keep many species, some of which need protection. Hence this aviary.'

'Brother Hugh. Hugh Balliston.'

'I was wondering whether you would recognize me, Daniel. My vows precluded me from reminding you of our previous and worldly acquaintance. But since you have penetrated under my hood, I see no reason to deny it.'

'Who is this?' said Piero.

'This is Mr Hugh Balliston—'

'—Just Brother Hugh, if you please—'

'—And he was once, not very long ago, a student at my college in Cambridge. A very good student,' Daniel said, turning from Piero to the friar. 'There has been speculation about what happened to you after you went down.'

'Now you know?'

'Why, Hugh? You had a splendid degree, you had every prospect—'

'—Don't ask me to explain, Daniel. It's much too difficult.
But I can tell you this much. You remember what happened to
Hetta Frith?'*

'Yes.'

'Well, the full ... the full meaning of it caught up with me a
few years later. The impact was delayed; when it came it was
horrible.'

'But it wasn't really your fault. The guilt lay with Mayerston.'

'Don't instruct me about guilt, Danny. I'm the expert.' Brother
Hugh ran his hand down his habit and looked very carefully at
Daniel. 'Or am I? Either way, we'll now leave the matter, if you
please. And indeed I must now leave here, since it seems this
contraption is ready. I'm due back on the island early this afternoon.'

'Tom Llewyllyn is in Venice,' Daniel said.

'Then perhaps I shall see him some time. And perhaps not.'

'Do you come over often?'

'Every few days I drive a small barge over, to do necessary
errands for the convent.'

'Then we could arrange—'

'—No, Daniel. I'm afraid we could not. I can't make arrangements of that kind.'

'We could all come to the island to see you,' blurted Piero,
who looked as if he might cry.

'You could come, and you'd be made most welcome, but
there's no knowing whether you'd see me. You'd see whom-
ever they sent to the door to show you round.'

'But surely ... your Order is not as strict as that.'

'*I* am as strict as that,' said the friar. 'Did I hear you saying
just now that you were too tired to walk any further?'

'You did.'

'Then it is my duty to render an office of corporal charity
and give you a lift home in my barge.'

'You will honour us by taking a meal?' said Piero.

'No, thank you. I'm expected on the island. So,' said the friar,
'we'll just get this aviary aboard and then we'll be off. See how
cleverly he's made it. Exactly the right use of space and shape,
as near as possible an asylum without being a prison. Come on,

*See *Places Where They Sing*, passim.

the barge is a few yards down from the church. Where am I to take you?'

In the end, since Brother Hugh's barge was too cumbersome to ride easily down the Rio Dolphin to the Palazzo, he dropped them at a quay by the Rialto Bridge. He had been too pre-occupied with steering to speak to them by the way, and so now,

'When do I see you again?' asked Daniel as the friar helped him up over the gunnels.

'Don't be awkward, Danny. You heard what I told you.'

Meanwhile, Piero had remembered something which Daniel had forgotten.

'For the good brothers of St Francis,' he said, leaning down from the quay and scrabbling a 10,000 lire note into the friar's hand.

'Thank you, my pretty one. We need everything we can get.' The friar raised his arm in farewell. 'We shall pray for you both on our island, my brothers and I.'

'All set for Saturday night?' said Max de Freville to Lykiado-poulos on the Thursday before the latter's Baccarat Bank was due to open.

'I think so. The new decor is sumptuous, the Casino personnel are making a considerable effort about the dinner, and the ar-rangements for the game itself are highly satisfactory. There is, however, one cause . . . I will not say for concern, but for serious thought.'

'Those Arabs you were talking of the other day?'

'Yes,' said Lykiadopoulos. 'They are not coming just yet, but it appears that they have reserved very heavily at the Bauer-Grünwald for early November.'

'How many of them are coming?'

'That is not clear. So far they have made no communication to the Casino. All we know is what we have from the manager of the Bauer-Grünwald, who has told us in confidence that two Arab princes of substance have engaged accommodation for themselves and their entourages from Friday, November the second for periods undefined but which in neither case are to be less than ten days. No precise numbers have been given: each prince has simply booked an entire floor. Now, my dear Max, one may readily assume that Their two Highnesses will come to play against my bank; but how many members of their entourages will they permit or encourage to come with them?'

'Ask me another,' Max said. 'But presumably places are now being booked at your table a long way in advance?'

'Certainly.'

'Then if these Arabs want to play they'll have to declare themselves to the Casino before very long.'

'Not necessarily. If all the proper places were booked when they came, they could always ask for chairs behind those of the other players, and play from those. It is a great nuisance when many people do that, but it cannot be stopped. And those of them humble enough to stand could play from the floor.

'In short, however many of them want to play, they'll find a means of playing.'

'Right, Max my friend. Now, if there were only the two princes, it would not be really dangerous. But if there were, say, ten more of their people, all playing on or near the maximum stake, as these Arabs are inclined to do, of ten thousand pounds a coup, then the affair would be very nervous for me. I must make certain preparations, I think.'

'You mean ... add more securities to those which you're putting up already?'

'I would not wish to, though it may be asked. No. As we were saying the last time we spoke of this, I must consider more deeply the mathematics ... or the metaphysics ... of a situation in which the resources of my opponents are approaching the infinite. I must have my equations ready. Tomorrow I go to Padua, to see a Professor of my old acquaintance at the University there.'

'You have a mathematician in the house – or at least in the tower. He is a metaphysician, too, if I am not mistaken.'

'I would not wish to involve Mr Mond. He is here to be quiet, I think, and must not be disturbed. Besides, I doubt his competence in that very specialized branch of learning to which I must address myself.'

'The theory of chance, I suppose? I should have thought Mond was well up to that.'

'Something rather more arcane than the theory of chance, Max. My professor and I must discuss an old discipline of the savants, which was once much prized both by mathematicians *and* by metaphysicians, but is now commonly ignored by both, and among them, no doubt, by Mr Mond.'

'I wonder how they all are in Venice,' said Baby Llewyllyn to Detterling, as they sat over tea in Ye Merlin's Pantrie on Saturday afternoon.

'I haven't heard anything.'

'I have, just a little. I wrote to Piero to tell him about some places in Venice, and he wrote back to say that Daniel and he would be going to them quite soon. But I haven't heard how they got on yet.'

'Why did you write to Piero of all people?' Detterling asked.

'He was kind to me. And then I want to keep in touch with Venice. I've written to Poppa, of course, and to Major Gray. Whatever happened to his face?'

'A bomb in Cyprus. There was a local truce, but even so a Greek Cypriot threw a bomb, and of course Fielding wasn't ready.'

'How unfair,' Baby said.

'But not surprising. Greek Cypriots are the nastiest people in Europe. Even the Greeks think so, though they don't often admit it.'

'One teacher at our school—'

'Be accurate, Baby. A master or a mistress?'

'They don't like being called masters or mistresses. They like being called teachers.'

'That sort, are they? Well, a man or a woman?'

'A woman. She says that Greek Cypriots are a fine, freedom-loving folk who have been exploited for centuries by Venetians and Turks and us British.'

'When did she say this?'

'In a history lesson. She was telling us how marvellous it was that since 1945 people all over the world have been throwing off the shackles of imperialism – particularly British imperialism. That's how she came on to Cyprus.'

'She deserves to be raped by a Cypriot.'

Baby giggled.

'I knew that would annoy you,' she said. 'Most things at my school would annoy you. A lot of them annoy me too.'

'What sort of things?'

'The teaching's so wet, for a start. It's difficult to explain this, but they just don't tell me what I want to know. Art Appreciation for instance – we do a lot of that, and the other day we were doing Claude Lorrain. We were shown a beautiful, dreamy painting of ships in a harbour and buildings with tall columns on the edge of the water. The teacher – a man this time – started talking about Claude's love of harbour scenes, and his nostalgia for a vanished world, and the romantic light. So then I asked what the picture was called, and he said it was called *Ulysses' Mission to Chryses*, because Claude often chose legendary subjects, it was part of the nostalgia thing. What *was* Ulysses' mission to Chryses, I asked, because although I knew a bit about his journeys I hadn't heard of this one. So he said it was a complicated story and didn't really matter – the point was the harbour and the nostalgia and the light, all that all over again. But *what* was Ulysses doing there, I asked, and *why* had he come to see Chryses, and *who* was Chryses anyhow? And then he got quite cross, this teacher did, and told me just to look at the picture and respond creatively to it. But you see, my lord, that was just what I wanted to do, and of course I know that means looking at it, but it *also* means knowing what it's supposed to be about, all the guide-booky things like that, so that one can understand roughly what was in the artist's mind when he was painting.'

'Agreed,' said Detterling. 'In this case your man probably didn't know the answer.'

'It's all in the *Oxford Companion to Classical Literature*,' said Baby. 'He could have read it there, as I did afterwards. It's the same with other subjects,' she went on, 'more scones, please, waitress, they don't teach you the hard and exact and necessary things you need to know or practise. It's all soft and flabby. In English Literature, for example, it's always "How do you react?" and "What do you feel?", never "What does he mean?" or "How is the poem constructed?".'

'In one word,' said Detterling, 'you want discipline.'

'I want to be made to work,' Baby said. 'I'm sick of just being told to express my own feelings about this, that or the other. How can you express anything unless you know something to express and learn the rules of expressing it? I want to play games,' she said, tucking into the new plate of scones, 'as they do at other schools, because if you don't get proper exercise you won't have a good appetite. I want to have tests and marks and competitions,' she said, flourishing the jam spoon, 'so that I can know that I'm the best.'

'And if you turn out not to be?'

'Then I shall make myself keep on until I am.'

'That's my girl,' said Detterling, rather wanting to cheer; 'I'll see what can be done.'

At much the same time that Saturday, Piero and Fielding Gray arrived for tea with Tom and Daniel in the Casino dei due Professori. This had become a habit agreeable to all four of them, though Piero could only attend when Lykiadopoulos was not at home (for Lykiadopoulos, while allowing and encouraging Piero to go on expeditions with Tom and Daniel, still forbade him to 'pester' them in the tower or the garden). This afternoon, of course, Lykiadopoulos was well out of the way at the Casino, supervising the final preparations for the dinner and the open-ing session of his bank. None of these at the tea-party in the tower had been invited to the dinner (nor had expected to be), but Tom and Fielding proposed to go to the gaming-rooms that evening and watch Lykiadopoulos in action at the Baccarat Table.

'It could be amusing,' said Fielding, 'and God knows I need some amusement. I've been slaving away at those archives all week long and not a sniff of Mr Humbert fitzAvon. The consular staff are sick of the sight of me. This afternoon they gave me a letter of introduction to the Italian chappie who's in charge of the City records – a pretty broad hint to take myself off there.'

He put his hand in his pocket to make sure he had the letter safe, and brought it out, along with another one which he dropped on the floor. Tom picked it up for him.

'That's Baby's writing,' said Tom in a carefully neutral voice which none the less suggested that an explanation was required.

'Is it? I collected it from the Gritti on my way here. A lot of people don't know I've moved.' He looked at the postmark. 'It must have been at the Gritti some time,' he said, facing down Tom's curiosity. 'I ought to go there more often. Come to that, they ought to send my stuff on to the Gabrielli – they know perfectly well that I'm there. It's typical of these places : once you've paid and left you can drop dead for what they care.'

'Come on, Fielding,' said Tom. 'Let's hear what Baby's got to say for herself.'

Fielding put the letter of introduction back in his pocket and opened Baby's. He read out loud her first phrases of greeting, then paused and read on in silence, irritated, puzzled, sceptical by turns, but always attentive.

'She writes a lively letter, your Tullia,' he said to Tom when he had finished it, 'in a fair round hand. But I'm not quite sure what you'll make of it. "Now, listen, Fielding", he read out to them all, ' "and don't laugh at me. Last night I had a dream. I was in the Palazzo Albani with you, looking at those paintings, and I wanted to go to the loo, and you told me, just as you did after that dinner, that I'd find one on the top floor. So up I went, but the stairs and the top floor were all different: I found myself going up a ladder and climbing out through a hatch; and instead of a penthouse, there was just one little tiny hut in the middle of the roof. Well, this hut certainly looked like an outdoor lav, so I dashed over and opened the door. But it wasn't a lav at all, it was a miniature version of a room that really is up there – I went into it when I was exploring that night – a room which is full of toys. Beautiful toys, some of them, and two lovely old rocking-horses, which were just the same in my dream as they had been when I really saw them, only of course much smaller.

' "And in this room somebody was crying. Not a child, as you might expect in a room full of toys, but a man, quite an old man, I thought, was crying his heart away. And after a bit, though I couldn't see him, I knew who he was: he was the father of the children in that picture which interested you so much – Fernando Albani. He had come to look at his children's rocking-horses – only he wasn't *up there with me*, he was wherever the rocking-horses had been when he was really alive, in a nursery somewhere on a lower floor, and he was deciding that it would be best to store the horses away. At first I thought that was because his children were grown up and gone, and this was what was making him sad. But then I knew it wasn't this, it was something quite different, something really horrible, which he didn't want anyone to know about and was somehow connected with those rocking-horses. It was almost as if the horses had seen something dreadful and he was afraid that unless he hid them away they might open their mouths and tell people. I knew, too, that he was ashamed as well as sad, most bitterly ashamed, but still, try as I might, I could not find out the cause of this. Then suddenly he stopped crying and was gone . . . and there I was, looking at the little rocking-horses and wanting to pee like mad. I woke up at once, but I only just made it, because at this school, though it's meant to be so modern, the night loos are down a corridor a million miles long.

' "Fielding, don't think that I'm silly, but since you're interested in Fernando's family and that man at the back of the painting, why not have a good look at those rocking-horses? Piero knows just where they are. I mean, if Fernando in my dream was afraid they might tell somebody something, why shouldn't they tell you?"'

After a silence Tom said:

'She never mentioned a room with toys while she was still here.'

'She didn't tell us anything much about what she'd seen,' said Fielding, 'because she'd promised Piero not to.'

'I should not have minded her telling you about the toy-room,' said Piero; 'and now ... that we all know each other as we do, I should not mind you knowing about the other things that are up there, though I shall not tell you just at this minute. The only thing is that you must never go up there. Mr Lykiado-poulos and Mr de Freville would be angry.'

'Then how am I to examine those horses?' said Fielding.

'You really think it's worth following up?' said Tom.

'I do.'

'You think those horses might open their mouths and tell you something?'

'Not literally. But they could be a clue of some kind.'

'I'm afraid you cannot go up to see them,' said Piero. 'No one can go up there.'

'You,' said Fielding. 'You can go up there.'

'Yes. But what would I do if I did?'

'You would look very carefully at those rocking-horses, and see if they suggest anything to you that is out of the ordinary.'

'Very well,' said Piero; 'if you promise not to be cross if you are disappointed in my report. Since that kettle is so slow, I shall go now.'

'Very civil of him,' said Tom when Piero had gone, 'going off on a fool's errand so readily.'

'Your daughter is very percipient,' Fielding countered; 'so is Piero, though in a different kind of way. In this instance the combination may turn out to be helpful.'

'Perception is one thing,' said Tom; 'but you seem to be crediting Tullia with some sort of second sight.'

'Let's say ... that I think her imagination, aided by her in-telligence, assists her to make particularly sensitive speculations. If her mind had been working on the mystery of the stranger in that picture, there is no reason why it should not have reached certain conclusions and presented them to her in a dream. Have you ever heard of a man called Rivers?'

'Psychologist,' said Daniel; 'flourished in the early decades of this century. A kind of common-sense English edition of Freud.'

'Right. He was in charge of mental cases at the Military Hospital where they put Siegfried Sassoon during the 1914 war. But that's by the way. In Rivers' published work he makes it very clear that he believes that our minds often sort out problems while we're asleep and then we dream the answer – or what the mind thinks is the answer. He adduces several alleged cases as proof. Now, if this faculty were especially intense, it might well produce the sort of dream experience described by Baby. What her mind was telling her, in a highly metaphorical way, was that the presence of a stranger in that picture, plus the fact that nobody can or will tell us anything about him, adds up to the possibility of some kind of disaster which involved the stranger and one or more of the Albani children, thus very much grieving their father. And so, her mind is telling her, if you want a clue to it all, take a good look at the children or, since they are long dead, at the places and things once associated with them.'

'These, I suppose, being collectively symbolized by the rocking-horses,' said Tom. 'But I cannot see how they themselves could possibly help you.'

'Nor can I. But they make somewhere to start.'

'Pretty tenuous thinking.'

'Perhaps,' said Fielding. 'But there could just be something in it. You see,' he said hesitantly, 'although I've tried to give a rational explanation, I also believe it to be at least possible that Baby has something ... something extra ... going for her in this field. Extra-sensory perception would be a respectable name for it.'

'Not to me, it wouldn't,' said Tom. 'I resent having my daughter exploited as a witch.'

'No one's exploited her,' said Fielding. 'I never asked her to write to me, about her dreams or anything else.'

'Well,' said Daniel the peace-maker, 'granted that Baby may be able to help you by tuning in on some unusual wave-length, what has Piero to offer? You had hopes, you said, of the combination.'

'Piero's main asset at the moment is that he alone of us is allowed up to that top floor. But I should also say that he has the gift of very speedy and very accurate practical awareness. If there is anything odd to be seen up there, Piero will see it – just as he'd see a coin lying in the gutter. It's part of his survival kit, like his ability to parrot English.'

'Unfair,' said Daniel. 'His excellent use of English comes from his ability to understand the mental processes which lie behind our idioms.'

'If you like. Whichever way you put it, there's no doubt that he's very quick to hook on to new usages. That's his speciality: *hooking on* to things. He doesn't have to be told twice. If he plays his cards right, I see a great future for Piero.'

'I don't,' said Daniel; 'he's vulnerable.'

'We all are. The thing about Piero is that he's smart enough to know where he's vulnerable and to take constant and necessary measures for his protection.'

'I wonder how he got that limp,' said Tom.

'Street accident,' said Daniel, 'or so he told me. A cart ran over his leg when he was small and it was never properly set. Vulnerable, you see. Any other street boy would have avoided that cart by instinct.'

'But not any other street boy would have cleverly turned an ugly limp into an important part of his charm.'

The door opened and Piero appeared, looking uneasy.

'I found nothing, nothing indicative,' he said, glancing at Daniel to receive his approval of the word, 'about those rocking-horses. But then it occurred to me that though dreams often tell us things, they do not tell us exactly.'

He gave a look that expressed genuine deprecation of this insight and sharp distaste for what he had achieved by it.

'In that room are uniforms hanging in frames, a child's uniforms. Some of them are of the Cavalry. Cavalry, I thought; horses. One of these uniforms had a kind of wallet.'

'A sabretache,' said Fielding.

'A sabretache,' repeated Piero carefully, storing this rare word away. 'Inside it was this. It may or may not be of interest to you.'

He put his hand under the waistband of his trousers and drew out a sheaf of rustling papers, quarto size.

'No need to look so miserable about it,' said Fielding; 'let's have a look.'

Then he saw what had upset Piero. On the top sheet, as Piero passed the sheaf to him, was a line of writing, probably a title or description, in bold capital characters of a kind known to him but not at all familiar: underneath was a detailed and delicate water-colour painting, life-scale, of a cluster of some five or six crocuses, in the middle of which burgeoned a flower that was not a crocus but an erect phallus, beautifully and variously tinted over the bulb by a band of primary chancres.

PART THREE

A BEAST IN VIEW

Lykiadopoulos fingered a card face down from the Baccarat shoe and slid it to his right. He fingered another card to his left, and a third he kept in front of himself. He then repeated the process, after which he watched the senior croupier as the latter scooped up the two cards on the right with a long spade of plywood and set them down before a little old lady in a mauve dress who had staked fifteen million lire and was playing the cards for the punters on her half of the table. The little old lady picked up her cards with reverent tenderness, as if lifting a newly discovered papyrus which might crumble to pieces at any moment, and examined them with enormous concentration, as though fearful lest she might overlook some apocalyptic message contained in them.

'*Non*,' she said, 'no card.'

Lovingly she lowered the two cards face down on to the table.

The croupier now scooped up the cards on Lykiadopoulos's left and presented them to a near-pithecoid German who had staked only two million lire but was the most highly committed player among his comrades on the other half of the table. He seized the cards, flexed them brutally, squeezed one out from under the other and flung them down.

'*Carta*,' he grunted.

But before he could have the card for which he had asked, Lykiadopoulos must show his own. He slid them apart with his two index fingers and flicked them both on to their backs, revealing a Queen and an eight.

'Another natural,' said Fielding to Tom. 'He's having a pretty decent run.'

The senior croupier checked the old lady's cards (a five and a two) and then the pithecoid's two tens). The junior croupier swept all the stakes into a heap in the centre and with a few flicks of his wrist had all the plaques piled according to their respective denominations, which ranged from 100,000 lire, represented by a modest blue rectangle no larger than a wafer of butterscotch, up to the permitted maximum of fifteen million, which was celebrated by triumphant figures of gold set in a slab of ivory a foot long.

The senior croupier checked the piles of plaques.

'*Cinquanta milioni*,' he proclaimed.

'Thirty-three thousand quid,' said Fielding to Tom.

The croupier scribbled on a coupon, tore it from a book, thrust it through a slot in the table, and sent three plaques of medium size after it.

'Less five per cent,' said Tom.

Tom and Fielding were leaning over a bronze rail which encircled the Table de Banque at a distance of about five yards. Inside the rail were the seated players (eighteen of them at the table and another three or four snuggling up as near as possible on extra chairs) and a mob of infantry (as Fielding had nicknamed them) who prowled about restlessly and from time to time tossed plaques over the heads of those seated and on to the enticing green baize. By leaning over the rail from outside Fielding and Tom declared themselves as spectators only; but this class was by no means contemptible, as there was a special admission fee of twenty-five thousand lire to be paid before one could even poke one's nose into the 'private' rooms in which the bank was being conducted. Fielding might have grudged the money, had it not been for the sumptuous decorations which Lykiadopoulos had commissioned and supervised during the last few weeks. The theme of these was Metamorphosis : the walls were decked with Ovidian scenes, at once delicate and voluptuous, of nymphs sprouting leaves or feathers to the frustration of the inflamed gods who pursued them; while carpets, chair-backs, looking-glass frames and even ashtrays carried supplementary legends of lesser importance but greater indecency.

Only the Table de Banque itself was strictly functional and innocent of venereal addition; and at this the play had now been going on steadily for half an hour. According to Fielding's rough estimate, Lykiadopoulos, who had started badly but then produced a series of naturals, had won on average three coups in every five so far played and was about a hundred and fifty million lire ahead. The betting on Lykiadopoulos's left had been mostly in millions and half-millions; on his right it had been rather higher, though only the little old lady in mauve was consistently betting in maximums.

'You know,' Fielding now said to Tom, 'if a few more of them started betting as high as they're allowed to, this game would get very fierce indeed.'

'It's quite fierce enough already. I'm not a prig, I trust, but I still retain vestiges of my youthful socialism, and it makes me uneasy to see billions of lire shunted back and forth over this table just to make a Venetian holiday.'

'But do admit: the spectacle is rather splendid. Lykiado-poulos has won again, if I'm not mistaken.'

'*Settanta milioni*,' called the croupier, and then, as an after-thought, '*e tre cento mila*.'

Lykiadopoulos looked modestly, indeed primly, in front of him, clasping his hands together almost as if in prayer.

'*Prego, Signore*,' called the senior croupier, initiating the next coup.

Lykiadopoulos's right hand slid out of his left, snaked across the green baize, reared up in front of the Baccarat shoe and darted out one quick finger to flick a card down from the frame.

'The way he does that,' said Tom, 'is curiously offensive.'

'The movement of the hand and the finger?'

'Yes. It reminds me of a particularly nasty gesture they make in Corsica to cast the evil eye.'

'The evil eye,' said Fielding in sudden excitement. 'That's it. It must be.'

'What must be what?'

'That picture on the front of the manuscript Piero found this afternoon. It's an example of the standard magical use of an obscene object to ward off unwanted intruders. Not quite the same thing as casting the evil eye, because in this case the idea is to protect oneself or one's property rather than to broadcast malice; but it's pretty sinister all the same. What that diseased limb among the flowers means is, "Watch out, or you'll be pick-ing something nasty".'

'A kind of curse? But why should anyone write a manuscript and then put a notice saying "*Don't* read on" at the very be-ginning?'

'We don't yet know what the MS is. It might be some kind of heirloom – a family document which they wanted to pre-serve but didn't want just anyone to look at. Or it could be a

will, or some piece of pure pottiness about buried treasure, or
directions how to find the unmarked grave of a criminal or a
suicide – it could be anything. Or nothing.'

'But of course you're going to have a go at it?'

'Of course. If Piero and Daniel hadn't been so upset by that
phallus on the front I'd have started there and then. As it is, it's
now safe in the Gabrielli, and I shall start on it tomorrow.'

'But if you're right,' said Tom, 'about that thing on the front
page . . . if it is a warning . . . then surely Piero and Daniel were
very wise to behave as they did. They refused to have that MS
examined or discussed in their presence because, they said, it
repelled them. On your theory they had good reason to be repelled. It's what they were meant to be – and you too, Fielding.
Doesn't that make you nervous?'

'Because I have explained a superstition, it doesn't mean that
I share it. And I'm sure you don't, Tom.'

'I don't share the superstition. But the use of that appalling
sign . . . according to you . . . does indicate that somebody at
some time was anxious that that MS should not be widely read.
Perhaps there was good cause for his anxiety. Perhaps one
should not pry.'

'Oh, come, Tom, come. If no one ever pried our libraries and
museums would be empty. You're a scholar – you *live* by
prying.'

'But you are not a scholar, Fielding. You're just inquisitive.'

'I don't think curiosity will kill this cat. In any case, I
imagine that that sign is only a modified warning. The use of
such symbols, remember, was to protect property from the
malignant, not to bar men of integrity. In this case, the probable
intention is just to stop that MS from falling into the wrong
hands.'

'What makes you think that yours are the right hands?'

'Look,' said Fielding, 'it is at least possible that that MS may
have something to do with Fernando and his family and that
stranger in whom I am interested. If so, it might save me the
trouble of going through hundreds more archives, and after the
experience of the past few days that is something I am keen to
avoid. And so tomorrow morning I start reading. All right?'

'That's up to you . . . and I don't say I shan't be interested to
hear what you find, if you're ready to take the risk.'

'You cannot believe that there's a risk.'

'Let me just repeat that Piero and Daniel don't like the smell

of it ... and then leave it at that. But there's another thing,
Fielding: the letters on that cover looked like a Greek script of
some kind. Why should anything to do with Fernando and his
family be written in Greek? Or is the text in something different?'

'No. I had a brief look through in the Gabrielli before meeting you for dinner. It's all in Greek, and a very awkward style
of lettering at that. Some sort of decorative late Byzantine type.
But the words and the syntax seemed very simple from what
little I saw. Schoolroom Greek, *nursery* Greek, Tom. You see?'

'I suppose so. If that MS consists of Greek exercises, say, done
by the Albani children ... and then discarded in the nursery
where they were written, tucked away in any old place for
want of a waste-paper basket ... yes, that might explain how
it came where Piero found it. But what could you learn from
children's Greek proses? And *why* that horible thing on the
top page?'

'Why indeed? Perhaps we shall know before very long... By
the look of it, my dear, Lyki has nearly come to the end of the
first shoe. Let's get into the bar before the rush.'

The bar had been decorated in much the same style as the
Salle de Baccara, but here was not so much Metamorphosis as
Metempsychosis. The murals carried a somewhat camp version
of the Platonic myth of the afterlife, displaying the descent of
a group of human souls, their trial before the nether judges,
and their subsequent rebirth as beasts or reptiles.

'A curious motif for a bar,' commented Fielding. 'I wonder
what on earth he's put in the restaurant.'

'The elevation of pure souls through the hierarchy of Ideas
to the level of the True and the Beautiful,' said Lykiadopoulos,
who had just come up behind them. 'Good evening, Mr
Llewyllyn, Major Gray.'

'Good evening, Mr Lykiadopoulos. And in what style is the
ascent of the pure souls portrayed?'

'The same as this. A frivolous style, I admit, but appropriate,
in my view, to the fumbling notions of a mere heathen philo-
sopher. My intention, you see, was to present a kind of pagan
Human Comedy: the inferno in the Baccarat room, the Pur-
gatory in here, and Paradise in the restaurant. I am afraid the
allegory will be wasted on most of the customers, but not on
you two gentlemen, I think. How did you enjoy watching the
game?'

'It was very instructive,' said Tom. 'I hope you are happy with the outcome.'

Lykiadopoulos shrugged.

'I do not think you approve,' he said in a courteous and indifferent tone; 'but then neither do I. Mr Mond is not here, I see?'

'He is tired this evening.'

'It is just as well that he has not come,' said Lykiadopoulos. 'The company would not suit his sensibilities. Do you think,' he went on with the tiniest hint of anxiety in his voice, 'that Mr Mond will come some other time?'

'I very much doubt it,' said Tom.

'And yet,' said Lykiadopoulos, with the gingerly persistence of one probing an incipient pimple, 'he did express an interest in the game ... that night when you all came to dinner.'

'Like all mathematicians,' said Fielding, 'he is always interested to hear about unfamiliar games, because the rules of these constitute new sets of dimensions, so to speak, and make for new quirks of chance inside them.'

Max de Freville came up to them.

'Just arrived,' he said. 'How goes it, Lyki?'

'Fair, Max, fair,' muttered Lykiadopoulos. Then, turning back to Fielding, 'So Mr Mond's interest in my bank is purely theoretical?' he asked.

'His interest – what there is of it – is not in your bank at all, nor even in the game as such, but in the mathematical ideas it suggests to him.'

'I always wanted to be a mathematician,' said Max de Freville, 'but I just wasn't up to it.'

'But,' said Lykiadopoulos, ignoring Max's autobiographical fragment, 'if Mr Mond is interested in such ideas, he could come here to the Casino and observe some actual passages of real play. The calculation of the odds against any given series of results, for example – would that not amuse him?'

'Not much,' said Tom. 'He has – forgive me – more absorbing problems to consider.'

'But of course,' said Lykiadopoulos with genial self-deprecation. 'How stupid of me to think Mr Mond should be much concerned. He expressed a polite interest in the game and perhaps entertained himself for half an hour the next morning with a few mathematical excursions which it might suggest; but that is all, eh?'

He still seemed in need of reassurance.

'I should say so,' said Tom.

'Lucky chap,' said Max de Freville. 'With that sort of mind he need never be bored.'

Lykiadopoulos, who had visibly relaxed after Tom had spoken, now tightened up again and shook his head sharply from left to right. A liveried footman approached and bowed. Lykiadopoulos acknowledged the bow with a quick wave of his hand and followed the man out of the bar without any further word to those about him.

'He's off back to the table,' said Max. 'You must forgive him if he's a bit edgy this evening. It's a prickly business, running a bank, and he's anxious to get off to a good start.'

'He's done well enough so far.'

'And he'll need to go on like that. In a few weeks some high-flying Arabs are coming, and the more he can stack up now, the better. What about some supper? Lyki tells me the food in the special restaurant they've put in is quite something.'

'So, apparently, are the murals,' said Fielding: 'the ascent of the pure souls, he told us, to the True and the Beautiful.'

'Poor Lyki,' said Max; 'he's always hankered after that. But he's incurably earth-bound if ever anybody was. It's all Plato's fault,' he went on as they entered the restaurant, 'for presenting the love of the ideal as a kind of spiritual pederasty. Plato only intended a metaphor, but old queens like Lyki get themselves into delicious and deliberate muddles about it, and end up by thinking that the True and the Beautiful just means a more than usually pretty little boy.'

They all looked up at the murals. Sure enough, enthroned at the top of the end wall, above the layers of the geometrical Ideas through which the pure souls (pneumatic water babies) floated dreamily upwards, sat a naked, very white, and pre-pubescent Piero.

'You see what I mean,' said Max. 'The True and the Beautiful – a high class fancy boy with his hairs shaved off. No more appropriate, logically and philosophically, than a grilled lobster – which would make a much better God in a restaurant.'

In the Casino dei due Professori, Piero said to Daniel:

'Why did you not go with the others to the gambling?'

'I've seen gambling once, and that was enough.'

'Where was that?'

'Years ago, in a place in Germany. It wasn't a proper Casino, just a low night-club where they played some wretched game with a ball and a wooden board with numbered holes in it. In Hanover it was, a club called the Oo-Woo Stube.'

'What a peculiar name.'

'It was a very peculiar place. There was an obscene cabaret, I remember – uncommon, back in the 'fifties. I was taken there by Fielding Gray and some of his friends. He was still in the Army then. We had a horrible row with a German, who called me a disgusting Jew. Perhaps that's why I've never been able to stand gambling establishments – I associate them with that German.'

'What was Major Gray like in those days?'

'Good-looking. Overbearing. A discontented officer in a smart cavalry regiment.'

'Ah. That was how he knew that word this afternoon ... sabretache. What do you think is in those papers, Daniel?'

Daniel shifted restlessly in his chair.

'I dare say we shall know soon enough,' he said. 'Fielding is a determined man.'

'He should be careful.'

'Because of that ... that sign on the top page, you mean? That won't stop him,' said Daniel, and jerked his head sharply, warning Piero that he had had enough of the subject.

'I do not understand,' said Piero, breaking the silence which followed, 'why you were in Germany with Major Gray. You were not in the Army?'

'No. It's a long story.'

Daniel's head jerked again, several times. His body twisted in the chair. His hand went to his throat, then flew away from it and pointed across the room .

'That drawer,' he gasped. 'There's a packet of powders. Put one in water.'

'There is no water in the jug.'

'Cold tea. . .'

Piero poured the remnants of the afternoon's tea into a dirty cup and emptied a sachet of powder into it. Daniel seized the cup and gulped. He breathed heavily, writhed a little, and was still. Piero came up behind him and started to massage his scalp.

'What is the matter, Daniel?'

'Nothing . . . now.'

'The pain will come again, I think.'

'Yes. But not for a while. And there are always the powders.'

'The pain will come more and more. The powders will help less and less, and then not at all.'

'Before then I shall be dead. It is time I told you.'

'Ah,' said Piero coolly; and then again, 'Ah.' He lowered both hands and stroked Daniel's ears. 'I shall not tell Mr Lykiado-poulos or Mr de Freville. Nor will we talk of it any more, Daniel . . . do you wish that I should be kind to you?'

'You are being kind to me.'

'I could be much more kind than this.'

'To please a dying man?'

'I said, we will not talk of that. I have wished to be kind to you for many days now. But until this evening there was no chance for me to say it.'

'Soon I shall sleep a little. When I wake I shall need all my strength. Please do not rouse me, Piero. Comfort me, as you have been doing. Do not seek to rouse me.'

'Very well,' said Piero, and raised his hands from Daniel's ears back to his scalp.

When Tom, Fielding and Max had finished eating their supper underneath the True and the Beautiful, they returned to the Salle de Baccara. Lykiadopoulos, who was now going through the third shoe of cards, still appeared to be winning, though not in such large amounts as when Tom and Fielding had watched him previously. The little old lady in mauve had de-parted, and her place had been taken by a dark, cross young woman who was betting in plaques of only half a million, these being reluctantly supplied by a stout middle-aged party who was standing behind her. Fielding wondered idly whether the old lady in mauve had been cleaned out or merely bored.

'God knows,' said Tom, when Fielding asked his opinion in this, 'but the play seems very tame now she's gone.'

'The punters are holding back,' said Max, 'because Lyki's been having a good streak. They'll sniff the air until they think they can smell his luck turning sour, and then weigh in hard. That could be interesting . . . particularly if they get it wrong. You see that Lyki's now putting on a pinched look and sitting rather hunched?'

'Yes.'

'He's doing it on purpose, to make them think that *he* thinks that he's going to start losing. This could encourage them to bet heavier while his luck still lasts.'

'But will it last?'

'You can never tell, of course. But obviously Lyki thinks it will. When he reckons he's in for a bad patch he starts grinning like a vampire to put them off.'

'They must see through him after a time.'

'Then he does it the other way round. Double bluff. And when that's stale, he goes into an entirely new range of expressions. Impassive one minute, jittery the next – they always bet high if they think the banker's jittery – humble, arrogant and even crazy. It's a non-stop performance.'

'Well, I'm afraid I can't stay for any more of it tonight,' said Fielding. 'I've got a long day tomorrow on that manuscript,' he added to Tom.

'What manuscript?' said Max.

Silently Fielding cursed his clumsiness. Lyki and Max must not know that he was in possession of something taken from the forbidden part of their house; taken by Piero, it was true, but at his, Fielding's, bidding.

'Something I found in the Biblioteca the other day,' he lied; 'didn't I tell you?'

'No. Something to do with that man in the picture?'

'Perhaps. I don't know yet.'

'How are you getting on with all that?'

'I'm getting nowhere,' said Fielding. 'It's time we had another trot round Venice ... if you're still interested in making restorations.'

'I'll give you a ring next week. I've got several ideas for raising money.'

'Perhaps Lykiadopoulos will help?'

As Fielding spoke the senior croupier announced a handsome win for the bank.

'Not a penny,' said Max. 'Anyhow, I want to do it myself.'

'Come on,' said Tom to Fielding; 'I must get back to Daniel.'

Tom and Fielding, having descended to the ground floor of the Casino, decided to walk together to the Rialto, where their ways would part.

'I shall be glad when this winter is over,' said Tom as they crossed the bridge into the Campo Santa Fosca. 'I'm scared, Fielding.'

'Scared of Daniel's death?'

'Scared of his dying. Of what may happen first. It's because I'm scared that I choked you off when you started to talk of it the other day ... of how that boy may behave and so on. I'm sorry, Fielding. I should have listened. You were saying that if Piero starts to pity Daniel it could be an ugly spectacle. What then?'

'There will be loss of dignity. It is important that Daniel should do this with dignity, Tom. You see that statue over there – Paolo Sarpi?'

'Sarpi the Servite. Sarpi the rebel and reformer. I can't imagine he's much to your taste, Fielding.'

'No, but he was an impressive man. You remember what he said? "I never tell lies but I do not tell everyone the truth." That has always been Daniel's way, Tom. He has never told lies but he has always seen fit to keep much of what he knew to himself. And so it is now. He is keeping his feelings, his troubles, his fears, his pain as far as possible to himself, and this, Tom, is the true dignity. But if once Piero shows him pity, it may weaken his resolve; he may be tempted to let it all out – to voice his fears, complain of his troubles, to whine about his fate.'

'Perhaps Piero will not pity him when he knows he is dying. Perhaps he will shun him.'

'That would be better, even if it hurt Daniel.'

'Then what am I to do, Fielding?'

'We must find Daniel something to do. If he is occupied, he might be proof against Piero's pity, or his disgust – whichever it turns out to be.'

'What possible occupation can we find him? Soon he will be too ill to leave the tower.'

'I was thinking this evening of what Piero said some time back – that Lykiadopoulos is somehow afraid of Daniel, afraid lest Daniel might see through his skin and find him out. Max, too, has said something of the kind. What reminded me of this was the anxiety Lykiadopoulos showed, when he spoke to us in the bar, about the possibility that Daniel might come to watch the play. He kept on reverting to it. So you don't think Mr Mond will come here, he said; and then, a few minutes later, are you *sure* that he won't come? Three or four times he asked that, though each time in a slightly different way. It was as though he had some secret which he thought Daniel might penetrate. If so, why not occupy Daniel by getting him to do so?'

'I've told you. Before long Daniel will not even be able to go out. Anyway, what should he care about Lykiadopoulos's secrets ?'

'It was just a thought. Lykiadopoulos's sort of secrets might be particularly diverting.'

They crossed a bridge and turned sharply into a narrow passage.

'As long as Lykiadopoulos is afraid of Daniel,' Fielding went on after a while, 'it will be a sign that Daniel still has his powers, powers which depend on his still being himself and so in good part depend on his dignity. Perhaps Lykiadopoulos has told his boy to destroy Daniel's dignity, by whatever means, so that he need have nothing more to fear. Or perhaps he has told Piero to spy on Daniel.'

'He has forbidden Piero the tower.'

'So Piero says. And comes there almost every day.'

'You are devising conspiracies like a Jacobean dramatist.'

'Yes. We'd better let it rest for a bit and see what happens. I'll have plenty to do with that manuscript to translate.'

'That manuscript. Do you really think it can help you?'

'Why not?' They came to the steps of the Rialto Bridge. 'Remember Tullia's dream.'

Tom started up the steps, shaking his head.

'I shall be glad when this winter is done,' he called down softly; 'plots, dreams, diseases ... gamblers and their catamites...'

'The stuff of Venice,' Fielding called back, and went on his own way.

In London, Detterling said to Isobel and Gregory Stern.

'I've found just the sort of school she says she wants, and they're willing to take her straight away. So what about it?'

'After Christmas perhaps,' said Gregory.

'She wants to move now. She wants to *start*.'

'Tom would forfeit this term's fees at the present school and have to pay them in full at the new one.'

'I'll see he's not the loser.'

'Perhaps,' said Gregory, 'he might not care for such a benefaction. He might even consider it to savour of interference.'

'I think Canteloupe is right,' said Isobel, who had so far been silent. 'If we simply tell Tom that the present school has turned out unsuitable, that we've found a good new place, and that we've made it all right about the fees, he'll be satisfied.'

'But, Isobel my wife, we must get his permission before we move her.'

'No,' said Isobel; 'let's not worry him just now. Let's serve it up as a *fait accompli*. He will trust us to have done what is best.'

'The school she is at will not release her,' said Gregory, 'until they have it from her father in writing.'

'They'll release her,' said Isobel, 'if the Most Honourable the Marquess Canteloupe of the Estuary of the Severn asks them to. He might have to pay them a big fat sweetener, from the sound of the place, but since he's so keen about Baby's future I don't think that will bother him.'

'No,' said Detterling, 'it won't.'

'Very well,' said Gregory; 'since you both seem so sure of your ground, I suppose I must agree to what you propose.'

'To what Baby herself has proposed,' Detterling said.

'So what is this new school you have found for her?'

'Radigund's School, near Dorchester.'

'Radigund,' said Isobel, 'Queen of the Amazons.'

'Motto,' said Detterling, 'from Lucretius. *Nil fit de nilo* – nothing comes from nothing. Headmistress : Miss Clodia Wentworth Rex, M.A. (Hons. Cantab.) – as tough and as beautiful as any Amazon of them all. Extensive woods and playing fields, hockey, lacrosse, cricket, Eton fives, squash racquets, tennis, badminton and swimming – in an open-air pool, unheated, no cosseting. Equitation as an extra on request; occasional attendance arranged at meets of the Devon and Dorset Stag Hounds under personal supervision of Miss Wentworth Rex. Seven open awards to the Universities (by which Miss Wentworth Rex means only Oxford and Cambridge) during the last academic year.'

'Fees?' said Gregory.

'You old *Jew*,' said Isobel.

'Stiff,' said Detterling, 'but no stiffer than the school she's at now .'

'Uniform?' said Isobel.

'Daughter of *Eve*,' said Gregory.

'Grey shorts and knee stockings,' said Detterling, 'with white shirts and blue jerseys. The school tie is worn with this ensemble on Sundays and November the eleventh; dresses only on formal occasions. School song: *Drake's Drum*. *No* termly exeat; girls may be visited but not taken out on the fifth and eighth Sundays of term – only. Miss Wentworth Rex does not believe in disruption.'

'I find it rather suspicious,' said Gregory, 'that she is so readily able to find a place for Tullia after the current term has started.'

'That was a stroke of sheer good luck,' Detterling said. 'One of the junior girls has just broken her neck while out with the Devon and Dorset Stag Hounds.'

'*Ἐγω Φερνανδος 'Αλμπανι,*' read Fielding in his room in the Gabrielli, '*ννν πεντηκοντα ἐτη βιωσας, ἐγραψα ταδε, ἀτε τονς παιδας ἐμονς την των ἀρχαιων 'Ελληνων γλωτταν διδαξων . . .*
I, Fernando Albani, being now fifty years of age, wrote what follows, in order to teach my children the language of the ancient Greeks.'

Just underneath this was written 'MAIUS MDCCC' (May 1800), the Latin intervention being explicable, Fielding thought, by Fernando's ignorance, common in amateur scholars, of the Greek way of expressing such tedious technicalities as dates. Under this again was a sentence which had been written in ink of a different colour from that used on the rest of the page and in rather cramped letters, as though the writer had penned them, with some difficulty, in a gap between passages previously completed.

'*Παντα ταντα γεγραφα, ὡς δονλος ὢν της ἀληθειας, ἱνα ἐκεινοι οὑς ἀν θελῃ ὁ Θεος ἰδωσι και ἐπιστωνται . . . .* All these things I have written, as the slave of truth, that those whomsoever God wills may see and comprehend.'

Tucked beneath this observation, in ink of the same colour was the date 'AUGUSTUS MDCCC'. This, as well as the sentiment expressed and the cramped writing, proclaimed that the sentence was an afterthought : clearly Fernando, having started with the intention of writing a Greek Primer for his children (the two younger children in the picture, thought Fielding, as the elder ones would have been fully adult by 1800 and indeed well before), had later decided that his work might appeal to a wider audience ('those whomsoever God wills') and had added his extra preface accordingly. This might reflect the vanity of an author, who was touting his MS round for publication, or it might amount to a prayer from Fernando that he would be properly understood – that his readers, whoever they might be, would 'see and comprehend'. In either event, thought Fielding, it could be taken to imply that Fernando was conscious of having in some way transcended his original purpose.

After the date of the second preface, the MS reverted to ink of the standard colour and now displayed a title in Greek capitals – the same title, and in the same elaborate style of lettering, as was written on the cover sheet above the abominable group of flowers.

Η ΤΟΥ ΝΕΟΥ ΑΥ̓ΚΟΥ ῾ΙΣΤΟΡΙΑ

THE STORY OF THE YOUNG WOLF

No difficulty here, thought Fielding. Plainly, Fernando intended to demonstrate the correct use of ancient Greek idioms through the medium either of a fable or a nature tract, the better to engage his children's interest. He had written an old-fashioned Reader; very well, now to read it. . .

The story began, simply enough, with the introduction of The Mighty Wolf (῾Ο *Κρατων Λυκος*) who was King of a Mountain in the Far North. To The Mighty Wolf were born two children, a male and a female, the former of whom, the Wolf-Prince or Lording of the Forest, was at once announced as the hero of the coming tale. Clearly a fable, then, rather than natural history; so far, so good. At this stage, however, the story became tiresome and prolix, for it entered into the details of the Wolf-Prince's upbringing. Fernando was obviously seeking to improve his children (and perhaps to impress the wider audience seemingly anticipated by his second preface) by laying down, in the manner of Xenophon or Cicero, the correct style of a gentleman's training. And the Wolf-Prince's training was interminable. Quite apart from the usual academic and moral disciplines of the period, he was put through a long and elaborate course, to prepare him for his duties as Lording of the Forest, in the Customs and Science of the Hunt, and another course in Tactical Deployment and Encampment of the Pack. He was later sent to a University for well-born wolf-cubs (thus giving Fernando the opportunity to express his copious notions on the proper conduct of such places of learning) after which he returned home for a final going-over in preparation for his despatch on the lupine equivalent of the Grand Tour.

At this point Fielding began to flag. Although the Greek was simple, clear and undemanding in its vocabulary, the florid and

finicky type of lettering wearied him, and the very simplicity of
the language, with its constant repetition of the same elementary
constructions, made it exceedingly monotonous. To top it all,
the tedium of the subject matter (for Fernando's views on pae-
deutics were in no way novel) began to irritate Fielding almost
beyond bearing. He now started to feel at his crutch the thick
sweat and lurking tumescence which were always with him, a
sign that mental desperation was about to lead to physical orgasm, which in turn would be followed by several degrading
hours of intellectual apathy and sloth.

However, before the crisis finally overwhelmed him he was
saved by pure chance. A few days before the Wolf-Prince was
to depart on his Grand Tour, one of his tutors took him into
the Forest to make certain he was still well up on his hunting
lore. In the ensuing passage, Fernando, for the first time, used
a word which Fielding did not remember. The Wolf-Prince was
described as '$\delta\iota\alpha\varphi o\iota\tau\omega\nu$' among the trees. Trying to ignore his
erection, which was now swollen dangerously close to climax
and defeat, and turning with some effort to the Greek Lexicon
which he had borrowed from the Biblioteca Marciana before
settling to his task, Fielding found that the word was a technical
hunting term which meant 'running up and down to catch the
scent'. Immediately after it, for some reason, Fernando had
written a similar word, '$\zeta\alpha\varphi o\iota\tau\nu\omega\nu$' in brackets. Further con-
sultation of the Lexicon revealed that this was the old Aeolic
form of $\delta\iota\alpha\varphi o\iota\tau\omega\nu$. Why bother to put that in, Fielding thought;
Fernando was simply showing off. Clearly, a man who had such
a limited vocabulary that he did not know the Greek equivalents
for May and August would have been only too glad to make a
big bang when using one of the few rare words he did know,
and might well have added a dialect form in brackets to ram
his point right home; it was all of a piece with his intolerable
display of his ideas on education – in short, sheer conceit. Still,
it was an attractive word, $\zeta\alpha\varphi o\iota\tau\nu\omega\nu$, thought Fielding, with
an interesting meaning; and as he looked at it once more
chance, or inspiration, caused him to picture it in English letters, a translation he sometimes effected with Greek words that
appealed to him. As he built up the word on the tablet of his
mind, the letters shifted and flickered, stirring some memory,
hinting at something familiar here. He wrote the word down,
both in Greek letters and in English :

ζ   α   φ   ο   ι   τ   υ   ω   ν

z   a   ph   o   i   t   u   o   n

He surveyed the letters. Something was there for him, waiting
for him to pluck it out. But what? What? His penis was beginning to throb. Any moment now he would squalidly come.
Quickly. 'z', 'a', 'ph' ... or 'f', 'i' and 't'. Surely; leave out the
'a' and transpose the 'z': phitz ... or fitz. What letters were
left? 'a' ... 'o' ... 'u' ... 'n'. But the first 'o' and the 'u' made
the Greek diphthong '*ov*', for which it was permissible to substitute an English 'v' – a reasonable if rough phonetic equivalent
in the present combination, after the 'a' and before the second
'o'. Thus the Greek '*αουων*' became the English 'avon' ... and
the whole turned to 'fitzavon', or, of course, fitzAvon ... which
was, surely was, the name given in the recent letter from the
Albani lawyers as being that of the stranger in the picture of
whom he had written to enquire. Fielding's penis, undischarged,
ceased to throb and curled away to nothing as he checked his
discovery, all danger of degradation now gone. Success had restored intellect to primacy. Now there was hope. For of one
thing he could be certain : there was some kind of trail. However Fernando's story meandered about, there was, there must
be, some sense in which the Wolf-Prince, the Lording of the
Forest, stood for the man whom the Albani laywers in Siena
had named as Humbert fitzAvon. Fernando had planted the clue,
and had indeed pointed directly at it, that those 'whomsoever
God willed might see and comprehend'. Be patient, Fielding told
himself; only be patient and play out the game in Fernando's
way, for there is no other.

'Those Carpaccios we could not see the other day,' said Piero
to Daniel, 'when the room at the Accademia was closed. I have
enquired, and I know the room will be open on Friday.'

'What about it?' said Daniel.

'We could go to see them then. We could also go to see the
other Carpaccios at the Scuola San Giorgio. It would make an
interesting morning.'

'A very long morning. Anyway, not on Friday, I think.'

'Why not, Daniel?'

'Friday is the thirteenth. Unlucky.'

'Saturday is the thirteenth. Friday is the twelfth.'

'Not Friday, *caro*. Next week perhaps.'

'Next week the Carpaccios at the Accademia may be closed again. Why not Friday, Daniel?'

'Because I shall not be well. There is beginning to be a rhythm in all this, *caro*. For several days I am all right and may need only a few of those powders. Then there will be a bad day, but with more of the powders I can see it through. Then there will be a very bad day, of which I will not speak. Friday will be one of those days.'

'And after that you will start to be better?'

'Yes. Only each time the bad days come they are worse than before, and it takes me longer to recover.'

'Oh,' said Piero flatly. 'Then I shall find out whether the Carpaccios will be open on Tuesday or Wednesday of next week.'

'All right,' said Tom to Fielding: 'I accept that Fernando seems deliberately to have drawn attention to that odd Greek word, and I accept that it is an anagram of fitzAvon. I also accept that since the Greek word is a participle describing an action of the Wolf-Prince, we can equate the Wolf-Prince, provisionally at least, with Humbert fitzAvon; and of course we know from that lawyer's letter that he is the stranger in the painting. But now for a few awkward questions.'

'Very well.'

'First, if Fernando wanted to write about fitzAvon, why did he write in Greek? And why cast the thing as a fable?'

'On the showing of the first brief preface,' Fielding said, 'he simply set out to write a story in elementary Greek to practise his two younger children in translation. On the showing of the second preface – the one in the different ink – he later realized that his fable had somehow ... taken him over ... and had changed into a disguised history of fitzAvon – with whom, for any number of reasons, he was obsessed. To judge from what I have read of the story—'

'—More of that in a moment. First let us be clear about what Fernando was trying to do. This clue, the word 'ζαφοιτνων', that identifies the Wolf-Prince as fitzAvon – it appears relatively early in the narrative. So Fernando Albani must have realized, even so early as that, that he was, in truth, writing about fitz-Avon; otherwise he would not have left so deliberate a clue to that effect. But whom was this clue for? For the two children? If I remember rightly what you've told me, they were twins,

Francesco and Francesca, who were about seven years old at the time when the family group was painted. Now, according to that lawyer's letter, Fernando first met fitzAvon late in 1794, and took a copy of the painting to the Count Monteverdi in Siena in the autumn of 1796. The painting, therefore, was almost certainly done in 1795 or '96. This means that the twins, seven years old then, were about twelve years old in 1800, when Fernando was writing his Greek fable. In which case he could hardly have expected them to spot his clue, unless they were very bright indeed; and in any event, if he had wanted them to know that the Wolf-Prince was fitzAvon, he could simply have told them so without playing word games. So whom is that clue for? And come to that, why the disguise in the first place?'

'Because what was to be told was scandalous and disgraceful. I haven't finished the fable yet,' Fielding said, 'but even as far as I've got the story is pretty shocking – once you transpose it into human terms, that is. Simply as an animal adventure it is no more than merely meaty—'

'—Fit for twelve-year-olds?'

'Yes, *so long* as it is read as an animal adventure. Now, suppose Fernando had promised his children a Greek Reader in the form of a fable, he would have wished, being a good parent, to carry the thing through in a suitable and consistent manner. As an animal story it had started and as such it must continue. But on my theory, as it stands so far, when he realized that he was also telling the story of fitzAvon, he inserted a clue to that effect, hoping that his children might come back to the fable when they were older and more perceptive, and learn the unpleasant truth they could not be told while still young. Fernando also hoped, if I am right about the second preface, that others too might learn this truth – 'those whomsoever God wills' – at some future date. In short, Tom : while he did not want his children, or anyone else, to find out straight away about a recent and appalling family scandal, he did wish the matter to be placed on record, so that posterity might have at least some chance to learn of it. It was his duty to his family to suppress the facts for the time being; it was also his duty, as a man of truth, to make sure that those facts remained, however remotely, available.'

'Why? What's so important about them?'

'Nothing yet. Spectacular they may be, but not in any sense important. Perhaps their importance may be revealed later.

Remember, Tom: I've scarcely read half of the text yet.'

'Very well,' said Tom. 'Take me through it as far as you've gone.'

'With pleasure. As I was telling you when you interrupted with all your questions, the Wolf-Prince was sent to a wolves' University and then came home to be prepared for his Grand Tour. There follows the hunting scene, with the verbal clue to the Wolf-Prince's identity at fitzAvon, and after it a long lecture from the Mighty Wolf about the dangers of foreign parts, in the course of which he dispenses a great deal of Polonian advice. And then, at last, the Wolf-Prince, Lording of the Forest, sets out on his travels...'

Detterling drove Baby Llewyllyn from the school she was leaving in Devon to the new one near Dorchester.

'I'm glad to get out of *that* place. Was it difficult to arrange?' Baby said.

'Not really.'

In fact, however, the progressive Headmaster and his wife (a female lout in long skirt and sandals) had insisted that Detterling pay three terms' fees in lieu of notice. They had become very fond of Baby, they snarled, and had been looking forward to having her under their care for the next four or five years. Since custom and the law only required one term's fees in lieu of notice, and since a letter from Tom, as parent, authorizing Baby's removal, would have compelled the school to release Baby on that consideration, Detterling had briefly reviewed the idea of telling Tom what was afoot and asking him to write. But all that would have taken time and time, he thought, was not on Baby's side: she only had to fix some silly crush on a boy or a male teacher, a thing which any girl of her age might do at any second, and she would want to stay where she was after all. So he had signed a cheque on the instant, helped Baby to pack her kit, and here they were now on their way to Dorchester.

'They'll fit you out with the uniform when you get to Radigund's,' Detterling told her; 'they're all ready for you.'

'Miss Clodia Wentworth Rex sounds jolly grand,' Baby said, looking at the brochure which Detterling had given her. 'Do you think I should do equitation? It's good for the thigh muscles.'

'I shouldn't do it just for that.'

'I'll see what kind of other girls do it, and then decide. It might annoy Poppa if I went stag-hunting.'

'Why should it?'

'He's still a socialist in his old-fashioned way and he some-times comes all over socialist about the most ridiculous things.'

'Then be on the safe side and drop equitation. No point in upsetting your Poppa.'

'Does he know about all this – my changing schools, I mean?'

'Not yet, no. Your Aunt Isobel and I thought it better not to worry him until it was all actually done. He's got his hands full as it is.'

'Yes,' said Baby, 'full of Daniel Mond. Poppa will need help later. Fielding Gray won't be much use; he'll just glide away somehow. And as for Piero, he's very young.'

'You know about Daniel then?'

'Of course, my lord. I wasn't born yesterday or even last week. You'll be there to help Poppa when it happens?'

'If he wants me. I shall be going to Venice fairly soon to see how things are getting on.'

As they drove up to the Tudor manor house in which Miss Wentworth Rex presided over the eighty odd members of the Headmistress' House (where Baby was to be) they passed two little girls who were trotting along in grey shorts.

'It's the sort of place where they make you run everywhere before six in the evening,' Detterling said.

'I wonder what I'll look like in shorts.'

'You will make a brave boy.'

The car stopped.

'Like Rosalind or Viola, you mean?'

'Say Viola. Then I can be your Orsino. "If ever thou shalt love,"' Detterling quoted, '"In the sweet pangs of it remem-ber me... How dost thou like this tune?"'

'Oh, good my lord,' whispered Baby, and kissed him on the temple.

Together they unloaded Baby's luggage, saying nothing.

'Drive away now,' said Baby: 'I must go in there by myself.'

'... And so,' said Fielding to Tom, glancing at the MS, 'the Wolf-Prince comes to the border of his father's territory and decides to spend the night there before crossing into foreign lands and beginning the Grand Tour proper. If we think of the Wolf-Prince as fitzAvon, it all fits quite well, I think.'

'Yes. For Mountain in the Far North we can read England, which fitzAvon is now about to leave, having received the education of an eighteenth-century English gentleman. So here he is, just before finally leaving. What happens now?'

'The Wolf-Prince falls in with bad companions over night. They all gorge themselves on the flesh of wild goats. Then one of them complains that it's too tough and asks the others if they've ever tasted lamb. The real delicacy, he tells them, is lamb which has been taken from the mother's womb before birth. So they all break into a sheepfold, find some pregnant ewes and gobble the unborn lambs. At first the Wolf-Prince hangs back, but the flesh the others are eating looks so delicious that finally he can resist it no longer. Then the sheep-dog comes along to see what's up, and the young wolves tear him to pieces and drink his blood.'

'Meaty stuff for twelve-year-olds, as you said.'

'It turns out that the sheep-dog and his sheep are under the protection of The Mighty Wolf, King of the Mountain, who has an agreement with the sheep-dog that his flocks shall not be molested provided that he sends in so many sheep a year as tribute to the royal household. So The Mighty Wolf is furious with his son, who has not only assisted in crimes of theft and murder, but has further dishonoured his royal birth by preying on defenceless beasts instead of hunting wild ones.'

'I thought wolves always preyed on defenceless beasts if they could.'

'Not royal wolves. Or not Fernando's.'

'But presumably The Mighty Wolf ate the sheep that came in as tribute.'

'That was different. Accepting tribute was one thing; breaking into a sheepfold and eating unborn lambs was quite another.'

'And how do we read all this in terms of fitzAvon's adventures?'

'As something pretty fierce, I'd say. A drunken orgy followed by child-rape, perhaps . . . that or something not far off. They got bored with the goaty old whores and sought out the tender little lambs. Despite the freedom allowed to the gentry in those days, they obviously went much too far, and wound up killing the night-watchman who'd come to investigate. How serious it was we can see by going back to the Wolf-Prince. He is told that he's put himself so far beyond the pale that he will be condemned to death by the Wolf Council and that not even The Mighty

Wolf, his father, can protect him. But the Wolf-Prince has a huge fit of repentance, and The Mighty Wolf manages to arrange that his son shall be allowed to leave the country in secret, on condition he undertakes a dangerous mission of *sub rosa* lupine diplomacy, which will keep him out of the way until the row dies down. And so now, instead of setting out on a Grand Tour, the Wolf-Prince is sent packing straight off through perilous country which is threatened by The Mighty Wolf's enemy, the Wolf Imperial, to the distant city of the Marsh Wolves ... which could, of course, mean Venice. And that's as far as I've got.'

'We deduce, provisionally, that what fitzAvon had done was so awful that he was threatened with hanging, but that someone important intervened and arranged for him to go away and get lost in a country under the threat of war – *i.e.* in an Italy which was about to be invaded by Buonaparte – and to fill in the time with a cloak and dagger mission to the Venetians?'

'That seems a reasonable equivalent.'

'But *who* intervened, Fielding? Unlike the Wolf-Prince, fitz-Avon was an orphan. Or so Fernando told His Excellency the Count Monteverdi ... according to your letter from the lawyers in Siena.'

'There could have been a guardian, or influential friends of the family to help him. Come to that, he may very well not have been an orphan at all. That lawyer's letter implied that what Fernando told the Count was very far from being the truth, and of course we now see why. He could hardly tell the Count, if there was to be any hope of an adoption, the real reason why fitzAvon had come to Venice. Nor could he tell him anything accurate about fitzAvon's family in England, in case the Count made enquiries and found out about the scandal. In fact it is very likely, I should say now, that fitzAvon was a false name assumed for concealment.'

'Then how did *Fernando* find out about the scandal? And why did he not reject fitzAvon once he knew about it?'

'Questions to be answered in our next instalment, Tom. Somehow, fitzAvon must have established a pretty strong hold on the Albani family in Venice – you can see that from the painting – and somehow the truth about him must have come to Fernando in such a manner and at such a time as to be acceptable ... if only acceptable perforce.'

'Well, I hope the rest of the story is going to be worth all your trouble.'

'I should say – wouldn't you? – that fitzAvon's travels have got off to a very promising start.'

'With child-rape and murder? After that there doesn't seem much left to go onto.'

'Oh, plenty, I assure you. If I know myfitzAvon – and I think that I am beginning to – he'll do much better for us than that.'

When Baby entered the Tudor manor house she found herself in a wide hall. On her left was a door which bore a highly polished brass tablet: HEADMISTRESS. Baby knocked and went in.

When she had closed the door behind her, she turned into the room and saw a tall, handsome lady, a kind of female version of Prince Philip (Baby thought), who was putting a large book back on a shelf.

'And who might you be?' said the lady, though she knew perfectly well, since she was expecting Baby and had observed her arrival through the window.

'I'm Tullia Llewyllyn, ma'am.'

'Are you indeed?'

The lady advanced, holding out a hand and smiling. Baby, without knowing why, did something which her mother had taught her to do long ago but which she had not done for years now: as she took the lady's hand she dropped a little curtsy. Considering her lack of practice (she thought) she made quite a good job of it. Anyway, the lady looked pleased enough.

'I am Clodia Wentworth Rex,' the lady said, 'and you address me, not as "ma'am", but as "Headmistress".' She looked Baby up and down and round and about, and then up and down again. 'You've got a bit of flab on you,' she said, 'but you'll do. You'll do very well, Tullia Llewyllyn.'

'Thank you, Headmistress.'

'Did no one bring you here?' asked the Headmistress, knowing the answer.

'Lord Canteloupe drove me down. He's gone now.'

'Has he indeed? Why didn't he come in?'

'Because I told him not to.'

'Why did you do that?'

'Because it would not have been the same if he'd been here when I first met you.'

The Headmistress considered this for some time.

'Your luggage is outside?' she said at last.

'Yes, Headmistress.'

'Come on then, Tullia Llewyllyn. I'll give you a hand with it.'

Detterling had decided, on his way home from Dorchester into Wiltshire, to send Tom a long telegram about what had been done with Baby. A telephone call, which would necessitate Tom's being summoned from the tower into the Palazzo, would be awkward; a letter would take too long. Now the thing was done, Tom must know at once.

As Detterling was walking after dinner in his rose garden, deciding on the style and composition of the telegram, his man-servant came through the darkness and requested an interview.

'It's like this, my lord,' he said, as he fell into step with his master; 'I find that I should be grateful if your lordship would desist from addressing me as "Corporal".'

'I've called you "Corporal" since you came to me.'

'Things are different now, my lord. The military title lays me open to mockery from the other servants. As you know, my lord, these are merely contractor's personnel, employed by the company, and they do not understand proper discipline.'

'Very well. What am I to call you?'

'The plain surname would be too peremptory these days, my lord. On the other hand, the addition of "Mister" before the surname would be merely vulgar.'

'Your Christian name then?'

'Unsuitable, my lord. My Christian name is "Tommy".'

'Suppose I called you "Thomas"?'

'That is not my name, my lord. I was christened as "Tommy".'

'Then what on earth would you like me to call you? Indeed what *can* I call you?'

'I have thought of this with great care, my lord, and I have decided on the title of "Chamberlain".'

'*Chamberlain?*'

'On the dictionary definition, my lord, a chamberlain is the chamber attendant of a king or a lord. I think you must agree that I qualify.'

'Yes, but don't you think something a little less archaic would be better? What about "Steward"?'

'Inexact, my lord. I do not cater for your lordship's house-hold.'

'In London you do.'

s.—8

'But your lordship's *seat* is here in Wiltshire. Anyway, the title of Steward is now cheapened by its application to delinquent boys who serve fried fish on channel steamers.'

'You don't think the other servants will laugh? I mean, if they laughed at "Corporal" they might find "Chamberlain" mildly comic as well.'

'The dogs bark, my lord, but the caravan moves on. I find the title of Chamberlain so satisfactory that I am prepared to be mocked for it. I am no longer prepared to be mocked as a mere Corporal.'

'So be it then.'

'I am greatly beholden to your lordship. Good night, my lord.'

'Good night ... Chamberlain.'

The Chamberlain bowed and backed off out of the rose garden. Had Detterling not known that his old friend and servant was a teetotaller, he would have assumed that he was drunk. He very much wished he could assume this, as the alternative appeared to be that the Corporal was going potty. If so, he must of course be humoured unless and until he became violent; for a man with his length of service could not be lightly put down or turned off. All the same, Detterling did not look forward to asking one of the other servants to fetch or find his Chamberlain. Shall I say 'the Chamberlain' or 'my Chamberlain', he wondered. He could of course just say 'Fetch Tommy', or whatever the other servants called him, but this would be to let him down behind his back. Detterling shivered, partly from the chill of the October night and partly from a sudden spasm of despair at human folly, and went indoors to telephone his cable to Tom Llewyllyn.

The cable arrived the next day at the Casino dei due Professori just as Tom and Daniel returned from a light lunch at a local café. Meals were getting to be rather a problem, as Daniel was less and less inclined to make the effort to go out for them, and Tom was more and more determined to keep him up to the mark for as long as possible.

'Just bring me back a sandwich,' Daniel would say.

'You must eat properly.'

'I've no appetite, Tom.'

'You must eat, Danny...'

On this particular day they had had a wretched luncheon of over-cooked omelettes, and Daniel went straight off to be sick as soon as they were back in the tower. What with this, and what with the sullen demeanour of the Major-Domo, who had brought the telegram over from the Palazzo, Tom felt low. After he had gone upstairs to his room and read the telegram, he felt even lower.

It was not that he objected to what had been done with Baby; far from it. Although he had formerly regarded Baby as a 'special' case and so had insisted on a 'special' school for her, he had come to doubt the wisdom of that decision while Baby had been with him in Venice; and if she had now been moved, at her own request, to a place at which she would (so Detterling assured him) learn much more and be much happier, it was quite all right with Tom. Nor was he in any way resentful that he had not been consulted; for he well knew that if such things were to be done, they were best very quickly done. Nor, finally, was he jealous of those who had acted for him, or fearful lest Baby's gratitude to them should divert her affection from himself; he was too big a man for that.

What bothered Tom was his own futility : his futility in choosing the wrong school for Baby in the first place; his futility in not changing his decision when he had begun to realize how well Baby was shaping now that Patricia was out of the way; and his futility, after Baby had left Venice for England, in simply putting the matter from him. He had, of course, the excuse of his preoccupation with Daniel. But in this area too he felt futile. He was letting Piero do the work for him, because himself he was too feeble to cope. Nor could he claim that much effort was going into his research – the research which, in any case, had been only a pretext for coming to Venice. All in all, he was just flabbily footling about, achieving nothing for those people he loved most (Daniel, Baby and himself) and having apparently abrogated both authority and control in the affairs of all three of them.

As if this wasn't enough to depress him, he now found him-self thinking of poor, sad Patricia in the lunatic asylum. Nor-mally he thought of her little, and then with thankfulness. For years before the disaster Patricia and he had been diverging: after a last violent flare-up in the early sixties all sexual relations had long since ceased between them; and many other causes had alienated and later entirely divided them. Patricia had be-come at first noticeably and then pathologically mean about money; she had begun to depreciate and then to mock savagely at his colleagues, at his concern with the affairs of Lancaster, at his intellectual and academic success; she had exercised a creepy and damaging influence over Baby during several crucial years of her childhood. So that when the Furies came to destroy Patricia, Tom had rejoiced both that his girl had been rid of a demon and that he himself would henceforth be spared a great burden of anxiety, inconvenience and hate. Nor had he ceased to rejoice in the months that had passed since. But this after-noon, as happened just occasionally, he remembered Patricia as she had been on the day when he married with her, loyal, loving and proud; he remembered the early years of what had been a true affection, intelligently served on both sides, and a true pleasure, hot and strong and loud with words of lust; and, remembering these things, he thought also of the poor fluttering and babbling thing in the asylum, and bowed his head.

But not for long. First, he made himself fetch paper and pen and write letters of assent and thanks to Detterling and Isobel. Next he wrote, more easily now, to his daughter to wish her luck. Then, mindful of past failures and future perils, he descended to Daniel's room, to try what he could do for him. Because he had failed in skill and virtue, he need not, he must not, fail his friend in love.

After the Wolf-Prince had been smuggled off on his mission, his adventures, Fielding found, were for some time very dull. Although he was supposedly travelling through perilous and almost embattled lands, the narrative eschewed danger or ex-citement and provided instead a crudely informative docu-mentary about the terrain between Nice and the Veneto, both of which, along with all the places *en route*, were now openly named by Fernando. The Wolf-Prince apparently reached Nice by ship and proceeded across Italy by the main roads, staying as he went in important towns and cities. To explain this sudden emergence into the actual world, Fielding conjectured that Fer-nando had decided to use the journey as an opportunity for teaching his children some geography (after all, he still pur-ported to be writing a work of education) and at the same time as a means of making absolutely clear, to such mature readers as had understood the clue to the story, precisely where fitz-Avon was going. To avoid any possible confusion, VENEZIA was spelt out in Roman letters instead of Greek and repeatedly named by the Wolf-Prince as his destination; and only when the point had been laboured *ad nauseam* did the story at last return to the terms and territory of fable. Thus the Wolf-Prince, having engaged rooms for the night in a posting-house in Vicenza and having ordered a carriage to take him on to Venice the next day, had nevertheless reverted, by the following afternoon, to procedures more proper to his species, being discovered slinking through the reed beds towards the nearby City of the Marsh-Wolves, 'which lay by the Ocean of the Winds'.

Once the Wolf-Prince had arrived in the city, the inhabitants of which appeared to live more in the manner of water-rats than of wolves, the tale livened up considerably. The Wolf-Prince's mission, it appeared, was to carry secret oral instructions to his father's representative at the court of the Grand Wolf of the Marshes. These had to do with action to be taken and policy to be followed in the various contingencies which might arise if the Wolf Imperial pursued a projected campaign eastwards and attacked the City of the Marsh Wolves. Having delivered these instructions, the Wolf-Prince was simply to stay on in the city, ready to assist The Mighty Wolf's representative to carry out his master's bidding in the light of whatever events might ensue. In other words, thought Fielding, fitzAvon came to Venice with secret orders for His Britannic Majesty's Minister in residence about what he was to do if Buonaparte crossed Italy and threatened Venice. For the rest, fitzAvon's brief was to hang about in Venice on the ostensible pretext that there might be further duties for him, thus ensuring that he kept some 300 leagues out of sight and out of mind of anyone, back in England, who might have it in for him on account of the atrocity he had committed there. So far, so good; very good, in fact.

But even more interesting than the story of the Wolf-Prince's mission (the conduct of which did not, of its nature, engage much of his energy) was Fernando's description of the young blade's diversions off duty. Predictably, the Wolf-Prince soon came by dubious and debauched companions, with whom he indulged in appalling revelries in dens along the bank of the river. But although the scope and kind of fitzAvon's iniquities could hardly be mistaken, Fernando continued, doubtless out of regard for the tender years of his children, to clothe his deeds in the disguise of animal metaphor. His actions were reported, as they had been in the earlier scene of depravity, in terms of ferocity rather than of sexuality. Now, however, the vocabulary, still simple but more ample, told its own tale : instead of his former monotonous use of the all-purpose word 'κακος' or 'evil', Fernando was resorting to such words as 'lustful' or 'corrupt' and to such phrases as 'with enticing movement of the limbs'. It was quite clear, if one paid close attention to the text, that fitzAvon was sampling the whole Venetian repertoire of sexual talent, at every level from elegant dalliance with the most famous courtesans down to zestful ruttings in the most infamous stews. And then, as Fielding read on, the Wolf-Prince and his friends made plans to organize a vast banquet of 'luxurious flesh, forbidden fowl and dainty sweetmeats' in their favourite waterside den – all unaware that a treacherous jackal had reported them to the stern Conclave of Black Wolves, whose office it was to preserve in the city the ancient lupine virtues. Which being interpreted, thought Fielding, can only mean that fitzAvon and his chums were getting up a sumptuous all-rounders' orgy in a friendly bordel, not knowing that one of their servants had peached to the Officers (formerly, if no longer, *Black* Dominican Friars) of the Holy Inquisition...

'... And so,' Fielding told Tom over lunch the next day, 'there they all were capering about in the bawdy house, when the doors suddenly flew open and in poured the men from the Holy Office to arrest them. Consternation and bare botties everywhere. Brawls and denunciations. But fitzAvon, who knew a thing or two about Venice by then, was off and away by a back passage before anyone spotted him, pausing only to assist a young man – a *very* young man – whom he rather liked the look of. As it is given in animal terms, "The Wolf-Prince descried a cub, who was almost grown but was too young and weak to save himself in such affairs as this; and the Wolf-Prince having pity for the cub, led him out by the hidden way and brought him to safety".

'Later on, when they were well clear of the fracas, the cub introduced himself as the eldest son of a wolf who was very important in the city, though in fact the family had originated elsewhere. They were called the White Wolves of the Green Mountains – a near enough correspondence to the Albani dei Monteverdi.'

'And so that was how fitzAvon came to meet Fernando,' said Tom. 'He rescued his son and heir from arrest in a brothel. And here is where the story which you're after really begins.'

'Unfortunately,' sighed Fielding, 'it is also where Fernando's manuscript ends. Or almost. After the rescue there is only one paragraph left. This just states, in so many words, that the cub brought the Wolf-Prince to his father, who was grateful and entertained him much among his family. The family looked on the Wolf-Prince with favour; the cub and the Wolf-Prince became blood brothers; the Wolf-Prince took a liking to the cub's sister, who returned it; and the pair of them declared their mutual love. And that's that . . . except for an indication that at this stage the Wolf-Prince was pretty much of a mystery to all of them. "He could not yet tell his true name and parentage because of the troubled times," writes Fernando. This may explain why there's no mention of any plans for a wedding. The last sentence, apart from a P.S. addressed by Fernando to the twins, is simply : "And so it came about that the Wolf-Prince told his love to the White Wolf-Maiden, and she told her love to him, little knowing to whom she told it".'

'This P.S.,' said Tom after a pause : 'what does Fernando say there?'

' "These things I have written for you in my chamber in the tower in the garden. Take what I have written when you go hence, and read. I shall write more of these matters while you are gone. When you return new pages will await you, against such time as you may read them, among the books in the tower." It is dated,' said Fielding, 'SEPTEMBER MDCCC. September 1800.'

'Plague,' said Tom the historian. 'In the autumn of 1800 there was plague in Venice. He must have sent the twins away, and finished off the first bit of his story in a hurry so that they could take it with them.'

'Why would he stay behind himself?'

'Business,' said Tom. 'In time of plague there are many complications. Banks and merchants collapse, and later on perhaps there are looters. He had to take care of his property and look after his money.'

'So he packed his children off with this MS, and promised to write more which they would find, should anything happen to him, among the books in your tower . . . all of which, of course, have long since vanished. He was planning a second instalment,' Fielding said, 'which they could read when they were older and wiser. And which, perhaps, others could read too . . . anyone who got hold of this' – he plonked his hand down on the MS – 'and learnt from the postscript where to find the continuation.'

'What form,' said Tom, 'would the next instalment have taken? Would he have gone on with his fable?'

'If we are right,' said Fielding, 'we have now reached just the point where the story really hots up. fitzAvon has performed a service for the Albani family and now moves in on them. He has the elder son right under his thumb, and the elder daughter has fallen in love with him. Clearly, there are the makings of real trouble here – given fitzAvon was the brute he appears to be – and scandal and disaster are looming. Now we have posited that Fernando began to write a Greek Reader for his younger children, found himself writing the biography of fitzAvon in the form of an animal fable, and decided to continue so that the children and possibly others should have a fair chance of later access to the truth which, for the time being, must stay disguised. In short, Tom, Fernando had got himself into a dreadful mess. He wanted the children to know – but not yet. He wanted the truth to be left to posterity, but he was committed to telling it in a code that would become increasingly difficult to decipher as the years went on and as all points of reference gradually became obscured. What was more, this code was already proving immensely cumbersome for himself to operate. So what does he do now? I think he says: "To hell with writing this Greek rubbish; the twins are off to the mainland, so they can take it with them, as far as it's got, and make what they can of it, and that gives me the chance to change my horses and tell the rest of the story in plain words. That Greek bit is unlikely to have made them much wiser, they probably won't get the point for years yet – but whenever they do they can come to the tower where the sequel will be waiting for them, and by that time they'll be old enough to know the worst. Meanwhile, there's plague threatening Venice, so I'd better get on with writing the rest of it while I still can." I think that's what he says – and does.'

'You could be right,' said Tom. 'A pity that we shall never see the second instalment, whatever form it took. *Did* Fernando Albani die of the plague?'

'No. He lived, according to the records, until 1812.'

'Then he could certainly have finished his work. But we have no way of finding it. Either it stayed in the tower among the books there, and was removed and destroyed with them years ago; or the children got hold of it ... and did what with it?'

'Hid it away perhaps ... just as they, or somebody, hid away the first part. We found that, but we can't expect such luck a second time.'

'No,' said Tom. 'Or can we? *That phallus,*' he said.

'What about it?'

'It's got to be explained some time.'

'I thought we were more or less agreed. It's some sort of warning to tread carefully. It's certainly worked on Daniel and Piero. They haven't even asked how I'm getting on. Have they asked you?'

'No. But I think it's the MS itself they're shy of – the paper on which that thing is painted. I dare say they'll listen to the story – if ever we get to the end of it.'

'I wouldn't be so sure. I think they're in favour of letting sleeping dogs lie.'

'But since you're so determined to wake them,' said Tom, 'let me put to you the following proposition. Whatever that phallus may or may not mean, it would certainly not have been on the cover sheet of the MS when Fernando gave it to his two twelve-year-old children. Somebody must have painted it on later.'

'All right. Who and when?'

'We can only guess. But first let us hypothesize a little. Let us assume that the two younger children were given that MS, with the declared purpose of furthering their Greek, and that they took it with them in the autumn of 1800 to the family villa in the Veneto or wherever they were sent to avoid the plague. Let us assume that they read it, did not take the clue about fitzAvon (though they probably remembered him quite clearly), and then wrote the whole thing off as a piece of silly old Papa's boring educational rubbish. However, they wouldn't want to hurt his feelings, so when he sends for them to return from the Veneto they bring the MS with them and put it in a cupboard in the schoolroom, ready to be trotted out if he asks about it. Meanwhile Papa, they know, has been working on a second instalment, which, according to the P.S. at the end of the first, is stored away in the tower in the garden. But they certainly don't want to read another load of what they assume will be the same old ballocks, so they deliberately "forget" about it; and Papa says to himself, well, if they're not interested, so be it, they haven't yet seen what I'm really at and just as well, I never wanted them to know as early as this and I'll leave it all till later.

'So the years go on, and then in 1812 Fernando dies—'

'—Rather suddenly,' said Fielding. 'According to the gossip books, of a "flux".'

'But nevertheless,' said Tom, 'he has time on his death bed to say to Francesco, 'Take another look at that Greek story I wrote for you and your sister when you were children, and this time pay attention." So Francesco, who by now is rising twenty-five, goes to the schoolroom, blows the dust off the MS, and has another gander.'

Yes, thought Fielding, that could be right. He thought of Francesco: Francesco sneaking away from the others who were kneeling round his father's corpse, tiptoeing through one of the circular anterooms with a candlestick in his hand. The chanting of the priest died away behind him, he went into a stone corridor, up or down some stairs and into the old schoolroom, set down the candlestick, looked around and remembered the rocking-horses (which if Baby's dream was anything to go by, Fielding thought, had been sent up to the attic by Fernando many years before); he smiled at the miniature uniforms, then went to the cupboard where the MS had been dumped when he and his twin sister came back from the villa in the Veneto, early in 1801, that would have been, after a sharp winter had rid Venice of the incipient plague. Francesco took up the MS, gave a sob as he thought how little attention he and Francesca had paid it despite all the trouble the kind old man had taken, and began to read...

'... And this time,' said Tom, 'the penny dropped. Or at any rate Francesco got inquisitive enough to follow the instructions in the postscript and to dig out Part Two from among the books in his father's study in the tower. And what did he find? In your view and, on balance, in mine, he found an undisguised narrative of what happened after fitzAvon had ingratiated himself with the family. Euphemia, the older girl, is in love with fitzAvon; Piero, the older boy, is fitzAvon's close friend, his "blood brother", bound to him by their memory of a sensational orgy and their escape from the Inquisitors' men; the two parents, whether or not they like the look of fitzAvon, must show their gratitude, and the more so as they understand that fitzAvon has an undoubted hold on them through his knowledge of Piero's delinquent habits. This is where the second part of the story begins. And Francesco, though fascinated, doesn't much like it. At the time when all this was happening, back in 1794, he'd been a tiny little boy who adored his big brother and sister, and now he's about to learn what they were really up to in the intervals of coming to the nursery and dandling him on their knees...'

'But where are they *now*,' said Fielding, 'his big brother and sister? What has happened to Piero and Euphemia? Are they kneeling with the others round Papa's corpse? Or have they gone away? Or what?'

'According to that lawyer's letter,' said Tom, 'fitzAvon left Venice for ever shortly after the Count Monteverdi refused Fernando's request to adopt him, and Euphemia went into a convent. But *could* one go into a convent in 1796 or '7 when Buonaparte was banging on the door of Venice? And anyway, what about Piero? If you ask me, what that letter said was just an official gloss. The real answers lie in the second MS, the one which Francesco has now found in the tower after his father's death. If that story has the kind of ending which you and I think it has, the answers will not be pleasant. I think we can assume that Piero and Euphemia had long since disappeared, and that the younger children had been given some suitable and ano- dyne explanation. But now, Fielding, in 1812, Francesco is about to find out what really happened.'

'And is not, as you say, going to care for it.'

'No. So let us continue to hypothesize. Francesco now reads about whatever disaster fitzAvon brought on the family, and takes his twin sister into his confidence – after all, the story was written for both of them – and they decide, being dutiful chil- dren, to honour their father's intention. This is that, while the story should not be shouted from the roof-tops, it should be available to posterity if posterity should have the wit to find it out. A civilized attitude, I think: the truth can be hidden from the vulgar but it must not be allowed altogether to lapse; an account must be rendered in order that history may be com- plete. Only God knows all things, but man should at least have the opportunity to discover as many as possible. This, to judge from the second preface to the MS which we *do* have, is obviously what Fernando thought and now his children think so too. So what are they to do? Here, Fielding, one becomes very speculative. But *I* think that Francesco and Francesca decided to leave the first MS in the nursery-schoolroom, in a casual but not necessarily obvious place—'

'—In that sabretache?'

'Why not? And then they had to think very carefully what to do with the second, which contained the real meat of the matter. Now, anyone who did find and read the first MS would be directed by its postscript to look in the tower for the second. But this, think Francesco and Francesca, is too easy; anyway, there may by now be excellent reasons for not leaving the second MS in the tower any longer. Possibly the tower is damp and the MS will be damaged if left there; or possibly Francesco, now the paramount male in the household if his elder brother has vanished, has a mind to use the tower .. for certain purposes, as a handy place for entertaining while his mother is still alive and encumbering the Palazzo itself ..., and does not wish the MS to be kicking about in the tower while he is giving his parties there. Possibly this, that or a hundred other reasons. So the second MS, they decide, is not to go back to the tower; but, to keep faith with their father, they must insert a clue as to its whereabouts in the first MS, so that anyone who gets that far—'

'—As we have done—'

'—So that anyone who gets that far, *as we have done*, may have a fair chance to know it all. Now then : have you seen anything, in any part of the narrative of the first MS, which might have been written in by another hand later?'

'No. All corrections are made in the same ink and in the same hand as the text – made, that is, while the text was being written. The only thing in ink of a different colour is Fernando's brief second preface, dated August 1800. And that can't be any help.'

'No. But it is the *only* thing in ink of a different colour?'

'Yes ... unless you count that phallus, which is in water colours.'

'But I *do* count that phallus, Fielding. It is the only thing there to count – the only addition to the original MS, and therefore the only possible thing that Francesco could have put there to be the clue we are after.'

'*If* he did. *If* such a clue exists.'

'We must believe it does, or we have no hope at all. So we are back, where my hypothesizing began, with that phallus. Why should a well-conditioned young man, as we imagine Francesco to have been, think of painting on that cover sheet a flower piece with a prick in the middle of it?'

'Well, why?'

'Because whatever else you may say of it, it would certainly be noticed. Almost anything else might be overlooked as mere decoration or doodling, but a phallus in that state is bound to receive attention.'

'Not after the first shock of the thing.'

'But for long enough – long enough for whoever sees it to notice that it is covered with primary lesions. Such a horrible thing is not forgotten, Fielding; it was not intended to be forgotten; it was intended, first, to arouse strong if horrified curiosity – "read this but read it with caution"—'

'—That I might accept—'

'—And secondly, Fielding, to give anyone who did find and read it a clue where to look for a sequel.'

'Not the most helpful clue I've ever been given.'

'But at least, as I say, unforgettable. One is compelled to think of it; its very violence ensures that. And if one goes on thinking of it long enough, it will sooner or later give up its secret.'

'I wish I had your faith.'

'Try, Fielding. Try, as I am trying.'

But there was no will left in Fielding's face.

'It's no good,' he said: 'one may as well recognize a dead end when one sees it.'

He rose from the lunch table and stretched.

'I'm due to meet Max de Freville in twenty minutes,' he said, 'at Florian's in the Piazza. We're going to have another look at a Palace which interests him. In the Ghetto. Want to come?'

'Why not?' said Tom. 'I could do with some fresh air.' He glanced down at the manuscript on the table. ' "*Mentula magna minax*",' he muttered.

'Catullus.'

'Yes. "A huge, menacing prick." It's got to stand for something, Fielding . . . if you'll excuse the pun.'

'Where is Tom this afternoon?' said Piero, arriving in the tower for tea.

'He went to have lunch with Fielding Gray in the Gabrielli. Fielding called in here this morning, bursting with news about that MS you found. I said I didn't want to hear it; but Tom did, so they went off together for lunch.'

'They will be coming back in time for tea?'

'I don't know.'

'Because if they do not come back, I shall make and pour it for you, but I cannot start until we are sure, because Tom would think I was presuming to take his place.'

'Then let's leave it for a bit,' said Daniel. 'I wish you'd never found that manuscript.'

'So do I. But at the time I was just trying to help Major Gray, and I did not think properly about that ... that sign. I only thought, "I do not like this". If I had thought longer, I should have put the papers back where I found them and pretended that I had found nothing. And yet, Daniel, I do not know that those papers can do any harm. The writing on the front had been done a long time ago; so whatever is in them – it must all be over now.'

'Nothing is necessarily over,' said Daniel, 'however long ago it was.'

Daniel had been wrong when he told Piero that Fielding and Tom were lunching at the Gabrielli. Although that had been their declared intention, Fielding had later remarked that he ate a lot of his meals there in the normal course and would welcome a change. So they had left the Gabrielli after having a drink in the bar and walked a few yards up the Riva degli Schiavoni to the Campiello del Vin, at the far end of which was (and is) the Trattoria Malamocco, well known for its plain but excellent table.

And so, now that it was time for Fielding to meet Max, they left the Malamocco, went back to the Gabrielli to park the MS in Fielding's room, and then again passed by the Campiello del Vin on their way to the Piazza.

'A very decent spot of lunch,' said Fielding, looking down the Campiello at the Trattoria which they had left a few minutes before.

'It was Mary McCarthy's favourite place,' said Tom, 'when she was here writing *Venice Observed*.'

'Malamocco,' reflected Fielding. 'I've heard the name recently. In another connexion, I mean.'

'No doubt. It's a port on the Lido. Once very important,' said Tom in a lecturing tone, 'but destroyed by an earthquake in the twelfth century, after which it—'

'—No,' said Fielding, suddenly impatient, 'nothing to do with that.'

'Sorry I spoke,' said Tom, and sniffed loudly.

They trailed up the Riva degli Schiavoni, both of them cross after too much noon-day wine.

'It made Baby laugh,' Fielding said, after some time, 'because it sounded so silly.'

'*What* sounded so silly?' snapped Tom.

'A name. Somebody da Malamocco.'

'Precisely,' said Tom, at once pained and smug. 'Somebody from the port of Malamocco.'

'*Rocco* da Malamocco,' said Fielding, ignoring Tom's exhibition of self-righteousness. 'He painted one of those portraits in the Palazzo Albani. Baby and I looked at it that night we all had dinner there.'

They turned into the Piazzetta.

'I've never seen the portraits,' said Tom in a deprived manner.

'They're not up to much. This one by Rocco is of a sixteenth-century chap who's holding a rose in one hand and a monkey on a lead with the other.'

'Very interesting, I'm sure.'

They trudged down the arcade towards Florian's.

'A monkey for lechery,' gobbled Fielding, 'and a red rose for the pox. Common symbolism all over Europe.'

'What are you blithering about?'

'Shit,' shouted Fielding as they entered Florian's. 'It's right under our bloody noses.'

Some elderly Americans looked startled. Max rose from a table, with a deprecating air, to greet them.

'Rocco da Malamocco,' boomed Fielding: 'the letters in the middle make CODA MALA. *Coda* is a variant of *cauda, cauda* means a "tail" or in obscene sense a "prick". *Coda Mala* – a bad, rotten or diseased prick. I must be off.'

And he was. The Americans gaped at the discomfited Tom. Max patted him rather hopelessly on the shoulder.

'Fielding's gone,' Tom said stupidly.

'But he was going to come with me to the Ghetto,' said Max.

'I know. He asked me to come too.'

'What's got into him?'

'I think ... that he thinks ... that he might have made a discovery, which he had almost despaired of making.'

Something to do with that portrait, thought Tom, pulling himself together. He's gone to the Palazzo Albani to investigate. Perhaps it will be best if I keep Max occupied; because then, with Lykiadopoulos off at the Casino, Fielding will have the place to himself. Better for him like that, thought Tom; for after all, the first MS, which started all this off, was taken from a forbidden part of the Palazzo without anybody's permission, and Fielding might be embarrassed if he had to make explanations. Aloud he said,

'Well, let's have a coffee and go to the Ghetto without him.'

'Very kind of you,' said Max courteously, 'to keep me company.'

'I think,' said Daniel to Piero in the tower, 'that you can start making the tea now. Since Tom's as late as this he won't mind.'

Piero took the kettle off the oil-heater and poured a little water to warm the pot.

'That's right,' said Daniel.

'The Carpaccios in the Accademia – the St Ursula ones – will be open on Wednesday,' Piero said. 'Will you come with me that morning? And then to see the others at the Scuola San Giorgio?'

'I'll come to the Accademia, and then see how I feel.'

Piero began to measure out the tea.

'It would be a pity to miss the Scuola.'

'There will be other days.'

'Let us hope so.'

Piero poured boiling water on to the tea in the pot and began to stir.

'Don't stir it.'

'Why not?'

'It's said to be middle-class.'

'It makes it stronger.'

'To make it stronger you must let it stand.'

'That takes longer, and we are already late having it.'

'Precisely; but that is a middle-class consideration.'

Fielding Gray came into the tower.

'I've read that MS,' he said without preamble: 'as I hoped, it's about the stranger in that picture.'

Daniel and Piero regarded him with displeasure.

'But it's incomplete,' Fielding said. 'There's another MS I must have – or something of the sort. I think I know how to find it.'

Piero fetched a third cup and poured tea for the three of them. Fielding explained that the phallus on the cover sheet of the first MS must be pointing to the sixteenth-century portrait of the man with the rose and the monkey. A monkey for lechery, he said as he had said to Tom; a red rose for the pox.

'Rocco da Malamocco,' he repeated in conclusion : *'coda mala* in the middle. That phallus must mean that we are to look at Rocco's painting.'

'*Who* is to look at Rocco's painting?' said Piero.

'Is there anyone in the house?'

'Only the servants.'

'Then will you take me there?'

'No. I should not have gone where you told me the first time. I shall not help you now. Whatever else that horrible sign may have meant, to me it is a sign to stand away. And to Daniel.'

'You agree with that, Daniel?' Fielding said.

'Yes.'

'I could go by myself.'

'You would not be allowed up to the portraits,' Piero said, 'unless Mr Lykiadopoulos or Mr de Freville or I myself were with you.'

'Then please come with me, Piero. I can't give up now. I must get to the bottom of it. Surely, Daniel, you understand?'

'Oh yes. I too once wanted, very much, to get to the bottom of something. I did ... and then I wished I hadn't. Leave this alone, Fielding.'

'But *this* is different. Your thing was scientific – it could have been abused. But this is just a very minor historical mystery.'

'It may reveal more than you know. It may open up something else which should not be opened up. My thing, as you call it – that too was just a minor mystery when it started. A minor mystery of mathematical notation which, if solved, might possibly suggest new methods for use in the most abstract realms of pure mathematics. Instead of which, Fielding, it opened up a new way to hell.'

'But all I want to know is what happened to some people who have been dead for well over a century.'

'Dead in their own private hells. If you open up the way to those hells, who knows what you may let out?'

'Daniel. . . This record has been deliberately left behind. There is a preface to the first MS which says it is written for whomsoever God wills to read it.'

'A pretty formidable curse it sounds.'

'Daniel, you are seeing this too darkly.'

'I wish I wasn't seeing it at all. I'm too tired to argue. Do what you want, Fielding. Piero, take him to that painting.'

'No,' said Piero, 'I won't. You are right, Daniel. Hidden things should stay hidden.'

'If Fielding is determined,' said Daniel, 'he will in any case uncover them. We shan't stop him for long. Better go with him now and do as he asks.'

'No.'

'*Please*, Piero,' Daniel croaked. 'I can't bear this conversation any more.'

'Very well.' Piero turned to Fielding. 'Come along, Major Gray,' he said. 'But understand this. If you stir up ghosts, I shall do everything I can to help them to rest again, because my master, Mr Lykiadopoulos, will not want them in his house. So much will be my duty.'

'What do you mean?' said Fielding.

'I do not want to help you. I am helping you only because I know you will bully Daniel until I do as you ask. So I will come with you now to the gallery – but on this understanding: should the ghosts whom you are summoning demand some payment for their journey before they will return, I shall help them to get it because it is just that they should have it.'

'You are saying,' said Fielding, 'that they may want their own back on me for poking my nose in?'

'They may want something of somebody, and if so they must be given it. That is the condition of raising them.'

'There will be no ghosts,' said Fielding, 'and if there are I know how to deal with them on my own terms.'

'I shall help them to get theirs. It will be the safer way for me. Now come with me, Major Gray, to the portrait gallery.'

'It has a lot of charm,' said Tom to Max de Freville as they looked at the Palazzo Castagna-Samuele in the fading light.

'My mind's almost made up. You see, Tom, I don't want to do anything obvious. But to save a back-street curiosity like this – I know Angela approves of the idea.'

'How will you go about it?'

'Angela agrees with me that I should raise the money for a survey of the fabric and the foundations. If the report is hopeful, then I shall pass it on to the organizers of the Venice in Peril fund, with some more money if I can get it. I think they'll take the hint.'

'So the next step is to find money. Not easy these days. The rich are in a mess, Max.'

'Angela thinks that Fielding Gray ought to help.'

'How? He's doing well just now, but he hasn't got *this* kind of money.'

'She wasn't very precise. She thinks he might produce some idea ... some new method of raising cash. After all, he owes a debt to both of us.'

Tom let this pass. He had heard various rumours as to the part that Fielding had played in bringing about Angela's death,* and he would have liked an accurate account; but Max's vague reference to the affair did not give him enough excuse for detailed enquiry. This being so, he preferred that the subject of Angela should be dropped altogether.

'How's Lyki's bank going?' Tom said.

'I can't expect any money from him.'

'I was just wondering how he was getting on.'

'Very fair, I'd say.' Max looked at his watch. 'If we walk down to the Casino now, we can watch the end of his afternoon session.'

Tom, who had seen and smelt enough of the filthy Rio which flowed round the Ghetto, was glad to assent. As they walked, Max said:

'All that excitement of Fielding's in Florian's just now... Was it something to do with this mystery of his – about the stranger in the family picture?'

'Yes.'

'I don't suppose any harm can come of it. But it *is* an Albani affair, and the Albani *do* rent the palace to us. So if something nasty comes out from under a stone, they might be cross with Lyki and me for letting Fielding meddle.'

'He's been doing most of his meddling in the public library. They can't complain of that.'

'But he did get his first notion about this business from looking at that picture in the Palazzo.'

And that's not all he's had from the Palazzo, thought Tom; not by a long chalk. Sooner or later, if anything more turned up, Lyki and Max might have some right to know what was going on .

'We gave him the address of Benito Albani in Siena,' Max went on; 'thinking back, I'm not sure that was wise.'

'Very little came out of that; only a lawyer's letter more or less dismissing the whole thing.'

*See *Come Like Shadows*, passim.

'But Fielding's still on the trail?'

'Yes.'

'Well ... just so long as he doesn't bother Benito or the lawyers again. It might make trouble. But I think,' said Max, 'that Lyki and I ought to know if anything startling comes of it. After all, we do live in the place.'

'I can tell you this, Max. Either nothing will come of it, or else Fielding will have his answer very soon. That's why he was so excited.'

'Well,' said Max, 'in a sense you live in the Palazzo too. So you'll see that Lyki and I know anything that we should.'

'Yes. I'll see that you know anything that you should.'

'Well,' said Piero to Fielding in the portrait gallery, 'there is your sixteenth-century portrait. There' – he tapped the canvas – 'is the red rose, and there is the monkey. What now?'

Fielding looked at the portrait. The man's face, indifferently painted though it was, suggested intelligence, self-control and worldly humour: it did not (for how should it?) suggest the whereabouts of what Fielding sought. What help, he asked himself, had he expected? The phallus had told him, so he thought, to come to the painting by Rocco da Malamocco: but as Piero said, what now?

'Will the picture come away from the wall?'

'Not easily, no. The frame is set into the woodwork round it.'

'Test it.'

Piero tried the frame. It remained quite steady. He ran his hand along the base, pulling, pushing, probing this way and that.

'It is very firm,' he said contentedly.

'Look down there. Just below.'

A few inches below the picture a small gilded and wreathed medallion was fixed on to the panelling:

TOMMASO ALBANI 1507–1560

it read; and underneath, in smaller letters;

Rocco da Malamocco pinxit

Clearly, the medallion was of far later date than the painting,

and had been placed there by some member of the family who
had taken an interest in the portraits, had perhaps had them
cleaned and catalogued. Then why, Fielding asked himself, looking along the row of faces on the wall, had not this pious person
placed commemorative plaques under all the paintings, as he
had under Rocco's – and, Fielding now saw, under Rocco's
alone. He felt the medallion. He pressed it. No response.

'You try,' he said to Piero.

Piero felt delicately round the gilt surface with his fingers,
then tried the chiselled wreath which surounded it.

'Nothing,' he said. But Fielding heard him catch his breath.

'Try again.'

Piero hesitated, then scrabbled with his finger-nails at the
wreath. Fielding shrugged and walked down the line of portraits.
Why is he suddenly so clumsy, Fielding thought: one moment
his touch was as tender as a girl's, the next he was clawing like
an impatient dog at a door; he was trying not to show that he
had found something. Fielding stopped and looked at fitzAvon,
where he stood at the back of the family group: he wanted to
appear relaxed, Fielding thought, but underneath he was as
fierce and tense as a cat about to leap – even this painter had
caught that. After a brief look at the rest of the family, all smug
and wooden (as though frozen into an appearance of content by
fear of him that watched them from behind), Fielding turned
from the Piero in the canvas to the Piero in the flesh ... who was
now standing away from the wall and shaking his head. I must
do what he did the first time he tried that wreath, Fielding
thought. He went to the medallion, placed his fingers round the
wreath, managed to ease the tips underneath it; then he pulled
wreath and medallion together gently out from the wall. They
were backed by a cylinder, which slid out behind them like a
drawer. The cylinder was about a foot long; from the far end
of it Fielding drew out a scroll of paper. Piero widened his
mouth, bared his teeth, and then spat, pointing the first and
fourth fingers of his left hand towards the floor. Fielding pursed
his thin, pink little mouth into a grin of triumph, then tucked the
scroll into the waistband of his trousers, as Piero, he remembered, had done with the first MS. Once more Piero spat and
pointed his two fingers at the floor.

'I'll just put this device back,' Fielding said. He inserted the
end of the cylinder into the opening in the wall and eased it in-
wards until the medallion, once again, sat right up against the

panelling as though fastened to it. 'There,' he said; 'I don't think anyone will notice that it's been interfered with. Do you, Piero?'

'You have no right to those papers, Major Gray.'

'I have every right. They were left there that "whomsoever God wills" should find them. It seems that God has chosen me.'

As Max and Tom entered the Casino from the Calle Vendramin, they were aware that the doorman saluted with unusual briskness. The lift-man, who took them up to the special floor on which Lykiadopoulos operated his bank, was positively leering with pleasure. Even the woman in the cloakroom, who normally radiated malignance, seemed to be happy about something and gave them tabs for their overcoats with a most uncommon good grace.

'There's a new air about the place,' said Max.

In the passage to the bar people hustled to and fro, laughing and chattering and waving. In the bar itself eager waiters darted about with trays, serving a clientele of at least three times the usual number, while the head barman, deploying bottles and cocktail-shakers with the skill and speed of an expert conjurer, pattered away with animation to nearby drinkers.

'An air of carnival,' said Max. 'What's got into everybody?'

When they entered the Salle de Baccara itself, they found out. As they wriggled their way through a dense crowd, excitement throbbed all about them and noises of oohing and aahing and Madonna-mia-ing rose shrill ahead of them; and as they broke through at last to the rail, they were almost dazzled by the profusion of brilliant plaques that lay strewn across the table and by the clusters of white robes which billowed on either side of Lykiadopoulos and threatened at any moment (Tom thought) to swirl right over him.

'Jesus Christ,' said Max, 'it's the bloody Arabs. They weren't expected till November.'

An Arab next to Lykiadopoulos turned his cards face upwards. There was a sound, somewhere between a high-pitched humming and a howl, from the spectators. Lykiadopoulos sat very still in his seat, while a delicate dewy red patina spread over both his cheeks.

'Part of his act?' said Tom to Max, remembering the latter's disquisition about this on the bank's opening night. 'Or genuine, would you say?'

Max shook his head and affected not to hear. While the humming of the spectators slowly quietened, Max and Tom watched the croupiers, who were doggedly paying out to the punters on both halves of the table.

PART FOUR

THE KILL

As soon as he had made his discovery in the portrait gallery in the Palazzo Albani, Fielding Gray returned to the Gabrielli Hotel. He did not even pause to look in again on Daniel in the tower. for Piero, he knew, would have accompanied him there, and he had had enough of Piero's disagreeable behaviour for one day. He simply walked out of the Palazzo into the Calle Alba and hence to the Accademia Bridge, where he caught a vaporetto which would take him the rest of his way home. Neither while he was waiting for the vaporetto nor while he was on it did he attempt to examine the scroll of paper which he had found, for the excellent reason that some of it might have blown away. The scroll stayed firmly tucked into the waist of his trousers, and only when he was in his room in the Gabrielli, with the door locked behind him, did he at last allow himself to extract and unroll it.

The sheets were covered with small and precise writing, not in Italian, as he had surmised, but in French. The moment he thought about it, the reason for this was plain : French would be understood by Fernando Albani's children, and by educated people of the kind to which the memoir was addressed, but it would not be understood by servants who might have happened on the sheets in the tower where they had at first been deposited. Although the French was more sophisticated than Fernando's Greek had been, it was not difficult to read and tended to avoid hypothesis or qualification. The opening paragraph (there was no title) was quite admirably blunt.

'I, Fernando Albani, offer the following account of the shameful events within my household between the years 1794 and 1797. The public evidence has been concealed in order to prevent or at least defer open disgrace. But I wish my younger children to know all, as a warning to be wary of their Albani blood. This blood has always been reported to be cool and wholesome; my story will suggest other possibilities. For the rest, it is written to preserve the truth for such as may come on it at some future time; the account is therefore rendered as truthfully as I would render it to God Himself.'

This was much the same declaration of motive as had prefaced the first MS, Fielding thought: the truth must be recorded in order that 'such as may come on it at some future time' (cf. 'those whomsoever God wills') may be fully and accurately informed. Very well; what was there to know?

'This history,' Fernando continued, 'concerns a young Englishman who first came under my eyes in the last months of 1794, introducing himself in the name of Humbert fitzAvon and as being of reckonable family. In an earlier tract and in another tongue I have written, under guise of a fable, of all that befell this young man in his life before he came here to Venice and before we knew him. I based that account on what he told me of his life and career as our acquaintance progressed; and it is of this acquaintance, how it quickened and then ripened into fruits of poison, that I must now write here.'

As the text continued, Fielding began to build a picture of fitzAvon in his intercourse with the Albani family in the early days after the first meeting. Where Fernando did not state, he most amply insinuated; where he omitted a concrete detail, he established it by the very manner of his omission; where he had not seen, he implied beyond doubt what he had conceived. A little imagination swelled the words into flesh and blood; a little insight transformed Fernando's hints and suggestions, his reported and compressed exchanges, into voices, conversations and whole scenes...

'... My son tells me you have done him a great service, Mr fitzAvon. We are grateful, my wife and I.'

'I was glad to be of use, Signore. A pleasant boy like your son should not be made to pay too high for one act of folly committed while he is still so young.'

'As to that ... act of folly ... I rely on your discretion.'

'You may do so. Discretion is a small thing to give, Signore, in exchange for the friendship of yourself and your family.'

'You are most welcome here, Mr fitzAvon. Consider this house to be yours and everything that is in it...'

... An invitation which was to be taken all too literally. For only a few days later:

'Why *were* you at that bordel, Piero?'

'I was curious, Umberto. A friend told me what was arranged there.'

'Did he indeed? Shall we walk in the garden and out to the tower?'

'If you like, Umberto.'

And they strolled in the garden, passing Fernando, who was coming back from the tower towards the house.

'We are going to the tower, father.'

'By all means, but please do not disturb anything in my study. I am happy to see you here today, Mr fitzAvon.'

'It is so pleasant in your garden, Signore. There are few gardens in Venice.'

'I'm glad you enjoy it. You must excuse me. Good afternoon, Mr fitzAvon, and Piero.'

'Your father will not be coming back to the tower, Piero?'

'No. He has business this afternoon.'

'Good. Let us walk a little and then go there. So, Piero. You were interested about what would happen at the bordel. Was your curiosity satisfied?'

'There was not enough time, Umberto. Those men came to spoil it.'

'What did you see before they came?'

'Men with women.'

'Was anyone with you?'

'No. I kept in the background. I was only there to watch.'

'I see. Come into the tower... And now tell me. Were you excited by what you saw before those men came?'

'Of course.'

'And you are excited now, remembering it?'

'Yes, Umberto.'

'Let me try you. Yes, you *are* excited, Piero.'

'I think you too are excited, Umberto.'

'Try me then ... *gently*, Piero. You Italian boys can be very rough. That's better. Do you trust me, Piero? Will you do what I say?'

'Yes. Only show me.'

'All you need do is stay still. For I think, *this* time, that it will be best for you ... like this. Quite still, Piero. My pleasure, *this* time, is to give you pleasure. So I kiss you there, and there, and there ... such a soft skin you have ... yes, you may stroke my hair, Piero ... while I am kissing you ... here.'

And a few days after that :

'I thought perhaps I should find you alone, Signora. I passed Signor Albani on my way in.'

'I am very often alone, Mr fitzAvon. I expected you before now.'

'Why?'

'Because of the way you have looked at me. You made sure the others would not see, and then looked at me.'

'I wonder what I meant.'

'Do not mock me, Mr fitzAvon. From the time you first looked at me, I have waited for this. I am impatient. My husband is no longer young, and *I am impatient*. Come with me. Behind that screen is a little door, and behind the door there is—'

'—One moment, Signora. Please don't move yet. Let me sit here beside you and let us talk for a little. Like this. What beautiful arms you have. Beautiful arms mean beautiful legs, they say.'

'Umberto ... no, Umberto, not here. What is it you wish to talk of?'

'I want you to say a word in my favour ... to your daughter.'

'My *daughter*?'

'Euphemia. Do not worry, Signora. My intentions ... there ... are honourable. Ah ... such a soft skin you have. Like warm satin.'

'Umberto ... oh, stop, Umberto. Come with me now. Behind that screen—'

'—There is a little door. So you have already told me. But first : you will talk to your daughter?'

'We do not know anything about you. Marriage in Italy is a very serious matter.'

'In that case, I had better cease ... to amuse myself like this ... with a married woman.'

'No. No. Don't stop. I only meant that the making of a marriage for a young girl is a grave responsibility.'

'I shall use her well. Presently you may see how well I shall use her.'

'But money, family ... who *are* you, Umberto?'

'I think I can satisfy your husband as to all that. Will you speak a word for me to your daughter?'

'You are well able to speak your own.'

'It will make her more trusting if her mother approves.'

'I am not sure I do approve. Oh, stop, Umberto, please stop. If anyone came in now—'

'—He would see your pretty bare thighs splayed all over the sofa. You *will* speak to Euphemia?'

'*Take me behind the screen.*'

'I will make you spend your pleasure like this, just on my hand, like a kitchen-slut here on this sofa, unless you promise to speak to Euphemia.'

'God, oh God ... *Umberto.* Yes; I will speak to her.'

'Good. *Now* we will go behind the screen, Signora, and through your little door...'

That same evening:

'How old are you, Euphemia?'

'I am sixteen, Signore.'

'You should call me "Umberto" as your brother does.'

'Umberto. Umberto.'

'In English, "Humbert". Try it.'

'Uh... Uh... 'Umburt.'

'Not bad, for a first attempt. Should you like to be able to speak English?'

'To whom would I speak it?'

'To me. Then the others would not know what we were saying. We would have a private language.'

'We are alone, Sign – Umberto. We do not need a private language.'

'We are not often alone.'

'We can be. My mother says I may be alone with you.'

'Does she now? Still, there are things that are better said in a private language, even when we are alone.'

'Teach me then.'

'Very well. Repeat after me: "What is love? 'Tis not here-after".'

' "Wot ess luff? 'Teez nat 'ereefty".'

'Very good. "Present mirth hath present laughter".'

' "Preesent mith heth preesint lefty." Tell me what it means, Umberto.'

'It means that if we wish to love somebody, we should not waste time, because soon we grow old.'

'Oh.'

'It is poetry. But there is other poetry, which tells us that we should not be in too much haste to have what we want, because when we have had it we no longer want it. It tells us to prolong the pleasure of waiting, of imagining.'

'Oh.'

'That is what I am going to do with you, Euphemia, and you with me. We are going to tempt one another; to tempt one another, but to remain covered and veiled, until we are almost frenzied. And then, after a long time of this delicious frustration, we shall marry and come to each other at last. We shall have guessed many things but seen and known nothing. We shall lust to compare what we have guessed at with what is really there.'

'I do not quite understand, Umberto. As for marrying, that is as my father may command me.'

'I will take care of your father.'

'But what is this . . . about tempting each other?'

'I will tempt you another time. To begin with, you see, I am tempting you with the mere idea of temptation.'

And on fitzAvon's way downstairs, a quick visit to the nursery :

'Francesca. . . Francesco. . .'

'Rock me on my rocking-horse.'

'You are big enough to rock yourself.'

'I want *you* to rock me. Francesca says you rocked her yesterday and made her feel nice. I want to feel nice.'

'Very well. Climb on to your horse and grip tightly with your knees.'

'I want to ride too.'

'Then get on to the other horse, Francesca, and sit as I showed you yesterday. Not sideways, but as your brother sits. That's right. Now, first I rock you both slowly . . . then a little quicker. See what your sister is doing, Francesco, sliding up and down along the saddle . . . faster and faster. . . Push yourself up towards the head as it goes up, back towards the tail as the head goes down.'

'It tickles.'

'Now try to do it the other way. Back towards the tail as the head goes up, down towards the head as the head goes down. Is it nice, Francesca?'

'Yes, but help me as you helped me yesterday.'

'Help me too.'

'Ladies first. I will help your sister first, Francesco, and then I will help you.'

And so the weeks went on :

'Umberto . . . come with me to the tower.'

'Not today, Piero. I must see your mother.'

'What do you want with her?'

'We have matters to discuss.'

'Then promise you will come tomorrow.'

'Tomorrow, Piero, we will go in my gondola together. The one which your father has lent me. That will be much better than the tower.'

'Promise?'

'I promise, *caro*. Now I must go to your mother. . .'

'. . . Euphemia is beginning to yearn for me, Maria, but I do not touch her.'

'You still wish to marry her?'

'Yes. She will not regret it.'

'You have spoken to my husband?'

'Not yet. I want you to prepare him.'

'He does not trust you.'

'He has lent me a gondola.'

'He does not trust you, Umberto.'

'The times are dangerous, Maria. Italy is threatened, Venice is threatened. Euphemia may need me by and by, and I Euphemia.'

'Fernando will never let his daughter marry a man of mystery.'

'I shall not be a mystery to him much longer. Meanwhile, prepare him, Maria.'

'I want you for myself.'

'For as long as possible you shall have me – if you do as I say.'

'Very well, I will speak with him. Now kiss me, Umberto. Have me. Take me. *Do it to me.*'

'I have already done it to you once.'

'Again.'

'But we have dressed ourselves and I must go.'

'*Again.*'

'Quickly then. Quick, Maria, down on your knees, Maria. Like the dogs do it, Maria. Up with your dress and . . . a nice, plump bottom you have, but getting slack and dimpled. Now Euphemia's, which I have never seen—'

'—Do not talk of her *now*—'

'—Euphemia's will be smooth and firm. And Euphemia will

have a neat, tight virgin cleft. It will not be like ploughing in a muddy ditch.'

'*Umberto.*'

'Be grateful for what you can get, Maria, and next time do not ask for too much. Do not ask at all until you have talked as I told you with your husband.'

'But don't stop now please don't stop.'

'You have one minute to reach your pleasure, Maria, and then I am going down to the garden to talk with Euphemia...

'... And so yesterday I tempted you, Euphemia, by telling you what little boys do, what I did and what my nurse did to me. Today you must tempt me. What do little girls do?'

'Once, when we were on a journey, I was put into the same bed as Piero. He was tired and fell asleep at once. When he undressed I had seen that thing of his. And now I was curious and put my arm round him to feel it.'

'Now you *are* tempting me, Euphemia. But I shall not touch you. What happened?'

'It went stiff under my hand ... as you told me yours did under your nurse's. But he did not wake. So I took my hand away and felt myself in that place. I found a tiny piece of flesh, but it would not go stiff like Piero's.'

'Did you feel nothing?'

'Something began to stir inside me. But then our mother came in, and pulled back the bedclothes to rearrange them. When she saw Piero's thing, sticking out under his shirt, she looked at me and said, "Have you been touching Piero?" I said, "No", and she said no more. But we were never put in the same bed again.'

'Did you wish to be?'

'Perhaps. But to make up there was a little black page, who used to let me play with him. I never let him touch me, but I would get him in the nursery cupboard and play with him and make stuff run out of him. When the stuff came out he used to whimper like a little dog. When I was in bed later, I would play with myself and think of him whimpering and the warm stuff running over my hand. Umberto, could we not ... play together?'

'No, Euphemia. We can only talk and tempt. Now I must go...

'... Good evening, Francesco. Where is your sister?'

'She is ill, Umberto.'

'Would you like a ride on one of the rocking-horses?'

'No. On your knee, like last time.'

'Come here then. You shall have an especially nice ride, Francesco, if you will promise to help me.'

'All right.'

'Just tell your father and mother that I have been kind to you and how much you like me.'

'Shall I tell them about our rides?'

'No. I shouldn't tell them about those.'

'Why not? Are they wrong?'

'Of course not. How could it be wrong just to have a nice feeling? But mothers and fathers sometimes get jealous and angry if their little children have fun with somebody else. So just say that I have spoken kindly to you from time to time.'

'All right. Now give me my ride. Someone will come soon to take me to bed.'

And some days later Maria and Fernando together:

'The twins like him, Fernando. And we know what he has done for Piero.'

'Yes. I have a shrewd idea what he has done for Piero.'

'What do you mean?'

'Nothing. Go on, Maria.'

'Why should he not marry Euphemia?'

'We do not know anything about him.'

'But if he sets that right?'

'We will see what he has to say. If anything. I mistrust him, Maria. He has a way with him which makes me uneasy. I know we must be grateful, but I could wish my family saw less of him. I do not like his visits to the nursery. There is a funny look about Francesco when he speaks of him, and Francesca is very sly.'

'Do not forget, Fernando: a word from fitzAvon, and Piero would be in trouble with the Inquisition.'

'A word from Piero, and fitzAvon would be in trouble with the Inquisition.'

'No. fitzAvon is a foreigner. He has a post under the British Minister – that at least we know. The Inquisition would not make trouble for him.'

'The French would, if they came here.'

'The French would make trouble for us all. At least fitzAvon could take Euphemia to his own country.'

'If the French let him go. Anyway, the French will not come for a while yet.'

'We should be prepared.'

'I am not at all sure that fitzAvon can help us with our preparations. I am not at all sure that I want Euphemia to leave Venice – least of all if it is he that is taking her.'

'But at least talk to him, Fernando.'

'Yes. I have been meaning to talk to him for some time...

'... And so now, Mr fitzAvon, let us converse together. You have been making rather free of my household, I think.'

'At your invitation, Signore.'

'You have interpreted my invitation ... somewhat loosely.'

'I do not think any member of your household is the less happy for it.'

'Perhaps our notions of happiness differ.'

'We are at least agreed that if Piero were ... shown up ... to the Inquisition, that would be most unhappy for him.'

'They would deal leniently with Piero. He is only a boy.'

'Nevertheless, Signore, it is not what you would wish. Another thing on which we could agree is that Euphemia has arrived at an age when she is not averse from being courted.'

'When, and by whom, my daughter is to be courted is for me to decide, Mr fitzAvon.'

'Would you reject me as a suitor?'

'We know nothing of you.'

'You know my name and my condition.'

'We have a name by which we can call you. We may accept that you are a gentleman. But beyond this we know nothing – not even why you are here in Venice.'

'To serve his Britannic Majesty's Minister here.'

'But in what capacity? It is not the kind of employment that most English gentlemen would choose at a time like the present. At times like the present, gentlemen take up arms. They do not lurk in foreign cities, or not without a clearly defined office to perform. What is your office, Mr fitzAvon?'

'I grant that I must be something of a mystery to you. Soon, very soon, I will make everything clear to you, for I shall owe this to you if I am to solicit your daughter's affection. I understand that.'

'Pray understand also that even when you do declare yourself you will not necessarily have my support in your approaches to my daughter.'

'When you know everything about me, I think you will be very happy that I should approach her. Although there is one ... circumstance ... which may displease you, it is more than outweighed by others.'

'Perhaps so. How soon can I expect your revelations?'

'In a few days.'

'Very well. In the meantime, though I can hardly object to your intimacy with my son Piero, I should prefer that you visit my two younger children only when others are present.'

At this stage, Fielding knocked off for lunch; it seemed a suitable place for an interval. The state of play was that fitzAvon, like the imported 'Greekling' in Juvenal's satire on Rome, had debauched an entire family – except Euphemia, whom he had enslaved but not yet seduced, and except, of course, for the paterfamilias himself, an omission which, if Fielding remembered aright, had not been made by the canny Greekling. So now the paterfamilias was entering a mild protest, to meet which fitzAvon had promised to reveal himself very soon in his true colours – *i.e.* to give Fernando Albani the information on which, Fielding supposed, Albani was later to base his fable of the Wolf-Prince. Now, at last, both Fernando and Fielding in their separate generations were about to learn who and what fitzAvon really was.

Meanwhile, Fielding asked himself, was he sure that his interpretation of this second MS was not too licentious? Fernando had never said in so many words that his wife and his elder son shared fitzAvon's favours, that his two youngest children had been corrupted, and that his elder daughter had been enticed in a fashion far more sinister than outright seduction. The only conversations reported *verbatim* were those in which Fernando himself had taken part; all the others, and the activities which accompanied or concluded them, had been imagined by Fielding. And yet Fielding reckoned he had good warranty for his imaginings. They might be due in part to prurience, or in part to the lack of sexual exercise in his own recent life; but nevertheless everything which he had pictured to himself was there in Fernando's MS; by implication, or between the lines, in metaphorical palimpsest, so to speak, it was all there quite as surely as if Fernando had described it word for word. The comparison which occurred to Fielding was with Henry James's *Turn of the Screw*: there was not a syllable, in that novel, which spoke directly of physical acts, but the reader was none the less cer-

tain – as certain as if James had spoken in the roundest terms –
that Miles and Flora had been sexually manipulated and, more
or less, how.

He would, in any case, ask Tom to adjudicate; if level-minded
Tom agreed with him, he must be right. Tom's opinion would
also be very useful in the area which Fernando was just beginning to enter – the whole question of fitzAvon's actual identity and provenance. If, as now seemed the case, fitzAvon was
about to be revealed as someone whose standing corresponded
with the splendid title of Wolf-Prince, under which he had gone
in the fable, then Tom the historian's knowledge of eighteenth-
century grandees and their families would be invaluable.

'I think,' said Max de Freville to Lykiadopoulos in the Palazzo
Albani, 'that Fielding Gray may have found out something about
that picture. He was very excited yesterday afternoon.'

'Found out what about what picture?' said Lykiadopoulos indifferently.

'That stranger in the Albani family group. You remember he
was interested. He may have a clue about him. Tom Llewyllyn
says he'd almost given up, but now it seems he may have discovered something important after all.'

'Discovered what?'

'I don't know. Tom has promised to let us in on it if it's anything to our purpose.'

'How could it be to our purpose? Our purpose is to make
money out of this Baccarat Bank.'

'Well, we might be concerned,' said Max. 'After all, if Fielding
found out something disagreeable about the family from whom
we're renting this house—'

'—It would still make no difference whatever to the Baccarat
Bank,' said Lykiadopoulos sullenly.

'You . . . don't sound too happy about that.'

'I'm not. Those Arabs have arrived before they were expected. I haven't had time to prepare my defences.'

'You mean your reserves aren't big enough?'

'Partly that, yes. Since I began, I've won a handsome sum
which the Casino is holding for me as a liquid asset. But yesterday I lost at least half of it. It just isn't large enough, Max my
friend. Another day like yesterday – with those Arabs betting
in maximums – and it'll all be gone.'

'The luck could change. Anyway, the Casino is funding your

bank on the strength of the securities you've lodged. They're still sitting there intact.'

'And must continue to do so. As we have said before, if the Casino demands the sale of any of those securities, we could be in trouble. So what I want is to be sitting on a nice healthy pile of ready money *over and above* any other surety.'

'Of course that's what you want. But you're too old a hand to think you can have your own way all the time.'

'Indeed I am. What I'm really saying, Max, is that those Arabs are making things happen too quickly. They're forcing the pace. I had hoped to take precautions against that, but they are here too soon for me.'

'Let's get this straight, Lyki. Do you just mean that you'd hoped to build up a large reserve of winnings before the Arabs arrived? Or had you . . . something else in mind?'

'Both. You see, I could never be sure of building a large reserve, let alone one large enough to protect me against really heavy betting. So as you may remember, Max, I went to see an acquaintance in Padua.'

'I remember. A professor. An expert in metaphysics.'

'A special branch of metaphysics.'

'Like Diabolism?' said Max sarcastically. 'I don't know of any other branch that could help you.'

'You are very near. My friend has made a study of the Black Art. Being a sane man, he does not believe in sorcery but he is fascinated by the methods of sorcerers. Such men did produce remarkable illusions.'

'Conjurors, Lyki. Shit,' said Max dully, 'you're not going to try to rig the game like that? They'll have you in prison.'

'Don't be silly, Max. As we know, there are only two ways of rigging the game like that: to insert the cards into the shoe in a predetermined order, favourable to oneself; or to substitute a specially prepared shoe of cards in place of the one in proper use. With the surveillance they have here in Venice, either method would be far too risky, even with the cleverest of conjurors to operate it. A single slip – and one would indeed, as you say, be in prison.'

'Thank God you've got that straight. So where does your tame Black Magician come in?'

'That is just the trouble. He can't come in yet, as he has not had enough time to make his preparations.'

'For Christ's sake, Lyki. What is he going to do when he has made them?'

'For one thing, he is going to need your help. That is why I am telling you this.'

'I don't like the sound of it.'

'Nor do I, but I have no choice. It is these Arabs, Max. So many of them, staking so high. Now, my academic friend has devised a method, not necessarily of ensuring that I win but at least of limiting those Arabs to stakes which I can reasonably afford to lose if the luck goes sour on me. It is quite undetectable, and even if it goes wrong there can in no case be discovery or accusation against him, or you, or me.' Lykiadopoulos lowered his voice. 'Listen, Max,' he said : 'you are aware that there are certain sounds which animals can hear but are either too high or too low in pitch for human ears?'

'I've heard something of the kind.'

'It was early realized by sorcerers and Diabolists that the waves caused by noise had definite effects on the nervous system. If you wanted to alarm a crowd, or to soothe it, certain tunes and sounds could be a great help – and even more help, my friend, if they were the kind which could not actually be heard by the ear. If you hear a shrill noise, you start; if you don't expect it, you start even more; and if you do not even hear it but just receive an unpleasant shock on the nervous system for no reason you can discern, you will come near to panic. You follow?'

'I think so.'

'My friend has investigated descriptions of instruments with which the old Magicians produced such influential but unheard vibrations. Very soon he hopes to have made and tested some of them. Then ... he will come to the Casino and soothe or alarm the punters.'

'It'll look pretty odd if he stands about blowing subsonic whistles or whatever.'

'He need not – should not – be too close to the table. All his instruments will resemble such commonplace objects as cigarette-holders and so on. No one will be aware what he is doing; everyone will respond to the vibrations ... or so we hope. When the gamblers are alarmed or uneasy, they will bet low; when they are soothed, they may bet high.'

'Where do I come in?'

'I shall not be able to communicate with my friend, even by

signs. It might be observed. You will be able to talk to him, quite naturally, whenever you wish. You will be able to tell him, at any time, whether in your judgement I am in for a good streak or a bad. If a bad – and you will of course lean heavily on the side of pessimism – you will tell him to alarm the punters and so keep their stakes low. But if you feel really confident, you will tentatively try soothing them and thus enticing them to increase their bets.'

'Those instruments could affect my judgement too.'

'No. You will know about them and so discount their influence.'

'What makes you think these Arabs will respond?'

'They are very much the kind of people that the old Magicians had to cater for. Ignorant and impulsive.'

'As to that, we shall see. When will your chap be ready?'

'He has had great difficulty in the manufacture of the instruments. I hope he will be ready for his first serious trial in three or four days. It is longer than I would wish, and meanwhile one can only pray that the cards will be kind.'

'... And so,' said Fielding Gray to Tom Llewyllyn, 'a few days after his conversation with Fernando, fitzAvon kept his promise and told him who he really was.'

'And who was he?'

Fielding took a deep breath.

'He was Charles Humbert fitzAvon d'Azincourt Sarum, called by courtesy of England Viscount Rollesden-in-Silvis, only son and heir apparent of the Earl of Muscateer.'

'He was what?'

'He was Charles Humbert fitz—'

'—Just the last bit.'

'Viscount Rollesden-in-Silvis, only son and heir apparent of the Earl of Muscateer.'

'Canteloupe's lot?'

'Yes, Canteloupe's lot. Come to think of it now, there were signals right from the start. In the first MS, the Wolf-Prince was also Lord of the Forest – Rollesden-in-*Silvis*, Tom. The Mighty Wolf was κρατῶν λύκος in Greek. KRATON is not far from an anagram of CANTE, and λύκος – wolf – equals and resembles the French *loup*. Put 'em together and you get something pretty near Canteloupe – which was Muscateer's title by the time Fernando got round to writing the fable. And then the

names Humbert and fitzAvon – both sometimes used in the
Sarum family as subsidiary Christian names. I should have
spotted them.'

'You seem very knowledgeable about the Sarums.'

'I ought to be. I went through a lot of the family stuff with
Detterling when old Canteloupe died last month. So here's a
little more about them. Fernando is here relating the events of
1795. This Earl of Muscateer just referred to was made first
Marquis Canteloupe in 1799. By that time his only son by his
first wife – *i.e.* Viscount Rollesden-in-Silvis, alias Humbert fitz-
Avon – was dead. According to the family records, he had died
abroad, in 1797.'

'That fits. Does Fernando get around to telling us about his
death?'

'He does. And more of that later. Meanwhile,' said Fielding,
'note this : the first Marquis Canteloupe, when so promoted in
1799, had no male heir. His wife was now mad (which may incidentally explain some of his dead son's behaviour) and was in
any case too old for child-bearing. So he arranged for the new
title to be passed on through the male issue of his daughter,
the Lady Julia Sarum, who married a Detterling. Then his mad
wife died and he managed a son by her successor, so in the
event there was no need of the special arrangement about the
issue of Lady Julia ... or not until the other day, when the main
line ended with poor old Canteloupe, and the Sarum/Detterling
side of the family came up with our friend Captain Detterling,
who has now inherited.'

'Why are you telling me all this?'

'You'll see. Oh my paws and whiskers, Tom, *you'll see*. But
first : what do you, as an historian, know of this Earl of Muscateer?'

Tom thought carefully. Then he gave a satisfied nod, as of
one who has just fitted an awkward piece into a jigsaw puzzle.

'He was never a really big man,' Tom said, 'but he was clever
at managing things behind the scenes. According to the gossip,
he ingratiated himself with the Royal Family by having George
III to stay down in Wiltshire and keeping a discreet eye on him
when he first started having the funny spells which afterwards
became lunacy. Muscateer was later made a marquis in return
for his services, and these being what they were the powers
that be would doubtless have been happy to oblige him in the
matter of the special remainder. He had also been previously

granted another and less official favour – again, according to the gossips. In 1794 his son had been involved in the Maids of Ty-burn Affray – a very nasty business in which a Roman Catholic Priest interrupted some noblemen, who were amusing themselves with some young Irish children in a brothel, and was killed for his interference. There was a blazing scandal, and young Lord Rollesden-in-Silvis was in the middle of it. But before the affair could come to trial, he was spirited away, with official con-nivance – and then never heard of again until reported dead ... in 1797. It was said that he had been serving the Government under the rose in Europe, and had been killed in a brawl with some French agents, several of whom he took on single-handed. All this was generally held to wipe out, to some extent, his guilt in the Maids of Tyburn case, and to justify the Government men who had smuggled him abroad when he should have been stand-ing trial.'

'They must have been whitewashing him, Tom. According to Fernando, later in this memoir, he was certainly killed in a brawl in 1797 – but *not* with French agents. Apart from that, what you say—'

'—What the contemporary gossips said—'

'—Seems to square pretty well with Fernando's account, both in the fable of the Wolf-Prince and in the memoir.'

Fielding patted the memoir with affection.

'Yes,' said Tom. 'I should have seen the resemblance – be-tween fitzAvon's activities and those of Rollesden-in-Silvis – much earlier. It was a celebrated scandal in its time.'

'Anyway, we agree, now, that the mystery of the stranger in that picture is solved. He was called Rollesden-in-Silvis; he was son and heir to Lord Muscateer, who was later promoted Mar-quis Canteloupe—'

'—And he died in Italy, in some kind of fight, in 1797. A very ingenious piece of minor research, Fielding, and a very amusing conclusion.'

'The only thing is,' said Fielding, 'that this isn't the con-clusion.'

'You have discovered who the stranger in that picture was, and you know that he was killed in 1797. That sounds pretty final to me.'

'But I haven't yet told you what Fernando says of fitzAvon's 'goings-on between the time when he revealed who he really was and the time of his death. There is a nasty little joke to come,

Tom, which I hope you will enjoy as much as I do.'

'You mean ... he married Euphemia Albani before he died, perhaps?'

'Dear me, no. Nothing as wholesome as that. True, he went on trying, but it didn't come off.'

'Then what did happen ... which you find so funny?'

Fielding turned the pages of the MS in front of him.

'As soon as fitzAvon had revealed his true identity to Fernando,' Fielding said, 'Fernando remembered the story of the scandal in England some while before, and was quite horrified to think whom his family had been entertaining. But fitzAvon – we may as well go on calling him that – told Fernando not to be a silly bourgeois prig, and then proposed a deal...'

'Tom and Fielding are discussing that new MS again,' said Daniel to Piero, when the latter joined him in the tower that afternoon. 'Tom's been gone hours.'

Piero shrugged crossly.

'It's too late to worry about that,' he said.

'I know. But I still have the feeling that whatever they find out ... may do none of us any good.'

'Meanwhile, there is something actually happening, now, that may do none of us any good. Mr Lykiadopoulos is worried about his Baccarat Bank.'

'If he should fail, you know by now where you can turn.'

'To you? To a dying man,' said Piero neutrally. 'There is little comfort in that for either of us.'

'There is some money you can have.'

'Mr Lykiadopoulos will not fail ... entirely. He will retain, somehow, much more than you could ever give me. But he will be unhappy. You see, Daniel, if this bank fails, he will have failed all those Greeks who depend on him. It will not console him that he will still have enough for himself and me.'

'Will it console you?'

'A little. But it will be miserable living with him.'

'Then leave him and take what I can offer.'

'He is ... he is my career. He is my living and my parents' living. He is my master, in a way you do not understand, and he has bound me to him. I may be disobedient to him, even in quite important things, but I am still his to command, Daniel, and I cannot leave him, however disastrously he should fail here

in Venice. Anyway,' said Piero, picking up the kettle, 'he may
not fail at all.'

'So the terms were drawn up,' Fielding told Tom Llewyllyn.
'Fernando took a great deal of persuading, and the bargaining
went on for some months, but at last the thing was agreed. What
Fernando would be getting was fitzAvon's absolute oath of
silence about Piero's presence in the brothel at the time of the
raid by the Inquisition; an ancient and noble name, and eventually the title of an English Countess, for his daughter Euphemia;
and a guarantee of financial aid (for fitzAvon already enjoyed a
considerable fortune in his own right) in the event of the
Albani fortunes' being wrecked by the troubles which were
sweeping over Italy.

'What fitzAvon would receive in return was, first, Euphemia,
whom in some way he seems to have coveted; and secondly,
protection. He could not return to England for a long time – not
until the Maids of Tyburn scandal had finally fizzled out; and
he might have considerable difficulties, as things appeared in
1795, in establishing himself anywhere in Europe. But in Italy,
he said, Albani could arrange for him to be adopted into the
family of the Monteverdi on the occasion of his marriage to
Euphemia, and once he was known as the adopted son of the
influential Count Monteverdi, and went under the same name,
he would probably be safe – even if Buonaparte conquered the
entire country .

'But here, as Fernando told him, there was one nasty snag. The
Count Monteverdi was an honourable and also a pious man,
and he would never adopt fitzAvon if he knew him to be really
Lord Rollesden-in-Silvis, the notorious debaucher of the Maids of
Tyburn and the murderer of a priest. Therefore fitzAvon must
be presented to the Count in the guise in which he had first presented himself to Fernando – as an orphaned English gentleman
of means. And if that wasn't good enough for the Count, it
would be just too bad for fitzAvon.

'Here, of course, we revert to that letter I had the other day
from the Albani lawyers in Siena. As the letter related, in the
autumn of 1796 Fernando took himself off to Siena to see Count
Monteverdi, carrying with him a copy of the family group
which had recently been painted and in which fitzAvon was
portrayed in the family's company. When asked by Monteverdi
to account for his prospective son-in-law, Fernando trotted out

the orphaned-English-gentleman-of-means-and-education story – and was turned down flat. So back he came to Venice with news of his failure. And then the trouble really started. fitzAvon was furious at this rejection, and was by now a frightened man as well; for Buonaparte's forces were rapidly crossing the North of Italy, and it looked as if he might be trapped – without the benefit of Tuscan papers and passport, which adoption by the Count Monteverdi in Siena would probably have procured for him. As a mere English agent in Venice, dubiously employed and without official diplomatic standing, he knew he would get very short shrift from the French – a cell or even a firing squad.'

'But surely,' said Tom, 'if we've interpreted the fable correctly, the Wolf-Prince, *i.e.* fitzAvon, had definite and official duties, should Venice be threatened with capture, in aid of the British Minister. Wouldn't this have given him some kind of diplomatic standing?'

'No. His instructions had always been secret. He had never been properly accredited. And according to this memoir no arrangements had been made for him. If things got dangerous, he was to help the Minister destroy certain records and papers – after which the Minister would be taken up by a British frigate and returned to England; but of course there was no such passage home available to the Maids of Tyburn murderer. Once the Minister left, fitzAvon was on his own.'

'He hadn't even a special passport?'

'Not special enough for the Armies of the French Revolution. No doubt about it. In a very few months or even weeks, fitzAvon was going to be up against it. No adoption, so no Tuscan papers, and no Euphemia – for in the circumstances Fernando was certainly not going to marry her to a man, Viscount or no, who would confer on her the taint of British nationality without being able to take her off to safety in Britain. So the game was nearly up. But fitzAvon still had enough pull with Maria to persuade her to arrange a hiding place for him in the family villa in the Veneto; and there was enough time, before he would have to leave, for him to have a last little fling with other of his favourites in the family. He would seem to have devised it partly as a farewell pleasure, partly as an act of revenge for his disappointments. From what Fernando writes, I imagine something rather like this. . .'

'. . . But there is one thing we can do before I go, Piero. One final delight we can enjoy together. We . . . and another.'

'And another, Umberto?'

'Your sister, Euphemia.'

'I do not understand.'

'You have often said that there is nothing you would not do for me. Surely you will not go back on that, now that I must leave you?'

'No, but I still do not understand.'

'Then listen. Euphemia has told me that when you were both children you were put into the same bed, in an inn. Do you remember what happened?'

'I was tired and fell asleep.'

'But Euphemia was not tired. She can remember what happened. She will show you and me.'

'But she is grown now, Umberto, and so am I. We cannot ... lie down together.'

'You will be children again, and so it will all be quite innocent. We shall be reverting to paradise, where all pleasures are the innocent pleasures of children...

'... So you see, Euphemia, you will simply do what you did that night in the inn, and leave the rest to me.'

'But what will happen?'

'We shall be playing. You have often urged me to play, but until now I have refused, so that we could have the more pleasure in tempting one another. Now that I must leave you, the time for temptation is over; at last, Euphemia, it is time to play.'

'It is only a game then?'

'Yes. A game of children, innocent. For you and Piero will again be children.'

'And you, Umberto? What will you be?'

'That you will see. It is my surprise. Now. Piero tells me your father will be out tomorrow afternoon. So at three o'clock you will meet us both in the tower...

'... Good afternoon, Signor Albani. I have come to say good-bye to you and your family. The French are very near, and to-night I must leave for your Villa at Oriago.'

'Rooms are prepared for you, my lord, and the servants are expecting you. Or rather, they are expecting Mr Humbert fitz-Avon. You will be wise to keep to the humbler designation ... though I do not think the French will worry you at Oriago. But you cannot stay there for ever. What shall you do? Where shall you go?'

'I shall hide at Oriago until things settle again. Then I shall make a plan to escape.'

'Where to?'

'Perhaps I shall be able to return to England sooner than I had thought. I hear my father gains daily in influence. What a pity, Signore, that you could not serve me with the Count Monteverdi. Think what a son-in-law you would have had.'

'Indeed.'

'You should have tried harder with the Count, Signore.'

'He is an obstinate old man. Perhaps it has turned out for the best. Although you would have made a rich and noble husband for my daughter, you might not have made a good one. But let us not part unkindly. I must go now. I have business, though what it will lead to in such times is hard to say. Allow me to wish you good fortune, my lord, and a safe journey to Oriago.'

'Good-bye, Signor Fernando, and thank you for your hospitality...'

'... Your father has gone. Your mother is resting. The twins will not disturb us here. And so now, Piero and Euphemia, let us remember. Let us remember that night in the inn. First you undressed ... Piero down to his shirt, Euphemia down to her shift. And as you undressed, Euphemia glimpsed Piero's childish maleness. Show her, Piero.'

'Umberto...'

'*Show her*, Piero. Briefly, as if by accident as you undress... Good. Then you both lay down on the bed – this rug will serve – and Piero was so tired that at once he fell asleep. Euphemia, made curious by what she had seen, was restless ... and made investigation of her brother. Tell us what you did. Show us, Euphemia.'

'I put my arm across him ... like this ... played with him ... like this.'

'And then?'

'I felt his flesh grow under my hand, as it is growing now. But he did not wake. So then I tried what I could do with myself.'

'Show me.'

'Like this. And after a time I felt a warmth stir within me ... as it is stirring now, Umberto.'

'But then your mother came in?'

'Yes.'

'*I* shall be your mother. She lifted the bedclothes and saw that Piero was roused. She lifted his shirt to look more closely, and she felt him ... like this ... to make sure of what she was seeing.'

'Yes.'

'Then she said: "Euphemia, have you been touching Piero?"'

'And I said: "No, mama".'

'You *have* been touching Piero, Euphemia. Show me how.'

'No, she did not say that.'

'But now, today, the story takes a different turn. Remember only that I am your mother and that you must obey me. You have been touching Piero, Euphemia, and you have been touching yourself. See there, I can tell. We must wake Piero so that we can tell him. Wake up, Piero... *Piero.*'

'What is it, mama?'

'Euphemia has found a new game, Piero. Show him, Euphemia. Show him how you played with him as he slept.'

'It was like this, Piero.'

'Oh, God. *Euphemia.*'

'And how you played with yourself, Euphemia ... so that he may learn to do it for you. There. Go on, Piero.'

'But Umberto—'

'Not Umberto. Your mother, your mother in the inn, commanding you. Play with her, Piero. Kiss her and fondle her as you long to do. Kiss him, Euphemia. Love him. Open to his hand. Wide. Wider. Good children, pretty children. Obey your mother. Your mother will show you what to do.'

'Oh God, Piero, Piero...'

'Oh God, *Euphemia...*'

'No more like that, Euphemia, or you will pleasure him too much and too soon. Kneel to her, Piero. Open to him, Euphemia. This is the right true game of love. Open to your brother. Guide him. Do not hasten, Piero. Let her relish the passing of her maidenhood, for she can never have it back. Easily, easily, trying not to hurt her...'

'*Piero.* It is hurting.'

'Yes, but not much. Open wider to him. Help him. There will be a little blood but there will also be ecstasy. Can you feel it, Euphemia, the ecstasy that is coming? Ah, how I love to watch you both. So pretty, so obedient. Pretty Piero, pretty Euphemia. How beautiful you are in your game of pleasure...'

'And so this is the little joke you found so funny?' said Tom to Fielding Gray.

'No, as it happens. The real joke comes later.'

'I see. Well, to confine ourselves to what has passed so far,' said Tom, 'aren't you reading rather a lot into that memoir? I grant I haven't looked at it as carefully as you have, but are you sure you can build . . . all *that* . . . on it?'

'The details are mine, I admit. But something like that must have been.'

'Obviously fitzAvon/Rollesden had a hold on them. But to *that* extent?'

'Fernando writes : "I know that what took place in the tower on the last afternoon before our accursed guest left us was shameful beyond imagining".'

"You seem to have imagined it all right,' said Tom. 'How can you be sure you are not imagining too much?'

'Because of what comes next. You see, Tom, the events which followed, the *facts* which Fernando now goes on to give – and from here on he is explicit – make the whole thing clear beyond any possible doubt.'

'Very well. Convince me, Fielding. *What* events followed that torrid afternoon in the tower?'

In the Casino, that same afternoon, Lykiadopoulos was facing up again to the white-robed princes of Araby. This time the edge of luck was paring the game narrowly in his favour; and by the time the afternoon session was nearing its close, he had recovered perhaps a quarter of what he had lost to the initial Arab attack the day before. So far, so good, he told himself : but there would be another session to face after dinner, and several more in the next few days before his friend from Padua would be ready to test his devices on the company; and at any or all of these sessions this high-playing mob might take ruinous sums from him, if the cards fell their way, in a matter of minutes. In normal circumstances, he would expect only one player at the table, at the most two, to be wagering the maximum stake; as it was, ten or twelve were doing so – at every coup which he dealt. No doubt about it : his reserves were not large enough to sustain an assault of this magnitude; if the Arabs were consistently successful, even at a margin as slight as four coups in seven, he would soon be in a very bad case.

The only thing to do (until the gentleman in Padua was ready) was to pray. Lykiadopoulos returned after the session to the Palazzo Albani, mounted to his private chapel in the pent-

house, and prayed most heartily. Later, when he left the chapel
and was walking along the corridor towards the stairs, he heard,
through a half-open door, the voice of Max de Freville. He must
be having one of his conversations with Angela, thought Lykiadopoulos, and paused to listen.

'It's all very well, Angie,' said de Freville's voice, 'to say that
Fielding Gray ought to help me finance the survey of that
palace; but he's earned his money the hard way and you can't
expect him to be too lavish with it."

De Freville was silent for a while. Then he said,

'All right. Detterling has inherited a good deal, I grant you,
but I don't think he can touch the capital. . . . Yes, he did have
quite a lot before he inherited, but he was always rather tight
with it. Anyway, Detterling's in England, so that's no help for a
start. . . . What's that? You say that Fielding could help me make
Detterling stump up? How, Angie? I just don't get it.'

Nor do I, thought Lykiadopoulos, as he crept on along the
corridor and started down the stairs; but one thing I do know:
if anyone's in a position to tap Detterling/Canteloupe, there may
well be a more urgent use for the money than any crazy scheme
of Max's for restoring ruined palaces. And then, as he prepared
for his bath, Lykiadopoulos began to think of the second of his
troubles: quite apart from the precarious situation of his bank
at the Casino, there were now signs that ugly pressures might
start to threaten his interests in Corfu in the very near future.
Although he had always expected trouble, he had hoped that
the pressures would not become serious until the spring, by
which time he would have the profits of his Baccarat Bank (God
willing) to enable him to fight off the dangers. But the most
recent news from Corfu made it clear that inflation and recession were working very much more quickly than he had anticipated; his supply of ready cash in Greece was running down
fast, and most of the securities against which he might have
borrowed were lodged with the management of the Casino in
the Palazzo Vendramin to guarantee his bank. No, Max, thought
Lykiadopoulos; if fresh money should become available, from
Detterling or any other source, this is no time to spend it on
gilding the decay of Venice.

'. . . And so you see,' Fielding Gray was saying to Tom Llewyllyn,
'there can be absolutely no doubt. Listen:

'"When Maria told me that Euphemia was with child, I at

first assumed that the child must be fitzAvon's – that is, my Lord Rollesden's. Since his lordship was still hiding in my villa near Oriago, the misfortune was not beyond repair. Euphemia could be taken to Oriago and there married to Lord Rollesden-in-Silvis, and the haste and secrecy of the wedding could later be explained by the dangers and uncertainties of the times. I therefore sent word to Euphemia to attend me in my study in the tower, meaning to tell her, with what kindness I could muster, of my purpose. However, when I reached the tower myself, my daughter, and with her Piero, were there before me. Doubtless they knew it had been my intention (before Maria's communication put all else from my mind) to meet with friends in the Piazza that afternoon; and so they thought to have the tower to themselves.

' "Their voices were raised in agitation, and, not expecting my intrusion, they did not hear me as I mounted the stairs ... upon which, troubled by the tone of their exchanges, I halted to listen. Piero was beseeching his sister to yield to his judgement in some matter, though I could not at first make out in what. Finally, however, he spoke to this effect : we have sinned the sin already, he said, and sown the seed of our punishment; but meanwhile we may yet enjoy the pleasures for a season without further increase in the penalty. As I crossed the threshold of the room, his arm had already gone about her, and she, for all her tears, was making ready to receive more than fraternal comfort. 'I wish that Umberto was here with us,' said Piero, then looked up, at the sound of my step, and shrank away, both from her and from me, trying to hide and repair the disorders of his dress". '

'Poor Fernando,' said Tom; 'not his day.'

'Nobody's day. But Fernando seems to have collected his wits pretty quickly. After all, he was a civilized and urbane man, not much given to antiquated superstitions and taboos. "Shameful" all this certainly was – but not incurable. Let his original plan hold, he said to himself; let fitzAvon be made to marry Euphemia – under pain of being kicked out of his refuge from the French at Oriago – and Euphemia's child would then be satisfactorily accounted for. So Fernando, all credit to him, simply proceeded to tidy up. He stopped the game that was afoot and forbade its resumption at any future time, but he eschewed moralizing. He dried Euphemia's tears, told Piero to brace himself up, and then explained to them both what would happen. After which, he despatched a reliable servant to Oriago,

with a message to fitzAvon/Rollesden to tell him that Euphemia
was in the club and that he, fitzAvon, must provide her with
respectable sponsorship. And all might have gone as merry as a
marriage bell, had it not been for recent events, of which Fernando as yet knew nothing, in the villa near Oriago.'

'Tom and Fielding are taking a long time with that manuscript,'
said Piero to Daniel in the tower. 'I must go now for dinner in
the Palazzo.'

'Please stay,' said Daniel.

'Mr Lykiadopoulos will be angry if I am not at dinner. He
might find out I was here, and then he would be angrier still.'

'You need only stay for a moment. Piero . . . I have been meaning to tell you all the afternoon. I shall not be able to come with
you to see the Carpaccios.'

'But you promised—'

'—And events have overtaken my promise.'

Piero considered this. At length he said,

'So it is to be sooner than you thought.'

'I think so.'

'But Daniel, there are doctors in Venice, for God's sake—'

'—I am thinking of my own. No doubt there are doctors in
Venice – who could prolong the agony for me, and the inconvenience to my friends, for weeks or even months. Common
sense and common decency reject such a notion. I shall simply
do as Plato tells me to : remain in my station until I am relieved
of it.'

Piero nodded and said nothing.

'Now you had better go,' Daniel croaked at him. 'There is no
point in upsetting Mr Lykiadopoulos or anybody else on my
account; that is specifically what I do not wish.'

Piero nodded again, rose, touched Daniel briefly on the cheek,
and went.

' "Meanwhile",' Fielding was reading aloud to Tom, ' "my messenger to Oriago was crossed by another who was coming thence
to Venice. It was the local priest that had written to me. My
guest (whom he knew only as Humbert fitzAvon) had shamed
my hospitality, he wrote. He had seduced and got with child a
peasant girl of thirteen years. The peasants had been likely to
kill him, but the priest had restrained them, urging that fitz-
Avon was under my protection and that in any case it was need-

ful that he should marry the girl whom he had abused, to make
the unborn child lawful and, so far as possible, keep disgrace
from the girl's family. To this all had assented. FitzAvon,
under constraint, had made some crude profession of submitting
to the Catholic faith – enough to satisfy the priest that he could
be married in the Roman Church – and the marriage ceremony
would happen that very day, would indeed already have happened by the time the messenger reached me".'

'Back to square one,' said Tom. 'No husband for Euphemia.'

'And a very grand husband, if she'd only know it, for a
thirteen-year-old peasant girl. From then on events moved very
fast. A few hours after Fernando received his letter from the
priest, his own messenger returned from Oriago – having found
fitzAvon both married and dead on the same day.'

'Dead?'

'Yes. As soon as fitzAvon and the girl were safely pronounced
man and wife, the peasants hanged him from the nearest tree.
"They still wanted revenge for the violation of the girl – for
such they said it was – and they were too foolish," writes Fernando, "to realize that fitzAvon, even only as fitzAvon, was a
man of substance who might have done much for them if treated
with respect. In him they saw only a fugitive from the French,
and they were, among other things, afraid lest the French should
discover they were harbouring him among them." Fernando
goes on to say some disagreeable things about the local
peasantry, who were "squalid creatures at best, made sullen and
cretinous by the vapours which are exhaled from the marshes,
and much given to intermarriage". Rather like the people who
used to live in the Cambridgeshire fens, I suppose.'

'Why did the Albani have a villa in such a district?'

'Lots of Venetians had their villas pretty much in that district.'

'But not bang in the marshes, which is where he implies this
one was.'

'The Albani owned other villas as well. Apparently they'd
picked this one up on the cheap, when the chap who built it
died. He was notoriously eccentric in several ways, and that
may explain his choice of site. Anyway, it seems it wasn't too
bad there in the summer, which was when the Albani would
want to use it.'

'And what time of year was it now – when all these high
jinks were going on?'

'The spring of 1797. But fitzAvon had been there for some time, remember, and it must have been horrid when he first arrived in the middle of winter. No wonder he needed diversion. The stupid thing about it was that he needn't have gone into hiding so soon. The French didn't get to Venice until the early summer of 1797, and he could have stayed on there months longer than he did.'

'Thereby avoiding death at the hands of the peasantry.'

'Yes. I expect he'd been panicked by rumours. Anyway, there it was. On top of all his other troubles, Fernando now knew that fitzAvon was decorating a tree near his own country villa. So off he went to sort *that* out. He saw the priest; he saw the little girl ("coarse and sturdy, eminently fit, and fit only, for the satisfaction of a brute and casual appetite"); and he saw the peasants. They were uncontrite, even quite pleased with themselves. Fernando, though angry with them for their mindless violence, and annoyed that by the enforced marriage and then the murder they had doubly deprived Euphemia of a possible saviour, had to admit that from most points of view they had done the world a favour. Together with the priest and a local apothecary, he fudged up what would pass for a death certificate, buried fitzAvon – under that name – in the local church, and returned to Venice to write an account "to Lord Rollesden's noble father, the Earl of Muscateer, as at that time he was still titled".

'But before he could get down to that, there was another job to be done. Piero, during his father's brief absence, had run amok. Whether it was grief at fitzAvon's death, or shame at being caught out with his sister by Fernando, or the realization that Euphemia's predicament was now absolutely desperate – whatever it was, something had proved too much for Piero, never, one suspects, a well-balanced character even at his best. He had, quite simply, strangled Euphemia and then blown half his own head off with one of an elegant pair of duelling pistols which fitzAvon had given him for his last birthday. There is some speculation, in Fernando's text, that perhaps Piero was trying to seduce Euphemia, despite his father's recent admonishment, that this time she refused him, and that he strangled her accidentally in the ensuing struggle. Equally, it seems possible that he did it to provide her with an infallible solution to her problem. In either case guilt and/or misery must have given him quite sufficient motive to make away with himself as well.

'Once again, Fernando showed great talent for tidying up. It seems he was a substantial benefactor of an institution called the Vecchia Scuola della Misericordia—'

'—I know, that huge barn of a building up near the Madonna dell' Orto—'

'—Right. Then as now, there was a tiny plot of grass, covered with weeds and brambles, tucked between one wall of the Scuola and a minor canal. If you go past there these days, you'll see what looks like a white stone hidden inside the bramble bushes. If you're very sharp-eyed, you may spot two or three of them. Under one of these are the remains of Piero and Euphemia, who were hastily buried there by discreet courtesy of the Councillors of the Scuola, who were doubtless mindful of benefits both past and potential. As Fernando himself observed, "Growing fear and conjecture in the city about the proximity of the French" (for now, Tom, they really were proximate) "caused at this period such laxity in official deportment as made possible the disposal, without enquiry or formality, of the bodies of my two unhappy children".'

'Having seen to which, Fernando now had the job of writing to Lord Muscateer. What did he tell *him*?'

'He very nearly told him nothing at all, because he only just managed to get his letter on to the last British ship to leave Venice before the frogs arrived. However, despatch it he did, at a steep price which was to be borne by Lord Muscateer on its delivery, and here is the summary Fernando gives of the information which his lordship was to receive for his money.

'Fernando wrote, first, that he had the honour to inform the Earl of Muscateer that his son and heir, Lord Rollesden-in-Silvis, was dead. About the circumstances Fernando tells us he was tactful : Lord Rollesden had been friendly with himself and his family, he wrote, so friendly that he had eventually revealed the true identity which underlay the *alias* of fitzAvon; when the French threat to Venice had begun to appear serious, Fernando had offered Lord Rollesden a retreat, in his less conspicuous identity of Mr fitzAvon, in his villa near Oriago in the Veneto; and there ... "Lord Rollesden, I wrote to the Earl, had been apprehended by those who wished him harm and, at the last, murdered by them, though honourable burial was later afforded him". If one considers the nature of fitzAvon's employment, the formula was quite plausible.'

'Yes – and also vague enough to account for the later rumour in England that he had been killed while fighting off French agents.'

'Certainly. It had the merit of being truthful as far as it went and allowing those who wished to put a charitable construction on it. As we shall see, Fernando Albani was anxious to let Lord Muscateer and the Sarum family down very lightly. He followed the announcement and account of the death with details of where the body was buried – "in case his lordship should wish to visit that melancholy spot when the times were more favourable to travel" – and an assurance that the death had been officially notified and recorded ... "although I had of course to tell his lordship that in the situation which then obtained in Northern Italy and the Veneto there could be no question of bringing the malefactors to justice".'

'Just what did he mean by "officially notified and recorded"?'

'Presumably that the details of the dead man had been logged by the priest in the register of the church where he was buried. With civil conditions growing more chaotic every day, I doubt whether anything further could have been done in that line, even if anyone had wanted it done.'

'But in fact we know from a little earlier in the memoir that the dead man was recorded as Humbert fitzAvon. Would that have amounted to proper official proof of the death of Lord Rollesden-in-Silvis?'

'Yes, I think so, because a lot of people other than Fernando knew about the *alias*. For example, those that first smuggled young Rollesden/fitzAvon out of England.'

'Fair enough,' said Tom. 'And of course one forgets that in those days people were not as fastidious in proving such matters as we are. The word of a *bona fide* gentleman-merchant like Fernando Albani would have been enough to satisfy even a court that fitzAvon-cum-Rollesden was dead. What else did Fernando write to the father?'

'A brief and formal commiseration, with which, he tells us, he concluded the letter.'

'Nothing about fitzAvon's marriage? Or the fact that the bride was pregnant?'

'Nothing. And so now, as you will appreciate, we are approaching the pith of the whole matter. Fernando states in this memoir that he did not inform Lord Muscateer of Rollesden's marriage, or of the child that was on the way, for the following reasons.' Fielding picked up the MS. ' "The family was ancient and noble",' he read. ' "It was not, in my view, fitting that it's line should continue through the coupling of such a vile man as I now knew Lord Rollesden to be and of such a woman (if woman she could be called) as the peasant hoyden whom he had been forced to make his wife; for the marsh peasantry, as I have already written, are brutish and sullen, and their stock degraded. By concealing the fact of Lord Rollesden's marriage, I should be leaving my Lord Muscateer free to assume that his heir was now dead without issue, and to make such arrangements as he could for the more proper inheritance of his Earldom and Estate. The bride, now the widow, knew only that she had married one Humbert fitzAvon, and neither she, nor her people, nor the priest, would ever be the wiser; there could be no chance, therefore, that she would claim or presume on the place that was now legally hers (and her child's) among the noble clan which her husband had dishonoured." Fernando,' said Fielding, 'seems to have had a touching regard for the English nobility. Listen to this. "Some time after I wrote to his lordship, I learned that he had been raised to the high dignity of an English Marquisate, as 1st Marquis Canteloupe of the Estuary of the Severn. This only confirmed me in thinking that I had been right to protect so illustrious a House against continuance through the get of a vicious criminal on a common country bawd." '

'Ah,' said Tom, 'but *what* get? Did that girl at Oriago have a son?'

'Fernando doesn't tell us. All he says is that he took early opportunity to persuade the girl's family that her name should be changed from fitzAvon, as it now was, to the more Italian-sounding Filavoni, giving as his reason that she would be happier in their community if so called. His real motive, of course, must have been stop the use in the area of the alien name of fitzAvon, which might later have attracted the attention of the curious. So the Signora fitzAvon became the Signora Filavoni' – he lifted the MS and let it fall back on to the table before them – 'and there the story ends.'

He grinned savagely at Tom.

'Except that it doesn't,' said Tom, returning the grin. 'Because if the thirteen-year-old Widow Filavoni gave birth to a boy, that boy was entitled to be called Lord Rollesden-in-Silvis, and was from birth the lawful heir apparent to the Earldom of Muscateer and to the Marquisate of Canteloupe when it was later conferred on his grandfather.'

'Exactly so. And if he grew and had children of his own, as peasants tend to even when they *are* of degraded stock and live in a marsh, then there is at least a possibility that the line of Filavoni is still extant.'

'And if *that* is the case,' said Tom with relish, 'then every single Marquis Canteloupe after the first has been bogus. Beginning with the son whom the first marquis got on his second wife, and ending with our good friend Detterling. They have all been standing in the shoes which should rightfully have been occupied by the rural descendants of Humbert fitzAvon and the barely pubescent slut with whom he was joined in holy wedlock.'

'If,' said Fielding, 'and only if, that barely pubescent slut gave birth to fitzAvon's posthumous son. A miscarriage, or a daughter, and the thing ends there.'

'Well,' said Tom, 'I think – don't you? – that we had better go and find out what happened at this momentous birth in the marshes. In the interest of historical truth.'

'And if there *is* still a family of Filavoni,' said Fielding softly, 'what duty do we have to that truth?'

'Let us consider that problem when and if it arises?'

'Very well,' said Fielding. He consulted a page of the MS. 'I have been talking loosely of Oriago,' he said, 'but in fact the Albani villa stood in a small village some way outside and called Samuele – after Moses Samuele, the architect and first owner of the villa, of which the village was a later accretion.'

'Samuele?' said Tom. 'He'd be the chap you were talking about just now – the notorious eccentric who liked marshy sites?'

'Yes. An interesting character – but that's another story. The point is, for us, that the church in which fitzAvon was married and buried is the village church, which was also built by Samuele, despite his being a Jew, in the eighteenth century. It was later named, for him or after him, the church of San Samuele – though God knows how he arranged that.'

'So we look for an eighteenth-century church near the villa, and we ask the priest to see the records.'

'That's about it,' Fielding said.

'And we'd better take Piero. We may need an interpreter.'

'That means letting Piero in on the story.'

'What harm in that? It'll be nice to have an audience to see how clever we've been.'

'Discretion?'

'We shall be telling Daniel in any case, and Daniel would certainly tell Piero, whether we wanted him to or not. They're thicker than ever, those two.'

'Piero's been so hostile to our investigations,' grumped Fielding, 'that he doesn't deserve to be told.'

'Don't be such a baby, Fielding. I'm not too keen on Piero myself, as you well know, but we're going to need an interpreter for an expedition like this, and he's the obvious choice.'

Piero was told the story on the way to Oriago the next morning. To Fielding's irritation, he showed little interest in it and no surprise. The only stage at which he was moved to comment was when Fielding was telling him about the little plot, by the Scuola della Misericordia, where Euphemia and her brother were buried.

'I knew there were sad ghosts there,' Piero said. 'Miss Baby Llewyllyn told me.'

'Baby told you?' said Tom.

'Yes. In a letter. So Daniel and I went by there in a boat one day to see the stones. Baby says that the ghosts rise up to go to the Casino degli Spiriti, where they mingle with the ghosts of the friends who once met there, and that with them they can be happy for a time. But now that you have found their secret,' Piero said accusingly to Fielding, 'they will stay alone by the Misericordia for very shame.'

'Piero . . . you cannot believe in all that.'

'Who are you, Major Gray, to say what I can believe? I believe it is better not to meddle with unhappy secrets.'

'Until you know what the secret is,' said Tom, 'you cannot know that it is unhappy.'

'You both knew . . . from that first manuscript which I found for you, just from looking at the picture on the front . . . that this secret must be horrible and unhappy. Why did you have to meddle?'

'There is another secret still to come,' said Tom. 'You'd better get on with the story, Fielding. Piero needs to know it all if he's to be efficient, and we're not far off Oriago.'

'*Oriago – dieci minuti*,' said the driver of the car which they had hired. Since the fellow did not know English, Fielding reflected, he had seized on the word 'Oriago' as an excuse to remind them, in the officiously democratic mode of modern Italy, that he too was of the party.

'*Grazia a voi,*' Fielding said, deliberately choosing the brusquest form of the second person pronoun and bringing a scowl to the driver's face. And then to Piero, 'Now for the rest of it.'

'Today or very soon,' interrupted Piero, 'I should have been going with Daniel to see the Carpaccios in the Accademia. But now he says he is too weak. Yet we, his friends, are not sitting with him for company. We are going to Oriago. Why is this?'

'*Oriago nove minuti,*' interjected the driver.

'Daniel prefers that we do not make a fuss,' said Tom. 'Now listen to Fielding.'

Piero shrugged, but now listened quite attentively as Fielding rehearsed the actions taken or omitted by Fernando Albani after the death of Lord Rollesden and started to draw the necessary deductions.

'You are going to say,' said Piero, cutting Fielding short, 'that perhaps your friend Lord Canteloupe is not Lord Canteloupe; that perhaps this Lord Rollesden left successors in Oriago.'

'Yes,' said Fielding.

'*Oriago cinque minuti,*' said the driver venomously.

'There you are, you see,' said Piero, quietly triumphant: 'that is what comes of meddling with such manuscripts.'

'Please tell the driver,' said Fielding, refusing to be baited, 'to enquire for a village called Samuele.'

Piero spoke quickly to the driver in Italian and received a gleeful answer.

'He says there is no such place,' said Piero. 'He hates me because I come from Sicily and speak English, and he hates you because you are paying him, and he will do his best to disoblige us. I shall have to enquire myself.'

The driver reluctantly obeyed an order to stop. Piero limped from the car to a group of men who were standing in front of a tavern. There was much shaking of heads and one venerable old gentleman crossed himself.

'They say it is a difficult place to find,' said Piero when he was back in the car, 'and that it is better not to find it. But I think I now know the way.'

Piero instructed the driver to turn left over a broad canal, shouted at him when he tried to turn right instead, and then directed him, when they were about a furlong beyond the canal, to drive down a minor road which forked away to the left across low, damp fields that were intersected by frequent willow-lined ditches. The driver started whining at Piero.

'He says the road is bad,' Piero told Fielding and Tom, 'and he must be given extra money.'

'Tell him we'll settle all that with his boss when we get back to the Piazzale Roma.'

On receiving this information, the driver stopped, got out, urinated at the side of the road, and then, after some leisurely stretching and scratching, lit a cigarette. At this point, Piero called to him through the window in a low voice, whereupon the driver reeled slightly, seemed to lose an inch or two in height, got back into the car, and drove on across the fields.

'What did you say to him, Piero?'

'That unless he drove on, I would put a spell on his pool of urine that would make him impotent.'

'He can't have believed you.'

'Probably not. But Sicilians have always been famous as witches, and since this man is a fool and a poltroon – poltroon means a coward, yes? – he will not care to risk it.'

A few minutes later Piero told the driver to turn off down a cart-track which ran along the top of a dyke between two flooded fields. The man sniffed, blinked piteously, and obeyed. On the far side of the fields, the dyke ran into a bank; the track continued through the bank in a small cutting, then passed through a copse. When the car emerged from this, it was forced to turn, with the track, and proceed alongside a high stone wall, behind which was a thick forest of pine trees. Eventually they came to a gateway without a gate, followed the track through it, drove on through about a hundred yards of pine forest, and came out into a meadow, at the edge of which the track abruptly ceased. On the far side of the meadow were a few small houses of dull red brick, beyond these a ridge perhaps fifty yards high and on the spine of the ridge a handsome villa with a pillared portico.

'Samuele,' Piero said.

'But where is the church?'

'We shall enquire.'

Piero took the car keys out of the dashboard, climbed out, and started to limp across the meadow. The driver, torn between a desire to execrate the village for its remoteness and the need to preserve his *bella figura* by pretending the place did not exist, compromised by closing his eyes tightly and shaking both fists in the air, and so did not discern the sequestration of his keys for some minutes. When he did so, he hurtled out of the car, took three steps on to the meadow, and then realized that it was very damp and that Piero, followed by Tom and Fielding, had by now almost reached the far side of it; which being the case, he blubbered noisily for thirty seconds, went snivelling back to the car, and shortly afterwards fell childishly asleep.

'The church,' said Tom to his companions, 'will be more or less a private chapel to the house. I expect it's on the far side.'

'There don't seem to be many people about,' Fielding said. 'But the villa appears to be cared for. I wonder whether the Albani still own it.'

'No,' said a sharp voice; 'I do.'

A trim man, in his late forties and a short fawn overcoat, walked from behind one of the little brick houses and came towards them. As he came, he picked violently at the skin round his left thumb.

'Shit,' muttered Tom; 'Jude Holbrook. We all wondered where you'd been, Jude,' he said, 'this many a year.'

'Hong Kong, I heard,' said Fielding, remembering, with a resentment much diluted by the passage of fourteen years, that the last time he'd seen Jude Holbrook Jude had threatened him with an open bottle of acid.

'Hong Kong for money,' said Holbrook; 'now here for peace and quiet. Not to mention obscurity. I do not like being disturbed. Why have you come, you two? And who's your little friend ?'

'Our interpreter,' said Fielding. 'We didn't know, you see, that we'd find an English-speaking acquaintance here. How is that amiable mother of yours?'

'She lives here and reads books.'

'What do *you* do, Jude?' said Tom. 'You were never one for books.'

'I mind my business. What do you want?'

'To look at the church of San Samuele; to inspect a tombstone which should be in or near it; and to examine the parish register.'

'Why?'

'Tom is doing historical research.'

'Yes,' said Holbrook. 'I remember he was always nosing into something or other.' He wrinkled his mouth, like a bookmaker calculating a difficult shade of odds. 'If I show you the church and the rest,' he said, 'will you go away and not come back?'

'Gladly.'

'And will you promise to tell no one that you've seen me?'

'Yes, if that's what you want. But can you trust us?'

'Short of killing you, which would displease my mother, trust you is all that I can do.'

'Who is this gentleman?' Piero asked.

'Never you mind,' Holbrook said. 'Come on to the church, all of you. The priest's away but it's open. And I know where he keeps the register.'

He led the way up the gentle slope of the ridge. They skirted the villa itself, which stood in rough open grass, without garden or proximate adornment of any kind. Then they descended towards a grove of holm-oak, beyond which was a small building with a classical portico (a replica of the one in front of the villa) and without tower or transept.

'You don't realize it's a church,' Holbrook explained, 'until you get inside. When you do, there's all the usual Catholic paraphernalia, also two or three slabs in the floor carved with the names of the bodies buried underneath. Samuele – the chap who built the place – is one of them.'

'Where are the villagers buried?'

'There's a cemetery out by the marshes for them. What's left of them. Most of them went away fifty years ago – or so the priest tells me.'

They all walked up the steps into the portico and through a narrow wooden door into the church.

'Slabs,' said Holbrook, and pointed to one: 'there's Samuele's.'

MOSES SAMUELE
Natus Kal. Jan. 1705 Obiit Kal. Jan. 1780

'Neat,' said Holbrook. 'Exactly seventy-five years old. Tidy number.' He picked at the skin round his thumb. 'That one over there is worth looking at. Rum sort of name for a wop.'

HUMBERTUS FITZAVON Armiger
Ob. 1797

'Only the year,' murmured Fielding to Tom. 'Discreet.' And to Holbrook, 'What about the register?'

'In a cupboard behind the altar. The priest is very proud of it because it's been kept up properly since 1745. Most of the

registers in Italy – or in England, come to that – are unreliable
any time before about 1830. But this one was taken special
care of. And there's a very odd tale about why.'

Holbrook led them behind the reredos (a rather chilly low-
relief of the raising of Lazarus) and opened a cupboard.

'I have to dine the priest once in a way,' Holbrook went on;
'my mother likes it. Not that she's a Rom. Cat., far from it, but
she thinks it's the thing to do. And when the priest comes to
dine, he tells his stories – the same ones every time, but this one
about the register isn't at all bad.'

Jude's really being quite pleasant, Fielding thought; I wonder
why. Making the best of a bad job? Wanting to send us away
happy so that we'll keep our side of the bargain? Very possibly;
he always had a sound sense of business.

'It seems,' Holbrook was saying, 'that this man Samuele moved
into the villa after he'd built it and encouraged several peasant
families to come and live nearby and form a new village – for
the benefit of which he built this church. All this would have
been around 1735, when Samuele was thirty. Well, in 1743, three
small children disappeared out of the village, and another two in
1744. They vanished just like that – there one second and gone
the next. But the funny thing was, the parents didn't seem to
mind. When the priest of the time went round asking questions,
the parents shrugged the whole thing off and muttered some
excuse about how the children had gone off to visit relations or the
like. But since the children never came back, the priest at length
knew that something was badly wrong, and eventually he got a
notion of what was happening from an old woman on her
death bed. Although her tale was very garbled and unclear, the
gist seemed to be that Samuele, who had several commissions
to build villas for rich clients in the Veneto, was buying children from their parents in the village and burying them alive
under the foundations of his buildings, in order to recommend
the buildings to the old gods and protect them against floods
and so on – a common practice, I understand, in certain pagan
eras. Apparently the clients knew all about it – or so the story
went – and gladly paid a considerable extra sum to have these
human sacrifices performed.

'Given the rather curious nature of Samuele's erudition and
the reported contents of his library, the priest was disposed to
believe the dying woman; but he had no proof – he hadn't even
got official proof that the children had ever existed, because his

predecessors, and up till then himself, had kept the register so
slackly that most births and baptisms had simply gone un-
recorded. So in order to make certain that from now on he had
at least had a proper roll of his flock, the priest determined to
keep an immaculate register, a determination of which he informed Samuele, with a quiet hint that any further unexplained
disappearances would be reported to the Inquisitions both of
Church and State. After which caution, I'm told, Samuele gave
up his previous practice or went elsewhere for his victims. But
the custom of keeping a precise register persisted up to his
death in 1780 and by that time was too well-established a tradi-
tion to be discontinued. Any priest would have felt himself
ashamed not to keep up the high standards of those before him.
Hence we have a detailed record of birth, marriage, mis-
demeanour and death in the village of Samuele from around
1745 to this very day.'

Holbrook produced a pile of leather-bound volumes and
dumped them on top of the cupboard.

'But why,' said Piero, 'if Samuele was so wicked, did this
church continue to be named for him?'

'For the same reason,' said Tom, 'as the Greeks called the
Furies "the Kindly ones". Or so one may presume. It is prudent
to flatter what you fear.'

Holbrook gave a sour chuckle.

'Always the pedant, Tom,' he said. 'Even in the old days,
when you were a cheque-bouncing, whore-grubbing drunk, you
were full of sly classical precedents for your behaviour.'

'Were you ever a cheque-bouncing, whore-grubbing drunk?'
Piero asked Tom .

'Yes,' said Tom. And to Fielding, 'Where do we begin with
this register?'

'With the wedding and burial of our hero,' said Fielding, 'and
then the widow's change of name – it should certainly be in
here – from fitzAvon to Filavoni—'

In England, Detterling obtained special permission from the
Headmistress of Radigund's School to take Baby out for two
hours on a weekday.

'I don't mind telling you,' Miss Wentworth Rex said to Baby,
'that I'm breaking the rule simply and solely because he's the
Marquess Canteloupe.'

Baby smiled with polite scepticism.

'Don't grin at me like that, Tullia,' said the Headmistress. 'The truth is that I'm a colossal snob, and I may as well admit it.'

In the end, Detterling did not take Baby out; they walked all round the school and its grounds instead, because Baby, who was proud of Radigund's, wanted to show it to her friend.

'You like it here, don't you?' Detterling said.

'Yes. And I like the things we do I wouldn't want to miss what I'd be doing now – for anyone except you.'

'What would you be doing now?'

'Statics.'

'Sounds a bit dry.'

'Yes,' said Baby : 'but it gives you such nice exact answers.'

After a little while, as they walked round the cricket field, Detterling said :

'Bad news, sweetheart. That's why I'm here.'

'Daniel?'

'Daniel. It can't be long.'

'Did Poppa write to you?'

'Oddly enough, no. It was Piero. He thinks that Tom – your father – doesn't quite realize how near it is for Daniel. He thinks that Daniel is deliberately misleading Tom, so that it can happen very suddenly, without a long and ghastly time for everyone to wait first.'

'But Daniel must be showing – well – signs, however hard he's trying.'

'Piero says not. Or rather, he says, there are signs, but only very slight ones, and everyone else, even Tom, is too busy and selfish to see them.'

'Rather conceited of Piero to say that.'

'Yes. But apparently he spends more time with Daniel than the rest – or has done just lately. Do you think he's telling the truth?'

'He has no reason not to.'

'That's rather my view. So I'm going to Venice tomorrow. As good a day as any, and an old friend of mine is going there on business, so I can fly out with him.'

'Be careful of Fielding Gray, my lord.'

'What did you say?'

'Be careful of Fielding Gray,' said Baby in a puzzled voice. 'The poor ghosts say that he has learned their secret and that from this he will learn others.'

'What ghosts, sweetheart?'

'I have heard them before. When I was in Venice.'

'Their secrets can have nothing to do with me.'

'Fielding Gray knows their secrets. Be careful of Fielding Gray.' Baby paused for a mere second .'I'm glad you're flying out with a friend,' she said, as though continuing the conversation from the point at which Detterling had mentioned this; 'it will be more fun like that.'

'. . . So there it is,' said Tom to Fielding, as he closed the last volume of the Register of the Church of San Samuele. 'Paolo Filavoni, now aged ten years and odd months. Orphaned son and only issue of Giuseppe and Susanna Filavoni, who were drowned in the floods of sixty-six. Taken into care by a spinster sister of his mother's, one Anna Tomasino.' He consulted the notes which he had taken while going through the register. 'And so now, we gather, this Paolo is the sole surviving descendant, in the male line, of Umberto and Cara fitzAvon, who were married in this church on April 7, 1797 : of which happy couple, Umberto died of "violent misadventure" on the day of the wedding, while Cara, subsequently *"per gratiam et officium Episcopi"* called Cara Filavoni, was delivered, on November 10 of 1797, of a male child baptised as Nicolo. In the course of time, Nicolo begat in wedlock Giacomo, Serena and Giovanni, the last of whom died in infancy; Giacomo begat in wedlock Maria and Pietro; Pietro lawfully sired Giorgio, Teresa and Serafina . . . and so on and so forth. Small families, you notice, by peasant standards, and a high rate of early mortality, doubtless due to the unwholesome climate of these marshes, particularly in the winter. A curse to the Filavoni, perhaps, but a boon to us, because it simplifies the family tree and now reduces the field, beyond any question, to one. And so where,' said Tom, turning to Jude Holbrook, 'can we find the spinster, Anna Tomasino, to whom Paolo Filavoni is in ward?'

Holbrook smiled urbanely and gently picked at his thumb.

'What's your interest?' he said.

'As Fielding has already mentioned,' said Tom, 'I am doing historical research.'

'Into peasant brats of the Veneto?'

'I am studying the decline and fall of the Serene Republic – which, as you will remember, Jude, finally fell in 1797, the same year as that in which Umberto fitzAvon, whose name you showed us on that stone over there, died here in Samuele. Now,' said Tom, in the most plausible manner he could muster, 'fitz-Avon, before he came here, had been prominent in social affairs in Venice in the days when her collapse was imminent, and so he will figure in a chapter which I am preparing about the social scene of the Serenissima in its death throes. Out of sheer curiosity,' he concluded smoothly, 'I should like to see this Paolo Filavoni, who is fitzAvon's direct descendant. He might be good for a footnote.'

'You're taking a lot of trouble for a footnote. Who was this fitzAvon anyhow? As I said earlier, it's an odd name for a wop.'

'He was probably the son of an English tourist and a Venetian courtesan,' Tom lied easily, 'called La Rotella. Hence his own name – the sort of fantasy name which an Italian tart might invent for her English bastard – and hence also the young man's need to take refuge here in 1797.'

Holbrook looked very sharply at Tom, and then, to Tom's relief and Fielding's, lost interest in the whole matter. His face turned suddenly grey, he fumbled in his pocket and rapidly swallowed two tablets which he found there, and then he tottered away down the church.

'Jude . . . are you ill?'

'Yes. Go and see this child, if you must, and then leave here. My mother and I want to be left alone. It isn't much to ask.'

'Why not sit down for a moment?'

'I must go to my mother.'

With some difficulty, Holbrook negotiated the steps down from the portico and stumbled slowly away through the grove of holm-oak.

'He didn't tell us where to find the boy,' said Fielding.

'Let us trouble him no more. I will find out for you,' Piero said.

He led Tom and Fielding back on to the raised ground (where they overtook Holbrook, who curtly gestured them on their way), past the villa and down towards the brick houses. He knocked on the door of the first of these, talked briefly to a humped old woman in black, and then led on to a cottage which stood slightly apart by a small, black pool. A large and slovenly woman with long, grey, greasy hair eventually answered his knock. After arguing with her for some minutes, Piero beckoned to Fielding and Tom.

'She wants to know why you wish to see the boy,' he said: 'he is only one more orphan.'

'Tell her,' said Fielding, 'that we are journalists who are investigating families that were broken up during the floods of sixty-six.'

Piero argued further with the woman. At length he said, 'If you are journalists, she says it will cost you five thousand lire to see the child.'

Fielding handed a new note to the woman, who examined it with a mixture of delight and suspicion, then yapped something at Piero.

'She wants the money in single thousands,' Piero said: 'round here they are not familiar with anything larger.'

Fielding produced five crumpled and dirty notes of a thousand lire. The woman took them, reluctantly returned the larger note which Fielding had first given her, and then backed into the living-room-cum-bedroom-cum-kitchen which apparently comprised the entire interior of the cottage. Still walking backwards, she crossed the room to a window which overlooked a small allotment. She turned, opened the window, and signed to her three guests to come to it.

Quietly digging in the allotment was an exceedingly handsome little boy who had auburn hair, wide and strong shoulders for his age, and classically formed bare legs.

'There you are,' said Piero indifferently: 'Paolo Filavoni. If I have been understanding all your talk this morning correctly, the rightful Marquess Canteloupe of the Estuary of the Severn.'

The boy stopped digging, stuck his spade into the mud, and smiled at them, pleasantly enough but rather slyly, Fielding thought. Then, with a quick movement of his left hand, he jerked his shorts down from his haunches, and with his right hand, skipping and cackling for glee, he began to waggle his penis at his audience.

'Paolo,' called the woman sharply.

But Paolo merely cackled the louder, skipped and waggled the more heartily, until the woman rushed from the cottage and appeared in the allotment. As she approached him, Paolo flexed his knees gracefully, pointed his piece at her, and then, emitting a series of deep and imbecile grunts, began to piss fiercely up into her face.

'A chip off the old block,' said Fielding; and the pinched little mouth began to throb and twist and gape like a fresh scar in his ruined face, issuing pipe after pipe of thin and self-congratulatory laughter.

PART FIVE

THE SURVIVORS

The friend with whom Detterling was flying out to Venice was Peter Morrison, who had succeeded the previous Lord Canteloupe as Minister of Commerce. Detterling had discovered that Morrison was going to Venice when he had called on him in London, some days before, to request his help in disposing of his man-servant. Since the corporal had now gone almost totally if quite harmlessly insane, and appeared to imagine that as Detterling's self-styled 'chamberlain' he was a high-ranking officer in the service of some semi-Royal prince palatine, it had occurred to Detterling that the man needed a change of scene along with some therapeutic occupation which would take his mind off his fantasies of court and castle. He had therefore proposed to Peter Morrison, who was an old and understanding ally, that the corporal should be sent down to Morrison's farm in Norfolk, where he could be employed on elementary tasks in the company of Morrison's once brilliant but now imbecile son, Nickie. Nickie and the corporal, he pointed out, had been on friendly terms since Nickie was a little boy, and they might now derive some solace from each other's companionship, if either of them could still remember who the other was. Furthermore, the corporal could make himself useful in tidying up after Nickie, who was apt to be rather messy in habit and in person.

Peter Morrison had seen the possibilities of this arrangement and agreed to a trial run of two months. It was after this that he had told Detterling he was going to Venice.

'You remember that tour you went on for your cousin Canteloupe just before he died?' Morrison had said.

'Very clearly. The idea was to check up whether anyone had caught on to the old man's new methods of industrial swindling – the ones he'd worked out with Somerset Lloyd-James.'

Morrison winced.

'You mean, new methods of industrial diplomacy,' he said:

'and your conclusion was that these were still valid?'

'Right. No one had rumbled them, as far as I could make out.'

'Well, I'm sorry to tell you, Canteloupe, that now somebody has. Or so we think. There's a big deal afoot with an Italian corporation in Mestre, which is being negotiated under the aegis of my Ministry. We are using the Canteloupe style of diplomacy aforesaid, and the whole thing seems to be turning sour on us. I'm going out to take a hand myself in a day or two.'

'To Mestre? Rotten luck.'

'Oh, I shall put up in Venice, of course.'

Whereupon Detterling had remembered that he too must go to Venice before long, and the two men had agreed to fly out together.

During the few days before the flight, Detterling had done three things. First, he had persuaded his 'chamberlain' to undertake a 'delicate mission' to Norfolk, where he would be required to act as tutor and bodyguard to the eldest son of one of Her Majesty's Ministers of State. Secondly, he had gone to see Baby Llewyllyn, had told her of his fears for Daniel and had heard of hers for himself. Thirdly, he had rung up his friend, Leonard Percival:

'Can you take a few days away from Jermyn Street, Leonard?' he had said.

'What for, Detterling – sorry, Canteloupe?'

'I want you to meet me in Venice. I've had a ... rather curiously based but very sincere warning that someone there might make trouble for me.'

'Who?'

'Fielding Gray.'

'Why should he? What's up?'

'That's just what I want you to find out.'

'This warning: what do you mean by "curiously based"?'

Detterling had swallowed and then come straight out with it.

'The person who gave it was relaying a message from ghosts.'

But Percival had been unexpectedly lenient.

'Or relaying a message from the sub-conscious,' he said. 'Bearing in mind all the help you gave me last year with the Lloyd-James business, I think they'll let me off to meet you. Time and place, Canteloupe?'

And so Leonard Percival would be joining him in Venice, Detterling reflected now, as he seated himself next to Peter Morrison

for the journey. It would be pleasant to see Leonard again. They
had dined together twice since getting to the bottom of the
Lloyd-James affair, but somehow Leonard was not very good
company unless there was some immediate problem or crisis to
be discussed. Given such a problem, Leonard and he could not
only wrangle at it, they could exchange, for hours on end,
theories and instances and memories of which it put them in
mind. But given no problem there was no catalyst to get them
going; and the two occasions on which they'd met in the last
year had been quite dismal. Now, however, thought Detterling,
there will be a problem again : Baby's warning – that should set
them up. For even if Fielding Gray was up to nothing at all and
the warning therefore false, there would still be the problem of
what had got into Baby (ghosts, as she said? a mistaken instinct? or sheer malice?) to make her give it.

'Very pensive, Canteloupe,' said Carton Weir (who was accompanying Morrison as his PPS from the other side of the
gangway.

'I'm going out to see a man die.'

'A friend?'

'No. I hardly know him, beyond the odd meeting in Venice
last month ... and in Germany more than twenty years ago. I
did him a bad turn that time, though I couldn't really help myself. So now I'm trying to make it up to him.'

'By going to watch him die, my dear?' said Carton.

'I'm hoping I shall say the right thing before he does.'

'What does one say to a dying man?' said Morrison.

This question brought the conversation to a stop. A little later,
when the aeroplane had taken off and champagne had been
served to them, Detterling raised a different subject.

'What shall you do,' he said, 'if this deal in Mestre goes
wrong?'

Carton Weir fluttered his hands reproachfully; but Peter Morrison, having made sure that the three of them were alone in the
first-class section, was prepared to talk of the matter.

'Your late cousin's diplomacy,' he said to Detterling, 'consisted in discrediting rival products by causing them to receive
praise which was so obviously inflated that it was then assumed
to emanate from the producers themselves, and so made them
appear ridiculous and untrustworthy. It was a kind of anti-
advertising, and he had several agencies who practised it very

skilfully, most notably an important merchant bank – the Corcyran.'

'That I knew. Ivan Blessington works for it.'

'Correction. Used to work for it. Ivan has boobed. Or so we
think.'

'Unlike him.'

'Ivan was too decent, dear,' said Carton Weir, 'and too clean.
He should have spent the whole of his life at school playing
footer and having showers.'

'He did well in the Army,' said Detterling. 'He was Military
Attaché in Washington and had some important appointments
on the Staff. And I understood he was doing well with the Corcyran Bank.'

'Too decent, dear,' Carton insisted, 'too wholesome – like
bread and butter pudding. And like bread and butter pudding,
too soft. He went and got religion the other day, rather late in
life as his sort often do. And then of course he started thinking
that dear old Canteloupe's tricks weren't frightfully Christian,
and so he split.'

'We *think* he did,' said Morrison.

'We had enough evidence to get the Corcyran to sack him.'

'To pension him off. You do no one a service by exaggerat-
ing, Carton.'

'Anyway,' said Detterling, 'it appears that the code has been
cracked. So what do you do now?'

'Think up a new diplomacy.'

'You were always good at that. I shall never forget how you
handled that business in India in forty-six.'*

Morrison gave a look of mild distaste.

'I was lucky,' he said, 'and the circumstances permitted a certain licence.'

'So do these. The old country's up against it. We *need* this
deal at Mestre and many more like it.'

'Indeed.'

'So what are you going to do?'

'In general,' said Morrison carefully, 'I'm not yet quite certain. But over this affair at Mestre, there's a relatively easy
solution. If this corporation there will let bygones be bygones,
forget how we've tried to flannel them, and go ahead and clinch
the deal, then we shall promise them, in return, the British Government's moral support at the next international conference

*See *Sound The Retreat*, passim.

about the future of Venice. As you know, there are some nasty rows brewing.'

'But Peter. The industrialists on the mainland want to destroy Venice. You can't mean the British Government will support that?'

'You exaggerate as badly as Carton. The industrialists do not want to destroy Venice, only ... to trim it a bit, so that they can have more room for their installations.'

'As well as polluting the air, and wrecking the fabric of the city, and letting their horrible tankers wash away its foundations. You'll support them in all that?'

'We need this contract from Mestre to go to a British firm. As you say, the old country's up against it. Venice is a beautiful city, Canteloupe; but I think the tide of progress may be allowed to claim a few of her outlying churches in the popular interest. The people – both British and Italian – want a certain kind of wealth, and Venice is one of the things which stands in the way of their getting it.'

'Venice is one of the richest parts of their inheritance.'

'Only they don't think so, Canteloupe. They want cars and washing machines and fish fingers, not Venice. They don't understand it and they resent the pleasure it gives to those that do.'

'But Peter ... you can't sympathize with such attitudes?'

'If I don't, someone else will. And that someone else,' said Peter Morrison, 'would very soon be Minister of Commerce.'

The day after the visit to Samuele, Tom Llewyllyn went to see Max de Freville.

'You may remember,' Tom said, 'that as my host you asked me to let you know if anything came of Fielding's investigation into that picture in the gallery ... anything that might make trouble for you and Lyki as tenants of this Palazzo.'

'I remember. Has Fielding found anything?'

'Nothing that need obtrude on your convenience.'

Tom had already given much thought to what should or should not be said about Fielding's discovery. The previous night, after the party had returned from Oriago, he had given Daniel a full account of their findings, and asked him what he thought should be done about them. Daniel, who had seemed feverish but alert, opined that nothing should be done about them. The scandal of Piero Albani and his sister, Daniel said, now had no consequence for anybody, save as an antiquarian freak; and as for the matter of the Canteloupe inheritance, what possible point could there be in revealing to the world that the real Marquess Canteloupe was an idiot Italian boy called Paolo Filavoni who lived with his aunt in the marshes? To present the proof in legally valid form would be difficult (albeit not impossible) and exceedingly expensive. Who would have the time and money (certainly not Tom) to undertake such a suit, on whose behalf, and in any case *cui bono*? The marquessate would be no good to poor Paolo, while the loss of it would seriously discommode Detterling.

'The probability,' Daniel had concluded, 'is that whichever of them has it, it will die with him. Detterling suits the place and the place suits Detterling. Let's just leave it at that.'

With this judgement Tom was in complete accord; indeed he had already decided on just such a course even before consulting Daniel, whose opinion he had sought only from academic interest. And so now, while talking with Max de Freville, Tom's sole concern was to keep his promise. He had promised Max, on the afternoon when they had gone together to the Ghetto, that if Fielding's enquiries brought anything to light, he would tell Max if it was something that he and Lykiadopoulos, as tenants of the Albani family, should know about. The answer now, in Tom's view, was 'no'. Fernando's manuscripts had been addressed to his two younger children and to anyone thereafter who might happen to come across them; it was no fault of Max or Lyki that someone had done so during their tenancy. If the Albani should subsequently find cause for complaint, let them blame their own ancestor.

In any case, unless the facts revealed by the manuscripts were subsequently published, the Albani need never know of the discovery, let alone complain of it. He himself intended to publish nothing, if only because the right to use the material was undoubtedly Fielding's. As to Fielding's intentions he was not altogether clear; but Fielding had said one thing on the way back from Oriago that was indicative.

'Pity Detterling and I were in the same regiment,' Fielding had said: 'otherwise one might have raised rather a stir.'

This Tom understood to mean that the prescribed loyalties of the British caste system forbade Fielding from using what he had learnt to embarrass an old companion in arms. So far, so good; both Fielding and himself were determined on silence or at least discretion. But what of Piero?

'Perhaps you are sorry I know of this?' Piero had said. 'But you needed an interpreter; any interpreter would by now have known more or less what I do; and better that I should know it than a stranger. And besides' – he echoed what Tom had previously told Fielding – 'you will be telling Daniel and he would have told me. I was bound to know sooner or later.'

'What is your ... opinion of it all?' Fielding had asked.

'A curious story which is none of my business. It could, I suppose, injure your friend who is now called Lord Canteloupe. It is no business of mine to do that.'

'So you will not repeat the story?'

'I cannot say quite that, Major Gray. In all things a man must render account of himself ... of himself and his conduct ... where that account is due. At one time or another I shall be required to render account of myself, from the time I found that first manuscript for you up to the time of what we have done and seen today.'

After that he had been silent. Tom had supposed, and now still supposed, that Piero was referring to the confessional. As a Catholic, the boy would have to search his conscience to decide whether the part he had played was a worthy one; and if he decided that in any respect it was not (if, for example, he felt that he should not have appropriated the first manuscript, an action which he clearly regretted), then he would have to make confession and some small part of the story might have to be told to his confessor. This in itself could do but little harm; the trouble was that Piero's language had been ambiguous; Tom could not be sure exactly to whom Piero's account was to be rendered, or how comprehensive it must be in its scope.

But there was nothing to be done about that now. Now Tom's task was to reassure Max, who was beginning to press him.

'You say that nothing Fielding has discovered need concern Lyki or myself,' Max was recapitulating, 'as the Albani's tenants here; but presumably it is of interest to somebody?'

'To scholars.'

'But amusing too?'

'You could call it that.'

'Then let's hear it.'

'I'm sorry, Max. Fielding has completed a very intricate piece of research, the results of which he will not want generally known until he has decided what use he himself will make of them. It's quite normal for writers to be secretive in such circumstances.'

'I hadn't thought of that,' said Max. 'But though I quite see
he wouldn't want anyone else cashing in, I'm not exactly a rival.
And it was in my house – mine and Lyki's – that the whole hunt
started. So I should have thought you might tell me a bit more.'

'I promised you, as your guest, to tell you anything which
you and Lyki ought to know. Well, you ought to know that the
investigation is concluded and that what has come out of it poses
no worries for you or Lyki. I've only raised the matter to set
your minds at rest for once and for all. I knew you were
bothered about what Fielding was up to, and I've come to tell
you it's finished with.'

'Very scrupulous, I'm sure. Scrupulous to the letter, Tom. So
let's exercise a few more of your scruples : oughtn't Lyki and I
to know what's happening to Daniel Mond? Whatever it is, it's
happening in our garden.'

'You need not worry about Daniel. He is living quietly in the
tower and one day – quite soon – he will leave it. There will be
no embarrassment.'

Max considered this. At last,

'No,' he said kindly, 'I'm sure there won't be. But do you
know where he will go? I suppose they'd have him at San
Michele – I think they've got sections for all sorts – but San
Michele's a dismal place. Not right for Daniel.'

'Funny you should speak of him like that. You hardly know
him.'

'I saw him that night at dinner ... and every now and then,
when he still came over for baths. That's how I knew something
was wrong, because he's stopped coming over any more. We
used to have a word or two sometimes,' said Max lightly. 'I
looked forward to it. Did you know that I too am a thwarted
mathematician? In a different way of course : he was too good
at it and I just wasn't good enough. But I knew enough to sympathize, and I liked – well – I like his spirit. I tell you, Tom :
San Michele's no place for Daniel.'

'He could go back to Lancaster.'

'Would he want that?'

'He was ... contented there.'

'But now the yobs are beginning to break the place up, Tom.
There was that business the other day when the chapel was
savaged by hooligans – one of the tombs was pick-axed, Tom –

and now they've found out that your own undergraduates did it.'

'I know.'

'Who wants to go back to a college chapel where that sort of thing can happen?'

'Does it really matter where he goes – when he leaves the casino in the garden?'

'I think so. Piero will too, if I am not mistaken.'

'Then I shall be glad to know,' said Tom crisply, 'what you and Piero may decide between you.'

In the Hotel Gabrielli Fielding Gray settled to work. It had become quite clear to him, after a little thought, what he should do with the secret which he had discovered. He was an entertainer by profession; he would therefore use the story – or rather, one very like it – in order to entertain. Although he had some pretensions as a literary critic, he was not a scholar as such, and to prepare a scholarly presentation of the facts, complete with proof and documentation, would have been exceedingly irksome to him. He had no wish to displace Detterling; and to initiate proceedings on behalf of Paolo Filavoni, in the courts or the College of Arms, he found quite unthinkable. Finally, he was not a busybody and cared very little about notions of justice, social or otherwise; and so to confront Detterling with the facts and urge that Detterling had a duty to set matters to right would have seemed to Fielding the grossest piece of impertinence. (Besides, as far as he knew Detterling was in England, which would have made confrontation a cumbrous affair at the best.) No, he told himself now, there could be no question of it: this tale was just what he needed to provide the substance of a new novel, which would be of a rather different kind from anything he had written heretofore. He would write of just such a search (but not the same) as he had lately been engaged in; he would gradually disclose just such mysteries (but not the same) as he himself, with Tom's help, had recently uncovered.

Fielding spent some hours drawing up a table of fictional equivalents. He decided, provisionally, on a narrative in the first person; the narrator should not be anyone like himself, he thought, but a young man who was in Venice for the first time and would therefore have to contend with the terrors and deceits of a strange city as well as with all the other obstacles that lay between him and the secret which he sought. His first inkling (that there *was* a secret) would not be given to him in a private gallery but in a public museum (the Correr); it would not come from an eighteenth-century picture but from a nineteenth-century ball dress, so displayed as to reveal some peculiarity in cut which in turn suggested some unusual (but not necessarily repellent) physical deformity. The dress, it would transpire, was that which had been worn by the wife of a prominent Austrian officer at a banquet in honour of a visiting Archduke. The lady, tormented by obsessive hankerings, had returned home early from the banquet, had mounted to her eldest son's quarters ... and had there found, or herself committed, God knew what of horror or delight, which the son had subsequently committed to a secret diary. This diary Fielding's hero would track down, through libraries and dank palaces and murky chantries, creeping from one to the other along the treacherous passages of snow-bound Venice....

Ah, thought Fielding, as he began to plot the outline of the early chapters, what it is to have work again, something to put my mind to day after day, something to wrestle with and curse at and be wholly possessed by, while the hours pass like minutes and the pile of written sheets slowly grows at my left hand.

The telephone rang in his room.

'Lord Canteloupe is in Venice,' said Max de Freville; 'at the Gritti.'

'Oh?' said Fielding. 'I'll call on him if I have time.'

He put down the receiver without saying good-bye to Max and returned to the half-filled sheet before him.

'I have disobeyed you,' said Piero to Lykiadopoulos in the Palazzo Albani. 'I have spent many hours with Mr Mond in the casino in the garden while you were at the Casino Municipale.'

'Why do you tell me now?' said Lykiadopoulos.

'Because I owe you a duty and must render my account.'

'Then render it.'

'You said I might go out with Mr Mond and Mr Llewyllyn, but that I must not be with them in the tower. But Daniel is dying and cannot leave the tower.'

'At least he can do no harm by dying,' Lykiadopoulos said. 'I was afraid of something quite different. That is why I forbade you the tower.'

'You were afraid that through me he might come at things which you would wish hidden.'

'Yes.'

'There is small danger of that now,' said Piero. 'Nevertheless, I have disobeyed you, and I must offer something in reparation.'

'They have certainly taught you a lot of English in that tower. What is this . . . reparation?'

'Major Gray and Mr Llewyllyn have discovered that Lord Canteloupe is not Lord Canteloupe. There is a prior claimant whom nobody knew of – until now.'

For almost the first time in his adult life Lykiadopoulos was wholly and genuinely surprised. He had often been partly surprised, as he was, just the other day, when the Arabs suddenly appeared in Venice some weeks before he had expected them; but since their arrival had always been a possibility, since talk of them had been in the air for some time, he had been merely startled rather than astounded. What Piero had now told him, however, would never have occurred to him in a thousand years. To fake noblemen of various nationalities and degrees he was altogether accustomed; but that Canteloupe should not be Canteloupe, that an English marquess, upheld as such by all the authority of the Heralds' College in London, should turn out to have inherited his dignity in error – this, to a man of Lykiadopoulos's conservative and anglophile disposition, was quite beyond his intellectual scope.

'Tell me more,' he said hoarsely.

Piero told him.

'By telling you this,' he said in conclusion, 'I have done some good, to make up for my part in disturbing the ghosts; for I have done my duty, my service, to you who are my master. Captain Detterling, we hear, was a rich man, Lyki *mou*; the Marquess Canteloupe is even richer.'

The day after Detterling arrived in Venice, Leonard Percival waited on him in his rooms at the Gritti.

'Here am I,' said Percival; 'what now?'

'You remember Tom Llewyllyn's girl, Baby? We met her briefly last year when we went to Cambridge?'

'Vividly. A vicious little sex-trap.'

'She's changed since then.' Detterling gave Percival some account of the improved Baby and what had improved her. 'It's she,' he concluded. 'who . . . listened to the ghosts and warned me. The threat, as I told you, appears to be Fielding Gray.'

'Where's he staying?'

'The Gabrielli.'

'I'd better start there, I suppose. You've no idea why Fielding Gray should spell trouble for you?'

'None.'

'And incidentally, Canteloupe, why are you in Venice?'

Detterling told Percival about Daniel Mond and what he deemed to be his obligation to him. Percival was brusque.

'A long time ago, that business with Mond in Germany,' he said. 'I don't think you need hold yourself to much on that account.'

'I like to say proper good-byes.'

'Fair enough. You attend to Mond and I'll try to sniff out whatever savoury little dish our friend Fielding Gray is cooking up.'

Detterling, anxious to see Daniel but uneasy lest he should intrude at an awkward time, went to the Palazzo Albani and made enquiry, since Max, Lyki and Piero were all out, of the Major-Domo. The Major-Domo, sycophantic of marquesses but contemptuous of the tower and everyone in it, said that he knew of no reason why the *due professori* should not receive the *Excellenza* if the *Excellenza* was so gracious as to wish to be received by the *due professori*. Rather uncertainly, Detterling crossed the garden, and having knocked on the door of the casino found Tom, Piero and an animated Daniel within.

Daniel was examining, with evident interest, an object which looked like a detachable cigarette filter. This, as Piero explained to Detterlng, had been left behind in the Palazzo earlier that afternoon by a gentleman who had now gone off to the Casino with Max and Lykiadopoulos. It had excited Piero's idle curiosity because engraven on its metal rim were some symbols and figures which were far too elaborate to be a trade mark and appeared to be some kind of mathematical formula.

What Piero did not tell Detterling was that he had seized on this toy in the vague hope that it might amuse Daniel for a few minutes, since Daniel, who had altered much in the last two or three days, was now only to be entertained, and that intermittently, by trifles of this nature. What Piero *did* tell Detterling was that Daniel was finding the formula on the rim of unexpected interest and was busy trying to solve its meaning.

But after a little longer Daniel handed the object to Tom and

sank back in his chair, clearly exhausted by his temporary show
of energy.

'Something to do with friction and velocity,' he muttered. 'I
could have done it properly once. God knows what it's doing on
that thing.'

Then Daniel fell asleep.

Detterling, who had so far not exchanged a single word with
Daniel, asked Tom when it would be convenient for him to call
again.

'Any time,' said Tom. 'Just take a chance. You're more likely
to find him approximately himself if you come in the morning.
It rather depends when he takes his powders ... not that they
work for very long now.'

'Will he wake up this afternoon?' said Detterling. 'I'd gladly
wait.'

'Please don't. You wouldn't like what you saw when he wakes
from his afternoon sleep. Leave Piero and me to cope.'

So Detterling, disconsolate and yet somehow relieved (for
since he had said nothing to Daniel, at least he had not said the
wrong thing), wandered away down the passages, came to a
vaporetto stage, got on to the first boat that came by, and got
off, without really thinking what he was doing or why, at the
Palazzo Vendramin. Then his head cleared, and he remembered
that the afternoon session of Lykiadopoulos's Baccarat Bank
would now be in full swing. He asked for a ticket to the special
rooms, winced as he paid for it (for the charge had gone up to
fifty thousand lire soon after the arrival of the Arabs), and went
up in the lift.

Standing some distance from the rails round the Table de
Banque was Max de Freville. Detterling waved, as to an old friend
whom he had not seen for some weeks, and was surprised at the
perfunctory way in which his greeting was returned. Then he
realized that Max was in close conversation with a man who
was standing next to him in the crush, a man with a long, seedy
face and wearing a long seedy suit. The man nodded, took a
cigarette straight from his pocket, and inserted it into a holder
which he was carrying in his other hand. He placed the holder
between his lips but did not light the cigarette. Why he was
bothering to watch these commonplace actions, Detterling did
not know; if asked, he would have said that there was something nervous and rehearsed in the man's manner, as though he
were taking part in an amateur play. He might have added that

there was a look of strain in the man's long face, the kind of look Detterling had seen on the face of a ventriloquist somewhere (one of those Gyppo conjurers during the war, perhaps) who had been striving to keep a still countenance while throwing his voice through clenched teeth.

After a while, the man took the holder from his mouth (the cigarette being still unlit) with a more relaxed movement than any he had so far made. Detterling now turned his attention to the table. He noticed that the stakes for the coup about to come were fairly light, and that Lykiadopoulos had an indefinable air of satisfaction and relief. In the event, Lykiadopoulos lost the coup to both sides of the table but retained his air of content.

Detterling went over to Max.

'How's Lyki getting on?' he enquired.

'Rather well. These Arabs are being more cautious than usual, and on the few occasions they have been greedy Lyki has usually beaten 'em.'

'Good. Who's your friend?'

'No one you'd want to meet,' whispered Max. He turned and nodded twice, each time with two very distinct movements (down with his chin and then up), to the man with the holder.

The man nodded back and once more produced a cigarette. A prime neurotic, this one, Detterling thought. Once again the cigarette went into a holder – but a different holder, Detterling noticed, from the one he had used before. Once more the holder went to the man's mouth, once more the muscles of cheek and jaw tightened in strain.

'How are your plans to save Venice going?' said Detterling to Max.

'One good idea,' said Max shortly, then craned forward to watch the table. The stakes for this coup were much higher, Detterling noticed, indeed many of the players must have wagered the maximum.

'What idea?' he asked Max.

But Max wasn't listening. He was absorbed in the cards which Lykiadopoulos flicked out of the shoe, gazing at them as though he hoped to see through their backs. A further card was called for on the right; a natural eight was displayed on the left; and then, as Max inhaled breath with a long hiss of his nostrils, Lykiadopoulos turned up a natural nine.

'What idea?' persisted Detterling.

'A palace that needs doing up. Fielding Gray found it. Look,

Canteloupe,' said Max, 'will you excuse me? I'm rather tied up in Lyki's fortunes just now.'

Detterling, who resented such incivility, hated crowds, and despised Arabs, went downstairs and rode home to the Gritti, where he had anchovy toast for tea and waited for Leonard Percival to come and report his day's findings.

Daniel was in the Forest near the Warlocks' Grotto, looking for Fielding Gray. If only he could find his way through all these trees. But of course! He needn't go forward, he could turn back, trace his path back, become a thread through space and time, threading back to where he last saw Fielding, so that he could speak to him just once more. Daniel was a particle reversing through space and time, tracing its path back – back and back and back – to find Fielding Gray. There were no trees now, only emptiness and, very far away, a dull red sun. In the sun was Fielding, but he would never reach him now, because the particle that was Daniel had gone as far back as it could go. There was a blinding flash which had once, aeons before, been its birth, and then Daniel was alone in no-space, before the universe and before time.

Funny, thought Detterling, as he drank his tea and waited for Leonard Percival, that cigarette holder which the chap with Max was using – it was very similar to the filter (or whatever) that Daniel was so interested in. There was the same oddity of line, the same kind of elaboration in the curve which led to the rim. But of course Piero had said that the filter had been left behind in the Palazzo by a man who had gone off to the Casino with Lyki and Max – so presumably this was the same man and he had a whole collection of the things. He'd used two different ones in the Casino just in the short time during which Detterling had been watching him there. What had Daniel said about the formula on the filter, before he went to sleep? 'Friction and velocity' – that was about it: 'Something to do with friction and velocity'. Well, thought Detterling vaguely, it might be interesting to find out what.

It was some time before Tom and Piero realized that Daniel was dead. When they did, Tom looked rather helpless and said:
'Where must he go now?'
'I shall arrange,' Piero said.

Then Piero crossed the garden to the Palazzo and rung up Lykiadopoulos's doctor, who agreed to come to Daniel and see that he was taken where he must go first. But the more important question was where Daniel should go at the last, and to this question, which Piero had pondered for many days, he had, he believed, found the right answer ... if only the necessary permission could now be obtained.

Piero left the Palazzo and went to a quay from which motor-boats plied for hire. It was beginning to rain, and there was only one boat waiting in the dusk. Piero gave his instructions. The driver gagged slightly and opened his mouth to refuse.

'Help me, brother,' Piero said, 'for the love of God – and double the fare.'

Piero stood by the driver as they drove slowly down the Grand Canal, more quickly along the Riva degli Schiavoni, and then slowly again as they turned left to cut through to the Fondamente Nuove; of which once clear, they sped past the island of San Michele (no, that was never for Daniel, Piero thought) and then skirted Murano. The rain was very heavy now and a strong wind blew from the East, but still Piero remained outside with the driver, not caring to sit in the comfortable cabin while the man who was serving him in his need must stand in the wet and the cold. They passed little islands, whose crumbling farm-houses they could just make out in the darkness, they passed sandbanks covered with low, creeping bush, they ran through dense, high beds of reed, and once they nearly struck an empty punt which was moored to one of the lantern-poles that marked their route. Then they turned off the marked route and edged carefully away to the right. After a time they approached a line of trees, which appeared, in the boat's headlight, to grow straight out of the water; but as they came close, the trees were seen to be growing from a low bank of mud, through which ran a gradually narrowing creek.

'We cannot go far up the creek,' the driver said : 'the tide is too low.'

So Piero let himself down off the boat and struggled through mud and reeds, aided but little comforted by the headlight which the driver played ahead of him; and at last, wet through to the bone and cold to the marrow, plastered with stinking mud and throbbing with pain in his maimed leg, Piero came to wooden steps. He scrabbled his way up these and along a platform, and reached a door in a wall of stone. He pulled a bell rope.

'They must, they *shall*,' he said between his chattering teeth as he waited .

At last the door opened. A large robed figure stood between Piero and a dully lit hall.

'Please bring me to Brother Hugh,' Piero said.

'You may see only who is sent.'

'Bring me to Brother Hugh,' said Piero; 'I have come here to him.'

'What do you want with Brother Hugh?'

'I want . . . his intercession for a friend, that the Good Brothers of St Francis may receive him.'

And now, overcome by pain and weariness and grief and chill frustration, Piero began to cry, in a fashion neither weak nor effete, but wild, savage and horrible.

'Hugh, Hugh, Hugh,' he howled through his tears, 'DANIEL IS DEAD.'

As the last of his strength left him with his howls, he fell forward into the dark.

'You're late,' said Detterling to Percival. 'I expected you before dinner.'

'Long day,' said Percival; 'one damn thing after another. Can you order me up a snack? Warm milk and digestive biscuits. That's about my mark these days.'

A little later, when Percival was settled with his humble refection,

'Fielding Gray was most co-operative,' he began. 'Since *you* wished to know what was up, he said, he had no choice but to tell. I'm afraid, Detterling, I've got rather a surprise for you.'

As he sipped his milk and nibbled a biscuit, Percival reported the facts which Fielding and Tom had discovered, just as Fielding had reported them to him that afternoon.

'I . . . don't quite understand,' said Detterling unsteadily. 'Can all this be proved?'

'With some difficulty and enormous expense . . . probably.'

'But you say Fielding has no intention of making it public?'

'Fielding intends only to write a novel loosely based on the true story. No harm there. But others, I suppose, could take a more awkward line.'

'Baby said the threat came from Fielding.'

'Ultimately it does. I mean, even if he's not out to expose you, he was the chap who dug it all up.'

Detterling went to the sideboard in his sitting-room and poured himself a quintuple whisky from a bottle labelled "With the Compliments of the Management".

'Who else knows?' he said after a long swallow.

'Tom Llewyllyn – who will do nothing, if Fielding is to be believed. And an Italian boy called Piero, property of one Lykiadopoulos. He might do anything, Fielding says, but should keep quiet if handled right.'

'Jesus. I can't believe it, Leonard. It's just not possible. A potty boy of ten in a tiny village in the Veneto ... *him* the real Marquess Canteloupe?'

'Some of the story is pretty shaky. But the bit about Lord Rollesden and his descendants by that Italian girl – that certainly seemed to stand up.'

'But whatever am I to do?'

'Nothing.'

'I could have a word with Piero. The sooner the better. He seems to be the most likely to make trouble.'

'You'll not be having a word with him just yet. He's gone.'

'Gone?' said Detterling hopelessly.

'When I'd heard the full tale from Fielding, I went round to the Palazzo Albani to see Llewyllyn and Piero and get their line on it all.' Percival paused, then said mildly : 'Daniel Mond died this afternoon.'

'But I was with him—'

'—And later on he died. Tom was off talking with doctors and policemen, I was told, and Piero had done a bunk. Then, just as I was leaving, a Franciscan Friar turned up. English, of all things – Brother Hugh, he called himself. He said he'd come from the Island of San Francesco del Deserto to tell Lykiadopoulos that the boy was there, suffering from exposure and concussion – he'd fallen down on arrival and hit his head on the offertory chest they keep just inside the door.'

'What in God's name did Piero want with the Franciscans?'

'He wanted them to find room on their island for Daniel. He was raving about it, according to this Brother Hugh. When they promised him Daniel could come, he calmed down a bit, though they had to keep repeating the promise. They're rather afraid he may die on them.'

The day of the funeral dawned with a low grey sky, a sharp north wind, and thin, spiteful rain. But at about ten o'clock the

cloud rose, allowing a watery yellow sun to filter through, and
the rain ceased.

Fielding Gray and Leonard Percival, both of whom disliked
burials too much to attend this one, had nevertheless stationed
themselves where they could see the procession pass, on a bridge
just off the Canale della Misericordia. This was the bridge on
which Daniel and Piero had first seen Brother Hugh, a stone's
throw from the little plot in which Euphemia and Piero Albani
lay buried. Fielding explained this latter curiosity to Percival,
and then,

'Do you believe in ghosts, Leonard?' he said.

'No.'

'Then where did Baby Llewyllyn's hunch come from – that
I had discovered something which might injure Detterling? You
did say that's what started your enquiry off?'

'Yes,' said Percival. 'I think Baby's instinct told her that your
research might end up with something nasty.'

'But why should she have guessed that the something nasty
had to do with Detterling?'

'It seems she is very close to Detterling. When anything nasty
is likely to turn up, one's first thought is, "Will it affect me?",
and one's second, "Will it affect those I love?" From this it's a
short step to an irrational fear that it will.'

'But Baby's fear was amply justified. In slightly different circumstances, this information of mine could have been very dangerous to Detterling indeed. It might be even now. Baby was
bang right.'

'Pure chance,' said Percival.

'At very long odds against.'

'Anything that ever happens has very long odds against, if
you think of all the other things that might have happened instead. If that bomb which got you in Cyprus all those years ago
had been thrown a moment earlier or later, you might now be
a corpse. Or you might have gone unwounded and become a
poor general instead of a rich author. Or it might just have
blown your balls off, in which case God knows what you'd have
become. But it was thrown exactly when it was thrown, and
things are as they are. One must accept everything, including
Baby Llewyllyn's hunch, as having come about in the natural
and logical continuation of prior events – any one of which
might have been different, given a split second here or there,
but wasn't. The most commonplace events are fantastically im-

probable,' Percival said, 'and the most improbable, if properly regarded, are entirely commonplace. Here he comes now.'

Up the Canale della Misericordia came a tawdry, gilded barge. A black canopy was held aloft by barley-sugar shafts, and under it was a coffin draped with a Union Jack.

'Military Honours?' said Percival.

'Yes. We found he'd kept his badge – the one he wore when we hid him in my squadron. All these years he'd kept it, Leonard. He never let us down, though it cost him very dear later ... as indeed you of all people must know.* Surely he qualified as an honorary soldier?'

'Then how to salute him as he passes, Fielding? No hats....'

'Stand to attention, I think.'

So Fielding and Percival stood to attention as Daniel went by, and then Fielding, absurdly, waved after him.

This was observed by Tom Llewyllyn, who was riding with Detterling, Max and Lykiadopoulos in the cabin of the first boat after the barge. Baby Llewyllyn (whom Detterling, somewhat to Tom's annoyance, had insisted should fly out for the funeral) was standing in the open at the rear of the boat, and waved to Fielding for Daniel. Lykiadopoulos nodded kindly approval of this little scene, then leaned forward and tapped Detterling on the knee.

'I need money, my friend,' he said.

'Do you indeed? For your bank at the Casino?'

'No. My Baccarat Bank is now safe—'

'—How do you know?—'

'—Because the conditions are in my favour. But this bank will not bring in enough.'

'Enough for what?'

'To keep things tidy in Corfu. There are difficulties there.'

'There are difficulties everywhere.'

'None of which cannot be solved by ready money.'

'Good,' said Detterling; 'a simple solution.'

'If the ready money is there,' said Lykiadopoulos.

'And if it isn't?'

'In this case, it is. I want you, my good friend, my lord Canteloupe, to let me have half a million pounds.'

'Out of what?'

'Out of what you have.'

'Why should I?'

*See The Sabre Squadron, passim.

'Compassion. For my people will be thrown out of work if the money is not forthcoming.'

'Including you?'

'*I* shall not be beggared,' said Lykiadopoulos, quick to preserve face, 'whatever happens.'

'Then count yourself lucky and stop scrounging.'

'I am not – scrounging. I have a basis for business.'

'Ah. You are offering interest on this half-million pounds?'

'In a sense, yes, but not in money.'

'Not very businesslike, Lykiadopoulos.'

'Lord Canteloupe, can you find me half one million pounds?'

'Candidly, no.'

'Then candidly ... you will have to part with your new marquessdom. And the new estate that has come to you with it.'

'Neither is saleable or transferable.'

'You haven't understood me, my lord.'

'Understand *what*, *Kyrie* Lykiadopoulo?'

'Either you pay me this money, or I tell the Heralds' College and your solicitors in London all I know about that boy in the marshes near Oriago.'

The barge and the first attendant boat passed into the wide Sacca della Misericordia, heading for the lagoon.

In the second boat, Peter Morrison said to Lord Constable of Reculver Castle, Provost of Daniel's college:

'That's Fielding Gray up there on the bridge. Do you ever regret that you kept him out of Lancaster?'

'No. He was a shallow, treacherous boy.'

Morrison, who did not know Daniel, had come to the funeral nominally to honour a faintly distinguished compatriot who had died far from home but in fact to give himself a trip round the islands and an excuse for spending twenty-four hours longer in Italy. He had concluded his business in Mestre, and had earned a brief period of holiday and celebration, for his terms had been accepted: the contract which he was so anxious to win for Britain would now go through as he had hoped – on condition that the British Government played its part, at the forthcoming international conference, in betraying Venice. And so Peter, who was pleased with himself this morning and expected (in this autumn of 1973) to have almost two more certain years of power and office ahead of him, did not want his agreeable mood to be spoiled by Constable's grating assessment (however accurate) of his old friend, Fielding. He therefore changed the subject:

'Tell me, Provost,' he said to Lord Constable, 'did the left-wing element in Lancaster make a fuss when you accepted your peerage?'

Jacquiz Helmutt and Balbo Blakeney listened from the other side of the cabin. As Fellows of Lancaster, they knew very well that Constable had done a deal with the left-wing element: there were to be no rows about his barony, provided he undertook to pardon and recall to the college, as soon as their prison sentences were done, the undergraduates who had been found guilty of robbing and desecrating the chapel. This being the case, Jacquiz and Balbo were very interested to hear how Constable would answer Morrison's question.

'There has been no fuss,' Lord Constable now replied. 'I made it quite plain that nobody, not even the college servants, need address me as "my lord".'

Whether or not his audience might deem this explanation to be adequate, Lord Constable was clearly going to say no more on the topic. As a matter of fact, Balbo Blakeney reflected, most of the college servants did call the Provost "my lord" and seemed very happy to do so. It made a change for them, Balbo supposed.

'I met Provost Constable once,' said Percival to Fielding on the bridge. 'Interesting man: an expert at transforming the plain into the devious. And now what have we here?'

The third boat contained Alfie Schroeder, the famous columnist of the Billingsgate Press, who had been in Venice to do his routine three-monthly article on the city's decay and had heard of the funeral through an accidental meeting with Tom Llewyllyn. Alfie, who had come a very long way since his one and only encounter with Daniel in 1952, was following the coffin party in a mood of humility, as a journalist paying tribute to a scholar, and partly in one of immense satisfaction, as a man whose professional prestige had continuously mounted since that encounter in 1952 while Daniel's had done little but stagnate. Conscious that this was an ungenerous and (if the gods were paying attention) a perilous sentiment, Alfie tried to expel it from his mind by speculating on the personalities of the three men with whom he shared the cabin. Two of them, one fat and one stringy, obviously were or had been soldiers: short hair, the same regimental tie, well-pressed grey suits of indifferent material and cut – all of this to Alfie spelt Warrant Officer. The third man, however, was a mystery: a dapper man, middle-aged yet smooth-faced, wearing highly polished black leather slippers.

'Perhaps we should introduce ourselves,' Alfie said.

'I know you,' said one of the soldiers, the fat one: 'you're the journalist who came nosing round the squadron in fifty-two, when we had Danny with us on the run.'

'You broke my box Brownie,' said Alfie, remembering the grey afternoon and the rotting piles of bricks and the sullen soldiers who were sweeping away rubble to make a football pitch: 'in Kassel.'

'God, what a dump,' said the second soldier.

'Not any more,' said the dapper man in the polished slippers. 'Kassel is now rebuilt and very prosperous and has been for years. This place ... Venice ... is the dump,' he said, in a just detectable American accent, 'I expect we shall be doing away with Venice before very long.'

'But there's this fund—' Alfie began.

'—Indeed there is,' said the American, 'if anyone can find where the Italians have hidden it.'

'What a funny little boat-load,' said Percival to Fielding on the bridge. 'That tittle-tattling Schroeder and the two old muckers from your regiment. How did you dig them up?'

'Through the Regimental Association. Tom Chead and Basil Bunce. I also tried to get hold of some of the officers who knew him.'

'But none of them came, I see. A rotten lot, the officers in your regiment.'

'Detterling came.'

'Detterling's rich. Chead and Bunce have paid their fares out of Sergeant-Majors' pensions.'

In fact Fielding had paid their fares, and put them up in the Gabrielli the previous night, but he let this pass.

'I see Earle Restarick's there,' he said.

'Yes, I got hold of him, through Jermyn Street. We still have close contacts with the Yanks. It turned out that Restarick was working in Mestre. The wops there want to scrub out Venice, and the Yanks are helping with the dirty work – in return for future concessions.'

The third and last boat passed on into the Sacca della Misericordia.

'Back to my book,' said Fielding contentedly. 'And you, Leonard?'

'Back to the Gritti, to wait for Detterling. Canteloupe, I suppose I'd better say. I don't think anyone's going to mess that up for him.'

'Not me at any rate.'

'He's going to make me his personal secretary. He reckons that he'll need someone like me about – just in case, Fielding.'

'You're not giving up spying, Leonard? The Service won't be the same without your nose for turds.'

'Jermyn Street and ulcers don't mix,' Percival replied. 'They'll be glad to be shot of me.'

'And you of them?'

'It's time I settled. I'll miss it all.' Leonard removed his wire-framed spectacles and wiped his red eyes with a grubby hand-kerchief. 'Oh, I'll miss it, turds and all. But it's time I settled.'

The two men turned to leave the bridge, then turned back to take a last look at the distant line of boats, as it veered slowly left and into the Laguna Morta.

In Lykiadopoulos's boat there had been silence ever since he had made his demand of Detterling. Only as they were passing San Michele did Detterling break that silence, quietly enquiring,

'Who told you about the boy in the marshes?'

'Piero,' said Lykiadopoulos. 'He is mine, you see.'

'No one told me,' said Max. 'Tom said there was nothing I need know.'

Max looked reproachfully at Tom Llewyllyn.

'Nor there was,' said Tom. 'What was it to you?'

'To me it is money,' Lykiadopoulos persisted calmly.

'Blackmail,' said Detterling.

'In a good cause. Like your Robin Hood. If I do not have this money, I shall have to close two-thirds of my hotels and there will be much misery on Corfu.'

'I have no money for you, Lykiadopoulos. My new estate is tied up. The money I had before is not enough.'

'If my affairs must come down,' said Lykiadopoulos, 'so must yours.'

'That's mere spite,' said Tom. 'Especially as you've already told us that you personally will be safe.' He shifted uneasily and took a small object from his pocket to fiddle with.

'Where did you get that?' said Max sharply.

'Piero found it and brought it over to amuse Daniel.'

'I mean exactly what I say,' said Lykiadopoulos to Detterling. 'I know that somewhere you can find this money.'

But Detterling hardly heard this. He was looking at the object in Tom's hand. What had Daniel said about the formula engraved on it? Friction and velocity. And the man in the Casino with Max had been ... sucking ... or mouthing ... on something very similar.

'You're up to something in the Casino,' Detterling said to Max, speaking on impulse, having no idea what if anything the accusation could mean. 'I saw that man who was there with you the other day.' He gestured at Tom's object. 'He was using a thing like that. Put it to your lips, Tom. Blow.'

He had no idea of where all this could lead, but he did know that both Max and Lykiadopoulos were disquieted.

'Go on, Tom. Blow,' he said.

'No,' said Max.

'Let him,' said Lykiadopoulos. 'What harm can he do here?'

Tom blew.

There was absolute silence while he did so – until, one second after he had begun, Baby Llewyllyn flung open the doors at the rear of the cabin. Her face was contorted.

'Did none of you feel it?' she cried. 'What was it? That horrible jarring feeling.'

The boat began to rock in the light wash made by the funeral barge ahead.

'Blow again, Tom,' said Detterling.

Tom blew. Baby shuddered.

'Stop it,' yelled Max at Tom. 'You may upset the driver. He's already got too close to the hearse.'

'So,' said Tom; 'I blow this thing, my daughter shivers with horror, and it upsets the judgement of the driver. What did you feel, Canteloupe?'

'A sort of pricking. I expect Baby is more sensitive than most of us. You remember what Daniel said, Tom? Something to do with velocity and friction.'

Tom turned to Lykiadopoulos.

'You were always afraid that Daniel would find you out,' Tom said. 'I'm not quite sure *what* he found out, but since Canteloupe has seen an associate of yours using one of these things in the Casino, I fancy the directorate might care to investigate further.'

'Only there will be no need,' said Detterling. 'We shall repay Lykiadopoulos's silence with our own. I shall continue to hold my title, and Lyki will continue with ... whatever game he is playing in the Casino. Both of us undisgraced, and undisturbed by the other.'

'Daniel Mond,' said Lykiadopoulos in a soft, sick voice. He peered at the barge ahead. 'I thought he was harmless once he was in his coffin.'

'So he is. If *you* keep quiet, and *we* keep quiet. This trick of yours, Lyki . . . could it bring you in a profit?'

'It is a means of control, of influencing the players' nerves and thus their bets. If we take risks . . . if we make them bet high when we think they will lose . . . then it *could* bring profit.'

'Enough to keep the hotels open,' said Max. 'We shall not try – shall we, Lyki? – to make enough to build more. Angela wouldn't like that.'

'We shall need much luck even to make the bare minimum we need,' said Lykiadopoulos, 'the way things are now going on Corfu.'

'But it could be done?' said Detterling.

'Yes.'

'Then from one fraud to another,' said Detterling, 'let me wish you joy of it.'

And now the procession had rounded Murano and was sailing straight ahead for San Francesco del Deserto. From the window of the friars' infirmary, Piero watched the boats as they approached. He was still too ill to go outside, the Brothers had told him, but they had arranged it all so that he could watch his friend complete his journey. Time and tide, he knew, were right : Daniel could come straight up the creek to the gate and need not flounder in the mud as Piero himself had done. Here he came now, under his Union Jack, while the Good Brothers stood to receive him. Four of them stepped forward, one of these being Brother Hugh, to bear him away; and after him followed those whom he had loved and some whom he had feared; those who had wounded and those who had cherished him.

Daniel's grave was near the caged bird sanctuary, under a tree which would bloom white next spring. Daniel would not see the blossom on this tree, but Piero would, for he too was to stay on the island with the Good Brothers. As he watched through the infirmary window, while Daniel's friends and enemies came forward one by one to scatter earth on Daniel, Piero considered the farewells that he must make after the burial was done. . . .

'Let me stay here, Lyki. Give some money to my family, and some to the Brothers, and then forget me.'

'Why do you wish to stay?'

'All prostitutes must seek refuge from their trade in the end. It is better they do so before they are worn out. This will be my refuge...

... Your secret is safe here with me, Lord Canteloupe. I told it to Mr Lykiadopoulos, I admit, but I gather it is now safe with him too. So will you do one thing for me?'

'If I can.'

'Give money, what you can afford, to Mr de Freville, so that he can make his restorations in Venice.'

'I don't know ... that it's worth it any more.'

'Please, my lord. Do as Piero asks.'

'If *you* ask, Tullia.'

'Piero and I, we both ask.'

'Very well.'

'Thank you, Lord Canteloupe. Thank you, Miss Baby. You will say good-bye to your father for me? He has never liked me, but he has tried hard not to show this. Take him my thanks.'

'You know,' said Baby to Detterling, as they walked from the infirmary to join the others by the boats, 'I shouldn't mind if they did all find out and you were plain Captain Detterling again tomorrow. I think Miss Wentworth Rex at school would be rather sick – she only let me come out here because you asked – but I shouldn't mind one bit.'

'I should. Keep it quiet, Baby, for my sake.'

'I shall do whatever you wish, my lord, both now and later. You know that.'

As Baby and Detterling came up to the landing stage, a curious thing occurred.

While Lord Constable of Reculver Castle, who had suddenly recognized Brother Hugh as the former Hugh Balliston of Lancaster, was reintroducing him, as it were, to Jacquiz Helmutt and Balbo Blakeney;

and while Tom Chead and Basil Bunce were talking of the brave days when Daniel had 'served' with them in the 10th Sabre Squadron;

and while Peter Morrison and Earle Restarick, having sensed what they had in common, were quietly discussing American plans for the erasure of Venice;

and while Max de Freville and Lykiadopoulos were planning

the tactics which they would follow that evening in the Casino;

and while Alfie Schroeder of the Billingsgate Press was asking Tom Llewyllyn about his plans for future books, hoping to get a free gobbet for his column;

while all this was going on :

a dark stain crept up the creek towards the landing stage, at first just a trickle of black, then spreading until it covered the entire width of the creek, coming fast and strong with the tide as more and more poured in behind it, lapping against the banks where the birds nested, lapping round the shining boats, finally coming right up to the steps of the landing stage and settling there, barely an inch below the bottom rung, silent, filthy and opaque.

And yet nobody noticed except Piero, who was staring down from the infirmary window and saw that the black stain was over all the lagoon, whichever way he turned his eyes.

PRINCIPAL CHARACTERS IN
ALMS FOR OBLIVION

The *Alms for Oblivion* sequence consists of ten novels. They are, in chronological order : *Fielding Gray* (FG), set in 1945; *Sound the Retreat* (SR), 1945–6; *The Sabre Squadron* (SS), 1952; *The Rich Pay Late* (RPL), 1955–6; *Friends in Low Places* (FLP), 1959; *The Judas Boy* (JB), 1962; *Places Where They Sing* (PWTS), 1967; *Come Like Shadows* (CLS), 1970; *Bring Forth the Body* (BFB), 1972; and *The Survivors* (TS), 1973.

What follows is an alphabetical list of the more important characters, showing in which of the novels they have each appeared and briefly suggesting their roles.

Albani, Euphemia : daughter of Fernando Albani *q.v.* (TS).

Albani, Fernando : Venetial merchant of late 18th and early 19th centuries. Author of manuscripts researched by Fielding Gray *q.v.* in 1973 (TS).

Albani, Maria : wife to Fernando (TS).

Albani, Piero : son of Fernando (TS). Not to be confused with the Piero *q.v.* of no known surname who lives with Lykiadopoulos in Venice in 1973 (TS).

Balliston, Hugh : an undergraduate of Lancaster College, Cambridge in 1967 (PWTS); retreats to a convent of Franciscan Friars near Venice, and is recognized in Venice by Daniel Mond in 1973 (TS).

Beatty, Miss : a secretary in the firm of Salinger & Holbrook (RPL).† 1956 (RPL).

Beck, Tony : a young Fellow of Lancaster College, well known as a literary critic (PWTS).

Beyfus, The Lord (life Peer) : a social scientist, Fellow of Lancaster College (PWTS).

Blakeney, Balbo : a biochemist, Fellow of Lancaster College

(PWTS); still a Fellow of Lancaster and present at Daniel
Mond's funeral in 1973 (TS).

Blessington, Ivan : a school friend of Fielding Gray in 1945 (FG);
later a regular officer in the 49th Earl Hamilton's Light Dragoons (Hamilton's Horse); ADC to his Divisional Commander
in Germany in 1952 (SS); by 1955 an attaché at the British Em-
bassy in Washington (RPL); by 1972 retired from the army
and working at high level for a prominent merchant bank
(BFB); pensioned off from the bank for indiscretion in 1973
(TS).

von Bremke, Herr Doktor Aeneas : a prominent mathematician
at the University of Göttingen (SS).

Brockworthy, Lieutenant-Colonel : Commanding Officer of the
1st Battalion, the Wessex Fusiliers, at Berhampore in 1946
(SR).

Bunce, Basil : Squadron Sergeant-Major of the 10th Sabre Squad-
ron of Earl Hamilton's Light Dragoons at Göttingen in 1952
(SS), and on Santa Kytherea in 1955 (FG); present at Daniel
Mond's funeral in 1973 (TS).

Bungay, Piers : Subaltern officer of the 10th Sabre Squadron at
Göttingen in 1952 (SS).

Buttock, Mrs Tessie : owner of Buttock's Hotel in the Cromwell
Road (RPL, FLP, JB, CLS), a convenient establishment much
favoured by Tom Llewyllyn and Fielding Gray q.v.

Canteloupe, The Marchioness (Molly) : wife of The Marquis Canteloupe (FLP, SR).

CANTELOUPE, The Most Honourable the Marquis : father of
The Earl of Muscateer (SR); distant cousin of Captain Detterling q.v. and political associate of Somerset Lloyd-James q.v.;
successful operator of his 'Stately Home' and in 1959 Parliamentary Secretary for the Development of British Recrea-
tional Resources (FLP); Minister of Public Relations and Popular Media in 1962 (JB); Shadow Minister of Commerce in 1967
(PWTS); Minister of Commerce in the Conservative Government of 1970 (CLS); still Minister in 1972, though under heavy
pressure (BFB). †1973 (TS).

Carnavon, Angus : leading male star in Pandarus/Clytemnestra
Film Production of The Odyssey on Corfu in 1970 (CLS).

Carnwath, Doctor : a Cambridge don and historian; an old friend
of Provost Constable, and a member of the Lauderdale Committee;† early 1950s (BFB).

Chead, 'Corpy': Corporal-Major (*i.e.* Colour Sergeant) of the 10th Sabre Squadron at Göttingen (SS); present at Daniel Mond's funeral in 1973 (TS).

Clewes, The Reverend Oliver: Chaplain to Lancaster College (PWTS).

CONSTABLE, Robert Reculver (Major): demobilized with special priority in the summer of 1945 to take up appointment as Tutor of Lancaster College, Cambridge (FG); by 1955 Vice-Chancellor of the University of Salop, and *ex officio* member of the Board of *Strix* (RPL); elected Provost of Lancaster in 1959 (FLP); still Provost in 1962 (JB) and 1967 (PWTS) and 1972 (BFB); ennobled as Lord Constable of Reculver Castle in 1973 (TS).

Corrington, Mona: an anthropologist, Fellow of Girton College, Cambridge. Chum of Lord Beyfus *q.v.* (PWTS).

Cruxtable, Sergeant-Major: Company Sergeant-Major of Peter Morrison's Company at the O.T.S., Bangalore, in 1945–6 (SR); 'P.T. expert' at Canteloupe's physical fitness camp in the west country (FLP).

DETTERLING, Captain: distant cousin of Lord Canteloupe; regular officer of The 49th Earl Hamilton's Light Dragoons (Hamilton's Horse) from 1937; in charge of recruiting for the Cavalry in 1945 (FG); instructor at the O.T.S., Bangalore, from late 1945 to summer 1946 (SR); by 1952 has retired from Hamilton's Horse and become a Member of Parliament (SS); still M.P. in 1955 and a political supporter of Peter Morrison *q.v.* (RPL); still M.P. in 1959, when he joins Gregory Stern *q.v.* as a partner in Stern's publishing house (FLP); still M.P. and publisher in 1962 (JB) and 1970 (CLS), and 1972, at which time he gives important assistance to those enquiring into the death of Somerset Lloyd-James (BFB); inherits his distant cousin Canteloupe's marquisate by special remainder in 1973 (TS), and insists that the spelling of the title now be changed to 'marquess'.

Dexterside, Ashley: friend and employee of Donald Salinger (RPL).

Dharaparam, H.H. The Maharajah of: an Indian Prince; Patron of the Cricket Club of the O.T.S., Bangalore (SR).

Dilkes, Henry: Secretary to the Institute of Political and Economic Studies and a member of the Board of *Strix* (RPL, FLP).

Dixon, Alastair: Member of Parliament for safe Conservative
seat in the west country; about to retire in 1959 (FLP), thus
creating a vacancy coveted both by Peter Morrison and
Somerset Lloyd-James q.v.

Dolly: maid of all work to Somerset Lloyd-James in his cham-
bers in Albany (BFB).

Drew, Vanessa: v. Salinger, Donald.

Engineer, Margaret Rose: a Eurasian harlot who entertains Peter
Morrison q.v. in Bangalore (SR).

fitzAvon, Humbert: otherwise called Lord Rollesden-in-Silvis,
the man with whom the manuscripts of Fernando Albani q.v.
are principally concerned (TS).

de FREVILLE, Max: gambler and connoisseur of human affairs;
runs big chemin-de-fer games in the London of the fifties
(RPL), maintaining a private spy-ring for protection from possible welshers and also for the sheer amusement of it (FLP);
later goes abroad to Venice, Hydra, Cyprus and Corfu, where
he engages in various enterprises (FLP, JB, CLS), often in
partnership with Lykiadopoulos q.v. and usually attended by
Angela Tuck q.v. His Corfiot interests include a share in the
1970 Pandarus/Clytemnestra production of The Odyssey
(CLS); still active in Corfu in 1972 (BFB); still in partnership
with Lykiadopoulos, whom he accompanies to Venice in the
autumn of 1973 (TS).

Frith, Hetta: girl friend of Hugh Balliston q.v. (PWTS).† 1967
(PWTS).

Galahead, Foxe J. (Foxy): Producer for Pandarus and Clytemnestra Films of The Odyssey on Corfu in 1970 (CLS).

Gamp, Jonathan: a not so young man about town (RPL, FLP,
BFB).

Gilzai Khan, Captain: an Indian officer (Moslem) holding the
King's Commission; an instructor at the O.T.S., Bangalore,
1945–6; resigns to become a political agitator (SR).† 1946
(SR).

Glastonbury, Major Giles: an old friend of Detterling p.v. and
regular officer of Hamilton's Horse; temporary Lieutenant-
Colonel on Lord Wavell's staff in India 1945–6 (SR); officer
commanding the 10th Sabre Squadron of Hamilton's Horse
at Göttingen in 1952 (SS).

Grange, Lady Susan : marries Lord Philby (RPL).

Gray, John Aloysius (Jack): Fielding Gray's father (FG). †
1945.

Gray, Mrs : Fielding Gray's mother (FG).† *c.* 1948.

GRAY, Major Fielding : senior schoolboy in 1945 (FG) with Peter
Morrison and Somerset Lloyd-James *q.v.*; scholar elect of
Lancaster College, but tangles with the authorities, is deprived of his scholarship before he can take it up (FG), and
becomes a regular officer of Earl Hamilton's Light Dragoons; 2 i/c and then O.C. the 10th Sabre Squadron in
Göttingen in 1952 (SS) and still commanding the Squadron on
Santa Kytherea in 1955 (KG); badly mutilated in Cyprus in
1958 and leaves the Army to become critic and novelist with
the help of Somerset Lloyd-James (FLP); achieves minor dis-
tinction, and in 1962 is sent out to Greece and Cyprus by Tom
Llewyllyn *q.v.* to investigate Cypriot affairs, past and present,
for BBC Television (JB); in Greece meets Harriet Ongley *q.v.*;
by 1967 has won the Joseph Conrad Prize for Fiction (PWTS);
goes to Corfu in 1970 to rewrite script for Pandarus/
Clytemnestra's *The Odyssey* (CLS); in 1972 is engaged on a
study of Joseph Conrad, which is to be published, as part of
a new series, by Gregory Stern (BFB); derives considerable
financial benefit from the Conrad book, and settles tempor-
arily in Venice in the autumn of 1973 (TS). His researches into
a by-water of Venetian history cause trouble among his friends
and provide himself with the material for a new novel.

Grimes, Sasha : a talented young actress playing in Pandarus/
Clytemnestra's *The Odyssey* on Corfu (CLS).

The Headmaster of Fielding Gray's School (FG) : a man of conscience.

Helmutt, Jacquiz : historian; research student at Lancaster College in 1952 (SS); later Fellow of Lancaster (PWTS); still a
Fellow of Lancaster and present at Daniel Mond's funeral in
1973 (TS).

Holbrook, Jude : partner of Donald Salinger *q.v.* 1949–56 (RPL);
'freelance' in 1959 (FLP); reported by Burke Lawrence *q.v.*
(CLS) as having gone to live in Hong Kong in the sixties; dis-
covered to have retired, with his mother, to a villa in the
Veneto 1973 (TS), having apparently enriched himself in Hong
Kong.

Holbrook, Penelope: a model; wife of Jude Holbrook (RPL); by 1959, divorced from Jude and associated with Burke Lawrence (FLP); reported by Burke Lawrence (CLS) as still living in London and receiving alimony from Jude in Hong Kong.

Holeworthy, R.S.M.: Regimental Sergeant-Major of the Wessex Fusiliers at Göttingen in 1952 (SS).

Jacobson, Jules: old hand in the film world; Director of Pandarus/Clytemnestra's *The Odyssey* on Corfu in 1970 (CLS).

James, Cornet Julian: Cambridge friend of Daniel Mond *q.v.*; in 1952 a National Service officer of the 10th Sabre Squadron at Göttingen (SS).

Joe: groundsman at Detterling's old school (BFB).

Lamprey, Jack: a subaltern officer of the 10th Sabre Squadron (SS).

La Soeur, Doctor: a confidential practitioner, physician to Fielding Gray (FG, RPL, CLS).

Lawrence, Burke: 'film director' and advertising man (RPL); from *c.* 1956 to 1959 teams up with Penelope Holbrook *q.v.* in murky 'agency' (FLP); *c.* 1960 leaves England for Canada, and later becomes P.R.O. to Clytemnestra Films (CLS).

Lewson, Felicity: born Contessina Felicula Maria Monteverdi; educated largely in England; wife of Mark Lewson (though several years his senior) and his assistant in his profession (RPL). † 1959 (FLP).

Lewson, Mark: a con man (RPL, FLP). † 1959 (FLP).

Lichfield, Margaret: star actress playing Penelope in the Pandarus/Clytemnestra production of *The Odyssey* on Corfu in 1970 (CLS).

LLEWYLLYN, Tom: a 'scholarship boy' of low Welsh origin but superior education; author, journalist and contributor to *Strix* (RPL); same but far more successful by 1959, when he marries Patricia Turbot *q.v.* (FLP); given important contract by BBC Television in 1962 to produce *Today is History*, and later that year appointed Namier Fellow of Lancaster College (JB); renewed as Napier Fellow in 1965 and still at Lancaster in 1967 (PWTS); later made a permanent Fellow of the College (CLS); employed by Pandarus and Clytemnestra Films as 'Literary and Historical Adviser' to their production of *The Odyssey* on Corfu in 1970 (CLS); still a don at Lancaster in 1972, when he is reported to be winning esteem for the first volume of his *magnum opus* (published by the Cambridge University Press) on the subject of Power (BFB); comes to Venice in the autumn of 1973 (TS), nominally to do research but in fact to care for Daniel Mond.

Llewyllyn, Tullia : always called and known as 'Baby'; Tom and Patricia's daughter, born in 1960 (JB, PWTS, CLS, BFB); on the removal from the scene of her mother, is sent away to school in the autumn of 1973 (TS). Becomes a close friend of Captain Detterling, now Marquess Canteloupe.

Lloyd-James, Mrs Peregrina : widowed mother of Somerset Lloyd-James (BFB).

LLOYD-JAMES, Somerset : a senior schoolboy and friend of Fielding Gray in 1945 (FG); by 1955, Editor of *Strix*, an independent economic journal (RPL); still editor of *Strix* in 1959 (FPL) and now seeking a seat in Parliament; still editor of *Strix* in 1962 (JB), but now also a Member of Parliament and unofficial adviser to Lord Canteloupe *q.v.*; still M.P. and close associate of Canteloupe in 1967 (PWTS), and by 1970 Canteloupe's official understrapper in the House of Commons (CLS), still so employed in 1972 (BFB), with the title of Parliamentary Under-Secretary of State at the Ministry of Commerce; † 1972 (BFB).

Lykiadopoulos, Stratis : a Greek gentleman, or not far off it; professional gambler and a man of affairs (FLP) who has a brief liaison with Mark Lewson; friend and partner of Max de Freville *q.v.* (FLP), with whom he has business interests in Cyprus (JB) and later in Corfu (CLS); comes to Venice in the autumn of 1973 (TS) to run a Baccarat Bank and thus prop up his fortunes in Corfu, which are now rather shaky. Is accompanied by Max de Freville *q.v.* and a Sicilian boy called Piero *q.v.*

Maisie : a whore (RPL, FLP, JB) frequented with enthusiasm by Fielding Gray, Lord Canteloupe and Somerset Lloyd-James; apparently still going strong as late as 1967 (ref. PWTS) and even 1970 (ref. CLS), and 1972 (BFB).

Mayerston : a revolutionary (PWTS).

Mond, Daniel : a mathematician; research student of Lancaster College (SS) sent to Göttingen University in 1952 to follow up his line of research, which unexpectedly turns out to have a military potential; later Fellow of Lancaster and teacher of pure mathematics (PWTS). † in Venice in 1973 (TS).

Morrison, Helen : Peter Morrison's wife (RPL, FLP, BFB).

MORRISON, Peter : senior schoolboy with Fielding Gray and Somerset Lloyd-James *q.v.* in 1945 (FG); an officer cadet at the O.T.S., Bangalore, from late 1945 to summer 1946 (SR) and then commissioned as a Second Lieutenant in the Wessex Fusiliers, whom he joins at Berhampore; by 1952 has inherited substantial estates in East Anglia and by 1955 is a Member of Parliament (RPL) where he leads 'the Young England Group'; but in 1956 applies for Chiltern Hundreds (RPL); tries and fails to return to Parliament in 1959 (FLP); reported by Lord Cante- loupe (CLS) as having finally got a seat again after a by- election in 1968 and as having retained it at the General Elec- tion in 1970; in 1972 appointed Parliamentary Under- Secretary of State at the Ministry of Commerce on the demise of Somerset Lloyd-James (BFB); appointed Minister of Com- merce on death of Lord Canteloupe *q.v.* in 1973 (TS); soon after is in Venice to take a hand in industrial intrigues in Mestre.

Morrison, 'Squire' : Peter's father (FG), owner of a fancied race- horse (Tiberius). † *c.* 1950.

Mortleman, Alister : an officer cadet at the O.T.S., Bangalore, 1945–6, later commissioned into the Wessex Fusiliers (SR).

Motley, Mick : Lieutenant of the R.A.M.C., attached to the Wes- sex Fusiliers at Göttingen in 1952 (SS).

Murphy, 'Wanker' : an officer cadet at the O.T.S., Bangalore, 1945–6; later commissioned as Captain in the Education Corps, then promoted to be Major and Galloper to the Viceroy of India (SR). † 1946 (SR).

Muscateer, Earl of : son of Lord and Lady Canteloupe *q.v.*; an officer cadet at the O.T.S., Bangalore, 1945–6 (SR). † 1946 (SR).

Nicos : a Greek boy who picks up Fielding Gray (JB).

Ogden, The Reverend Andrew : Dean of the Chapel of Lancaster College (PWTS).

Ongley, Mrs Harriet : rich American widow; Fielding Gray's

mistress and benefactress from 1962 onwards (JB, PWTS, CLS), but has left him by 1972 (BFB).

Pappenheim, Herr : German ex-officer of World War II; in 1952 about to rejoin new West German Army as a senior staff officer (SS).

Percival, Leonard : cloak-and-dagger man; in 1952 nominally a Lieutenant of the Wessex Fusiliers at Göttingen (SS), but by 1962 working strictly in plain clothes (JB); friend of Max de Freville, with whom he occasionally exchanges information to their mutual amusement (JB); transferred to a domestic department ('Jermyn Street') of the secret service and rated 'Home enquiries only', because of stomach ulcers in 1972, when he investigates, in association with Detterling, the death of Somerset Lloyd-James (BFB); joins Detterling (now Lord Canteloupe) in Venice in 1973 in order to investigate a 'threat' to Detterling (TS). Becomes Detterling's personal secretary and retires from 'Jermyn Street'.

Percival, Rupert : a small-town lawyer in the west country (FLP), prominent among local Conservatives and a friend of Alistair Dixon q.v.; Leonard Percival's uncle (JB).

Philby, The Lord : proprietor of Strix (RPL, FLP) which he has inherited along with his title from his father, 'old' Philby.

Piero : A Sicilian boy who accompanies Lykiadopoulos q.v. to Venice in 1973 (TS). Becomes friend of Daniel Mond. Not to be confused with Piero Albani q.v.

Pough (pronounced Pew), The Honourable Grantchester Fitz-Margrave : Senior Fellow of Lancaster College, Professor Emeritus of Oriental Geography, at one time celebrated as a mountaineer; a dietary fadist (PWTS).

Pulcher, Detective Sergeant : assistant to Detective Superintendent Stupples, q.v. (BFB).

Restarick, Earle : American cloak-and-dagger man; in 1952 apparently a student at Göttingen University (SS) but in fact taking an unwholesome interest in the mathematical researches of Daniel Mond q.v.; later active in Cyprus (JB) and in Greece (CLS); at Mestre in autumn of 1973 in order to assist with American schemes for the industrialization of the area (TS); present at Daniel Mond's funeral.

Roland, Christopher: a special school friend of Fielding Gray
(FG). † 1945 (FG).

Salinger, Donald: senior partner of Salinger & Holbrook, a printing firm (RPL); in 1956 marries Vanessa Drew (RPL); is deserted
by Jude Holbrook q.v. in the summer of 1956 (RPL) but in
1959 is still printing (FLP), and still married to Vanessa; in 1972
is reported as having broken down mentally and retired to a
private Nursing Home in consequence of Vanessa's death by
drowning (BFB).

Schottgatt, Doctor Emile: of Montana University, Head of the
'Creative Authentication Committee' of the Oglander-
Finckelstein Trust, which visits Corfu in 1970 (CLS) to assess
the merits of the Pandarus/Clytemnestra production of *The
Odyssey*.

Schroeder, Alfie: a reporter employed by the Billingsgate Press
(RPL, FLP, SS); by 1967 promoted to columnist (PWTS);
'famous' as columnist by 1973, when he attends Daniel Mond's
funeral (TS).

Sheath, Aloysius: a scholar on the staff of the American School
of Greek Studies in Athens, but also assistant to Earle Restarick
q.v. (JB, CLS).

Stern, Gregory: publisher (RPL), later in partnership with Captain Detterling q.v. (FLP); publishes Tom Llewyllyn and Fielding Gray q.v. (RPL, FLP, JB, PWTS, CLS); married to Isobel
Turbot (FLP); still publishing in 1973 (TS), by which time
Isobel has persuaded him into vulgar and profitable projects.

Strange, Barry: an officer cadet at the O.T.S., Bangalore, 1945–6,
later commissioned into the Wessex Fusiliers, with whom he
has strong family connections (SR).

Stupples, Detective Superintendent: policeman initially responsible for enquiries into the death of Somerset Lloyd-James in
1972 (BFB).

Tuck: a tea-planter in India; marries Angela, the daughter of a
disgraced officer, and brings her back to England in 1945
(FG); later disappears, but turns up as an official of the Control
Commission in Germany in 1952 (SS). † 1956 (RPL).

TUCK, Mrs Angela: daughter of a Colonel in the Indian Army
Pay Corps, with whom she lives in Southern India (JB, FLP)
until early 1945, when her father is dismissed the Service for
malversation; being then *in extremis* marries Tuck the tea-

planter, and returns with him to England in the summer of 1945 (FG); briefly mistress to the adolescent Somerset Lloyd-James *q.v.*, and to 'Jack' Gray (Fielding's father); despite this a trusted friend of Fielding's mother (FG); by 1955 is long separated from Tuck and now mistress to Jude Holbrook (RPL); in 1956 inherits small fortune from the intestate Tuck, from whom she has never been actually divorced *pace* her bibulous and misleading soliloquies on the subject in the text (RPL); in 1959 living in Menton and occasional companion of Max de Freville *q.v.* (FLP); later Max's constant companion (JB, CLS). † 1970 (CLS).

Turbot, The Right Honourable Sir Edwin, P.C., Kt : politician; in 1946 ex-Minister of wartime coalition accompanying all-party delegation of M.P.s to India (SR); by 1959 long since a Minister once more, and 'Grand Vizier' of the Conservative Party (FLP); father of Patricia, who marries Tom Llewyllyn (FLP), and of Isobel, who marries Gregory Stern (FLP); by 1962 reported as badly deteriorating and as having passed some of his fortune over to his daughters (JB). † by 1967 (PWTS), having left more money to his daughters.

Turbot, Isobel : *v.* Turbot, Sir Edwin, and Stern, Gregory.

Turbot, Patricia : *v.* Turbot, Sir Edwin, and Llewyllyn, Tom. Also *v.* Llewyllyn, Tullia. Has brief walk-out with Hugh Balliston *q.v.* (PWTS) and is disobliging to Tom about money (JB, PWTS, CLS). In 1972 is reported by Jonathan Gamp to be indulging in curious if not criminal sexual preferences (BFB); as a result of these activities is finally overtaken by disaster and put away in an asylum in 1973 (TS), much to the benefit of her husband and daughter.

Weekes, James : bastard son of Somerset Lloyd-James, born in 1946 (BFB).

Weekes, Mrs Meriel : *quondam* and random associate of Somerset Lloyd-James, and mother of his bastard son (BFB).

Weir, Carton : Member of Parliament and political associate of Peter Morrison (RPL); later official aide to Lord Canteloupe (FLP, JB). P.P.S. to Canteloupe at Ministry of Commerce in 1972 (BFB); becomes P.P.S. to Peter Morrison *q.v.* when the latter takes over as Minister of Commerce on the death of Lord Canteloupe.

Winstanley, Ivor : a distinguished Latinist, Fellow of Lancaster College (PWTS).

'Young bastard' : assistant groundsman at Detterling's old school (BFB).

Zaccharias : an officer cadet at the O.T.S., Bangalore, 1945–6; commissioned into a dowdy regiment of the line (SR).

Bestselling British Fiction in Panther Books

Bestselling British Fiction in Panther Books

GIRL, 20	Kingsley Amis	40p ☐
I WANT IT NOW	Kingsley Amis	60p ☐
THE GREEN MAN	Kingsley Amis	30p ☐
THE RIVERSIDE VILLAS MURDER		
	Kingsley Amis	50p ☐
THAT UNCERTAIN FEELING	Kingsley Amis	50p ☐
BEST SUMMER JOBS	Patrick Skene Catling	60p ☐
FREDDY HILL	Patrick Skene Catling	35p ☐
THE CATALOGUE	Patrick Skene Catling	35p ☐
THE SURROGATE	Patrick Skene Catling	40p ☐
GEORGY GIRL	Margaret Forster	25p ☐
THE FRENCH LIEUTENANT'S WOMAN		
	John Fowles	75p ☐
THE COLLECTOR	John Fowles	60p ☐
THE SHY YOUNG MAN	Douglas Hayes	40p ☐
THE WAR OF '39	Douglas Hayes	30p ☐
TOMORROW THE APRICOTS	Douglas Hayes	35p ☐
A PLAYER'S HIDE	Douglas Hayes	35p ☐
THE GOLDEN NOTEBOOK	Doris Lessing	£1.00 ☐
BRIEFING FOR A DESCENT INTO HELL		
	Doris Lessing	60p ☐
A MAN AND TWO WOMEN	Doris Lessing	60p ☐
THE HABIT OF LOVING	Doris Lessing	50p ☐
FIVE	Doris Lessing	60p ☐
WINTER IN JULY	Doris Lessing	50p ☐
THE BLACK MADONNA	Doris Lessing	50p ☐

All-action Fiction from Panther

SPY STORY	Len Deighton	60p	☐
THE IPCRESS FILE	Len Deighton	60p	☐
AN EXPENSIVE PLACE TO DIE	Len Deighton	50p	☐
DECLARATIONS OF WAR	Len Deighton	60p	☐
A GAME FOR HEROES	James Graham*	40p	☐
THE WRATH OF GOD	James Graham*	40p	☐
THE KHUFRA RUN	James Graham*	40p	☐
THE SCARLATTI INHERITANCE	Robert Ludlum	75p	☐
THE OSTERMAN WEEKEND	Robert Ludlum	60p	☐
THE MATLOCK PAPER	Robert Ludlum	75p	☐
THE BERIA PAPERS	Alan Williams†	60p	☐
THE TALE OF THE LAZY DOG	Alan Williams†	60p	☐
THE PURITY LEAGUE	Alan Williams†	50p	☐
SNAKE WATER	Alan Williams†	50p	☐
LONG RUN SOUTH	Alan Williams†	50p	☐
BARBOUZE	Alan Williams†	50p	☐
FIGURES IN A LANDSCAPE	Barry England	50p	☐
LORD TYGER	Philip José Farmer	50p	☐

* The author who 'makes Alistair Maclean look like a beginner' (*Sunday Express*)

† 'The natural successor to Ian Fleming' (*Books & Bookmen*)

Bestselling Transatlantic Fiction in Panther Books

THE SOT-WEED FACTOR	John Barth	£1.50	☐
BEAUTIFUL LOSERS	Leonard Cohen	60p	☐
THE FAVOURITE GAME	Leonard Cohen	40p	☐
TARANTULA	Bob Dylan	50p	☐
DESOLATION ANGELS	Jack Kerouac	50p	☐
THE DHARMA BUMS	Jack Kerouac	40p	☐
BARBARY SHORE	Norman Mailer	40p	☐
AN AMERICAN DREAM	Norman Mailer	40p	☐
THE NAKED AND THE DEAD	Norman Mailer	60p	☐
THE BRAMBLE BUSH	Charles Mergendahl	40p	☐
TEN NORTH FREDERICK	John O'Hara	50p	☐
FROM THE TERRACE	John O'Hara	75p	☐
OURSELVES TO KNOW	John O'Hara	60p	☐
THE DICE MAN	Luke Rhinehart	95p	☐
COCKSURE	Mordecai Richler	60p	☐
ST URBAIN'S HORSEMAN	Mordecai Richler	50p	☐
THE CITY AND THE PILLAR	Gore Vidal	40p	☐
BLUE MOVIE	Terry Southern	60p	☐
BREAKFAST OF CHAMPIONS			
	Kurt Vonnegut Jr	50p	☐
SLAUGHTERHOUSE 5	Kurt Vonnegut Jr	50p	☐
MOTHER NIGHT	Kurt Vonnegut Jr	40p	☐
PLAYER PIANO	Kurt Vonnegut Jr	50p	☐
GOD BLESS YOU, MR ROSEWATER			
	Kurt Vonnegut Jr	50p	☐
WELCOME TO THE MONKEY HOUSE			
	Kurt Vonnegut Jr	75p	☐